Advance Praise for
One Thing I Know

"*One Thing I Know* has everything I want in a feel-good romance: chemistry, banter, humor, heart—and a charming hero from the mighty Midwest. Faith without a sugar coat, families that walk through broken spaces onto firmer footing, a love that finds its way toward 'always'—Isaac's novel is a total gem."

—Kimberly Stuart, author of *Heart Land*

"Winsome and wholly satisfying, Isaac delivers a fresh take on love, regret, and the secrets that breathe between them."

—Carol Award–winning author Nicole Deese

"Once again Kara Isaac reminds us why she is a RITA award–winning author with her fabulous new release. *One Thing I Know* is the perfect balance of hilarious dialogue, exquisitely appealing characters, and a flawless sense of pacing. This lovely, unforgettable story will resonate with anyone who has struggled to stay true to the person God has called them to be."

—Tammy L. Gray, RITA Award–winning
author of *My Hope Next Door*

READ MORE KARA ISAAC NOVELS

One THING I Know

KARA ISAAC

HOWARD BOOKS

NEW YORK   LONDON   TORONTO   SYDNEY   NEW DELHI

HOWARD BOOKS

An Imprint of Simon & Schuster, Inc.
1230 Avenue of the Americas
New York, NY 10020

First Howard Books trade paperback edition February 2019

Design by Michelle Marchese

Manufactured in the United States of America

10 9 8 7 6 5 4 3 2 1

Library of Congress Cataloging-in-Publication Data

Names: Isaac, Kara, author.
Title: One thing I know / by Kara Isaac.
Description: First Howard Books trade paperback edition. | New York : Howard Books, 2019.
Identifiers: LCCN 2018033163 (print) | LCCN 2018035450 (ebook) |
ISBN 9781982103354 (eBook) | ISBN 9781982103347 (paperback)
Subjects: | BISAC: FICTION / Christian / Romance. | FICTION / Romance /
Contemporary. | GSAFD: Christian fiction. | Love stories.
Classification: LCC PR9639.4.I83 (ebook) | LCC PR9639.4.I83 O54 2019 (print) |
DDC 823/.92—dc23
LC record available at https://urldefense.proofpoint.com/v2/url?u=https-3A__lccn
.loc.gov_2018033163&d=DwIFAg&c=jGUuvAdBXp_VqQ6t0yah2g&r=VLL
wScFhq9g5kj6m7mvdZkSQKElssXlHhCgJv-2hn0_QhgQ6fft8ZGRVAsiOB8I
P&m=KL2aRwZIT-PaVbMwor7b3RMApPdnFZDTJonCFCbpj80&s=A5zW
S3hY-BGuMBZ7UegZ_a9pipLGsbgR61AW8q0vzo4&e=.

ISBN 978-1-9821-0334-7
ISBN 978-1-9821-0335-4 (ebook)

For the "dream team,"
who are not only incredible friends
but are like a second family who love our kids,
step in when the wheels fall off, keep our house from
becoming a haven for toxic mold, and shamelessly
flog my books off to their friends and family.

Ann-Maree Beard, Liv Williams, Fee Conway,
Anna Holmes, Team Harper, Team Benson, Nicola Goodman,
and Stephanie Howe. You are the actual best.

One
THING I
Know

- *1* -

*R*achel Somers wasn't sure what bothered her more: conning most of America, or the fact that they'd been doing it for almost a decade and no one even suspected.

She glanced around her tiny living area crammed with her three coconspirators. Afternoon sun through the smudged side window cast a shimmering halo through the room, dancing across surfaces covered with either people or papers.

"So, Dr. Donna, tell us how you came up with the topic of your latest book, *He Wasn't the One that Got Away*." Lacey O'Connor, their publicist, leaned forward in her chair, role-playing a talk show host.

Her question was directed at Rachel's aunt Donna, who slouched back on the brown leather couch, face coated in an oatmeal-and-cinnamon-scented beauty mask. "Well, Suzanne, one night I was facilitating a speed-dating event—"

Rachel winced. Oh brother, this was not a good beginning. "It was a call-in radio show." *Lost in Translation*, their third book, was the one inspired by speed dating.

Donna looked Rachel's way. "What was?"

"You were guesting on a call-in radio show," Rachel reminded her.

"I was?" Donna's brow crinkled, or tried to, anyway. "Really? Max, can you check?"

Rachel pressed her lips together. Throttled the indignant response rising within. It was fine that Donna wanted to check. Really.

Their agent's stubby finger slid across a line on the spreadsheet in front of him. "Rachel's right. *Lost* was speed dating."

Of course she was right. She'd written them both. With each book, the juggle got harder, the stakes higher. She liked to think that if they'd had any idea how big the deception would get, they never would've suggested it. They were worse than those manufactured tweenage pop bands. At least nobody took twelve-year-old boys crooning about true love seriously.

Now here they were, a week from release, and Donna couldn't even remember this book's inspiration. This was it. Finally. The book that was going to doom them all. *Deep breath, Rachel.* "You were on—"

"Drive Time with Debbie, and we got all these phone calls from women who were living in the past, wondering if they'd missed their chance at love back in 1993." Donna's gray eyes sparkled with mirth underneath the goop. "I know. I was just teasin' y'all."

"Don't do that!" Rachel reached out for a pillow to throw at her aunt, but Lacey got there first, taking off her stiletto and swiping at Donna's heel.

Donna pivoted sideways, moving her feet out of striking distance and pulling herself upright. "C'mon, how long have we been doing this now? And when have I ever let you down?"

Rachel blew a breath out between the gap in her front teeth. Nine years. Nine long years. And her aunt was right: the one time they'd almost gotten busted, it had been Lacey's fault, not hers.

"All right, enough, ladies." Max's hand rose midair, stopping as though frozen halfway through a hallelujah moment. "Since you're so cocky, Donna, I think it's time for rapid fire." He tossed one rubber-band-bound stack of cue cards to Rachel, then a second to Lacey, keeping the third for himself. "Rach, you start."

Rachel took a swig of her ice-cold Diet Coke, then pulled a crisp cue card at random. "Do you really believe that revisiting the past is always a mistake?"

Donna's shoulders went back, eyes narrowed, and in an instant, Rachel's oatmeal-faced, tracksuit-wearing aunt disappeared, and Dr. Donna Somerville, relationship guru and bestselling author, showed up. "Of course not. In fact, revisiting the past is very important, because it's our past that defines who we are today. What I'm saying is that *living* in the past, that's the mistake. You'll see in Chapter Three I talk about the difference . . ."

Two and a half hours later, the last cue card hit the floor. Where it joined six cans of Diet Coke, two bags of Hershey's Kisses, and both of Lacey's stilettos.

Rachel locked her hands together, stretching out her aching shoulders. It looked like they were going to live to fight another round after all. She shook her arms out, trying to shake off the strange sense of disappointment that had grown as her aunt nailed question after question, never stumbling.

"Good work, everyone." Max snapped his last spreadsheet back into the black binder on his lap. "Lacey, you need anything more or are we done?"

Their publicist tapped a glossy red nail across her iPad, the screen showing Donna and Rachel's calendars side-by-side. "One final thing. Got a last-minute request for a two-hour call-in slot with Lucas Grant next Tuesday. Donna's in Atlanta and has an early start. Rach, can you sub?" She kept her gaze focused on her iPad as she asked the question.

"Doesn't he do a sports show now?" At least he had the last time she'd heard anything about him. Which admittedly was a couple of years ago.

The edge of Lacey's mouth tipped up. "Lucas would *like* to do sports. Unfortunately for him he's single, very eligible, and can't seem to escape all the women calling in to get his advice on their love lives."

"And he wants Donna on his sports show for *two hours*?"

Lacey shrugged. "No idea. I only deal with his producer, but as your publicist I am telling you that two hours on Lucas's show is like filling a stadium with fifty thousand Wisconsin women. We'd be nuts not to do it if we can make it work."

"Okay, fine." Rachel could use a break from staring blankly at her computer screen, grasping for inspiration.

"Great." Lacey put her phone to her ear, stepping back into her shoes. "Ethan. Lacey. Tuesday sorted. Donna will call at ten your time. Ciao." She slung her navy leather purse over her shoulder and grabbed the matching suitcase from where she'd parked it in the corner. "Mwah, mwah." Air kisses all around, and she was heading for the door.

Twenty-one-year-old Lacey, with her crazy curly hair, wouldn't have recognized her perfectly groomed decade-older self. Or understood the well-worn tension that undergirded their every interaction.

Max, meanwhile, piled folders into a battered Wal-Mart tote. Between that and his rumpled thrift-shop suit, you'd never know he was one of the biggest literary agents in the country. He paused and turned as he opened her front door. "Rach . . ." Green eyes loomed large over his bulbous nose and gray spiked mustache.

"I know. I know." Rachel didn't meet Donna's eyes, sure of what she would see there. "Soon, I promise."

"I'm just saying, next Thursday . . ."

"Max, as soon as I know, I'll tell you." She crossed her toes. Childish, yes. But she wasn't quite up to telling their agent their decision just yet.

Max picked up his tote, then draped his coat over his arm. "Okay, then. I'll see you both at the lunch." They both watched as the door clicked shut behind him.

"Raaaachel." Donna was using *the* voice.

She knew. "I will." Rachel pulled the trash can out from under the sink and started picking up the detritus littering the floor.

"You have to tell him. He fought hard to get us such a great offer. It's not fair."

"Tell me about it." Fairness. Now *that* was something her life knew nothing about. "It's not like there's not time. We've still got one book to go."

"Speaking of which . . ."

"Nada." Not a bean, not a blip.

"Nothing?" Donna flipped open a silver compact.

"Sorry." And she was. There was nothing more she would like to give her aunt to take to their publisher than the premise of her next book. But given that in three months she'd come up with three possible book ideas and abandoned them all less than five thousand words in, she didn't put much hope in the next few days being any different.

Her aunt shrugged. "It'll happen. You didn't think you could write *one* book and yet here we are."

Yes, here they were, still in the same dingy one-bedroom condo the whole charade had started in. "Indeed."

"You okay?" Her aunt snapped her mirror shut and peered Rachel's way.

"I just . . ." Rachel struggled to put her thoughts into words. "Do you ever . . ."

"Of course." A sigh escaped Donna's lips as she slipped the compact back into her oversized purse. "Rach, you're a brilliant writer. And what you write is good, and true, and it *helps* people live better lives. Do I feel bad that people believe those words come from me? Of course I do. But we made the best decision we could at the time. No one could have ever guessed it would have turned into this."

"I guess." They were the ones who'd suggested the charade. Yet the most noble of reasons in the world didn't make it right.

"Oh, I almost forgot." Her aunt dug around in her purse until a white envelope appeared.

Rachel slipped the crisp monogrammed sheet out of its

pocket. The certification from their accountants was standard. It was the check appended on the top that mattered. A twitch of a smile. $88,657.23. The Christmas season had been good to them. Only half a million to go before she would be free. Finally.

All that stood between the two of them was one more book. Well, one more book and another year of living a lie.

- 2 -

Cinching her bathrobe at the waist, Rachel snagged a still-warm chocolate chip cookie off the counter on her way to the couch. Pillows, check. Cocoa, check. Blanket, check. If there was one thing she'd learned, it was to make sure she was set up for comfort before a call-in segment.

Poor Donna usually had to get all gussied up and sit in the studio with the host for her marathon sessions. Give Rachel the fluffy socks, bathrobe, and call-in deal any day.

Settling on the couch, she opened her laptop browser, pulled up the WFM webpage and clicked to livestream *Sports with Lucas*.

A couple of seconds later, Lucas Grant's husky tones filled her living room. ". . . talking about the news just out today that Springer is out for the rest of the season after that terrible collision on third base Saturday night."

Rachel stretched out her legs and yawned. Sports, *blegh*. She checked the time. Still five minutes before she needed to call in.

". . . facing months of physical therapy and even possible early retirement. I spoke to Chris Green last night and he advised it's a waiting game at the moment to see if surgery will be required. Devastating for Springer, but a great opportunity for Sampson or Little to prove themselves. Time for one more call before the news. What are your thoughts, Bill?"

There was a pause while a line opened up. "Hi, Lucas, it's Billie. Not Bill." A woman's voice came over the air.

"Hi, Billie. Welcome to the show. What are your thoughts on Springer's accident?" Something in Lucas's voice had changed. It sounded tighter somehow.

"Oh, I don't really follow hockey."

"Baseball."

"Or baseball. But I do have a sports-related question for you."

"You do." Lucas sounded skeptical.

"Yes. My boyfriend and I had a fight because he wants to go on a guys' weekend away to some racing thing, but he's supposed to be saving up to buy me an engagement ring and I told him it's too much money."

"That's not a sports question." Lucas didn't sigh, but he might as well have.

"It is. Sort of. Because it's sports that are getting in the way of Ross finally proposing."

Rachel seriously doubted that.

"So Ross has told you he's saving up for an engagement ring?"

"Noooooooo. But we've been together two years and all our friends are engaged, so he'd better be."

"Does he have a job?"

"Yes."

"Do you live together?"

"Yes."

"Does he pay his share of the bills?"

"Sure."

"Are his friends law-abiding, responsible, decent men?"

"I guess."

"Since you got together have you gone on a weekend away with your girlfriends?"

A pause. "Yes. But—"

This time Lucas did actually sigh. "Look, Billie. If Ross has a job and he's paying his share of the bills and his friends are good guys, then until you're married Ross can do whatever he likes with his money. So I recommend you encourage him to go on this boys' trip. Men need friends just as much as women do. How would you feel if the roles were reversed and Ross was telling you not to go away with your friends because he wanted you to spend your money on something he thought was more important?"

Huh. That was exactly the advice Rachel would have given.

"You're right. I hadn't thought of it that way. Thanks." Billie actually sounded grateful. There might be hope for her and Ross after all.

"You're welcome. And with that, it's time for the news highlights. This is Lucas Grant and you're listening to *Sports with Lucas.*" With a definite added emphasis on the *sports*.

A commercial came on and Rachel closed out of the browser, then put her laptop beside her.

He hadn't said anything about Dr. Donna being on after the news. Could she have gotten the date wrong? Rachel opened her calendar and checked. The invite from Lacey was definitely for today and now. Tapping in the studio's number, Rachel wedged the phone between her ear and shoulder as she arranged the blanket around her.

"Ethan speaking." The producer's brisk tone cut across the line before the phone even had a chance to ring.

"Ethan, it's Donna." Her impersonation was passable, but it had been a few weeks. There was room for improvement.

"And right on time. I'll put you through to Lucas in a couple of seconds. Sorry about his foul mood."

"Wha—"

Too late. He was already gone and the voice of Lucas Grant filled her ear: ". . . coming up after some words from our sponsors we have Dr. Donna Somerville, to chat about love, loss, and her new book, *He Wasn't the One that Got Away*. Sorry to all you guys out there who thought this was a sports show. Apparently my producer thinks otherwise."

Rachel winced. So he'd been blindsided by this. That was going to make for a real fun two hours.

An ad for a sporting goods store started and then Lucas came onto her line. "Evening, Donna. I would say I've been looking forward to this, but truth is Ethan only told me about it thirty seconds ago."

"So I figured. We can always cut it short if you want. I can plead a mix-up. Another commitment." Her Donna impersonation still wasn't quite right. It would probably take the first few minutes of the call to get back into the swing of it. Hopefully no one would notice.

"It's fine. Well, it's not really, but it's certainly not your fault that my producer seems determined to make me talk about feelings instead of football."

Rachel smothered a laugh. Lucas didn't know her from a bar of soap, but she'd known him since he was a hungry graveyard-shift host and she a no-name debut author prepared to take whatever publicity she could get. Even when the only people listening were probably a couple of geriatric insomniacs in Arkansas. "Well, according to my publicist you're apparently quite good at both, if that helps at all."

At least that got half a laugh out of him. "So, another book. What number is this one? Five?"

"Six."

"Are you on tour again now?"

"Yup. Atlanta today."

"And the next book already in the works?"

A groan slipped out before Rachel could stop it.

"That bad, huh?"

"Let's just say it's a work in progress." The three ideas that had gone nowhere had to count for something.

"You're back on in three . . . two . . ." Ethan's voice broke through their laugh.

"Welcome back." Lucas made the switch effortlessly. "Tonight, we have a surprise guest that my producer allegedly forgot to tell me about, Dr. Donna Somerville. She needs no introduction; many of you have read her books and, look at that, the switchboard is jammed already. Dr. Donna, welcome to the show."

"Thank you, Lucas. And thank you to all your listeners for having me this evening." The voice, the poise, it all came back when it mattered. They hadn't paid big bucks for Hollywood's best voice coach for nothing.

"Just before we start, I have a quick update for the sports

fans listening. The Olympic Committee has announced that Chicago will be making a bid to host the 2032 Summer Olympics."

Hardly breaking sports news, but then Rachel guessed there rarely was any this late at night unless it was coming from the West Coast.

"What are your favorite Olympic sports, Doc?" The man was clearly trying to avoid taking a call.

"Pole vault in summer, bobsledding in winter." At least he'd picked the only sports question she could actually answer. Even she liked the Olympics.

"Lucas," Ethan's voice cut in. "Stop stalling. Your first caller is Megan. Line one."

"Interesting choices, Doc." Lucas didn't even miss a beat. The people listening would have no idea he had Ethan barking instructions off air. "Would love to talk to you more about that, but my producer has told me we need to take some calls. Are you there, Megan?"

"Hi, um, hi!" The flustered but very excited voice of a woman who sounded in her thirties shot down the line. "Oh Dr. Donna, I am such a fan."

"Why thank you, Megan." Rachel wedged the phone against her shoulder and ran her fingers through her damp hair, securing it in a bun on top of her head.

"So, I know that you say if he doesn't have a job, he's not a keeper, but . . ." *Oh brother, the but. The struggling artist/ actor/super-talented-but-still-to-catch-a-break sponger boyfriend who every woman thinks is the exception.* ". . . gifted, and he's promised it would just be for six months, and I could support us both—"

"Run." Lucas's voice cut over Megan's self-justification.

"Excuse me?" Megan sounded shocked.

"Megan, you don't need Dr. Donna for this one. I'm telling you as your average American male, ditch this loser. Now. Tonight. Get off my phone line and throw him off your couch, or out of your bed or wherever he is."

"But . . ." The poor woman sounded as if Lucas had struck her.

Time for Dr. Donna to intervene. "Megan, I know it can't have been easy calling in tonight. So first of all I just want to acknowledge that." Call-in rule number one: you always catch more flies with honey. "Can I ask you a question?"

"Of course."

Rachel stretched out her legs, pressing her feet against the arm of the couch. Whoops, dropped the cookie. "When you think about the man that you want to spend the rest of your life with, what kind of characteristics come to mind?"

"Well . . ." A hesitation. "Someone who loves me and would make a good father and treats me well. Same thing any woman wants, I guess."

"Now you alone can answer this question, and I need you to do it honestly. I don't know your boyfriend and I don't care about him, I care about you. So even best-case scenario, if you pay the rent and buy the groceries and he 'finds himself,' do you think he is going to be the husband, the father, you want, that you deserve?"

Silence. Then a whimper. Ethan would be loving this. People's hearts breaking on air was great radio. "But what if he's my last chance?" The last two words came out a strangled sob.

Inevitably, this was what it came down to. Women of a certain age, giving up and settling for some subpar guy because they'd bought into the lie that it was better to suck it up and live with a dysfunctional relationship than be alone.

"What if he's not?" She modulated her voice carefully. It was in moments like these, when she was walking a finely tuned emotional tightrope, that she was liable to let Dr. Donna slip. "What if that guy who will make you happier than you can even imagine is out there? But he's never going to have a chance as long as you're with a guy who isn't right."

She was such a fraud. The Duchess of Cambridge had had three children since she last went on a date. And those dates had been purely for research. At least her aunt, having done a full lap of the marriage continuum, could say this stuff with some integrity.

The minutes slipped away as Rachel focused on call after call, broken up by the occasional sports update from a still-reluctant Lucas.

"Time for one more call, Doc?" Lucas's voice cut over a soft-drink commercial. Rachel glanced at the clock. Almost eleven, so nearly midnight in Wisconsin. She was on the right side of a time difference for once.

"Sounds good."

"Great, see you on the other side." He was gone as quick as he came, leaving her to the twangs of a used car salesman.

"And we're back, and we've got time for one more caller. Are you there, Jill?"

"Hi there." The woman's voice was hesitant. "I, um . . . I've never done this before."

"That's great!" Lucas was the master at calming first-time

nerves. "We're honored that you've chosen us for your radio debut. What's on your mind?"

A deep breath. "Well, I seem to have gotten myself into a bit of a situation." Another pause. Dead air on radio was never good. Rachel could imagine what kind of gestures Ethan would be making at Lucas right now.

"You and all the rest of us, honey." Rachel pulled out her most mothering Dr. Donna voice. "People and pickles are mighty good at finding each other." Man, she could use another cookie. She wandered over to the bench and ran her eyes over the remaining pucks of chocolate goodness, taste buds anticipating one disintegrating into crumbs of buttery bliss.

"I, um. Well, you see, Iseemtohavetwolives." Jill's words came out on top of each other, like a highway pileup. "I don't know how it happened. I love my husband. I really do. But I travel for work and two years ago I met someone in Ohio, and he's just amazing too. But now he wants me to move to be with him, and I can't, obviously. But I can't *not* be with him."

"So you want us to find you a way to have your cake and eat it too." Lucas wasn't exactly rude, but his tone was far from his usual charming one.

"I uh . . ." Jill's voice had the edge of someone realizing maybe this wasn't such a good idea after all. The cookie would have to wait. They had a couple of seconds before she hung up.

"Well, that is definitely a tight corner you've painted yourself into." Rachel tried to buy them both some time to re-gather their thoughts. *Dr. Donna. Channel Dr. Donna.* "Okay, the good news is you know what you need to do. The bad news is that you're going to break a couple of hearts doing it, including your own."

A muffled sob. "I . . . I—"

"Honey, there ain't no putting the toothpaste back in the tube. You can't undo what you've done. But both of these men deserve better than this, and it's time for you to do the decent thing and let one of them go. Being the old-fashioned gal that I am, I vote you do your best to mend a few of the vows you've broken." She had a long enough list of sins as it was; she wasn't going to add breaking up marriages to it.

"But . . . but . . ."

"But what? Oh I know, maybe we should petition for the great state of Wisconsin to legalize bigamy. Then you could be one happy *Big Love* family." Lucas's sarcastic suggestion snapped across the line.

What? Rachel was confused. Were they doing good cop, bad cop? The last time she'd been on his show, there had been a word he used to let her know he was about to pull that. She couldn't even remember what it was, but she was sure he hadn't used it.

"I don't know how to choose. I love them both." Jill's voice had taken on the beginnings of a petulant whine.

"No you don't. You love yourself." Lucas spat the words out like bullets.

Whoa. They had to wrap this call up and fast. This was not good cop, bad cop; there was something else going on. Lucas sounded like he was about to reach down the line and strangle the woman.

Rachel scrambled for something, anything. "Jill, we're out

of time, so what we're going to do is take you off air so you and I can talk further."

She had no idea what was going on in the studio, but she and Ethan were obviously on the same wavelength, as the show's theme music swelled over the end of her sentence.

LUCAS GRANT flicked off his microphone for the final time that evening, leaned back in his chair, and gulped down the last of his stone-cold instant coffee. *Gah.* He slammed the mug down on his desk.

"Dude! What was that about?" Ethan propped his heels up on the console opposite, tilting back to extract a beer from the small fridge in the corner of the cramped studio.

"What was what about?" Lucas eyed the clock above Ethan's head. Midnight and six. Usually he enjoyed debriefing, but he was still really hacked off with Ethan over his little stunt and he had to be up in six hours. The truck needed service and the guy at the shop had said if he got it to him by seven, he'd do his best to turn it around same day.

He didn't know how Donna did it. One a.m. in Atlanta, and no doubt she had to get up in a few hours for another full day on the PR circuit. The woman was a machine.

". . . people won't call if they don't feel safe."

"I have a sports show, Ethan. I'm not Dr. Phil. I don't want people calling to feel safe. I want them calling to talk about touchdowns and Davis's terrible defensive call last weekend." Lucas had long since mastered one of the survival skills of radio, the ability to track a conversation, so that even if he tuned out for a couple of seconds, the caller never knew.

"Look, I hate to break it to you again, but remember those great ratings you enjoy? The ones that dictate your paycheck. A decent chunk of those is because whether you like it or not, you have a lot of female listeners. If you want to break into the big time one day you need to keep them, and having Dr. Donna on for a couple of hours does that."

"Well, I don't want to keep this one. She was a lying, cheating piece of work. 'I don't know how it happened. I just woke up one day and found myself sleeping with two men.'" His falsetto imitation of Jill's voice was poor at best. "Seriously? How stupid do people think we are? You don't just wake up one morning and find yourself with lives in two states. She chose to flirt with that guy. Then she chose to sleep with him. Then she chose to do it again and again and again. Meanwhile, her poor schmuck of a husband . . ." His voice trailed off. It made him sick just thinking about it.

"I'm just glad we had Donna. She saved your butt big time, man, even if you don't care to admit it."

Okay, maybe he could've been a little less aggressive. Or maybe he let loose because he knew Donna could salvage any situation. Heck, the night she catapulted to national stardom, she'd talked a woman off a ninth-story window ledge, live on the air. It certainly hadn't hurt his career, either. Though he was pretty sure he'd aged about ten years from the stress.

"Tomorrow night it's all men. Got it? I don't care if it's discriminatory. No women calling me for advice or to ask about my love life. Just men talking about sports."

Ethan just swigged his beer with an eye roll like Lucas was the one being unreasonable. He was right, though. He did owe Donna. At the least for not giving her the sign he was about to go ballistic on that selfish, entitled brat. To be fair, by the time he knew he was, he already had.

Lucas shoved his chair back, wrenching his beaten brown leather jacket off the hook on the wall as he stood. "*Sports with Lucas.* That's the name of this show, Ethan. It may not be imaginative, but it's what I signed up for. I will talk about feelings all you want as long as they come attached to a game result."

- 3 -

*T*orrential rain hit a few minutes before Rachel's cab reached her North Nevada Avenue destination. The driver muttered obscenities as he crouched forward, nose almost against the windshield.

The white building leapt out in front of them, its entrance obscured by flailing construction signs buffeted by the wind.

"Thanks." Rachel flung the driver a twenty, racing against the hail of raindrops to the front doors. She was late. She hated being late.

"Hey, Loretta." The rain had won their race. She finger-combed her sodden hair, water trickling through her fingers, and pulled it into a ponytail.

"Hey, honey." The voluptuous nurse looked up from her notes. "He's in the activities room."

"Thanks. Any change?" The same question she'd been asking for ten years. Even though she knew the answer before she walked in the door. A question Loretta had long since stopped answering.

Her feet cut through the plush carpet. Paintings dotted the pale yellow hallway. No amount of decorating could hide what this place was. The truth was that for most of the people living within its confines, atmosphere was irrelevant. The colors, the artwork, the cheerful staff in the immaculate uniforms were all for the families. They helped assuage their guilt as visits dropped from daily, to weekly, to monthly. From hours to minutes.

Passing through the double doors, Rachel paused. Not to locate her father—he'd be in the same spot he was every week. In his bed, facing the garden, a seat placed beside him, ready for her arrival.

God, please don't let there be anyone. She wasn't sure why she still shot prayers up to someone she'd stopped believing in a long time ago. Maybe it was because a small part of her thought that if He did exist, He at least owed her a favor or two.

It was one thing for her to be here, hope long since gone. It was the new patients and their families that wiped her off the emotional map. The result of an ordinary day gone horribly wrong. A basketball game, a quick drive to the store, an unseen puddle on a wooden floor. The faces that leached hope as days, then months, disappeared without their miracle.

She had earned her place here, in this limbo on earth. So, too, had her father. Though most of the people who knew that were long since gone, or didn't care enough to remember.

Rachel walked behind an elderly patient watching a *Frasier* rerun and slipped into the wooden chair beside her father. It was all angles and hard edges, like her. When he'd first been relocated here, an orderly had regularly moved a large leather armchair into place for her, until she asked him to stop. It was too comfortable. There could be nothing comforting about these visits. Not after what she'd done.

"Father." She'd tried to say "Dad" once, but it had jammed in her throat.

He blinked. A slow motion, like a window shade being drawn. The first time it had happened she'd been convinced he was trying to acknowledge her. But the vegetative state was a cruel master, and she'd come to understand that its signs of life meant nothing.

"Latest royalty statement came in. We did good over Christmas." Of course, "good" was relative. In other people's worlds, eighty grand was a down payment on a loft, a year off to chase the dream, or college tuition. In hers, it paid for barely nine months at the intersection of Eternal Regrets and Hushed White Corridors.

She stretched her legs out, toes almost grazing the French doors. Chicken legs, he'd always called them. She'd never been so grateful for a fashion trend as she was when models sprung up with jeans tucked into their boots. Even then, the backs were still often so big they slapped into her shapeless calves.

"Latest book released a couple of weeks ago. Max and Donna think it's one of the best. Lacey, too, not that she'd ever admit it." A surge of regret traveled through her as she thought of the tense tightrope of professionalism that she and Lacey now traversed. If either of them had made a different decision that night—

"Excuse me." The words were so quiet she almost missed them. She knew the tone, though not the voice. It belonged to someone who had spent most of her recent days crying, until all she was left with was a hollow whisper.

Her gaze followed scuffed tennis shoes and worn jeans to a large Berkeley sweatshirt, engulfing the small frame it hung on. Brown hair pulled back in a ponytail, blotchy skin, long lashes framing red-rimmed brown eyes. The face of the person who represented both the best and worst moments of Rachel's life.

"I'm sorry to bother you, but . . ." The woman waved an empty drink bottle around, as if unable to grasp the words to complete the sentence.

Rachel pushed her chair back and turned on shaky legs to see her better. Maybe it was just the angle that had made a stranger look like a ghost from her past. She took in the small scar on the woman's forehead. The permanent result of a late-night stumble in the library quad after they'd spent hours cramming for an exam.

"Anna?" The question fell out in two jagged syllables.

They'd both gotten B-pluses on that paper. That was the random fact that came to her as she stood staring at her ex best friend.

The woman looked at her, then clutched her drink bottle to her chest as if she needed some kind of barrier between them. "Rachel?"

"Yeah."

Anna's gaze darted to her father. "Oh my gosh, is that your . . . I thought he was—" Her mouth slammed shut before she could finish her sentence, but she didn't need to.

Dead. Anna thought her father would have been long gone by now. At least from this building, if not from the planet. If she'd given it any real thought since their friendship fractured.

Rachel glanced at her father. "Yes. This my father, Dan." His name felt foreign on her tongue, it had been so long since she'd said it. No one who knew he still existed ever asked after him. As if speaking his name would cause her to remember they'd all abandoned him to shrivel and die alone. Anna had met him all of once. If you could even call hauling a drunk, abusive man out of a dim and sleazy bar meeting someone. "What are you doing here?"

Anna's body seemed to curl in on itself at her blunt question. "My husband—" Anna's rasping voice faltered for a second, but she caught it. "My husband, Cam, he got transferred here a few days ago."

Anna was married. To a man called Cam. Anna. Who had been determined that she would never join the patriarchal and oppressive institution that was matrimony. Rachel let herself absorb the information for a second.

"They said it's the best place in Colorado for brain injuries. I wondered why it sounded familiar. But of course. You told me your dad was here before . . ." Her voice trailed off.

Before Rachel had evicted Lacey and Anna from her life.

"I'm sorry about Cam." There were no other words. Not when Rachel knew that if Cam was still here in five years, Anna would no doubt think it would have been better if he'd died.

Anna's face sagged. "He fell off a ladder. A ladder he's used a hundred times before. It doesn't make any sense. And all everyone keeps talking about is how great it is that he's here. I just want my husband back."

At least she had that. Rachel couldn't even say she wanted her father back. Well, not the one who'd loved booze far more than he'd ever loved her. And invested the last years of his life turning into such a selfish, vindictive man not even the grave wanted him.

She shook her head. He was already sucking up all her money. No need to give him any more mental energy.

"Let me show you the water cooler." Her hand grazed Anna's forearm but Anna stayed rooted, staring out the French doors.

Outside, the rain still pelted down, barreling against the glass. "You know, I went home last night and painted my kitchen pink. Just slapped it over every surface I could find. It's a disaster." Anna shook her head. "I hate pink. Libby had to beg me for months before I gave in for her bedroom. I still hate it, but know what I hate more now?"

Rachel was pretty sure she did, but the question was rhetorical.

"Lemon. Stupid, sickening, insipid lemon. I chose it so that even in winter we still had sunshine. And now I spend all day, every day, living my worst nightmares, surrounded by blinking Pollyanna yellow, and it makes me want to break things. Which I did. And then we ran out of dishes, so now I have a pink kitchen." Anna's face scrunched with distaste just saying the last two words.

My father is a vegetable because of you and you think we can still be friends? If I never see you again it will be too soon. Those were some of the last words she'd spoken to Anna, and here they were talking interior decorating. "The lemon's new," Rachel said, gesturing toward the wall. "When my father came, it was duck-egg blue. I still won't stay in a blue hotel room. Or lemon. So I'm hoping they don't repaint again soon."

Anna glanced at her, gratitude in her eyes. "Has he . . . ?"

If only she could lie. But any idiot could see her father had nowhere to go but up. And still be alive, that is. "Nothing."

"Mommy!" A mop of carrot curls torpedoed into Anna's legs.

"Hey, sweetie." Anna lifted her up onto her hip.

Two curious hazel eyes peered at Rachel. "Who're you?"

Anna mouthed "sorry" over the top of Torpedo's head. "Libby, this is Rachel. Her daddy is here too."

Rachel just stared at the little girl. Anna's daughter shared her snub nose and long lashes.

"Look!" A pudgy fist shoved a crumpled piece of paper into the air. "I drawed this for my daddy."

"Ooooh, let me see." Anna peered over the paper.

The best Rachel could make out from the multicolored scribbles was something that might be an abstract tree.

"Can you tell me about it, sweetie?" Anna unfolded a crumpled corner.

A stubby finger stabbed the picture. "That's you, and that's Daddy in his bed, and Poppa and Grandma, and the angels making Daddy all better."

Anna gazed heavenward and forced a deep swallow. "That's right, baby girl. Daddy has lots of angels watching over him."

A sigh snuck through Rachel's lips. Everyone got religion in these walls. People who had never stepped foot in a church suddenly found Jesus, angels, and the power of prayer. Until none of them worked.

"Can we go gimmit to him?"

"Sure, baby."

Libby wiggled herself out of Anna's arms, entwining five pudgy fingers around her mom's. "Daddy's going to think it's my bestest one yet!" She made the pronouncement with the authority of someone who has never doubted for a second her place in her father's world.

Envy entwined itself around Rachel's heart. Her cornerstone memory of drawing her father a picture was of finding it in the trash the next day, jammed between leftover mashed potato and moldy bread.

Without warning, five little fingers wound around hers. "You too, Rachel. You come meet my daddy."

Her daddy. Anna's husband. Was here. Years ago, she'd wished that Anna would one day know how this felt. And here she was.

Rachel was glad she didn't believe in a god. Because she would hate to think one could be cruel enough to answer a prayer like that.

- 4 -

"Good show the other night, Luc. Especially Dr. Donna. Didn't realize she'd added sports commentator to her quiver of expertise." His brother clapped him across the shoulder, his other hand tossing the last bite of an oatmeal cookie into his mouth.

"You're hilarious." No doubt as soon as Donna had come on air, Scott had turned the show off. His brother would sooner plow his fields by hand than sit through two hours of talking about feelings. Same as any other average red-blooded American male. The supportive-older-brother act was nice, though.

"Uncle Lucas!" Three feet of pint-sized power barreled into the den and wrapped itself around his legs.

"Hey, champ." Lucas swung his nephew up by his armpits and spun him around, then dropped him back to the floor. "Man, I think you've gotten even bigger since I saw you last. Much more of this and you'll be taller than your dad before you're six."

"Let's hope not." His sister-in-law wandered into the homey

room, laundry basket tucked under her arm. "I have enough trouble keeping enough food in the house as it is." Her T-shirt was rumpled and her brown hair looked like it needed a wash. Something was wrong.

"Hey." Lucas dropped a quick kiss on her cheek. "How're you doing?"

"Okay." Grace ditched the basket on the sofa. "Lunch is ready."

"Yay!" Joey careened out of the room.

"Wash your hands first, young man," Grace called after him, then shook her head. "Let me just go make sure he does. He's lately taken to just running the tap."

Lucas grabbed the bottles of soda he'd brought and headed for the kitchen. Pulling the fridge open, he stashed a couple away and pulled out a tray of ice from the freezer. "Coke or Dr. Pepper?" His brother peered past him with an odd look on his face. "Scott? Everything okay?"

"What? Oh, whatever is fine."

Lucas pulled out three large glasses and Joey's Spiderman cup, tumbling ice into all. He twisted open the Dr. Pepper, filled two glasses, and handed his brother one. "What's Joey drinking these days?" Grace was a stickler about soda being allowed only on special occasions.

"There's some lemonade in the fridge. Add half water." Scott thumped into a chair at the dining table, landing like a sack of spuds.

"What's happened? What's wrong?"

His brother didn't say anything for a moment, his Adam's apple bobbing as he swallowed a couple of times. "The latest round hasn't taken. We found out a few days ago."

Not again. How much more could they take? Lucas crossed the room in a couple of strides, taking the seat beside his brother. "I'm so sorry." Three years of trying to give Joey a sibling. An endless carousel of angst, anticipation, hope, and despair. Secondary infertility. There was a phrase he wished had never been added to his vocabulary.

Scott shrugged his shoulders, then slumped against his chair. "I don't know how much longer we can keep doing this, Luc. It's killing us. Emotionally, financially, mentally. Not to mention what Grace's poor body gets put through." He took another gulp of his soda. "It had just looked so promising this time. She's taking it hard."

"I'm sorry." There was no time Lucas felt more useless than in these conversations. The ranch, Joey, everything else he could help out with. But this? Nothing.

"Okay, all done." Grace marched Joey into the room and he clambered onto the chair next to Lucas.

"I'm so sorry, Grace."

She offered a weak smile that failed to reach her cornflower-blue eyes as she took her chair. "Some things just aren't meant to be, I guess." Tears welled, but she swiped the moisture away. "Grace, Scott?"

They all joined hands, Joey standing on his chair to reach both his mom and uncle.

"Gracious God, we thank you for this meal and for the many blessings that you have bestowed upon us. Thank you that even when things don't make sense, we can trust you. Amen."

Lucas studied the pockmarked table as the words rolled over him. How could his brother believe in a gracious God when He kept dishing out defeat?

"Uncle Lucas." Joey tugged on his sleeve. "Pass the peanut butter, please."

Lucas slid the jar to his nephew, who dug his spoon in with a vengeance. "You want some help with that?"

"Nope." A boulder of peanut butter flopped onto the whole-wheat bread.

"Joey." Grace's voice held a note of warning.

"No, thank you." Joey swiped some spread up and popped it in his mouth.

An awkward silence settled over the table as everyone put together sandwiches. It wasn't like they could discuss the elephant in the room with Joey there.

"So." Grace cut her bread into two perfect rectangles. "Good show the other night, Luc."

"Thanks." He took a bite of his roast beef, cheddar, and pickle on rye. Mmmm, his sister-in-law did a knockout roast.

"Is Dr. Donna as great as she seems?"

He choked for a second, then swallowed. He'd thought she was just making polite conversation. Why on earth would she want to listen to a whole bunch of other people's issues when her dream for another child had been shattered, again?

She shrugged, reading his expression. "I know you would rather have been talking about the Brewers, but sometimes it's nice to know other people in the world have problems. I especially liked the serve you gave that last caller." She shook her head. "She doesn't deserve either of those poor guys."

"What happened?" Scott actually looked interested.

"Oh . . ." Grace flicked her hand, seeming to forget it was holding her lunch. A piece of tomato splattered on the table. "This married woman has a boyfriend and he wants her to move in. She wanted to know what to do. Lucas gave her a bit of a hard time."

"You did, huh?" Scott took a sip of his soda.

Lucas's blood boiled just thinking about it. With the benefit of hindsight, he wished he'd given the caller even more grief. "No more than she deserved."

Scott speared a pickle. "Fortunately, most of us don't get what we deserve."

Lucas was so not in the mood for a sermon today. "Well, most of us have the decency not to live a life of lies." He took a large bite of his sandwich. Hoping his brother would get the signal.

"I think everyone is capable of crossing lines they never thought possible, given the right circumstances." His brother either missed the hint or just dodged it.

Lucas stabbed an errant pickle. "Well, anyone capable of living a double life is not someone I want anything to do with. Not on my show, or in my life." And if anyone ever tried it again, he'd cut them loose so fast, they'd have whiplash.

- 5 -

"Donna!" Theodore Randolph's voice boomed across the private dining room. Not even the plush carpets or the velvet curtains were able to muffle the sound of a man used to having his every word obeyed.

"Theo!" Donna glided forward, regal in a burgundy wrap dress, perfectly painted face an expression of delight. Rachel trailed behind, her role so ingrained she didn't even need to think. Air kisses all round before Donna gestured behind her. "You remember my assistant, Rachel."

"Of course." Theodore Randolph IV, patriarch of the Randolph publishing empire, didn't even glance her way. The man couldn't pick her out of a lineup of one. Which was just how they wanted it.

She was here only because Donna, with her Southern sense of justice, wouldn't hear of Rachel not coming to her own celebratory new-release lunch. Which was a shame, since she would've preferred staying at home and conjuring up more terrible ideas for their next book over a brisk spring day in New York watching Donna being fawned over by the senior executives at their publishing house.

Cue received, she left Randolph and the head of marketing to schmooze with Donna, and she dropped into a seat opposite Kelly at the end of the table. All dark glossy hair and Fifth Avenue pearls, you'd never guess that under her perfect twinset, their editor spent her weekends as a competitive rock climber.

A waiter materialized, pouring fizzing champagne to the tops of their glasses.

"Hi, how's the tour going?"

Rachel placed her phone beside her plate. "Fine, I think. We're in Charleston next. Then Texas. I haven't been with her this last week, but Lacey says the crowds have been good."

"Randolph is desperate to know about the new offer." Kelly took a dainty sip, mouth puckering slightly. Whether because of the taste or the conversation topic, Rachel wasn't sure.

"I know." Rachel plucked a piece of bread from the bowl at the center of their table. She wasn't stupid. Donna was Randolph's golden-egged goose.

"Do you think she'll sign?" Kelly's voice was hopeful.

Rachel checked that everyone else was a safe distance away. "She's been talking about taking a break, a life-out-of-the-limelight sort of thing, so I'm not sure."

Kelly's face fell like a child's who'd just been told Christmas had been cancelled.

"But who knows. Anything could happen."

"Well, we'll all know soon enough, I guess." Kelly's hand tightened around her glass.

Rachel looked around for a waiter to order a drink. What was she even doing here? Her mind drifted to Libby and Anna.

Seeing her old friend in the last place she'd wish on anyone had created a hurricane of mixed emotions inside her. Ones that refused to be compartmentalized, no matter how hard she tried.

". . . do it." Rachel jolted to, only to realize she'd just missed everything Kelly had been saying.

"Sorry, Kel, zoned out for a sec. What was that?"

Kelly paused, champagne glass in her hand. She shook her head, dark hair swishing like a shampoo ad, and gave a little laugh. "Oh nothing. I was just saying that you've been with Donna so long, you could probably write the books yourself."

A cough erupted from Rachel's throat.

"You all right?"

Rachel smacked her chest. "Fine—something just went down the wrong way." She grabbed her glass, slurping some water to buy some time.

"So do you know what the next one is about?"

At least she could answer this honestly. "No idea. She's played with a few ideas but is going full tilt promoting this one at the moment." Her calm words belied the twisting in her stomach. The two of them had spent the entire previous evening in Donna's hotel room trying to brainstorm a concept, but even that effort hadn't come up with anything they felt good about. Which had never happened before.

Kelly leaned back and glanced up the table toward Donna. "You know, we were talking at the office the other day about how crazy her schedule is. Does she need some help?"

"What do you mean?"

They both paused as the waiter topped up Kelly's glass.

"Can I grab a lime and soda, please?" The man nodded at Rachel's request and disappeared.

"A collaborative writer. It's no problem to hire someone to get started with putting some words on the page. In fact, it's very common once people reach this level."

Donna didn't need a ghostwriter. The problem *was* her ghostwriter. "I don't think that will be necessary."

Kelly cast a look to where Donna and the executives were still standing and talking. "Well, you didn't hear it from me, but I'm pretty sure her sales are keeping half the company afloat. He put some big money into a couple of titles last year that didn't sell nearly as many copies as had been expected."

Rachel put down her fork and pushed her plate away. "You've got plenty of other big authors, though, right?" They had to. Randolph Books was an empire. *Publishers Weekly* was always packed with their latest and greatest deals.

Kelly's brow furrowed. "Well, of course we've got Bella and Mark in fiction, but even they're not doing as well as they used to. Some people think that books that take a year to write should cost less than a latte. And of course they're competing with the indies giving away their books." She shrugged her shoulders. "At the end of the day, if you're not a hard-core fan and just looking for an easy beach read, are you going to pay twelve bucks for a Bella Kingsley or download twenty for free on the chance that at least one will be decent?"

Rachel took a sip of water. "Can't say I've ever thought about it." Especially when Donna got sent more books than one woman could read in a lifetime.

"Well, so far Donna isn't suffering the same fate. Her sales are strong across all channels. Some of our mid-list authors should be sending her gift baskets. She's the only reason they still have contracts."

Rachel's stomach clenched. How did she end up responsible for a bunch of people she'd never even met? "I'm sure she'll let Max know what her decision is soon."

Kelly twirled her fork, half-eaten asparagus spear spinning. "Can you do me a favor then?"

"Of course."

Kelly leaned in a little, dropping her volume. "If she does decide not to sign, can you at least give me a heads-up? I'd like to at least get my résumé out the door before the stampede begins."

"What?"

Kelly shrugged. "It's pretty common knowledge. No new Donna deal and Randolph's going to start sharpening the knives, and cutting loose the authors who aren't making enough money. And when authors go, editors follow." She gave a short, sharp laugh. "No pressure."

"But surely you won't be at risk? You're one of the best."

Kelly laughed. "The only reason he knows I even exist is because of Donna. With him, no one's safe unless they happen to have some pretty impressive connections. Which definitely isn't me. Now Lindsey, who thinks Jane Austen is a woman Colin Firth dated once, her uncle's a senator, so she has nothing to worry about."

Rachel shoveled a bite of salad into her mouth. *Great, just great. Yet one more thing to feel guilty about.*

- 6 -

*T*he scent of gardenias wafted through the hotel window. Actually, Rachel had no idea what they were, but she'd read a travel review once that had gushed about Charleston in spring and gardenias, so either that's what they were or she'd chosen to latch on to a writer just as botanically clueless as she was.

"Good, you're here." Lacey marched into the hotel suite, not even bothering with the most cursory of greetings. "I need you to convince Donna schnoodles are out." She smoothed an invisible wayward hair back into her perfect chignon.

Rachel groaned. Donna was such a pushover. Every year, without fail, they had to intervene to stop her being wheedled into supporting some pointless cause that would have the rest of America die laughing if they heard about it. "What on earth is a schnoodle?"

Lacey just managed to get the words past her incredulous expression. "A cross between a schnauzer and a poodle. Schnoodles against starvation. Some crazy woman is having a fundraiser to raise money for the starving puppies in Africa."

"Now, that's not very kind," Donna remonstrated from the doorway to her bedroom, but her smile gave her away. "And please, give me some credit. Even I'm not going to get suckered into signing up for that one." She pottered into the room, her purple velour tracksuit in contrast with her professionally done hair and makeup.

Donna lowered herself onto the red chaise lounge, sitting ramrod straight to avoid crushing her updo. "So I've been thinking about our little situation."

"Which one?" Rachel pulled a couple of dresses out of the garment bag she'd draped over the back of a chair. "Black or navy?"

Donna wrinkled her nose. "Neither. Whatever happened to that nice floral one I gave you for Christmas?"

Rachel smothered the sigh that threatened to escape. Every few months the same old debate would flare up. Donna persistently bought her gorgeous, colorful clothes that she would never wear. There was nothing she wanted less than to be memorable, for any reason.

"Fine." Donna threw her hands up. "In that case, I don't care. Now back to our situation."

"What situation?" Rachel held both dresses up in front of her, then dropped her arms. Her aunt was right. It didn't matter which out of two equally boring dresses she wore.

"The book one. I've been thinking that maybe your problem is you need to change it up a bit. You know, get yourself out of the same old same old. It's no wonder that after years of being my assistant by day, Dr. Donna by night, with no love life to speak of, the well of inspiration is running a bit dry. So I've come up with something that I think will help."

"What's that?" Please don't let it be some kind of retreat where she'd spend a week eating legumes and cleansing her aura. She'd sooner take on the fundraising schnoodles.

"It's more *who's* that. We're going to bring in Lucas."

She knew exactly one Lucas, but it couldn't be him. "Lucas Grant?"

Her aunt leaned back, then remembered her hair and sat forward again. "Yes. Lacey talked to Ethan and he thinks it's a great idea too. He's just getting the clearance from his bosses."

Rachel stared at her aunt, trying to process what she'd just said. What did Lucas Grant have to do with coming up with a new book concept?

"The two of you always tag-team so well together and this is perfect. You'll get to spend lots of time on air, get some fresh ideas, and of course Lucas gets to have Dr. Donna on his show and gets the boost to his platform from being on the road with us."

"Hold on, hold on. Come again? What are you doing?"

"You're going to go on Lucas's show a night a week for a few weeks, and then he's going to come and join us for some joint events on the tour. Well, we're going to do one test event first, in a couple of weeks, to make sure it's as popular as I think it's going to be, but I know it will." Donna clasped her hands together like a girl who had just been invited to the prom.

She could not be serious. "You know about this." Rachel pointed a coat hanger at their publicist.

Lacey glanced up from her phone. "Donna's plan? It's pure genius. The actual romance expert and the accidental one live onstage. Tickets are going to fly out the door. Besides," she tapped her nose, "sources have it Lucas is making a name for himself and people in high places are watching. It's going to be a little awkward navigating all of Donna's existing commitments, but we'll make it work."

"Lucas will never agree to it." Thank goodness for that. There was no chance, no way, that Lucas Grant would agree to come on Donna's book tour and dole out relationship advice to rooms full of women.

"I wouldn't be so sure about that." Donna had the kind of Cheshire Cat smile she always had when she knew something Rachel didn't. But Donna hadn't heard how peeved Lucas had been when Ethan blindsided him with her appearance on the show. So Rachel was pretty confident she had this one in the bag.

"Want to know what we're calling it?"

"Nope."

"*The Feelings and Football Tour*. Ethan came up with it." Donna's grin widened, if that was even possible, and all of a sudden Rachel knew that Lucas was in just as much trouble as she was.

"MAN, DO I have some good news for you!"

Sweat dribbled down Lucas's arms, drops hitting the pavement like a summer shower. He didn't even look up at Ethan's yell. The last time he'd shown up at the basketball court yelling he had good news, Dunkin' had brought his favorite donut back for a limited time.

Lucas faked right, then drove left, swerving past his opponent. One, two, three steps and a clear shot into the basket. He finished the sequence off by running circles around his downtrodden competition, fists pumping the air.

Joey stood, hands on hips, scowl affixed, unimpressed by his uncle's smooth moves. "Uncle Lucas!" You could have built a cabana on the ledge made by the kid's bottom lip. "You said you'd play fair!"

Lucas picked Joey up in one easy move, lodging him under his right arm and spinning around. "Sorry, buddy, just couldn't resist." He swung him upright. Grace would have his hide if he delivered Joey home with another "Uncle Lucas spun me until I puked" tale.

He lifted Joey until they were eye-to-eye. "Ice cream or soda?"

Gray eyes crinkled as the decision-making process worked its way through. "Two scoops?"

"Sorry, little dude, I promised your mom. You know what happened last time you had two scoops." It had been over a year ago, but hearing Grace tell the tale, it was only yesterday her favorite rug had been enhanced.

Eyes clouded over. Poor little guy. A year ago was a fifth of your life when you were five. "Tell you what. Why don't you pick my flavor too, and I'll let you have some."

Sunshine returned. "Yeah!" A small palm high-fived his. "You're the best, Uncle Lucas!"

Joey scrambled down, chicken legs already churning

to race across the adjoining playground to the cart by the swings.

Lucas strolled over to Ethan, keeping an eye on his nephew, who had reached the cart and was bouncing up and down, trying to see into the ice cream freezer.

Ethan pushed himself up off the bleacher, brushing pieces of flaking white paint off his designer jeans. "Feel good beating a kindergartener?"

Lucas pulled his T-shirt off, swapping it for the clean gray one he'd left on the sideline. He used the old one to wipe down his face and arms. "Guy's gotta take his wins wherever he can find them."

He grabbed his water bottle off the bench and squirted some into his mouth. Ahhh. Icy goodness. He couldn't stand lukewarm water. Grabbing his keys and phone, he threw his dirty T-shirt over his shoulder and bounced the keys in his hand.

Joey bounced up and down on his toes, radiating impatience from across the playground. No doubt plotting to bargain an extra scoop for having to wait. Lucas loped across the distance between them.

"Well?" Ethan trotted beside him, needing to take three steps for every two of Lucas's.

"Well what?"

"Aren't you going to ask what the great news is?" Ethan ran his hand through his floppy hair.

Unable to take any more waiting, Joey ran back and came to a stop, doing some sort of jitterbug in front of them. "Uncle Lucas, I can't decide between cherry or fish or cookies!"

Ethan looked peeved at being interrupted, a harrumph escaping his lips.

Served him right for crashing their play date. Lucas only got to take Joey out once a week, but he was stuck in a closet with Ethan Monday through Friday.

"Tell you what, buddy." Lucas flipped open his phone cover and extracted a twenty. "Why don't you order one of each—Ethan needs one too, and I'm sure he'll let you have some."

Joey palmed the money and ran away, a blur of yellow.

Lucas shoved his phone back in his pocket. "Okay, tell me." This had better be better than donuts.

"Have you ever met Lacey O'Connor?"

"I don't think so."

"Well, you're about to, and when you do, I hope you make your appreciation clear, because that wonderful, wonderful woman has just opened up a whole world of possibilities. Also, for the record, very easy on the eyes and stupid smart."

Not this again. How many times did he have to tell Ethan that just because his sports—*sports*—show kept getting hijacked by women wanting relationship advice, it didn't mean he wanted one. In fact, he was pretty sure the gig worked because he was single. No girlfriend thinking everything he said was about her, about them. "Let it go, Ethan. I'm not interested."

Certainly not in Ethan's kind of setup, anyway. The man thought Lucas should be using his quasi-fame to sleep his way around the county. He was pretty sure his mother would blast down the Pearly Gates and hurl them on him if he ever so much as thought about taking a woman home for nothing more than the night.

"You can't be serious!" Ethan stared at him like this was the first he'd heard of it.

Lucas grabbed the toe of his sneaker and stretched his quad. Their ratings were just fine, as Ethan well knew. "Ethan, I don't need a girlfriend. I don't *want* a girlfriend. End of story. It doesn't matter how you try and frame it."

Ethan looked at him, a smirk on his lips. "Well, I'm sure her boyfriend will be happy to hear that. If she has one. But that's not what she's offering. Lacey is Dr. Donna's publicist."

Lucas grabbed his other toe, his sock poking through the worn sneaker. Ethan had lost him.

He cast his gaze to Joey, who was sitting in a patch of sun by the ice cream cart focused on decimating his ice cream. Two other containers sat behind him, scoops melting in the sun. "What are you talking about?"

"Lucas Grant and Dr. Donna Somerville on—get this— *The Feelings and Football Tour*." Ethan spread his hands out as he said the words like he was seeing them in lights.

Lucas rocked back on his heels. *What the . . . ?*

A grin split Ethan's face. "Yes, you *should* be speechless. Lacey just pitched it yesterday—well, the idea; the name is mine—and the bosses just okayed it this morning. Donna is going to come and be on your show for a few weeks and then you're going to join her at some events on her book tour for a couple of weeks. Maybe longer. They'll call them *The Feelings and Football Tour* and you should see the venues they are booking. There's one small pilot event next weekend to test to market, but that's just a formality. Donna will be in town Thursday to do your show and tell listeners about it."

So many swear words exploded through Lucas's head that he wouldn't have been surprised if Miss Margie—his old Sunday school teacher—rose from the grave to slap him upside the head. "Dr. Donna is coming on my show the next few weeks to talk about feelings, and I'm going on her book tour to talk about football." He uttered the words slowly, making sure there was no room for error.

Ethan shrugged. "Well, let's be frank. You'll probably talk mostly about feelings on that, too."

"Yeah, nah. I don't think so." Lucas lengthened his stride and headed toward where Joey was still sitting on the grass with his ice cream.

"What do you mean you don't think so?" Ethan jogged to keep up with him. "This is *huge*! Think of her platform. Think of the wonders this will do for your profile and the show's ratings. You keep saying you want to syndicate the show. This could be your golden ticket!"

"I do sports. I want to syndicate my *sports* show." Lucas shoved the words through his gritted teeth.

"Um, actually, I hate to break it to you, but according to your contract, when it comes to promotional work, if the station orders you to get dressed up in a chicken suit and walk down State Street clucking, you do it. And it doesn't get any more promotional than this."

"What about my show? Who's going to cover that while I'm doing these events?" He had worked his way up from the bottom of the radio food chain. It had taken years to build up the experience and profile needed to convince a station to take a chance on giving him his own sports show. He wasn't going to trust just anyone with it.

Ethan shrugged. "Some of this will be on the weekend, so you shouldn't miss too many. Once Lacey has confirmed the schedule we'll fill in any gaps."

"Uncle Lucas?" For a second he couldn't coordinate where the mournful words came from, then his sight bounced down. To a towheaded five-year-old with a mouth rimmed with brown and pink. "I don't think you should have spun me like that. I don't feel so good."

Well, that made two of them.

- 7 -

"*T*ell me why I had to come again?" Rachel mumbled the words to her aunt as the elevator doors swished open and deposited them into the reception area of WFM Madison.

She was crabby. Her rare couple of days off mid-tour had been hijacked by the radio station asking if Donna could come to Madison to do a photo shoot and kick off the tour live in the studio with Lucas.

Donna pulled a container of mints out of her purse and popped one in her mouth. "Lacey had something urgent come up. Besides, it will be good for you to meet Lucas since he'll be traveling with us."

They accepted their laminated visitor cards from the receptionist and then sat on one of the beige couches in the waiting area. All around them were signed posters of the latest "it" celebrities and musicians.

Rachel eyed the door behind the reception desk that Ethan or Lucas would be coming through any second now.

"I'd rather not, actually. Behind all that Midwestern nice-guy shtick is probably just another DJ playboy who thinks he's God's gift to women."

After tonight it would be Rachel doing shows with him. For four hours at a time. If it had been up to her, she'd have kept Lucas Grant safely at the end of the phone. She liked the Lucas Grant at the end of the phone. Didn't really want to risk discovering he was actually a jerk. But that bird had clearly flown the coop.

"Not all women. I prefer to leave the ones over fifty to Larry on the graveyard shift." The familiar voice came from behind them and rolled up her spine.

Rachel's head jerked up to find a broad T-shirt-clad torso standing right behind their couch.

Donna stood and turned, a smile playing on her lips. Rachel stood too, her ears burning. Not sure whether to be madder at herself or at him for having the temerity to not be in his office. Or whatever it was radio station hosts had.

"Lucas, this is my assistant, Rachel. Please excuse her. Red-eye flights don't bring out the best in her."

Rachel forced herself to look him in the face and her mouth went dry. Lucas Grant looked like a cowboy off one of the covers of the romance novels she used to read as a teenager. Tall. Brawny. Forehead a little too large. Pale blue eyes. Nose a little crooked. It had been years since she'd last seen a photo of him. Then he'd been in his twenties and with the fresh-faced look of someone just out of college.

Not now. The aging process had only been kind to Lucas Grant.

This was who was going to be touring with them?

"Rachel." Lucas held out his hand. In his other one he held a Starbucks tray with two venti-sized drinks.

"Hi." Rachel's hand crept forward, and his fingers wrapped around it firmly.

Wow. This wasn't awkward at all. She tried to coax a smile onto her face, but only the left side of her mouth cooperated. No doubt making her look like a stroke victim.

Lucas turned his attention back to her aunt. "I hope you haven't been waiting too long. The photographer said he was running a few minutes late, so I just ducked out to get you a coffee." Pulling one out, he handed it to Donna. "One white chocolate latte with extra whip."

Donna's favorite. *Smooth, real smooth.* Her aunt reached out and accepted her drink with thanks.

"I'm sorry, I didn't know you were coming, but you're welcome to my flat white." Lucas offered the remaining drink to Rachel.

"No. That's fine. Thank you."

Donna's gaze bounced between the two of them. "Lucas. I was just thinking. We should have breakfast in the morning to discuss the plans for the tour. Can you set that up with Rachel while I go freshen up?"

Lucas may have missed the speculative gleam in her aunt's eye but Rachel knew it well. "You already have a breakfast meeting tomorrow and then our flight is straight after." Rachel gave her aunt laser eyes. Which Donna refused to acknowledge.

"Coffee, then. After the breakfast. Just ring Jeff and get him to change our flights to late morning. Lucas darling, work it out with Rachel. I'll be back in a few minutes." Lucas opened his mouth, but Donna stopped his words with a raised hand. "No need. I remember where the ladies' is." Donna bustled past Lucas before he even had a chance to respond, pausing in the doorway and mouthing "be nice" to her furious niece.

DONNA DISAPPEARED faster than a whirling dervish, so Lucas turned his attention to her assistant, who looked ticked off, to say the least. She stared at the empty doorway, rosy lips pursed, then heaved a sigh.

Well, that made two of them.

He wasn't even sure what she was doing here. Ethan had called him in the morning saying that Donna's PR person wanted to set up some promo shots before the show. Hardly an assistant-worthy event.

"Look, I don't want to cause any difficulty. We can just—"

"It's fine." Rachel cut him off with the flick off her wrist.

"I know a nice—"

"Just give me a sec, okay? I need to look at tomorrow's schedule and see if we can make this work."

Fine. If she was going to be snooty, he'd just leave her to it. The photographer was still MIA, so he settled himself down on the couch and pulled out his phone. Scrolled through CNN to see if there was anything in the sports news that he could lever into the show. Just because Donna would be there didn't mean he was giving up without a fight.

Rachel pulled an iPad out of her purse and tapped the screen a few times, lips pursed and brow furrowed. Then she got on the phone and paced. Her beige dress was about the same shade as the couches. She almost blended into the furniture as she walked behind them. Though even the unflattering cut couldn't hide long legs and a slim waist as she lapped the reception area, debating connection times and layover airports with the person on the other end.

He forced his attention back to his phone, but the words on the screen couldn't hold his attention.

Behind all that Midwestern nice-guy shtick is probably just another DJ playboy who thinks he's God's gift to women.

The comment burned at the back of his brain. He wasn't unaware of the reputations of some DJs. Even at WFM, the breakfast and drive-time crews had a reputation for enjoying the benefits that came with fame. If you could even call it that when your so-called celebrity existed only in Madison and the surrounding counties.

But that wasn't him. And he'd worked really hard to never do anything that might give the appearance or perception that it was. So hearing his name besmirched by some woman who didn't know him from the back end of a bull got to him.

Lucas looked up from his phone as she ended her call and dropped down onto the other couch, tapping something into what looked like a calendar app. "I'm not." The words were out of his mouth before he realized he was speaking.

"I'm sorry." The assistant looked up from her screen. "Was that directed at me?"

Might as well finish what he'd started. "Yes. I just wanted to clarify. I'm not a player."

She studied him for a second, then shrugged. "Okay." Her gaze returned to her screen and she tapped a couple of times.

"I'm sorry. Was that a sarcastic 'if you say so' okay? Or an

'I believe you' okay?" What was he doing? He sounded like a teenager on his first date, overanalyzing every little detail. What did it matter? He'd never met this woman before and given he was in this thing under extreme protest, why would he give a dime about what she thought?

Rachel lowered her device and looked at him properly. She tilted her head, as if considering a curiosity. "Why does it matter to you that much? Surely you're used to people assuming things about you that may or may not be true?"

She had brown-blond, kind-of-wavy hair unraveling from a bun. Long oval face, nose slightly too large, lips slightly too small. No one would call her beautiful in the conventional sense, but she was definitely striking.

And she was right. He shouldn't care. People believed far worse things about him. Every day there were trolls on social media casting all sorts of aspersions and downright slander, keeping the station's PR people employed.

"You're right. Forget it." The doors of the elevator behind him swooshed open and he turned his head to see Ben the photographer walk in, large Canon slung around his neck and phone pressed to his ear. Lucas stood. He lifted his hand in greeting.

Rachel stood too. "No, you're right. That was unfair of me. The fact that I didn't intend for you to overhear me doesn't make it okay." She took a couple of steps toward him. "Can we just start over? It's been a long day."

He studied her for a second, then held out his hand. "Hi, I don't believe we've met. I'm Lucas Grant."

There was something in the way her gaze flickered that made him feel like he'd said something wrong, but it was gone the same second she pressed her palm to his. "Hi. I'm Rachel Somers, Donna's assistant."

"Nice to meet you, Rachel." He gestured toward the door beyond the reception desk. "We should head to the studio. Donna knows where it is."

Swiping his card, he stepped back to let Rachel and Ben go ahead of him. The photographer strode on ahead, but Rachel paused until he caught up.

"So, how long have you worked for Donna?"

"Since the beginning."

"Wow. So you've seen it all. The rise and rise of Dr. Donna."

He opened the door that led into the production booth for Studio 1. The largest studio, where they hosted guests with any kind of stature. He normally used Studio 3, but its small, cramped quarters were only suitable for when it was just him and Ethan.

Rachel looked around the booth and through the window into the studio, taking it all in. "I have. But then this isn't exactly Y92 Arkansas, either."

His first gig. Right out of college. Even he'd almost forgotten about that. He groaned. "I can't believe you know that. Please tell me you never listened." It made him cringe just thinking about what an earnest do-gooder he'd been back then. Seeing the world in only black and white.

Something he couldn't decipher flashed across Rachel's face. "I listened to all of Donna's interviews the first couple of books. Part of the job." Her mouth lifted in a genuine smile and it transformed her face. "I've always wondered. How was Mavis when you decided to move on?"

Mavis. His first-ever regular caller when he'd been covering the any-topic-goes graveyard shift. She'd rung almost every shift at one a.m. on the dot for three years. A spunky octogenarian who'd had an opinion on everything from gun control to birth control. Not that he'd ever asked her about either. But that hadn't stopped her from offering it to him and his other ten listeners.

"She attached herself to my successor with equal vigor. Though she always claimed that was only because she couldn't afford the toll calls to follow me to Wisconsin. But she'd still call me now and then. To keep me on my toes, she said."

Rachel laughed. "I wonder what she looks like. In my mind she's just like Sophia from *The Golden Girls*. White hair, big glasses, small frame."

"Close." Lucas leaned back against the console. "Minus the big glasses. She had this small pair that perched on the end of her nose and this way of peering over the top of them that always made me feel like I was a child who'd been summoned to the principal's office."

Rachel's eyebrows lifted. "You met her?"

Lucas shrugged. "Yeah. A few months in she didn't call for a few nights, so I checked up on her. She'd been in the hospital with pneumonia. It just went from there. Most of her family is far away and so was mine."

Rachel opened her mouth. He hardly ever talked about his friendship with Mavis because people—women especially—usually thought it made him some kind of saint. Truth was, he'd gotten more out of it than she had. Which was why he hardly ever talked about it. He started to interrupt her, but she just said, "Okay, I'm going to go see what is taking Donna so long, then I need to make some calls. It was nice meeting you, Lucas."

She flung the last few words over her shoulder as she disappeared back out the studio door.

Strange woman.

FOUR HOURS' sleep. That's what a restless conscience got you.

Rachel took a sip of her sugar-doctored coffee and tapped on her iPad, checking that their flights were on schedule. They had less than an hour before they had to leave for the airport.

She could get through this. Forget that Lucas Grant visited the elderly in his spare time. Just focus on the book. Maybe something on bad dates turned good? She could get some case studies on horrible first impressions leading to love. Dr. Donna's fans loved that kind of stuff.

Bad enough that Lucas had accepted her apology. Bad enough that when she'd pulled herself together enough to return to the studio they'd been taking photos of him and Donna and his gaze had occasionally caught hers, and she'd felt her heart stumble every time.

The worst part was that while the photographer had snapped photo after photo she'd been online trying to find something, anything, that would confirm her desire for him to be just like every other good-looking radio host under forty. When that failed, she searched for evidence of a significant other. She would've taken either.

Nothing. No articles featuring drunken nights out or

accusations from ex-girlfriends of rat-fink behavior. No feel-good articles with him and some gorgeous Wisconsinite showing off their stylish home and their perfect life. He didn't even seem to be photographed on the Madison social circuit. Just a whole lot of industry-related events sprinkled with the occasional movie premiere of the latest action flick that any guy would have jumped at free tickets to.

"Rachel?" Her aunt clicked at her from across the table. "Earth to Rachel."

"Sorry. What was that?"

"How did you think it went last night?"

"Great. It was great." While listening to the show, she'd also completed a more thorough exegesis of Lucas's career trajectory and online profile. Studying up. She knew times had changed since his late nights at Arkansas's lowest-rating station, but she'd had no idea how popular he'd become.

After last night's show she knew why. Sure, he started off his show talking about some sports team she'd never heard of. But the callers didn't seem to care that that was what he wanted to talk about. They called in to ask him for his take on the men in their lives, and he answered them truthfully. If she'd been a lovelorn lady in Wisconsin, after a few hours of listening to his straight-talking yet compassionate, authoritative, no-holds-barred advice, she would have found it difficult to resist hijacking his sports show as well.

"If it was so great, why is your face sagging like it's trying to fall off your skull?" Her aunt pulled a fluffy piece of pastry off her pain au chocolat and popped it into her mouth.

Rachel looked around. They were at an isolated corner table at the café facing the front door. There was no chance of anyone overhearing them. Or of Lucas surprising them with his arrival.

"How can you look so serene about this? He's a genuinely decent guy. I knew it would have been better if I hadn't met him. Now I feel even worse about being the one doing the rest of his shows. Not to mention totally stressed out that he's going to figure out I'm not you."

The guy had a phenomenal memory. Someone had called in and he'd remembered the details of her situation from three months prior. When he asked after her cancer-stricken mother, you could hear him capturing thousands of women's hearts on air.

Donna chewed, then swallowed. "The way I see it, it's a win-win. He gets ratings through the roof for the next few weeks, not to mention a huge boost to his profile from the tour. Both can only do great things for his career. And we, hopefully, get a book idea. Trust me. Lucas is not going to be looking that gift horse in the mouth."

"I guess." He was real, genuine. Everything she was not. She hated herself for agreeing to Donna's suggestion, but if she didn't find some inspiration soon, it was over. And returning the advance was not an option.

"Here he is." Donna nodded toward the doorway.

Shifting slightly, she lifted her gaze from the tabletop to see him approaching their table. Damp hair, fitted T-shirt, and a small person hanging onto the end of his arm.

A small person who looked like a miniature version of him. Wow. She did not see that coming.

"Sorry we're late. Had a bit of an unexpected diversion." Lucas pulled out a chair. "Here you go, buddy."

Nothing. Not a single thing in all of her internet stalking had even alluded to Lucas having a son. That was some impressive privacy protection in the internet age.

A son meant a mother. Which meant a wife or a girlfriend. Or a husband or boyfriend. You couldn't assume anything these days. And if he'd managed to keep a kid out of the limelight, who knew what else he had back there. So much for Lacey's claim about him being an eligible bachelor.

"This is Joey." Lucas slid easily into the other free chair beside Rachel while the kid—Joey—shrugged off his miniature backpack and climbed on his chair.

"Hi, Joey. I'm Donna, and this is Rachel." Her aunt didn't look in the least bit surprised by their extra guest.

"Are you the lady who writes the books?"

"I am. And Rachel's my assistant."

Joey looked her up and down with the openly calculating assessment that only small people could get away with. What was he, four? Maybe five? "Your top looks like our old curtains."

Rachel looked down at her blouse. A perfectly serviceable floral number that she'd gotten for a bargain at 80 percent off. Now she knew why. "Um, okay. Is it better as a top?"

The boy looked at her seriously. "Not really." And that would be two to small fry, zip to her.

"How about a milkshake? Or waffles? Or pancakes? Or some Angry Birds?" Lucas jumped in before the fashion critique could get any worse.

Donna smirked from behind her teacup. No help whatsoever.

"Sorry." Lucas muttered the words to Rachel as he handed

Joey his phone. "Five-year-olds apparently don't come with a filter."

"It's okay. It's old. I was planning to get rid of it anyway." Three weeks old, and she certainly was now.

Lucas flashed a smile at her and Rachel was glad she was sitting down. "Look, his favorite sandwich is peanut butter and spaghetti, so he's hardly a bastion of great taste." He unzipped Joey's backpack and pulled out a juice box, then expertly unwrapped the miniature straw and pierced the foil.

Donna snorted. "He is when it comes to this. That blouse looks like it belongs to someone named Mildred seeing out her sunset years in a rest home in Florida."

"Hey! It's not that bad. It's fine." Every clothing decision she made was about blending in. This top did just that. If she looked like a piece of drapery, so be it. Even better.

Though she could have done without being humiliated in front of Lucas, but whatever. Soon she would be thousands of miles away. "Anyway, we don't have long before we need to head to the airport. So why don't you two debrief while I go place our order. What will Joey have?"

"He'll just have the kids' waffles."

"And you?" Rachel stood. Self-conscious—for the first time ever—of the way her shapeless forest-green skirt hung off her like a sack.

But he had a son. And if what he said on his show about commitment was true, a wife. Or at least a significant other. So who cared what he thought? The best ones were always taken.

"The best what?" Lucas tilted his head at her.

She had not said that out loud. She had not. She grasped

onto the first thing that came into her mind. "Waffles! I've heard the waffles are really popular here. The best. So, um, often taken. But I'm sure it'll be fine."

Across the table Donna grinned, eyes dancing. "Though the same also applies to men."

Rachel gave her aunt a death stare. "What can I get you, Lucas?"

Lucas didn't even glance at the menu. "Whatever you think looks good will be fine."

How about you? Her aunt mouthed the words at Rachel as she raised her cup to her lips, and for a horrible split second Rachel thought she might have said them aloud.

She'd have to place that order fast. Who knew what else her aunt might say in her absence? Rachel took a step and tripped on her satchel. Feet tangling around its strap, she went tumbling. Right into Lucas's lap.

On instinct, her arms lassoed around his neck. Which stopped her from sliding headfirst onto the floor, but wrenched his head forward so that it stopped only a breath away from hers.

Joey looked up from his phone. "Nice catch, Uncle Lucas!"

ONE SECOND Lucas had been mortified at his nephew's observations about Rachel's clothes and the next thing he knew, the woman was sprawled across him.

And back on her feet almost before he'd had a chance to realize what had happened.

"Sorry about that." She swiped some hair away from her face. "It wasn't on purpose. I tripped on the strap. Of my bag. I tripped on my bag's strap." She gestured to where a brown leather satchel was lying on its side between their two seats. "It wasn't on purpose."

"Okay."

"It wasn't!" Her shoulders straightened and she glared at him like he'd pulled her into his lap.

Lucas held up both of his hands. "Whoa, whoa, I believe you."

She still looked at him skeptically.

"Look, if you'd done it on purpose, you hardly would have leapt off me like you'd landed on hot coals, would you?"

He knew what women trying to get his attention looked like. Even when they thought they were being subtle. Rachel was not one of those women.

Donna had disappeared from the table. Hopefully to place the order Rachel had been about to place. Joey was watching them both with unbridled interest.

"So . . ." Rachel sat back in her seat, pushing her iPad a couple of inches away from her. "Joey's not your son."

"I never said he was."

"You never said he wasn't. It's a fair enough assumption to make when you show up with a kid who looks like your mini me." Why was she looking at him all mad again? Most women found the uncle-looking-after-nephew thing endearing.

"No, he's not my son. He's my brother's son. And Scott also happens to look quite a lot like me."

Joey looked back up from his Angry Birds. "Uncle Lucas doesn't have any kids. He's just an uncle."

"That's me. Just an uncle. Joey's mom had an unexpected appointment, so I offered to take him for the morning."

Joey narrowed his eyes and looked between Lucas and Rachel. "To have kids you have to have sex, and Uncle Lucas doesn't have anyone to have sex with. Do you?"

Oh wow. That was next level. Lucas could feel his ears heating up. He'd give anything to go back to the clothing insults now.

"Um . . ." Lucas cleared his throat but couldn't come up with any other words. Everything he could come up with had the potential to make things even more awkward.

Joey looked at him expectantly. "What? It's true. You don't. My dad said—"

Lucas panicked. "Joey, if you don't finish that sentence I will take you for ice cream after this." Who knew what Scott had said. Especially if he didn't know Joey was listening. It would be worth Grace being cross with him just to end this.

Joey's eyes widened. "Ice cream before lunch?"

Lucas shrugged his shoulders. "Sure."

"Okay." Joey returned his attention to his screen, but Lucas's system was still flooded with adrenaline.

Rachel was trying to smother her laughter but doing a terrible job of it. "Are all five-year-olds like this?"

"I don't know. I only know this one."

She leaned back in her chair. "They should send them to all the CIA black sites. Imagine the intelligence they'd gather."

"I know." They smiled at each other and something seemed to be broken. "Can I ask you a question?"

Rachel tilted her head at him and took her time answering. "That depends on the question."

"Have we met before? Have I done something to offend you?"

Rachel sighed. Drummed her fingers on the table for a couple of seconds. "No, I'm sorry. It's not about you. It's just this tour has taken months to plan and Donna's got a book due in a few months that she hasn't even really started writing and things are just a bit crazy. I just . . ." She shrugged her shoulders. "I'm sorry, but I'm just not sure about bringing you on board and adding all this extra stuff into the schedule. Especially this late in the game. Call it an occupational hazard, but an assistant's job is to know what's going on. To have everything under control. And now you're on the scene and suddenly I don't."

"If it helps at all, I probably want to be doing this about as much as you want me to be."

That mustered a small smile out of her as she picked up her water glass. "I thought that might be the case."

"Since we're here, what *exactly* is awaiting me tomorrow at this test event? Ethan's been very sketchy on the details. Am I coming to a book signing? Some kind of meet-and-greet thing?"

They would be in Chicago. Where he was a nobody. Even if everything went well, they'd realize after Saturday night that he brought nothing to the table and they'd let him loose to go home and he could go back to his sports show, and Donna could just carry on with her tour without him.

Rachel raised her eyebrows over the rim of her glass. "You don't know what's planned for tomorrow night?" The way that she carefully placed her drink on the table with puckered eyebrows sent a prickle down his spine.

"Why? What's with the concerned eyebrows?"

Rachel glanced toward the counter, where Donna was

ordering. "It would probably be better if Donna or Lacey, our publicist, looped you in. This was Donna's idea, but Lacey is more involved with organizing it than I am and she has all the details. I can give you her phone number."

"As very competent as I'm sure Lacey is, I'd rather you just break whatever it is to me." He'd rather hear it from the woman who was as skeptical of the whole thing as he was. Not the person in charge of planning it.

Rachel shifted in her seat. "Well, it's set up in a talk show style. So you and Donna will be up front on a couple of couches. She'll speak for probably ten minutes or so about the latest book, then she'll introduce you, and then there's a Q-and-A session from the audience."

That didn't sound so bad. How many people could it be at such short notice? "So, maybe a hundred people?"

She winced. "Try two thousand."

"I'm sorry, what?" He had to have misheard. Or she had to be mistaken.

"The venue capacity is two thousand. And all the tickets sold out in a few hours. I hate to be the one to break it to you, but *Feelings and Football* is already a runaway success, before it's even a thing."

- 8 -

Rachel had no reason to lie to him, but Lucas had hoped—with the fingers-and-toes-crossed, fervent-prayers-to-a-God-he-hadn't-spoken-to-in-a-long-time type of hope—that she'd been mistaken. That Lacey had gotten this mixed up with some other event she was planning. Anything.

And then he'd found himself in Chicago at the Donald E. Stephens Convention Center in a room bigger than a football field, with uniform rows of chairs that seemed to stretch forever.

Lucas stood on one side of the stage, just out of sight of the women pouring into the room. His shirt already stuck to him from the heat of the lights. He hadn't brought a spare. It had been a last-minute thought to bring a dress shirt, full stop.

"Here's a copy of the latest run sheet." Rachel walked up to him and handed him a piece of paper. He looked down at the long list of items timed down to the second.

"Is someone going to tell me what to do? Where's Donna?" His voice was an octave higher than normal.

"Just think of it like radio. Except you can see the people."

"One of the best things about radio is *not* being able to see the people." He mumbled the words as he squinted at the page. Surely he didn't need glasses already?

There was a whoosh as a banner unfurled from the ceiling and down the back wall. An enormous banner, emblazoned with a photo of him and Donna, and *The Feelings and Football Tour* written across the bottom. *Feelings* was in cursive, and *Football* in block font.

"What is that?"

Rachel barely glanced up. "Oh, that's nothing. You should see some of the merchandise that's been ordered."

"Do I have to?"

Her face split in a smile. "You'll be fine. I promise. Just imagine them all in their underwear or something."

"That's even more terrifying." Two thousand women in their underwear. He'd rather imagine a zombie apocalypse.

Rachel pointed to a door that was set into the wall a few yards away. "Let's go to the green room and I'll talk you through it all. Watching people arrive is just going to make things worse."

Lucas took one look at the growing crowd just in time to see a woman wearing a hot-pink T-shirt emblazoned with *Lucas Lover* take a seat in the front row. He couldn't escape through the door fast enough.

It closed behind them and suddenly there was blessed silence, with just a muffled hint of all the voices in the next room.

Rachel sat down on the couch next to him and plucked the paper out of his hand. "Look. You really only have to remember three main parts. Stay in here until it starts. I'll tell you and Donna when it's time to go wait in the wings, and then you walk onto the stage when the two of you are called, then sit on a couch while Donna does her spiel, then just talk for a while. Like you do five nights a week."

"I talk about sports, Rachel. Sports. You can't tell me that there are two thousand women coming tonight to talk about baseball stats or defensive plays or ask about my draft picks."

Rachel lifted the paper to cover the bottom half of her face. Presumably to try to hide the fact that she was biting her bottom lip to contain her laughter. "Maybe not," she finally conceded. "But what's the worst that can happen? If you get up there and completely freak and just sit there mute, this will be the one and only event. And if you're a natural, then that can only do good things for your profile. Even if it's not *exactly* in your preferred area of expertise."

"Where is Donna?"

Rachel shrugged. "Probably out working the crowd, signing books. She loves things like this. Hates being in the green room. She says green rooms are extroverts' joy killers."

"You're not an extrovert, are you?" Even though Lucas barely knew her, he couldn't imagine Rachel as the life of the party.

She shook her head. "Absolutely not. That's why we make a good team. Lots of high-profile people fall out with their assistants because they secretly want to be in the spotlight too. That would be my worst nightmare. I'm definitely a behind-the-scenes woman."

"You and me both. Well, not the woman part. Obviously."

Rachel stood up. Helped herself to a couple of cookies from a plate on a table. "Want one?"

"Sure."

She threw it at him like a Frisbee and he caught it midair. Shoveled it into his mouth. He hadn't had any breakfast. Or lunch. The nerves had unexpectedly assaulted him from the moment he woke up. This had been the longest day in the history of the world.

"Don't you have things to be doing? Don't let me keep you."

Rachel checked her watch. "Nope. This is Lacey's gig. If Donna isn't in here in ten minutes, then I'll need to go and find her. Apart from that, my only other job is making sure the two of you are out there in time to go on the stage."

"But surely you must have other assistant-y stuff to be doing."

Rachel shrugged as she sat back down on the other couch. "Not really. If tonight goes well and *Feelings and Football* officially becomes a thing, then I'll have plenty to do, but this is the calm before the storm."

"Well, hopefully it doesn't become a thing, then. Then you can go back to your perfectly planned tour and I can go back to sports." Well, sports with a side of angst, since he had yet to come up with a magic bullet to stop all the women from calling in to his show.

Rachel didn't say anything for a couple of seconds, then asked, "Does it really bother you that much? People asking you for advice?"

"I'm a sports guy. Why do women call me to ask for relationship advice? Why do they even care what I have to say? I'm not an expert. I have no relevant experience. Heck, I'm not even married. I feel like such a fraud. They'd probably get better advice from a fortune cookie."

Now, there was an idea. For every call he got asking about anything that wasn't sports related, he could just crack open a fortune cookie and read them whatever it said.

Rachel didn't say anything. Just tapped her phone and studied its screen for a second. Her hair slipped down and shielded the expression on her face. She looked back up, tucking her hair behind her ear. "Want to know why I think women call you?"

"Fire away."

"Have you heard of Belle Gibson?"

"No."

Rachel drummed her fingers on the arm of her couch for a few seconds. "Okay. So Belle Gibson is an Australian who was building this massive wellness empire off the back of having terminal brain cancer. She claimed she'd shunned conventional medicine and that she'd gone into remission thanks to whole foods, detoxing, that kind of thing. She created this app that Apple promoted in the App Store, had a huge book deal, hundreds of thousands of followers on Instagram, you name it."

He could see where this was headed. "And she died? She wasn't in remission at all?"

Rachel shook her head. "She never had brain cancer. She'd made the whole thing up."

Lucas rubbed his hand through his hair. "She'd falsified her medical records?"

"No. She didn't have any medical records at all. At least not ones saying she had cancer."

"But how could she get a book deal based on a lie?"

Rachel shrugged. "She'd built a big social media following and everyone just believed the hype. They were so desperate to cash in on it that they never asked for any evidence. But the worst of it is that people who really had cancer believed her and thought that if they shunned conventional medicine and followed her diet, then they could beat cancer too."

"So people could be dead because of her."

"It's definitely possible."

"And I remind you of Belle Gibson." Talk about a soul-destroying thought.

Rachel leaned back on the couch. "What made me think about her was your comment about not being an expert. We live in an information age, where everything is contestable. Where people with PhDs and years of research have to compete with people who haven't spent a day in a science lab since they left high school but think their arguments should be given equal weight because they found some stuff on Google."

Better and better. "So I'm not like this Belle woman, but I'm like an internet nut job? This is what you want me to be thinking when I'm about to get on a stage with your boss in front of thousands of women?"

Rachel threw her head back and laughed. That kind of full-hearted laugh couldn't help but make him laugh too. "No." She managed to gasp out the word as she ran her fingertips under her eyes. "Okay, let me try again."

"To be honest, I'm really not sure if my ego can bear it."

"Okay, what I'm trying to say is that I think the reason that women find you so attractive—"

"That's definitely a more promising start."

Rachel rolled her eyes at him, but she couldn't hide the flush that hit her cheeks. Which he took a childish amount of satisfaction in. "It's because you're the anti-expert. And I don't mean that in a quackery kind of way."

"What other kind of way is there?"

"Women believe you because you don't have an ulterior motive. Like you said, you're the sports guy who has never solicited women to call your show and ask you for advice on their love lives."

He sure hadn't.

"And that's exactly what appeals to people. You're not trying to build some kind of self-help empire or land a book deal or be the next Dr. Phil. You're just a guy—and I'm not going to lie that being a single, eligible one doesn't hurt—who doesn't pull any punches, because what you really want is for them to get off your phone lines and let you get on with talking about the Dodgers or whoever your baseball team is."

"The Brewers."

"Whatever." Rachel checked her watch. "Okay, I really need to go and find Donna now. Was that a good enough pep talk for you?"

"Oh, is that what that was?"

Standing, Rachel rounded the couch and opened a door opposite the one they'd entered from. She cast a smile over her shoulder. "Yup, and it was a one-time-only deal. So don't go getting your hopes up for any more."

Their gaze connected, something seemed to spark, and suddenly Lucas found his hope rising for something completely different. Now *that* was something that hadn't happened in a long time.

CLOSING THE door behind her, Rachel sagged against the wall. The intensity in Lucas's gaze had spiraled something through her that she hadn't felt in years. If ever.

She didn't have time for this. Didn't have time to be distracted. Certainly not by a reluctant guy with a brooding gaze and a penchant for honesty.

Pushing herself off the wall, she headed down the silent hall toward the door that would take her out to the main foyer. No doubt she'd find Donna there mingling with her hordes of adoring fans.

"Sorry!" Donna rounded the corner at the end of the hall and walked toward her. "Though, in my defense, I am improving. I'm only a couple of minutes late and you didn't have to come find me. How's Lucas?"

"Okay. He's just waiting in the green room. Though I feel bad that we didn't really do anything to prepare him for this. He has no idea what he's in for."

Donna dismissed her concerns with a flap of her hand. "You can't prepare someone for something like this. They just have to do it. He'll be totally fine. His job is to be prepared for the unexpected."

"He asked me what I thought his appeal was. I told him I thought it was because this has landed in his lap despite his attempts to push it off. Unlike Belle Gibson."

Donna's lips formed a thin line. "That woman should be in jail."

"How are we any different?" Rachel dropped her voice to a whisper as they headed back toward the green room. "That was all I could think as I was telling him about her. We're just as bad."

"Nonsense. That woman was a pathological liar who preyed on the most vulnerable. People with terminal illnesses desperate to grab onto any scrap of hope they could find. And to make her money and fund her lifestyle, she sold them a complete lie."

"I know, but . . ."

Donna stopped walking and turned toward her. "You worry too much. Ghostwriters are totally standard. You know that. I could put a billboard in Times Square tomorrow announcing that I have a ghostwriter and no one would care."

Her aunt was right in some ways, but it did nothing to salve her conscience. "I feel so guilty when I'm with Lucas. Knowing that he thinks that it's you on his show when it's me." Ghostwriters might be common, but pretending to be Donna during interviews definitely was not. The advice that came out of her mouth during those interviews was all her, and people had no idea.

"We're not hurting anyone. You are giving the exact same advice that I would. That I do."

"I should have been braver back then. Done things differently. If I had, we wouldn't have to worry about any of this."

Donna put her hands on Rachel's shoulders and looked her straight in the eye. "But then I never would have met Rob. And who knows what would have happened with your father." Her aunt's voice rose. "We did what we needed to do. And I will never, ever apologize for that."

"I know." Rachel had revisited the scenario a thousand times in her head. The pressure had been unimaginable. The alternative options nonexistent.

The door to the green room opened and Lucas stuck his head out. "Hey, Donna. I thought that was your voice. Lacey's here. She says we're about to start."

"Great!" Donna's face transformed. "We're going to have such a great night." She patted Lucas's arm as she passed him by.

Lucas paused, looking at Rachel. "You okay?"

Rachel pasted on her own smile. "Yes, fine." She ducked past his arm and into the room where a sound tech had just handed Donna a microphone.

On the other side of the green room wall, what had been a muffled roar had ramped up as the emcee worked the crowd. Rachel checked her watch. Only a couple of minutes before they'd be summoned onto the stage.

Lacey was obviously thinking the same thing as she opened the opposite door and gestured at them to move into the staging area. Rachel followed Donna through, Lucas following her.

"I'm pretty sure I wasn't this nervous when I was a lineman at State." Lucas murmured the words into her ear as he palmed his mic from hand to hand. It was almost impossible to hear him over the sound of female hysteria and the emcee.

"Please, give a warm Chicago welcome for Dr. Donna

Somerville and Lucas Grant." The words rolled across the room and the crowd went into a complete frenzy.

Donna headed up the steps and then Lucas bounded up after her.

"You need to go and be one of the roamers." Lacey tugged on Rachel's arm and handed her a microphone.

"What are you talking about? I don't do big event stuff. You know that."

"Please." Lacey chucked her a black T-shirt. "We're down a couple and the whole middle left block is uncovered. It's easy. You just hand the microphone to the person asking the question and then take it back."

I wish I'd been braver back then. The words she'd uttered less than five minutes ago rang in her ears. She couldn't change anything about back then, but maybe, just maybe, she could start being a little bit brave now.

I WILL never, ever apologize for that. At least Lucas was pretty sure those were the adamant words Donna had been saying as he'd opened the door. Even if he hadn't heard them exactly, there was something about the vehemence in her words that signaled she and Rachel had been talking about something important.

The heat from the stage lights plastered his shirt to his skin, but Donna talked about her latest book as effortlessly as if she were having coffee with some friends. An exceptionally large and adoring group of friends. So far, Lucas had managed to avoid all the eyes staring at him by focusing his gaze slightly above their heads. He wasn't going to be able to get away with that for much longer.

"So, Lucas. Why don't you tell us a bit about yourself and how you ended up on this stage."

Lucas looked at Donna, who grinned back at him. That was not on the run sheet. The run sheet had them going from Donna's book sales pitch to the Q&A. Not a soliloquy from him.

He tipped his gaze down to all the eyes staring at him and a trickle of sweat rolled down his back.

"We love you, Lucas!" The scream came from somewhere to his left and was almost immediately drowned out by a loud cheer.

Awkward. He lifted his mic. At that moment he'd rather it were a live grenade. He cleared his throat. "Hi, everyone. Thanks for coming out tonight." His voice boomed across the room. No turning back now. "Anyone here from the mighty state of Wisconsin?"

More screaming. This was unreal. He gave the room a short wave. More screaming.

"Looks like you have some fans." Donna's voice was tinged with amusement and the screaming got even more piercing.

"So for those of you who don't know who I am, my name is Lucas Grant. I host a sports call-in show on WFM Madison, and for reasons that I'm not entirely sure of, Dr. Donna thought we should share a stage."

Donna lifted her microphone. "What Lucas means to say is he aspires to host a sports show, but unfortunately for him he often finds his lines clogged with ladies seeking relationship advice. Isn't that right, Lucas?"

He couldn't even get a response out as a combination of laughter and cheering rolled across the room.

"So, do y'all want to know why I invited Lucas here? Apart from the obvious reason." Donna said this with a wink, and Lucas wasn't sure whether to be offended or complimented. "Well, you're all about to find out. It's time for Q and A."

The emcee spoke from beside Donna. "Ladies—and I think I may have spotted one sole terrified-looking gentleman somewhere in the room—there are staff in black T-shirts roaming the floor. If you have a question, stick your hand up and they'll bring you a microphone. I apologize in advance if time constraints mean we aren't able to get to all of you with questions. You can also Tweet us using the hashtag *feelingsandfootball*, and we'll see if the technology allows us to answer some of those Tweets as they come rolling in."

The two screens lit up on either side of the stage with Twitter live feeds, but no hands went up. How many people would really be brave enough to ask a question in front of two thousand strangers? Maybe this would be a lot shorter than he'd anticipated.

Then a hand went up and a black-shirted helper hustled to give a redhead a microphone. "My question is for Lucas. Are you single?"

A burst of applause.

Really? They paid to come here for this? Sighing, he lifted the microphone to his lips. "I am. Yes."

More applause. This was going to be a long night.

"When was your last serious relationship?"

Seriously? "It's been a few years."

A few more hands went up and the redhead reluctantly relinquished the microphone.

"Can you tell us about your ideal woman?"

Lucas scanned the crowd to try and figure out where the voice was coming from but couldn't.

"Is that a question for me?" Donna raised her mic with a grin and the crowd laughed, along with a few calls of *"Lucas!"*

"Lucas, dear. For some reason they don't seem to want to know what my ideal woman is. Though I have plenty of great ideas."

Lucas barely smothered his sigh as he spoke into his microphone. "I don't have one. I figure I'll know her when I meet her."

"But surely you must have things you look for?"

He scanned the room but still couldn't work out where the questioner was.

"My bottom lines are honesty and integrity. Look." He settled back into the chair. Clearly he was going to have to do some talking if he wanted to avoid all the awkward personal questions. "If you want my opinion, which, apparently, some of you do, here it is. I think lots of women miss something great because you have this ideal man in your head and you won't give anyone else a chance. You decide you don't want bald or facial hair or a blue-collar guy or someone who's divorced or the guy who earns less than you or the guy with a few extra pounds. And great guys pass you by because you're looking for the perfect guy who doesn't exist."

Silence filled the room for a second, then Donna lifted her microphone. "Lucas, I'm pretty sure you just quoted one of my books right there."

"Will you kick me off the stage if I admit I've never read one of your books?"

"Would you admit it if you had?"

"Probably not." The room burst into laughter and he felt himself relax a little more. He could do this. Just keep his gaze on the back wall and pretend it was radio.

"Okay, next question," the emcee said.

"My question is for Lucas."

Again? This time it was a blonde near the front. "What are you looking for in a relationship?"

"Someone who likes to talk about sports. Football. Or basketball. Or baseball. Surely, there's someone in this room who would like to put the 'football' into *Feelings and Football*. Anyone?"

Resounding silence.

"Poor Lucas. We should move on before he never comes back to one of these things again. And that would be a shame when we've just spent so much money plastering him on banners the size of Texas. Yes, over there." Donna pointed to their right and Lucas shifted to see who she was indicating.

Someone looking an awful lot like Rachel was holding the microphone while a woman spoke into her ear. Maybe she had a look-alike, because she hadn't been wearing a black T-shirt when he last saw her.

Rachel, or Rachel's doppelganger, tried to give the woman the microphone, but the woman shook her head and pushed it back to her. Rachel held it out again. The woman pushed it back toward her. Did he even want to know what this question was going to be? Clearly it was something for him. Again.

"What's the lady's question, Rachel?" Donna spoke. "Everyone, this is my lovely assistant."

Rachel sighed into the microphone. "For Lucas. Again. Hypothetically, are you open to a woman asking you out on a date or do you think a man should be the one to make the first move?"

"Hypothetically, are you asking me on a date?" He didn't know where the impulse came from to tease her, but he couldn't help himself.

"You wish."

Lucas didn't know how to respond to that. He cleared his throat. "Hypothetically speaking, I couldn't care less. But I am old-fashioned about proposing. Unless, hypothetically speaking, you would like to."

Rachel shook her head at him. But she was smiling. So he considered it a victory.

9

"Lucas, my man. Another big night. Good luck!" Bill Robson's firm hand clapped on Lucas's shoulder as he walked the hallway to the studio.

"Thank you, sir." Lucas tried to choke down the gurgle in his stomach. Nothing quite like having the usually invisible owner of the station roaming the deserted building at seven thirty p.m. to pile the pressure on.

The Chicago event had been christened a raging success, and the station had gone nuts. Marketing had plastered the county with *Feelings and Football* billboards. Just yesterday he'd almost driven into the back of a bus when he'd seen his face staring back at him. He'd put his foot down, though, when they wanted to create life-size cutouts to put in bookstores. There were some things that were sacred, and walking into Barnes & Noble without running into a cardboard version of yourself was one of them.

On the upside, he'd had the afternoon free to clear out his gutters. No need to worry about having to prep some filler topics when there was no possibility of the phone lines drying up. The nights since the Chicago event had been crazy. They'd even fielded calls from outside of Wisconsin, which he was pretty sure was a first. He'd hardly been able to talk about sports at all, even though he'd instructed Ethan to stick to the sports callers and keep the relationship callers for tonight. Tonight would be the first night when Donna would do a phone-in for the entire show. He felt his shoulders bunch up just at the thought.

They'd never done a whole show remotely. A whole four hours on the phone. No being able to catch her eye. Read each other's expressions and body language. No scrawled notes. What if they disagreed? What if it was too much for her? Maybe they should have built up to it. He'd been doing radio for a decade and still found it demanding. Did she have any idea what she'd signed up for?

Last week's ratings had been through the roof with minimal promo work, so this time the show had been promoted all week on and off air. He sucked in a deep breath as he opened the studio door. He couldn't exactly pretend he hadn't heard the whispers, either. That this might be his big break. That if he made the most of it, the big guys might come knocking with his dream. Syndication. To be heard from coast to coast. To have the kind of clout he needed to talk about sports and things that brought men together and leave the emotions and relationships to people way more qualified.

Yet . . . if he managed to help keep one marriage together, help one woman turn down the guy trying to wheedle his way into her bed without any commitment, maybe there was an upside to all the feelings stuff. *Stop one guy from turning into my father.* He shooed the thought back into the recesses of his mind. Not here, not now. After everything his old man had destroyed, he wasn't going to let him distract him when he'd finally reached the cusp of his dream.

"Hey." Ethan was already in the production booth. "Ready for another big night?"

"As ready as I can be."

His producer tilted back in his seat. "You've never really told me about Chicago. How was it? How was Lacey?"

"Lacey? She's just what you said. A great publicist."

"That all?" A speculative smile was on Ethan's mug.

"What do you mean?

"Oh come on, Lucas. The woman is hot."

Lucas sighed. He had zero patience for his producer behaving like a frat boy. "Ethan. If you want to make a play for Lacey, then find a reason to come to one of the events and do it. As far as I'm concerned, Lacey is a great publicist and she'd probably kick your butt if she heard you talking about her like that." He'd met many beautiful and ambitious women just like Lacey O'Connor in his line of work and never been attracted to any of them.

Ethan tilted farther back in his chair. "So if it's not Lacey, then who is it?"

"Who's what?"

"You've had a weird look on your face every day since Chicago. Like you are thinking about someone. I'd assumed it was Lacey, but if it's not, then . . ." Ethan thought for a second, then grinned. "Is it the assistant? I mean she's not quite Lacey's caliber, but I can see how she might have some appeal. In an ice queen kind of way."

Lucas was silent. If he let Ethan bait him, he'd probably say something he'd regret. And it wasn't like anything had happened with Rachel. They'd had a disconcerting moment. That was all. He may have mildly flirted with her from on-stage. But it didn't really count when it was for show in front of two thousand people.

And when they'd all gone out for a drink afterward, she'd made her excuses and gone up to her room as soon as she'd finished hers. Hardly the sign of someone interested in him.

"Sorry, dude." Ethan said the words genuinely.

"For what?"

"I didn't realize things between you were that serious."

"What do you mean? There's no 'thing' between us."

Ethan shook his head. "You may want to believe that, but we have worked together for two years. And you have never looked like that before when I've mentioned any other woman. Ever."

"AND THAT'S a wrap." Ethan's voice came across the line, the sound of an advertisement for a motor vehicle dealer in the background. "Good work, team."

Rachel sagged down onto her bed, knocking off her glass of water in three gulps. In the last half hour Ethan had piled call after call through, trying to make a dent in the backlog.

"You still there?" Lucas's voice came down the line. His horrible, perfect-for-radio, soothing voice.

"Yup." Rachel's voice had started taking on a croaking quality three hours in. By the last couple of calls, she was struggling to put the oomph behind her words that radio required.

"How's the throat?" Lucas's words were slightly muffled, like he was talking through a mouthful of food.

"Okay. Do you think it went okay?" The words wheezed down the line. Lucas had been amazing tonight. Fair, just, brutally honest, but kind with a couple of people who had gotten themselves into a whole pile of trouble. Compassionate with callers who were struggling to pick up the pieces of their broken hearts. The man was wasted on sports, no matter how much he preferred them.

He was the kind of guy that any woman would want to come home to. Hear her name on his lips as they caught up on their day.

Stop it, Rachel!

"It was great. Going by the way Ethan's been flapping his arms at me all night, I'd say ratings are through the roof."

"Good. That's good." Rachel was struggling to hold onto her Donna voice. Not even the water seeming to help her dry and rasping throat.

"So how's the book tour going this week?" The sound of cellophane tearing came across the line. Her stomach rumbled. Reminding her that she'd skipped dinner because of nerves.

"Good." Rachel had lost track of the number of people who had asked Donna today if she was going to be coming back with Lucas. But no need to tell him that. "How are you feeling about joining it properly next weekend?"

"I still can't believe Ethan roped me into this." Lucas paused. "Actually, while I'm thinking about it, would you be able to give me Rachel's number?"

Rachel almost lost the ability to breathe. "Rachel, my assistant Rachel?" Something had seemed to flash between them in the green room, but she'd been telling herself that she was imagining it.

"Yes. She mentioned that she looks after your social media pages and the station PR people were wanting to talk to her about doing some cross-promotion on Facebook or something. I mean I could talk to her about it in LA next weekend, but I thought it might make sense to put them in touch sooner."

Of course they did. Lucas didn't want her number personally. Which was a good thing. It was.

If she were actually her aunt, no doubt she'd razz him about what he actually wanted her number for, but she wasn't that much of a sucker. "Um, sure, of course." She rattled off her number. "Okay, I should go now. It's late. Good night, Lucas." She hung up before he could answer and dropped her phone on the bed before striding into the bathroom. Trying to shake off the disappointment that had hit at the news that he only wanted her for her Facebook log-on.

She was a shadowy figure of no importance. That's how they'd set it up. That was how it had to stay.

This was a horrible idea. There had to be a better way to find an idea for a book than having to spend all this time with Lucas and being reminded of everything she didn't have. Might never have.

Stop it! She turned the cold tap on full, dousing her face, shocking herself back to the real world. Where good guys like Lucas weren't for women like her.

She dried her face. Tried to shake some of the melancholy off as she walked back into her room. Another book tour, another bland room for a night, just like all the others.

More cities stretched out before them. She wouldn't be back in Denver anytime soon. Not that it mattered. She had no one to go home to. If she never went back to her condo, the only person who might eventually wonder where she went was her regular Uber Eats delivery guy.

Her entire life was as small as four people. Donna, Max, Lacey, and her vegetative father. Four and a half, if you counted Anna and the few texts they'd exchanged since she left.

Rachel blew out a breath, then watched it mist on the window overlooking whatever the river was that ran through Minneapolis. Below her, people strolled along the boardwalk. Leaving restaurants after a late dinner. Heading home after a night shift.

A knock on her door jolted her from her thoughts. Rachel walked to the door and peered out the peephole.

Lacey?

Pulling open the door, she tilted her head at the publicist. "Hey. Is everything okay?"

"Fine. The charity auction was as expected. I just thought I'd check in and see how tonight went with Lucas." Lacey was still in her cocktail gown from the evening's event. A draped affair that made her look like she'd been dipped in silver.

"It was fine. I think. Have you heard otherwise?" Lacey lived on her phone. Juggling her clients. Wrangling interviews and publicity opportunities.

"No. I'm sure I'll hear from Ethan tomorrow." Lacey shifted on her feet. What was going on? In the eighteen months she'd been their publicist, she'd never shown up at

Rachel's hotel room. Lacey was all about efficiency. They could have had this conversation at their morning breakfast briefing.

"Was there something else?"

Lacey glanced down the empty corridor. "Can I come in for a minute?"

"Um, sure." Rachel stepped back to let her into the room.

"I spoke to Anna earlier." Lacey said the words carefully as she placed her clutch on the hotel desk.

Oh.

"She said your father is still alive?" Lacey lifted the hem of her long, shimmering skirt and then sat on the one chair in the room, leaving Rachel to perch on the end of the bed.

"That's probably overstating his situation." Rachel tugged her bathrobe around her.

"That's where your money goes. That's why this whole Dr. Donna thing is still going." It wasn't a question.

Rachel nodded. Lacey and Anna were the only people outside of Max, the acquiring editor at Randolph, and their original publicist who knew the truth about how Dr. Donna had been created. That was why Lacey had been a no-brainer when their old publicist retired. Lacey or Anna could have ruined everything at any point, but neither of them had ever breathed a word. Whether out of loyalty or penance, she'd never known.

"How is Anna's husband?"

Lacey leaned back in the chair, closing her eyes briefly. "No change."

"When did they get married?"

"Five—maybe six?—years ago."

"You're still close?" She didn't know whether to hope they were or weren't. The thought of their friendship continuing without her hurt. But then, so did the idea that it hadn't.

"We keep in touch. Nothing was ever the same after you . . ." Lacey's words trailed off.

Rachel swallowed. Anna and Lacey had been her best friends. The only true friends she'd ever had. The people who had given her hope that she could be more than the sum of her broken parts.

She'd believed they'd destroyed their friendship. Especially Lacey. But the truth was it had been her. She was the one who'd pushed them away, snapped every single olive branch offered, blocked their numbers and frozen them out.

She shook her head. Not even wanting to think about it.

"Rach?"

"I didn't know how to . . ." She couldn't go on, her words stuck in her throat. She wasn't even sure what they were. She'd had to share the blame for her father's accident with her best friends because she couldn't carry the full weight of it alone. But their friendship couldn't shoulder the weight of all that pain.

"What about you? Have you ever married?" It was the closest they'd ever gotten to a personal conversation. Some unspoken agreement had kept things purely professional since Lacey had come on board.

Lacey propped up half a smile that shadowed weary around the edges. "Only to my job." She shrugged. "I date, but mostly I get my romance vicariously through Emelia."

"How is she?" Rachel had met Lacey's cousin a few times. A clever, quiet woman. An unspoken understanding had formed between them when they'd discovered their similar hands dealt by life.

"She's great. She lives in England and is dating an Olympic rower."

Would not have picked that. "Wow, good for her."

"Indeed." Lacey shook her head as if dispatching memories. "Anyway, I should get going. Can you look in on Anna when you're back home this weekend?" Lacey pushed herself off her chair and grabbed her purse.

"She doesn't need me, Lace." Anna's husband's room had been filled with friends and family the day they'd met. "I'm probably the last person she wants to see."

"Just think about it, okay? She could use all the friends she can get right now. And you know what?" Lacey gave her a tired smile. "You could probably use one, too."

10

"And one and two and three!" At his brother's signal, Lucas threw all his weight against the obstinate fence post. He slammed his shoulder into the side and paused for a second before wrapping his arms around it and wrenching it back in the opposite direction.

They'd been at it for twenty minutes and the fight was now personal. So far the score was fence post six, Lucas and Scott zero, but they were about to win the war.

Lucas whipped his Stetson off and swiped his filthy, sweaty forearm across his forehead. "This is the last time I trust you, big bro. You wouldn't know the definition of easy re-fencing if it trampled you like Milton there." He nodded over to Scott's prize bull, grazing in the next pasture.

His brother leaned back against the rear of his pickup, a sheen barely breaking his brow. "You've just gone soft, little bro. All those hours sitting behind a microphone spoon-feeding people their emotions sent your body to seed. Shame. Used to be such a beautiful specimen, back in the day."

Lucas jammed his hat back down, trying to stop the blustery May wind from taking off with it for a third time. "Whatever." His brother was right and they both knew it. Not that anyone could accuse him of being a tub of lard, but he certainly couldn't compare to his brother, whose life on the land had him built like a brick outhouse.

"Tell you what." Scott satisfied himself with the unspoken victory. "Chuck me a water and then we'll finish her up."

Lucas fished into the cooler in the back of the truck and pulled out two bottles. Throwing one to his brother, he snapped open the other and took a deep drink. The self-proclaimed pure spring water provided welcome relief as it sloshed an icy trail down his parched throat.

His brother stared into the distance, water bottle still in his catch hand, unopened.

"What's up, Scott?"

His brother started. "Sorry, what?"

"Everything okay?"

"Fine, fine." Scott averted his eyes.

Lucas tossed his bottle back into the cooler. "You and Grace okay?" For all the unwanted practice he'd had, he should've been a pro at probing, but he shifted his feet. "I mean with the trying and all . . ."

His brother sighed, opening his bottle, only to toss the lid in his hand. "We're fine. All things considered."

All things considered? What did that mean? "Is there something wrong with you? With Joey? What is it?" A twisting fear hit him in the gut. They were all he had.

Scott shook his head. "No, nothing like that." He sighed.

"Look, it's no big deal, Luc. We've just leveraged ourselves a bit paying for these treatments. As long as it's a good summer, we'll be fine."

"And if it's not?"

His brother closed his eyes for a second, as if it pained him to even think of the possibility. "Well, then it will be . . . tight." He lifted his bottle to his lips and took a couple of long gulps.

Scott saying it would be tight meant it was anyone else's financial Armageddon.

Lucas opened his mouth to offer up the contents of his meager savings account, but his brother cut him off with a "don't even think about it" look.

Screwing his lid back on the bottle, Scott threw it to Lucas and turned back to the stubborn post. "I reckon another couple of shoves should have her. Ready . . ." They both positioned themselves on the same side of the post, arms gripping the top, heels digging into the ground at its base. "One, two . . ."

"All the single ladies, all the single ladies . . ." What the . . . ? Some pop chick belted out of Lucas's back pocket, the combination of surprise and volume sending both men flailing into the dirt.

Scott stayed there, his whole body shaking with guffaws. Across the paddock, Milton joined in with a series of bellows.

Lucas scrambled to wrench the phone from his jean pocket. He was going to kill Ethan. He should've known something was up when his producer, a country-and-western nut, exited the studio humming the catchy tune last night.

Blocked number flashed on the screen. Blasted telemarketers. Apparently the "do not call" registry didn't extend to India. Half the continent seemed to call him about changing his long-distance provider.

"Look, I've told you, I'm not interested!"

Silence for a second, followed by what sounded like some hybrid of a West Coast accent. "Will you at least hear me out first?"

"Who is this?" Lucas glared at his brother, who was still lying in the dirt, shaking like a bowl of Jell-O.

"First can I just confirm who this is?"

Lucas pulled the phone away from his ear and stared at it. Seriously? This guy wanted *him* to verify himself?

"Buddy, if you don't know who I am, then get off my line—I've got work to do." Not to mention some serious ribbing to get over and done with.

"Attitude, huh. I like it. Hear that's part of your charm. The no-holds-barred good guy."

Surely this guy wasn't hitting on him. "Who is this?" Lucas's finger hovered over the *end call* icon. He gave the guy one more sentence or he was gone.

"This is Brad Shipman."

"How stupid do you think I am, Ethan?" Lucas stabbed the button, then turned the phone off for good measure. He'd fix the song later. While plotting his revenge. How stupid did Ethan think he was? Like he was going to fall for the age-old trick of the fake LA producer call! He'd never understand how his producer managed to be so good at his job when he had all the maturity of a fourteen-year-old.

He turned his attention back to his brother, who had managed to raise himself from the earth and was propped against the obstinate post, a smirk still on his lips.

Lucas folded his arms across his chest, daring Scott to mess with him. "You want to finish this fence off or not?"

LUCAS LEANED back in his chair and stared at the screen in his palm. For the life of him, he could not work out how to get the hideous song off his ring tone. Blasted newfangled phones. Give him the old flip phone any day. Calling, that was all a man needed. Maybe the occasional text message. Not these ridiculous contraptions.

He spun the phone across the console. There was no way he was letting Ethan exit their booth tonight without fixing it.

Stretching his aching arms above his head, he scanned the news feed for possible topics for the evening. He liked to select both the ordinary and the slightly off-center.

His gaze lingered on a story about an aspiring NFL player arrested for domestic battery. That would get the airwaves pumping.

"So any interesting calls today?" Ethan's backpack hit the floor with a thud.

Lucas didn't even bother lifting his eyes from the screen. "Actually, yes. Dawson called; he wants his hair back."

"Seriously."

"Yeah, I'm sure you found it seriously funny doing the Beyoncé/Shipman double hit. FYI, Scott also found it so hilarious it's going to be Thanksgiving 2025 before he'll bother to find another story to tell over the turkey."

His eyes landed on a story about a fifteen-year-old girl drinking Drano after her boyfriend dumped her. Seriously, what was wrong with this country? Where was the father who should've taught her no guy was worth that?

It didn't matter. Tonight was about sports. Just sports. Not feelings. Or relationships. Or love advice from someone completely unqualified to give any. Sports.

"Brad Shipman *called*?" Ethan's puppy-dog tone demanded acknowledgment.

"Sure, Brad Shipman called." Lucas lifted his finger off the mouse long enough to denote bunny ears around the name.

"Well, what did he say?" Eager eyes peered over the dividing ledge. Lucas had to give it to him: the guy was a decent faker.

"Ethan. Give it up. You got me; now let's move on. In case you didn't notice, we're on air in twenty and we haven't even outlined the show yet." Lucas took a gulp of his water.

"Okay, Beyoncé was me. But I'm not joking, Luc—Brad Shipman wasn't."

Lucas stared at him. He couldn't be saying what he thought he was saying.

Ethan was fumbling with something on his side of the desk. "Listen." He held up his phone, set to loudspeaker, the electronic voice intoning he had one saved message.

"Ethan." The same voice he'd heard earlier echoed around the room. "Brad Shipman here. Hey, I've heard good things about your guy, Lucas, and listened to a couple of his shows. You guys have a nice thing going there. Just wondering if you can do me a favor and pass on his number. I'm interested in talking to him about some opportunities I have coming up." He listed a couple of phone numbers.

Lucas's head hit the desk about the same time the tone indicated Brad had hung up. He thumped it on the hard wood. Twice, three times, for being so stupid, stupid, *stupid*.

"What happened?" Ethan's voice was Mickey Mouse high.

"I hung up on him."

- *11* -

*L*ucas studied the discreet sign above the brick facade. *Matterhorn*. Trust Brad Shipman, a stranger from LA, to know the trendiest place in town.

He fisted his hands in his jeans pockets. Brad was the one who'd flown all this way only a few days after their initial phone conversation. The one who'd requested the meeting. It wasn't as if Lucas had done anything to make this happen. In fact, the hanging-up debacle only seemed to make Brad fall over himself more to meet him.

So here he was, a week later, fingers tugging at the collar of the designer shirt Ethan had made him go buy. No call for fancy suits and shirts when your job takes place in a cell. He'd almost had a heart attack when he'd managed to sneak a look at the price tag. A hundred bucks for some flimsy material with a couple of sleeves and some buttons. Unbelievable.

Brad Shipman. His fingers tightened around the mahogany door handle. Brad Shipman here, in Madison, to meet him.

"Hey, buddy! You coming or going?" The loud voice behind jerked him from his pondering.

"Sorry." He pulled the door, it opening with a swish to reveal an interior of paneled wood, red velvet, and starched tablecloths. A tall, slim hostess with gleaming white teeth stood behind some sort of podium. Glasses tinkled and the hum of conversation captured the air.

"Welcome to Matterhorn." The sparkling teeth got even more prominent.

"Hi." Sweaty palms wiped the outside of his jeans. "I'm Lucas Grant. I'm here to meet—"

"Mr. Shipman." She didn't even consult her book. "Right this way, Mr. Grant."

She cut through the room like the bow on a ship, Lucas trailing in her wake. The restaurant was heaving with men in suits and women in cocktail dresses. Not a pair of jeans to be seen. What on earth was he doing? He didn't belong here. Saints almighty, if there was a legion of knives and forks waiting for him at the table, he was done for.

"Mr. Grant?" The hostess stood behind a chair, holding it out for him. He'd never let a lady pull a chair out for him in his life. It just wasn't right.

"Lucas!" He was saved by the sole other occupant of the table launching up and grabbing his hand. "Thanks for coming—sit, sit, sit." His other hand windmilled toward the chair, which thank goodness, now had an empty space behind it.

"Mr. Shipman?" He didn't mean it to sound like a question. It was his voice, so clearly that's who he was. Except it wasn't. Not the Brad Shipman he'd conjured up, anyway. The Brad Shipman in his mind was all LA—buffed, bronzed, angelic looking. But if they were talking heavenly creatures, the man across the table owned a large amount of real estate at the cherub end of the angelic continuum.

Brad Shipman sat, the bench underneath groaning at the burden of his navy-blue-swathed girth. A platinum halo encircled a bald scalp, and his face segued into his chin, which disappeared into his collar. In the middle of it all sat a small pair of shrewd pale blue eyes.

"Call me Brad. Champagne!" He clicked his fingers at the waitress Lucas hadn't even seen hovering by their table.

Lucas's fingers trailed the intricately carved wooden arms of his chair as he sat. Whoever was bankrolling this place was loaded. Craftsmanship like he was sitting in did not come cheap.

A bucket of champagne appeared beside the table. The cork was popped and fizzing glasses landed in front of them before Lucas could say he didn't drink.

Brad's glass was already in the air, awaiting its partner for a toast. "Lucas, my man, I am going to make you a star."

A COUPLE of hours later, Lucas mopped up his plate with the last piece of the best-tasting steak he'd had in his life. Even though he'd managed to get away with barely a sip of champagne, his head spun as though he'd drunk a bottle.

Dinner had continued the same way it had started. Brad, waxing lyrical about the plans he had to syndicate Lucas, launch him into national stardom, punctuated only by pauses to down copious amounts of booze and eat a pile of ribs so big it must've required the sacrifice of a small herd.

From what Lucas could tell, so far there were a lot of big promises being spun like cotton candy, but not much detail.

"So, Lucas." Brad rinsed his sausage-shaped fingers in the bowl of water between them. "What do you say about all that?"

About all what? "It sounds very interesting, sir."

Brad threw back his head and roared. "Oh, I love you Midwesterners. So reserved. If I'd just told anyone in LA what I've said to you, I wouldn't have to worry about recruiting for my casting couch anytime soon, if you know what I mean."

Unfortunately he did, and it made him feel tainted just sitting at the same table as the man.

"Anyway, let's get down to business." Brad had a glint in his eye. "There's one little detail to my offer I haven't told you about yet."

"What's that?" He was going for nonchalant; it came out eager.

"Lucas, I want to bring you out to LA and set you up with a new show just like *Feelings and Football*. Some sports, some love advice. It's genius. I guarantee, within two years it will be syndicated across America. You, Lucas Grant, will be the person everyone calls when they want advice or to even just shoot the breeze about the Cardinals' win."

He hoped not. That would be pretty sad. People should be calling their parents, or siblings or girlfriends, not him. The fact that so many people called him—a complete stranger with no more expertise than the average man on the street—was proof of how disconnected people were from each other these days. Since when did talk radio and reality TV become a substitute for real relationships? Not that he was one to talk. Scott wasn't far wrong when he teased him about hiding in a closet behind a microphone so he wouldn't have to deal with real life.

". . . signing bonus of five hundred thousand dollars."

Brad's words screeched across his brain. Lucas was sure the whole restaurant had stopped to stare at the man. Half a million dollars? As a signing fee?

"Five hundred thousand dollars?" He struggled to get the words out, tongue tripping at putting the words "hundred" and "thousand" next to each other. He could help Scott and Grace, give them a bit of breathing room. Fund some more treatment, help Joey have the brother or sister he desperately wanted.

"I know, you were probably expecting more." Brad spread his palms across the table. "And there is more, but it comes with a catch."

"A catch?" Lucas took a slug of water. What could be worth even more money?

"Dr. Donna."

Ahhhhhh, now it all made sense. Lucas sensed his dream slipping out of his grasp. "I can't bring Donna with me. As far as I know, she has no interest in having her own show." He still couldn't believe that in the middle of being a bestselling author, she'd shown up for his show for four hours. Even if he'd rather be talking about the baseball picks. Not when she could have had countless shows with a bigger listenership than his.

"I don't want you to bring her along." Brad flicked his hand like she was an annoying blowfly. "You guys are friends, though, right?"

Were they friends? He'd never really thought about it. "I guess, in a way." She was funny and a fantastic cohost. But she was old enough to be his mother.

"Good. I want you to use your friendship to expose her."

His water glass stalled halfway to his mouth. "Excuse me?"

"I think she's hiding something. Something big. Something that if it got discovered would destroy her." Brad's piggy eyes gleamed at the possibility.

"Why on earth would you think that?" The guy was nuts. Must've had too much to drink.

"A man in my position hears things. Just little things, but after a while discrepancies start stacking up. One here, another there. Individually they mean nothing, but when taken as a whole . . ." A stubby finger poked the air, a whisker's distance from Lucas's nose. "Something isn't kosher."

"Well, I've known Donna for years; there's nothing there." It had been eight years since the first time she'd been on his show to promote her first book. He'd had the graveyard slot, where people called in about anything and everything, and she'd been so nervous that the first few minutes her voice sounded like something out of a cartoon.

"Maybe I'm wrong." Brad shrugged his shoulders. "Maybe what I've heard isn't right, or there's an explanation. But—" He leaned forward, which was only a slight movement given his size and the table penning him in. "What if I'm right? If I am, then she is a fraud, a con, of the highest order. Millions of people have bought her books. Doesn't America deserve to know the truth that their favorite therapist leads a double life?"

A double life. It wasn't possible. Donna was nothing like

his father. She was kind, passionate, warm, witty, intelligent. Besides . . . his head hurt even trying to think about how on earth she would have gotten away with hiding anything significant. Not in these days of 24/7 tabloid journalism.

"Can you give me an example?"

"Sure." Brad leaned back. "There have been times when she's been doing a signing in one part of the country while on radio at the same time somewhere completely different. How is that possible?"

Um, it was called a prerecord. And Brad being in the radio business knew that better than anyone.

"Her old publicist retired a couple of years ago. She's been saying things too. That Donna isn't what she seems."

Lucas raised his eyebrows. That was all the man had? Some prerecorded interviews that the station promoted as live and the ramblings of someone who was probably going senile?

"A million bucks." Brad folded his hands over his expansive girth.

"What?"

"A million bucks is what I'll add to your signing bonus if you can deliver proof I'm right, or, having looked into it, convince me I'm wrong."

Lucas stared at him, jaw scraping the tablecloth. "I . . . I . . ." His mind struggled to wrap itself around so many zeroes. With that kind of money he could help Scott and Grace out, clear all their debts, and pay off his own home with the change. But something didn't sit quite right. "Brad, I'm flattered, really I am. But I'm not a PI. Even if there was something there, I wouldn't know where to start."

Brad swiped his fat finger around his dinner plate to get the last of the sauce. "Don't worry. If I wanted one of those I'd hire one. All I'm asking is that you keep your ears open when you join them for the tour, ask a few questions, maybe dig around and see if you uncover anything that doesn't add up." He sucked the sauce off his finger with a slurp.

Lucas eased back in his seat, considering. There couldn't be anything there. Donna was so high profile that surely, if there was, it would have been discovered by now. And how could he live with himself if he said no and Scott and Grace lost their ranch?

Brad pulled out his wallet and threw a wad of notes on top of his plate. "Just think about it. You have my number."

Lucas made a snap decision. "No, I'll do it."

Brad hoisted himself off the booth, the whoosh of his bulk moving causing the candle on their table to flicker.

Lucas pushed back his chair and stood too. What had he just agreed to exactly?

"A man who knows how to make a quick decision." Brad thrust his hand forward, fleshy, sweaty fingers enveloping Lucas's palm. "I like that. It's been a pleasure, Lucas—I'll be in touch."

Moving with speed that defied his bulk, he disappeared, leaving Lucas standing at the table by himself.

- *12* -

*T*he carpet sucked her feet in. Not that Rachel made any attempt to fight it. The August deadline was getting closer by the day and here she was, in the one place guaranteed to not spring forth even a whit of inspiration.

"Hey, Rach."

"Hey, Harvey." Rachel threw a wave to the sturdy orderly who had been here so long, he was as much a part of this place as the walls.

She balanced the cardboard tray of coffees in front of her as the door to room 401 appeared on her left. She paused, her fingers on the handle. It had seemed like a good idea twenty minutes ago, but now it just felt weird. Like the loner in the playground doing anything to try and find a friend.

The glass sliding door was partly open, the steady beep of the monitors floating out. Anna sat curled up in the easy chair beside her husband's bed in the same Berkeley sweatshirt they'd met in. Alone. No pocket-rocket preschooler to be seen.

Rachel's heart retreated. There was something about Libby that had made the world feel alive, even within these four walls that specialized in bad news and long-term heartbreak.

Her knuckles tapped the glass and Anna turned her head, motioning with her hand to come in.

The door slid open and Rachel stepped into the room, pulling it closed behind her.

"Hey." Anna gave a glimmer of a smile. "Welcome back. Book tour finished?"

How . . .? Oh, Lacey. "Weekend off." Rachel gestured to her tray. "Loretta mentioned you're here pretty much twenty-four/seven, so I thought you might need some of the good stuff."

Anna's eyes lit up like the star on top of a Christmas tree. "You're an angel. I swear I've been dreaming about proper coffee."

"I wasn't sure what your poison is now, so I've got a latte or a mocha."

"Full fat?" Anna's words were painted with hope.

"Full strength, full fat, and I've even got some white magic if you also want full sugar."

Anna levered herself out of the chair and padded across the room. "If I wasn't worried about spilling the coffee, I would lay the world's largest hug on you right now."

Rachel held out the tray. "Left is the mocha, right is the latte."

Anna pursed her lips, eyes narrowed. "Oh what the heck, I'll take the mocha."

Rachel ejected it from the tray and handed it over. "Sugar?"

Anna already had the lid off and was slurping up the

foam, a ring of milky bubbles looping her mouth. She shook her head, mumbling something that Rachel semi-deciphered as "this is perfect."

The door slid open behind them and an older woman stepped into the room, purse hanging on her elbow, knitting needles and yarn visible in the open top.

"Hi, Marie." Anna licked some foam off her top lip. "Marie, this is my old friend from college, Rachel. Rachel, this is Cam's mom."

Old friend from college. Anna said the words easily. Like there hadn't been almost a decade of silence between then and now.

Marie nodded. "How's he doing?"

"No change." Anna sighed out the words, rubbing her temple with her free hand. "The doctor said this morning the swelling has gone down a little bit more, but not as much as they had hoped."

Marie patted Anna's arm. "Well, a little bit is better than nothing. Why don't you take a break, dear. Stretch your legs. I'll call you if anything changes."

"We can go sit outside; it's a nice day." The words were out of Rachel's mouth before she'd thought about them.

Anna popped the lid back on her coffee. "You know what? That sounds like heaven. I think I've breathed in about as much recycled air as my lungs can take." Placing the coffee on the table at the foot of Cam's bed, she grabbed a gray jacket off the back of the chair and slipped her arms into it. "Lead me on."

Rachel threw the tray and napkins in the trash beside the door. Sliding it open, she turned to glimpse Marie extract a large Bible from her purse and cross herself. Hopefully her God would hear her prayers, because from the look of the monitor tracking his brain activity, Cam needed all the help he could get.

"Has your father been here the whole time?" Anna took another sip of her mocha as they headed toward the closest set of doors leading to the garden.

"Yes. Straight from the hospital. The only thing that's changed is he's moved rooms a couple of times." She didn't look at Anna as she opened the door and ushered her ahead, choosing to stare at the still snow-capped Rockies in the distance.

A semi-choke from beside her. "No change at all?" It was spluttered more than said.

A bitter laugh. "Yeah, I didn't know it was possible either." She wrapped her fingers around her cup, trying to drain every last piece of warmth from it. It was a nice spring day, but not a warm one.

"What's . . . I'm sorry, I know this is weird. I've lost all my social cues with everything that's happened. I should have just said thanks for the coffee and let you go on your way."

"His actual brain was battered beyond any chance of recovering function. But somehow his brain stem remained intact. So mentally he's a vegetable, but physically all major organs work just fine. Part of me wishes he'd just stroke out so they can finally go to people who could really use them." She gasped as her ugly words were carried on the wind. Had she just wished her father dead to Anna, of all people?

She glanced sideways, expecting to see the judgment and damnation painted across Anna's face. Instead, her eyes crinkled in thought and she held her hair back with one hand to stop it from flying in front of her face as she drank.

Finally Anna swallowed and spoke. "I can't imagine much worse than Cam being here, the same, six months from now, let alone ten years. I could never wish him dead, but . . ." Tears flowed freely down her cheeks. "Hooked up to machines, unable to function in any sense? What is that? I'm not sure if it even qualifies as life."

Rachel patted her on the shoulder, the coarse texture of Anna's coat scraping across her fingers. "Try not to think about it. It's early days yet. I've seen people come in here like Cam is now and walk out well on the road to recovery." No need to tell her it had been all of about five.

Anna fished a tissue from her pocket and blew her nose. "I just pray that whichever it is, God takes it out of my hands. I've tried to get my mind around turning off his life support if they told me there was no hope, but I can't. How could I explain that to Libby? How could I live with myself?"

Rachel didn't answer. She had never had to make that decision since her father could breathe on his own.

"So, you and Lacey work together now." Anna changed the subject as she sat down on a wooden bench facing the gardens.

"She's a great publicist." Rachel sat down too, stretching her legs out in front of her.

"That she is."

"What about you? What do you do now?" It was horrible. Excruciating. She and Anna had used to talk about everything. Filling their apartment with laughter and yelled conversations across rooms. Now here they were. Worse than strangers.

"Me?" Anna shrugged. "Nothing really. I'm just a mom. Maybe soon-to-be widow." Something came out that sounded halfway between a laugh and a sob.

Rachel was silent. She couldn't promise it was going to be okay when clearly her situation said the opposite.

"How have you done it, Rach? What if Cam is like your father? How am I supposed to make a life for Libby if her dad . . ." Anna choked, unable to finish the sentence.

"I don't know." Rachel took a sip of her coffee. As far as she could tell, the only thing Cam and her father had in common was this building. "He wasn't a good father, Anna. I have a whole lot of guilt but very few good memories. If he were still alive he'd probably still be the same selfish, demanding drunk. I wasn't trying to build a life with him. It was the complete opposite. I was trying to build a life away from him."

"We should have just come with you that night. I've never quite forgiven myself that we didn't."

"We were twenty-one. It wasn't our fault." Even though she'd told herself the same thing many times over the years, for the first time ever, Rachel felt herself starting to believe it.

Anna leaned forward, hands tightening around her cup. "I tried to find you."

"You did?"

"Yeah. Six years ago. When Cam and I got engaged. I had this weird compulsion to have you meet him. Wanted to know if you'd approve. But I couldn't find you anywhere. Lacey couldn't either. I mean obviously we knew you were connected with Dr. Donna, but eventually I figured you had made yourself invisible for a reason. That you didn't want us to find you."

Rachel flinched. She'd only gotten in touch with Lacey when they had to find a new publicist, and she'd never reached out to Anna. Had always assumed that the things she'd said, the way she'd behaved, would mean they'd long since moved on. It had never occurred to her that they might one day come looking for her.

Would she have left some clues if it had? Would she have taken a chance and reached out?

Maybe three years would have been enough time. Maybe they could have found a way to rebuild what they had lost. Maybe if they had, right now she'd have a life with a footprint bigger than a postage stamp.

- *13* -

"Why do you think women always seem to go for the bad guy?" Lucas sounded more curious than anything else.

Rachel swallowed her last mouthful of orange juice and schooled her Dr. Donna voice. "Define a bad guy." She checked the clock on the wall. Less than ten minutes to go before the show was over. Thank goodness. Lucas hadn't been quite himself tonight. Distracted. Asking odd questions during breaks.

"You know, the one who drinks too much and flirts and treats women badly, and yet they seem to fall over themselves to date him?"

"Well, I have a couple of theories." Putting her glass down, she opened the cupboard, looking for a snack. "First off, it's not that women always want to go for the bad guy, it's more that they get tired of waiting for the good guy to finally get off his duff and make a move. Secondly, some women are just suckers for a challenge. Never satisfied with what they can have, they want to be the one to 'convert' that guy who has already run through all of their friends like water. Thirdly, I think it's a stereotype that's not true. I know plenty of good guys who have more than enough women falling over themselves to go out with them, and, to be blunt, often the women I see falling over themselves for the bad guy aren't the kind of woman the good guy should want anyway." *Oooh, marshmallows!* Fishing the bag out from the back of the shelf, she emptied the remaining sugary puffs onto the counter. She snagged a handful and padded back to the couch to settle in for the last part of the show.

"Nah, Doc, I've seen more than my fair share of smart, kind, good-looking women throw their hearts in front of the bad-guy train wreck and then be surprised when they get run over. But put a decent guy in their path and they don't give him a second glance."

"A decent guy like you?" Rachel teased him.

Lucas laughed. "I plead the Fifth."

"Well, why don't we ask our callers what they think? What do you think, Wisconsin? Do the bad guys really get the women, or is it just an urban legend? We'll be back after a few messages from our sponsors and a couple of sports updates."

Ethan synched up some ad as Rachel stretched out her legs and perused the chipped coral polish on her toenails. Definitely time for a new coat. After she'd finished the sugary, spongy candy.

"You really don't think it works like that?" Lucas was back faster than she expected, forcing her to swallow a half-chewed marshmallow.

"Of course it does sometimes. And like I said, sometimes it's because he actually gets in there and makes a move, while the good guy seems content to just warm up the bench. There's only so many weeks a woman is going to flutter her lashes over the back of a pew and drop hints about going for a coffee before she'll move on."

"Hmmmm." Lucas didn't sound convinced.

Rachel stood up and walked to her window, pondering the traffic and pedestrians passing by on the street below. "Here's what women want. Most of us, anyway. They want a guy with a bit of an edge who has confidence in himself and who knows what he's looking for in life. Combine that with someone who treats them well, makes them laugh and that they have chemistry with, and ta-da, magic. It's not rocket science."

Lucas groaned. "You make it sound so—whoops, ads are almost done." He disappeared into the ether, and radio Lucas reappeared a few seconds later. Rachel wandered back to the couch as he talked about teams she'd never heard of and players she had no interest in.

"Well, looks like we've sparked some conversations out there. We have time for one last call before it's time to call it a night and let Donna get some beauty sleep. Go ahead, Mitchell."

A guy cleared his voice. "So I guess you could probably say I used to be a bad guy."

"How so?"

"Well, you know all the stereotypes. Bit of a smooth talker, didn't call, cheated, took girls home when I knew I didn't want anything beyond a bit of nighttime fun, if you know what I mean."

"Yeah, I think we can interpret that."

Rachel almost laughed out loud at Lucas's dry tone.

"So what changed?"

"First of all, there wouldn't be any bad guys if women didn't let them treat them badly. I was a bad guy because I got away with it. Simple. I'd take a girl out for a date, not call for weeks, and then when I got bored and called her, she wouldn't call me on it or tell me off. She was falling over herself to go out with me again. What's with that?"

"So what happened?"

"Well, I guess it just got a little old. I mean, partying and picking up short-term flings when you're twenty-one is one thing, but I reckon it's a bit sad when you're twenty-five and still living like you think you're some kind of hot-shot frat guy. And secondly, I met a great girl who kicked me to the curb when I didn't treat her right."

"So you changed your ways to get her back?"

"Well, I tried. But it was too late—she'd moved on to a guy who was smart enough not to mess it up. But the next time I met a great girl, I'd learned my lesson."

"Mitchell raises an interesting point. Would we have bad guys if women didn't put up with it? Matilda, what're your thoughts?" Lucas asked the next caller.

"I think it's a bit rich to be putting it all on the woman. I mean, man up, take ownership for your actions. I get that it can be all very attractive if some woman is throwing herself at you. It requires no work for you to put another notch in the bedpost, but it takes two to tango." She sounded like she was in her twenties.

"You're absolutely right."

"You know what I think some of it is?"

"Go ahead."

"These days so few people have the luxury of being raised by both parents. So many times, there's not a father around. So we have a generation of girls who are growing up with no idea what a father is meant to be. Maybe Mitchell would have looked at that woman he took home for a night of fun differently if he'd asked himself if maybe she didn't have a father or had an abusive one and was desperate for some sort of male affirmation."

"You raise some good points. What do you think, Doc?"

Rachel almost couldn't talk. Her throat had closed over at putrid memories of her own. Ones that reminded her she knew all about doing dumb stuff out of desperation for male affirmation.

"You there, Doc?"

Get it together, Rachel. "Yes—yes, I'm here." She cleared her throat. "I think Matilda makes a good point. We live in a world where a lot of children don't know what a functional relationship looks like. They've never known what it's like to have parents who provide an example of what it means to be in a relationship that works. If you've grown up in a household where your dad beats your mom, then that is your normal, and statistics show that you are highly likely to do the same because you've never been shown anything different."

"There's no excuse for beating a woman, and any man who does so should be in jail." Lucas's voice was grim. "And on that cheerful note, it's time to wrap up tonight's show. Doc, a pleasure as always, and for all of you out there in our fair state, this is Lucas Grant. Sports fans, hang tight; we have a jam-packed four hours of sports—and *just* sports—coming your way tomorrow night."

Rachel pressed her forehead against the window, waiting for Lucas to come back on the line for their debrief. Outside the wind blew from the Rockies, an icy chill dancing through the streets. She had to be up to catch a plane to Texas in five hours and she hadn't even packed yet.

"Hey, Doc." Lucas yawned down the line. "You got a couple of minutes?"

"Of course." Rachel turned and leaned against the windowsill, jumping back up after the chill leached through her pajama bottoms.

"You know what you said about the research about if your father beat your mother then you'll probably beat your wife too?" There was something vulnerable in his tone.

"The correlation is higher, yes, especially if people don't deal with it. There are situations where people are determined they are going to beat their past and turn out to be wonderful parents. But the research shows that people do have a tendency to react to conflict the way their parents did, so if a boy used to see his father beat his mother, he's more likely to do so. If a girl grows up seeing her mother used as a punching bag, she's more likely to become one, because that's her normal."

"What about other things?"

"Like?"

"Well, if, say, a parent cheated or was an alcoholic or something like that?"

A memory flashed through Rachel. Her father, passed out on the kitchen floor, surrounded by vomit; her mother, weak from chemo, on her hands and knees trying to clean it up before Rachel saw.

"I'm not sure about cheating. I can have a look at the research. I know studies indicate a genetic component to alcoholism." She paused. "Is everything okay?"

A couple of seconds' silence down the line. "My father, let's just say he wasn't the world's greatest guy. Drank too much. Had another family we knew nothing about until he left us for them. Nothing scares me more than turning out like him."

She could relate. "You're nothing like him."

"How do you know?"

"I've known you for years. No one's that good at hiding who they really are." Except for her and Donna, of course. The masters of deception. He deserved better than this. "Lucas, I have to go."

"Okay." His voice was still laden with unspoken burdens. "See you this weekend, Doc."

"'Bye." Rachel hung up and placed her phone down on the table. In a few days Lucas wouldn't be at the end of a phone. He'd be traveling with them. In person.

The first person in a long time to make her want to be herself again. To stop hiding and take control of her own life. Despite the stakes. And he had no idea he was just part of the publicity-at-all-costs game.

- *14* -

"Hello?" Rachel's voice was so clear, it was like she was standing next to him.

"Hi, it's Lucas." He wiped his left palm on his jeans. What kind of idiot was he? She was going to see straight through his excuse for calling.

Silence for a second.

"Hope you don't mind me calling. Donna gave me your number." He jiggled his Bluetooth in his ear. Stupid thing never sat right.

"No worries at all. How can I help?" She didn't sound thrilled to be hearing from him, but she didn't sound unhappy, either. He'd take it.

"So, um . . ." He tapped his fingers on the steering wheel. "The reason I'm calling is I was thinking of getting Donna something—you know, to say thank you for the show and all—and I was hoping you might be able to give me some pointers."

Rachel groaned. "Really? She's a nightmare to buy for."

"Please, anything."

"Well, she likes nice lingerie."

His mind couldn't even go there. "I was, um, thinking more along the lines of something that wouldn't get me in trouble with her husband."

She laughed. "Look, I'll think about it, okay? And give you a call back. I honestly don't know of anything off the top of my head. It took me two months to source her birthday present. What's your budget?"

Oh cripes, he hadn't even thought about that. He scrambled for a figure. This was going to be one expensive ruse phone call. "A couple hundred?"

"Okay, I'll do my best. If I find something, do you want me to just buy it? You can pay me back."

"I would love you forever." He almost drove into a ditch as he realized what he'd said. *Love you forever?* He was trying to pump her for information, not make her think he was hitting on her.

"Right, well, I won't hold you to that." Thank goodness, she hadn't taken him seriously. "So what are you up to your last couple of days of freedom? Apart from cleverly shifting your gift-buying errand onto me, that is?"

Lucas gave up on the Bluetooth and pulled to the side of the road, tossing his headset on the passenger seat and putting his phone to his ear. "I'm just on my way to my brother's. I'm helping re-roof the henhouse in exchange for dinner."

"Is he doing the cooking?"

Lucas squinted his eyes at the glare bouncing off the road. Where had he put his sunglasses? "Grace, my sister-in-law, will be doing that, thank goodness. Scott probably couldn't boil an egg without supervision. Joey has more culinary skills than he does."

"If Joey remembers who I am, can you let him know I took his advice and got rid of that top he hated?" She sounded doubtful that Joey would remember her. Like she was used to being forgotten. Or never noticed at all.

He cleared his throat. "He will definitely remember you. So, um, how are things going?" *Smooth, very smooth, 007.*

"Fine, we're in . . . where are we? Sorry, it's a bit of a PR blur at the moment . . . Dallas, I think. Either Dallas or Houston. Or is it Austin? They all start to look the same."

"Don't let any Texan hear you say that. You'll be run out of the great state."

"Hold on a sec." A scuffle, then, "Lacey, where are we?" The line cleared. "We're in Houston."

Lucas groped through the glove box—no glasses. "Well, make sure you get yourself some good Texas barbecue while you're there."

A snort. "I highly doubt Lacey has worked that into the schedule."

"I'm deeply sorry."

"You know what? I don't think I've ever had Texan barbecue."

"My child, you have not lived." He salivated just at the thought. "Hickory-smoked goodness, tangy ribs, so tender the juice runs down your arms . . ."

"Okay, I get the picture. For the record, all I've had to eat today is a couple of bites of airplane breakfast, so that was just cruel."

"Where are you?"

"We're at the Marriott. Donna's set up in a room here doing PR for the next few hours."

"Okay, I know a great place in Houston. I'll text you the details. Promise me you'll try and get there if you can."

Another laugh. "I'll talk to the PR schedule controller and see if she'll loosen the reins."

Lucas flipped down the sun visor. There they were. He slipped the glasses over his eyes and put the truck back into drive. "Good luck. And thanks for the help with the gift."

"No worries. I'll let you know."

The beep of her disconnect vibrated through the cab. Lucas allowed a smile to play on his lips. He may not have gotten any measurable progress on the Brad mission, but something told him he'd managed to chink Rachel's armor a little.

THE KNOCK on the suite door caused the entertainment reporter to frown and lose her place in her question. "Cut—let's start that one again."

Rachel slipped the door open and peered out. A teenage boy in a red cap stared back and held up a large paper bag. "I have an order for a Rachel Somers?"

She hadn't ordered anything. "But I—" The pungent smell emanating from the bag interrupted her chain of thought. "What is it?"

The boy glanced at the receipt. "A dozen ribs, corn, some hush puppies, and an extra serving of special sauce."

Lucas. Just his name running through her mind caused a smile to twitch her lips. "Just let me get my purse."

"No need, already paid for. I just need you to sign." The boy held out the receipt and a pen.

Rachel scrawled her initials and took the bag. She dug into her pocket and extracted a couple of crumpled dollar bills. "Thanks."

Clicking the door shut behind him, she carried the deliciously aromatic bag over to the dining table. She pulled out paper napkins and plastic forks and saw a note scrawled at the bottom of the order sheet: "Rachel, hope this rocks your world as much as it does mine. Thanks for the help. Lucas."

"My word!" This time it was Donna who cut herself off. "Sorry, sorry." She waved at the reporter, who was making irritated cutting motions at her cameraman. "Rachel, what on earth have you brought in here? How is a woman supposed to do interviews with that smell tormenting her?"

Rachel shrugged. "I didn't order it. Lucas did."

"Lucas Grant sent you barbecue. From Wisconsin." Her aunt sounded more amused than surprised.

"Noooo." Rachel rolled her eyes. "From somewhere here. I may have mentioned I've never had it before."

Donna raised her eyebrows. "You did, did you? I didn't realize the two of you were trading culinary experiences."

Rachel pointed a finger at her aunt. "Don't you even start. He actually called about *you*. And if you want any of my ribs, you'd better be nice."

Lacey opened the bag and breathed in the scent, golden hair slipping across one shoulder. "You do realize those things have about a thousand calories each."

Rachel looked down at her ironing-board silhouette. "Do you promise?"

Lacey pointed a perfectly manicured nail at Donna. "None for you until you've finished this interview and Fiona says it's a wrap."

Rachel pulled a heavy plastic container out, snapped it open, and extracted a sticky, tender rib, holding a napkin underneath. She took a bite. Tangy, salty, spicy pork goodness coated her mouth and rolled down her throat. Just as Lucas had promised, juice ran down her wrist and dripped onto the table. Across from her, Lacey had stripped off her cropped jacket and was chowing down on a hush puppy, barbecue sauce smudged across her lipstick.

Rachel raised her rib in a toast to her aunt, who was pouting in her chair. "I'd advise you to hurry. I can't guarantee there'll be any left if you don't."

"Fiona, you call it a wrap right now and I promise you'll get an extra-special interview for the next one." Donna pulled out her best wheedling voice.

Rachel hoped she said no, just so she could have more rib time before her aunt got her hands on them.

"And that's a wrap."

Little did Fiona know that at the rate things were going there wasn't going to be a next book, so she'd just cut short her interview for nothing. Rachel tore the last remaining strip of meat off her first rib and grabbed a second from the container, her fingers sticking to the napkin like tar on a summer Texas highway.

Donna flopped into the seat next to her, kicked off her shoes, and nicked a hush puppy straight off Lacey's plate. "Mmmmm, God bless that boy."

Rachel set her rib down and sucked the sauce off each finger in turn. "Mmm-hmm."

Her aunt cast her a glance, letting her eyes speak since her mouth was stuffed.

Don't go there, Rachel. He's just a nice guy, thanking you for taking a pain of an errand off his hands. It took him all of about two minutes and twenty bucks.

Donna chewed and swallowed. "Anything you want to tell me, kiddo?"

Rachel picked up her rib again. *Keep cool.* "Nope." She took another bite to underline her point.

Lacey returned from dispatching the reporter and scowled at her empty plate. "Was it really that hard to get your own?"

"Yes." Donna smiled like an angel and turned back to Rachel. "Don't try and pull one over on me, Rachel—I saw that smile you tried to hide. By the way, just in case you happen to be interested, he has an excellent credit score."

Rachel stared at her aunt. "You ran a background check on Lucas?"

"Not a full one. Just the basics. Great credit score, no criminal record, no ex-wives, owns his own house. Mortgage is a bit more than ideal for his income, but that shouldn't be a problem soon."

"I can't believe you ran a background check on him."

"Why not? It's great advice from a renowned relationship expert." Her aunt grinned at her as she licked barbecue sauce off her fingers.

Never ever underestimate the importance of a good credit score. Butterflies come and go, but bad credit lasts for longer than many marriages. It was a line out of their second book, *101 Questions to Ask Mr. Perfect.*

The book had practically written itself after she'd realized that half the emails she got were the product of women not doing some basic due diligence at the beginning of a relationship. What she'd give for that to happen again.

"Except I'm not in a relationship with Lucas."

"But you like him?" Lacey had grabbed a replacement hush puppy and paused mid-dip.

Seriously? What were they in? High school? "C'mon. For a start, I barely know the guy."

Donna's forehead puckered. "Actually, you do; he just doesn't know it. Don't tell me you haven't chatted off air."

"That doesn't count—I'm you!" If anything, it made everything worse. Like eavesdropping on an intensely personal conversation and not being able to unhear the information. Especially the stuff about his dad. She had the feeling he hardly told anyone what he'd told her the night before.

She'd spent this morning's red-eye thinking about the vulnerability in his voice. Wishing she had been the one he was talking to, instead of Donna.

All of last night's show had felt off. For the first half, Lucas didn't seem to know if he was coming or going. During ad breaks he'd veered from distracted to asking odd, disjointed questions about Donna's life. Like he was trying to find out something but didn't know what.

"If it helps, I think he might have a bit of a thing for you." Lacey broke her hush puppy in half and tossed it into her perfectly lined mouth.

Her cheeks burned just at the possibility. *Deflect, deflect!* "You've only met him once. How would you know? Besides, I would have thought he was right up your alley. Single, good-looking, ambitious."

Lacey shook her head as she chewed. "He doesn't drink. Way too much of a good boy for me. A guy who won't even kick back and have a beer? No thank you. But that makes him perfect for *you*, Little Miss Goody Two Shoes."

Rachel snorted. "Lacey, in case you haven't noticed, we're engaged here in the self-help version of Milli Vanilli's lip synching."

Lacey rolled her eyes. "You wish it was that big of a deal. Regardless, soon enough you'll be free, and no one will ever know."

Rachel and Donna exchanged glances. They hadn't told anyone about the next book being the last. Agreed not to until they'd at least nailed down a concept out of the eight half-baked ones they now had.

Lacey laughed. "Oh come on, I'm blond, not blind. Anyone with a few neurons to rub together can see that you two are planning for a graceful exit. I'm guessing the only reason you haven't officially told us is because between the two of you, you still haven't managed to nail down a book idea."

"You got any?" There was no point denying it.

"Why don't you embark on a nice little fling with Mr. Grant? Might be just what you need to get some of those creative juices flowing again, if you know what I mean." Lacey flicked her a mischievous grin and reached for the last hush puppy.

Rachel slapped Lacey's hand away, distracting her mind

from places it shouldn't go. "You really think he wouldn't be able to smell a rat here if we let him get close enough? Or, worse, that eventually I wouldn't slip up somehow and give it all away?"

"C'mon, Rach, you've been doing this for years. And it could be over tomorrow if you wanted it to be. I've already got the PR all ready to go. Dr. Donna confesses to having a ghostwriter. Whoop-de-whoop. Now, the whole pretending-to-be-her thing to maximize media opportunities is admittedly next level. But even that would wash out in a week or two if we managed it right. Unless there's something you aren't telling me."

Rachel shoved her plate away, appetite gone. "You might be right, Lacc. But you could also be wrong. All it would take is one lawsuit and everything I've saved to take care of my father could be gone."

"Rachel's right." Donna took a sip of her soda. "We've only got one more book to go; her focus needs to be on getting that written and delivered. We can't afford distractions right now; we're too close."

"Then—"

"However," Donna continued with a twinkle in her eye, "I agree with Lacey. I'm pretty sure if my assistant were old and ugly, we wouldn't be eating ribs right now, and I can tell that you," she pointed her straw at Rachel's face, "have a soft spot for him. So, my dear, I wish you the best of luck in holding onto your heart."

- *15* -

*L*ucas hummed a made-up tune under his breath as he bounded up the steps to Scott and Grace's porch. The wood creaked beneath his feet, one plank giving a little more than it should. No doubt fixing that would be on the never-ending to-do list for the summer.

He let himself in. Hopefully he'd timed it right to grab a couple of minutes with Joey before heading out to give Scott a hand.

He checked the old wooden clock in the hall as he strode past. Right on three thirty. Rachel should have got the barbecue by now. He'd paid extra for express delivery. A smile played on his lips. What he would've given to see her face when it showed up.

He slipped his phone out of his pocket again and checked it. Just in case he'd missed anything, despite it being set on vibrate and high volume. Nothing.

Of course not. She was probably busy gorging on ribs. Sauce dripping down her fingers. Tender, juicy pork falling off the bone. He salivated just thinking about it.

Opening the door to the kitchen, his first glimpse was of Joey sitting on a stool at the breakfast bar, a cup of juice on the counter in front of him.

"Hey, buddy!"

Joey turned and his face lit up like a firefly. "Uncle Luc!"

Lucas picked him up and swung him around. Man, the kid got heavier every time. He set him back on the stool and ruffled his hair, then dropped his tool belt on the counter. "How was school today?"

"Good."

"Just good good or high-five good?"

Joey's brow folded in thought. "Well, Mrs. Ford said that I was a good helper in the morning, but then I got in trouble after lunch for calling Kayla a dummy."

Lucas stifled a smile. "Why did you do that?"

Joey shot him an indignant look. "Because she said the Badgers weren't the best because they didn't come in first. But they *are* the best, because Daddy says that having a good heart is just as important as winning."

Lucas nodded. "Which is true. But you know, some kids' dads think it is all about winning, so you shouldn't call Kayla a dummy. Instead it's probably better to tell her why you think the Badgers have more heart."

Joey pondered this for a moment. "Like when that guy kept playing even though he'd hurt himself?"

Lucas nodded. "Exactly." He gave Joey's hair one last ruffle. "I've gotta go help your dad now, but I'll see you for dinner."

The sliding door skated opened and Grace stepped through, arms full of flowers and foliage. "Joey, can you . . ."

Her words trailed off when she saw Lucas and surprise crossed her face. "Hey, Lucas."

A weird, awkward silence tripped into the room. She licked her lips and opened her mouth, closed it, then opened it again. "Is Scott expecting you?"

Lucas grabbed his tool belt off the counter and slung it over his shoulder. "Yup. He asked me last week if I could come help with the chicken coop today. Do you need a hand with those?"

She shook her head, placed the mound of greenery on the dining table, and then wiped her hands on her striped apron. "Actually, I think he's pretty much done out there. I'll go get him; he's about ready for a break anyway." She looked back over her shoulder toward the chicken run.

"I'll go. Need to stretch my legs anyway." Maybe they'd decided to give it one last shot and started another round? His brother had told him all the drugs wreaked havoc on Grace's system. That might explain her being so flustered.

"See ya soon, sport." He slipped past Grace and out the door, sliding it closed behind him.

He strode across the large backyard. Patches of grass had started to show signs that summer was coming, and he jumped over the back fence and headed for the coop. His tool belt bounced against his torso, hammering his ribs, and he reached a hand up to shift it farther onto his shoulder.

This was the perfect opportunity to tell Scott about Brad's interest. Probably best not to tell him about the offer, though. Ever since Scott had found God, his take on things had become a little less predictable.

His brother's familiar form stood by the coop. Lucas

slowed. There was a man next to him that he didn't recognize. Older, with a bit of a gut, and salt-and-pepper hair
that flicked off the back of his collar. Weird; Scott hadn't
mentioned anyone else helping out, and he wasn't one of his
usual hired hands. Maybe someone from his church. Fingers
crossed he was more of a worker than a preacher.

"Hey!" Lucas called when he was about twenty feet away,
just in case they were in the middle of some deep theological
discussion.

Scott jolted and turned. "Lucas." His voice was high,
with the same kind of stressed tenor it held whenever he'd
tried to lie to their mom. "Didn't realize you were stopping
by."

He closed the space between them. "You asked me last
week if I could—" His words met an abrupt end as the person
next to Scott turned.

No. *No.* The face was older, more haggard, but his profile
was the same. It was so unexpected, so out of place, the world
spun for a second, like gravity had shifted.

"Hello, son." His father spoke the words as if it had been
two days, not almost twenty years.

"What are you doing here?" He spat the words out like
darts. "No. Stop. I don't want to hear it." His heart thundered
in his ears.

"Luc." Scott put his hand up, as if trying to stop the train
wreck of emotion the sight of their father had unleashed. "It's
not—"

"Not what? What I think?" His fists clenched by his
sides. He took a step back, then another. "It doesn't matter
what I think, Scott, because there is nothing, nothing at all,

that could explain why he's here." He stabbed a finger in his father's direction. Let loose with an expletive for emphasis. "Either he leaves or I do."

"Lucas." The person he hated more than anyone else on earth spoke.

"Don't say my name. Not ever." His arms shook from the effort of holding them at his sides, quads burning as every muscle in his body clenched. "How could you? After everything he did?" He seared his brother with a look that contained more brimstone and damnation than he'd probably ever gotten from the pulpit.

"Let me know when he's gone and never coming back!" He yelled the words over his shoulder as he gave up any attempt at composure and bolted for the sanctuary of his truck and the open road.

LUCAS'S CHAIR creaked in protest as he leaned back, rubbed his eyes, and stretched his arms over his head. A dull throb permeated his head from staring at his laptop screen, trying to find a hint of anything shady about Donna. It had been a good way to spend the afternoon, trying to distract himself from the scene at Scott's house.

As far as he could find, her backstory seemed to check out. Not to mention, the single mom who worked two jobs and put herself through night school to get her psychology degree was the kind of Cinderella story the public loved. The only other thing he'd managed to establish was that she was a PR whirlwind. How one middle-aged woman could sustain such a grueling schedule was beyond him. Some days he'd pieced together she couldn't have managed to grab more than a few hours' sleep between commitments.

Something he was about to get a taste of. The schedule that had been sent through for his first official *Feelings and Football* events started with some schmoozing charity gala event on Monday night, and then went straight into a full day of media and PR appearances on Tuesday.

He shook his head. So Dr. Donna was a workaholic. Hardly anything to write a memo about.

I will never, ever apologize for that. The vehement words he was sure he'd heard Donna say to Rachel echoed through his mind. Could there be something of interest in them? Sadly, it was just as likely they were completely unrelated.

Pushing his chair back, he stood, shook out his legs, and wandered to the kitchen. Pulling open the cupboard, he yanked out a box of macaroni and emptied the packet into a bowl.

His phone flashed from its charger on the counter. Three missed calls from Scott. Three corresponding voicemails. Not that there was anything his brother could say to explain this afternoon.

He pulled out the milk and slammed the fridge door shut. How could Scott not have even mentioned he'd been in contact, let alone been standing there like they were any old father and son? His stomach curdled just at the memory.

A whiff of the milk confirmed his stomach wasn't the only thing that was off. Emptying the liquid into the sink, he tossed the uncooked macaroni into the trash and grabbed his car keys. Pizza en route to the studio it was.

His forgotten phone rang as he lifted his wallet off the hall table. He retraced his steps to the kitchen and paused at the name flashing on his screen. *Brad.*

Stifling a sigh, he plodded across the kitchen and picked it up just before it went to voicemail.

"Brad."

"Lucas! My main man! How's the detective work coming?"

Just the sound of his bold, brash voice vibrating down the line made Lucas cringe. Main man. What was that? Some kind of LA code?

"I'm doing my best, Brad, but it takes time." Lucas leaned against the counter and rubbed his temple. Ever since he'd agreed to look into Donna, the man had been all over him like a rash.

"All good, man. Actually, I was calling about something else."

"Oh." He pulled his phone off the charger and headed for the door. Might as well get something useful done while Brad got to the point.

"I was talking to the team today and they were so excited that you might be coming on board. So I checked your tour schedule and saw you guys are in LA next week. I'm assuming you have time to swing by and say hi. Let Stacey know your flight details and we'll have a car pick you up at the airport."

"I think Donna's assistant has arranged a car to pick me up." He paused halfway down his porch steps.

"Just let her know you've changed your plans and can make your own arrangements. You don't have anything on until the afternoon, right? Let Stacey know and I'll see you Monday."

The dial tone sounded before Lucas could even respond.

Opening the door to his truck, he tossed his phone on the dashboard and slipped behind the wheel.

He tried to summon up offense at Brad's presumptuousness, but it was like an escape hatch had opened up above him. A visit to his station would be good. A chance to see what his life might be like. Much better than staying here and trying to avoid the rotten apple on the family tree.

His phone trilled again as he pulled up in front of Burt's Pizzas, the multicolored flashing neon sign turning his cab into a mini-nightclub.

Pulling his phone out, he stilled at the name. *Rachel.*

Be cool, Grant. One more ring for good measure. "Hello."

"Hi. It's Rachel."

"Hey." He couldn't stop the slow smile that spread up his face. What was it about this girl that got to him? *Remember the goal, Grant; no distractions allowed.*

"Hey." Her voice was warm and comforting, like hot apple pie on a winter's day. "I just wanted to say thanks for the ribs. They were amazing."

"I'm glad you liked them." Noises in the background. "Where are you?"

A yawn echoing down the phone. "Gosh, sorry. We're at the airport. It's been a long day."

"I know what you mean." He leaned against the headrest. It was nice to have a normal conversation. He grasped for something to say to keep it going. "Oh, by the way, don't worry about sending a car to pick me up at LAX. I'm making a few plans for the morning."

"You sure? It's no trouble for you to use our driver to take you wherever you need to go. We have a generous budget."

"I'm sure."

"Okay. Well, our flight's boarding—I've got to go. But just let me know if there's anything you need before Monday."

"Will you be at the gala?" Monday night could be a great opportunity to do a bit more digging. See if he could get Rachel to drop her guard enough to give him any kind of hint as to whether Brad might be right.

She laughed. "No. I don't do schmoozing parties. They're Lacey's domain. But I'll be around on Tuesday."

Well, there went that idea. "Guess I'll see you then. 'Night, Rach. Safe travels."

"'Night, Lucas." The smile in her voice almost made him forget all about the resurrection of his long-lost drop-kick father and that he was trying to uncover dirt on her boss. Almost.

- *16* -

*B*rad's headquarters turned out to be housed in a gleaming silver skyscraper, with a foyer that rose for stories, uncomfortable designer couches dotted around the lobby. Everyone here looked like they'd stepped out of a catalog shoot.

Whisked up in a hushed elevator, Lucas stepped out into a plush reception area with floor-to-ceiling windows. The wall behind the front desk was emblazoned with *Shipman Productions* in curved letters.

His driver had waved him good-bye in the basement parking lot, promising his duffel would meet him at his hotel.

And here he was.

A door opened to the left of the receptionist and another woman entered. Perfectly tousled hair, skintight jeans, polished boots, trendy white T-shirt hanging off a coat-hanger body. She screamed money and success from every angle.

"Lucas!" She walked toward him, hand outstretched. "Hi, I'm Shawna, one of Brad's producers. He's in meetings at the moment but has asked me to show you around." She smiled, but the rest of her face didn't move with it. Who decided a plastic mask was something to aspire to? At least she had a good, firm grip.

"Hi. Thanks for having me."

"Oh, it's our pleasure. We were so excited when Brad told us you were thinking about coming to join the team. We're all big fans." She gestured him through the door and into a long, curved hallway. "We're just down here." Opening a door to the right, she stood back so he could walk through.

The view was so incredible, he stopped dead in his tracks. LA spread out before him, from glittering buildings all the way to the glistening ocean in the distance.

"Pretty amazing, huh?" A petite woman with copper hair and freckles stood beside him.

"Yeah." He looked around the conference room. About twenty people stood chatting, and there was a large buffet spread out in the middle.

"I'm Naomi. Casting."

"I'm Lucas."

She laughed. "I know. You're the one we're all here to meet. Your mug shot has been well circulated."

"Oh." He grasped for something to say, and saw out of the corner of his eye that Shawna was still in the doorway, talking to someone outside. "So, um, who are all these people?"

"Oh, you know, the usual." She waved a hand, bracelets clanging on her wrist. "Casting, production, advertising, PR, researchers."

"And they all work on the shows?"

"Well, we rotate a bit, but this is pretty much the team for a slot."

"For one slot." Lucas looked around and tried to absorb what she was saying. What did they need so many people for? It was call-in. People called. Ethan answered the phones and cued the ads and Lucas talked to them. It wasn't exactly rocket science.

He turned back to Naomi, who was still talking. "Though Jack over there"—she gestured toward a clean-cut guy who looked to be in his thirties—"he's just had a baby, so is about to swap to a daytime show."

"Fair enough; I wouldn't want to do night shift with a new baby either. No doubt his wife will be relieved."

"His partner. Geoff. They had a surrogate. One of their friends donated the egg. Actually, maybe that was Matt and Leo. Maybe Geoff and Jack bought one. Not sure who's the biological father, though. They just mixed all the swimmers up and let nature take its course."

Let nature take its course? Lucas pressed his lips shut. No point marking himself as a bigoted redneck before he'd barely gotten into the building. Not that he was one, but clearly what was unremarkable in LA differed from Wisconsin.

"Lucas." Shawna touched him on the elbow. "Come and grab a sandwich and meet some of your team."

Two hours later his head was spinning. There were too many blurred faces and he was on information overload. The biggest shock had been discovering what casting was. Apparently in LA, people didn't just get to call in. No, they had to audition to be a caller. *Audition.* To talk about Saturday night's game? Straightaway, there were three people who wouldn't have a job on his show.

His fingers tiptoed along a state-of-the-art production

desk. Ethan would have laid himself across it and wept in adoration if he'd found himself in its presence. It was wasted here. It should have been in a recording studio somewhere, mixing a Grammy-winning album.

"How's it going?" Shawna appeared beside him, a little too close for his liking. A pattern that had emerged over the afternoon. He glanced at her. Hair still perfect, lips glistening like they'd recently been retouched. She was attractive in a fashion-magazine kind of way, he guessed, but he preferred women who looked a little less Photoshopped.

But then every woman he'd met that afternoon looked like a version of the same. Slim, toned, tanned figures. Perfect hair of varying hues. Flawless makeup. Trendy clothes that looked like something out of a magazine spread. It was wearying being around so much perfection.

"Lucas? Are you there?" Shawna seemed to take his slow response as some kind of invitation and took a step closer.

"Sorry. It's been good. Thanks for showing me around. It's been great meeting everyone."

Shawna leaned in and bit her bottom lip in a way that he was pretty sure was meant to be alluring but came across as contrived. She tilted her head up at him with big eyes, and he had the distinct sense he was in some kind of scene from a daytime soap. "I could show you around some more if you like. Give you the more private tour." She ran her hand up his chest and Lucas froze. He'd been propositioned before, but it had been a long time since it was this shameless.

He had never understood the appeal of having sex with random strangers. And the idea of doing it in some closet somewhere in a populated high-rise on a Monday afternoon made his skin crawl.

"It's been a long day. I think I'm just going to head back to my hotel so I can relax before tonight. Alone." He added the last word just in case Shawna thought it was some kind of invitation.

She stepped back, and something that looked disconcertingly like relief flickered in her eyes. "Okay, well, your driver is downstairs, so you can head to your hotel anytime. Brad's still in his meetings, but says he might see you tonight at the *Feelings and Football* gala."

"The gala?" His insides twisted with panic at the idea of Brad coming onto Donna's territory.

Shawna flicked her hand. "He also said your date is going to meet you there at eight."

"My date?" Um, no, he had definitely not signed up for one of those. "Look, I'll be fine. I don't need a date."

She cast him what appeared to be the first genuine smile of the afternoon. Her eyes even threatened at a hint of pity. "Just roll with it. Trust me, it'll be easier."

- 17 -

What was she doing? Rachel reached one end of the hotel room, then pivoted back around. Bed, TV, bathroom, and turn. She pushed a couple of fingers to each temple and gave them a rub.

She did not play dress-up. Ever. That was the deal she had with her aunt. This schmoozing literary-gala stuff was Lacey's job, with her thigh-high slits, long legs, and easy laugh that made every male book buyer in the room place orders for thousands of whatever she was promoting on the spot.

Yet here she was. Sausaged into some ritzy cocktail dress that Lacey had magicked up from nowhere and levered her into. Her feet already hurt from her toes being scrunched up like discarded Kleenex into shoes half a size too small.

Rachel glanced down at the deep red dress. *Red*. It made the colorful clothes Donna gave her look tame in comparison. Not only was she jammed into the most attention-getting color of all, but the V-shaped neckline had somehow created cleavage that she'd never before possessed. It was like two strangers had suddenly attached themselves to her chest. She couldn't stop staring. And no doubt once most of the middle-aged men had bottomed a few drinks she wouldn't be the only one. At least that would be a new experience. No one had ever talked to her cleavage before.

Rachel tugged the bodice up. She could not see Lucas tonight looking like this. They hadn't spoken since she'd called to thank him for the ribs, but their good-byes had had her stomach twisted like a pretzel for the last two days. The only thing more terrifying than wanting a man to look at her twice was the thought that he might think she was dressed like this so he did.

A knock on the door. Rachel peered through the peephole and found Lacey on the other side. She slipped the dead bolt, opened the door, and stepped back. Lacey walked in, clad in a black backless number that swept to the floor, her hair in some kind of fancy braided updo. Half the guys in the room would probably get whiplash when she walked in. "You look great."

"Thanks." Lacey chucked her clutch on Rachel's bed and turned around. "So do you. I knew that dress would be perfect. Is Donna ready? I've just been downstairs and everything looks perfect."

"She texted a few minutes ago and said she would be ready in ten."

"Good. We probably don't want to arrive before eight thirty anyway. Make sure there are plenty of people already there when she walks in. Have you heard from Lucas?"

"No. He said he had some other plans this morning. But I asked downstairs and he's checked in, so he's around." Rachel tried to sound calm and unconcerned as she said it. Like he was just another person on her list to keep tabs on.

Lacey gave her a look that said she wasn't fooling her, but let it go. "Anna said you dropped by last weekend. She was really glad to see you."

Rachel shrugged. "It was the least I could do. Like you said. She needs friends right now."

Lacey sighed. "I wish I could have gotten there, but my schedule is just crazy at the moment and there are rumors of a partnership spot opening up."

"It's okay. She's got lots of people with her. And we'll be in Denver in a couple of weeks. Hopefully—" Rachel caught herself before she could say the words. She was no doctor, but even she knew that the longer Cam remained in a coma, the worse his outlook was.

"He doesn't die before then. That's what you were going to say, wasn't it." Lacey lifted her hand as if to run it through her hair and then stopped. Probably remembering her fancy updo.

"It's not good, Lace. He hasn't made any real progress in weeks."

"I know . . ." A breath whooshed out of Lacey. "It's just Anna, you know. And Libby. Her husband can't die. It just wouldn't be right."

Rachel put a hand on Lacey's arm as her lip wobbled. "I know. But that's not how life works sometimes."

Lacey pressed her lips together and then shoved her shoulders back. "Anyway, how are you feeling about seeing Lucas?"

"Fine. He'll be busy working the room. I doubt we'll

really speak." Especially since she planned to sneak back to her room at the earliest possible opportunity.

"You ready?" Donna's head poked through their adjoining door. Her eyes widened, then a very unladylike whistle split the room and the grim atmosphere. "Look at you. Hotter than a fried lizard on an Arizona highway."

Whatever. Rachel tugged at her full skirt. It was knee-length, practically a maxi compared to some of the skirt lengths that some women would be flaunting tonight, but combined with the lower-than-normal neckline she felt completely exposed.

"Now you stop that. If God meant you to be all covered up, he wouldn't have given you legs like that." Donna's bosom entered the room, followed by the rest of her. "Now where's your purse?"

Rachel gestured toward the bed, where a sparkly black clutch lay. "There."

Before Rachel could stop her, Donna had emptied it out over the bed and palmed her room key.

"Hey!"

"Nuh-uh-uh. No sneaking back to your room after ten minutes tonight, Little Miss Antisocial. You can have it back after two hours."

Two hours? Two hours was . . . Her gaze landed on her phone. Scrabble, Angry Birds, Risk—all she needed was to find a quiet bathroom. Not ideal, but far superior to death by a thousand mindless conversations. Or worse, standing alone trying not to look like a social outcast.

Donna, Lucas, and Lacey would be busy working the room. She wouldn't be getting any help from them.

Her aunt's talons ripped the phone from her sight. "And I'll take that, too."

Rachel's mouth wasn't working. Wasn't opening to voice her protests. She watched mutely as her phone accompanied her room card into her aunt's bag.

"Enough is enough, Rachel. You're thirty-one years old. Soon enough this charade will be over and you won't have your guilty conscience to hide behind anymore. Or a job as Dr. Donna's assistant. It's time to start getting used to the real world. And that, my dear, includes mingling with the masses. Now, let's go."

LUCAS STRODE into the room. And hid behind a large potted plant. His fingers tugged at his collar. He hated schmoozy parties. Even when they were supposedly half his.

The Feelings and Football Benefit Gala. The funds raised would be equally split between his and Donna's chosen charities, Kids in the Game and Books for Kids. For their sake, he would work the room like a pro and charm the checkbooks open.

In a few minutes.

Once he'd had a chance to get the lay of the land and dodge his d—

"There you are." The young blonde Brad had sicced on him for the evening wound her claws around his elbow.

He racked his brain for her name. Whitney? Stephanie? Melanie? Some well-connected mid-list romance author to introduce him around in exchange for some free promo for her latest book on one of Brad's stations. She'd leeched onto his arm as soon as they'd met and made it clear she would be happy to extend the arrangement to something of a more personal nature.

"Woo-hoooo! Justin, Lisa!" Her skinny, glittering wrist shot up, waving madly at a middle-aged couple a few feet away.

The woman turned their way. "Seonie!"

Seonie? Since when was that even a name? What ever happened to good old Sarah, or Katie, or—*Rachel*. His breath stalled. He'd only glimpsed the woman in a red dress for a split second in a gap in the crowd, but the profile . . . He shook his head. Wishful thinking. She'd made it clear that she wasn't going to be here tonight.

A tug by the terrier on his arm dragged his gaze downward. "Lisa Harvey, meet Lucas Grant. Lisa is in marketing at SouthSide House; Lucas is a radio host who Brad has his eye on."

Lisa's green eyes widened. "Well, Lucas, any friend of Brad's is a friend of mine."

"Thanks." He was being rude, but he couldn't stop his gaze from roving, trying to find the woman in the red dress again. What if Lacey was sick? Or Donna needed some help with something? It wasn't unthinkable that Rachel could be here.

He grasped for an excuse, any reason to dive into the crowd. "Can I get you ladies a drink?"

Lisa tilted her half-full glass. "I'm fine."

"Such a gentleman. I'll have a chardonnay, please," Seonie purred. Bad luck for her he couldn't stand cats. "Let me come with you."

"No, no, you stay and catch up with Lisa. No point two of us trying to part the Red Sea."

A pout. "Well then, hurry back."

No chance of that.

"Lucas, there you are." Lacey shouldered her way into the circle in a way that was somehow assertive without being rude.

"Lacey, this is Seonie, Justin, and Lisa." Lucas gestured around the circle. "Lacey is Dr. Donna's publicist."

Lisa nodded. "We've met in passing. Lisa Harvey. I'm in marketing at SouthSide House."

"Lacey O'Connor with Langham and Co.? I've been a big fan of your work with Bella Kingsley. And that campaign that you did for Kate McKenzie's last release was just inspired." Seonie sounded like a teenage groupie.

"Thank you." Lacey gave a polite smile. "Lucas—"

"Sorry." Seonie clearly wasn't. "I'm Seonie Rush. I'm an author with Watts Ryan. Would it be possible to pick your brain for—"

Something in Lacey's expression flickered, and she gave Seonie a look that was a combination of impatience and dismissal. "I'm sorry to be rude, but I'm working this evening and I really need to speak to Lucas for a few minutes. I'm sure you understand that when I'm on the clock I need to be dedicated to my client."

"How about a drink after? I just have a couple of questions. It would only be a few minutes of your time to help out a fellow book lover." Lucas winced as Seonie's tone turned petulant, and Lisa and Justin both took subtle steps back as if to distance themselves.

Lacey's expression turned icy. "Unfortunately, giving away advice to fellow book lovers doesn't pay my mortgage, but if you'd like to work with Langham and Co., please feel free to contact the office and one of the associates will be more than happy to talk to you about our publicity packages. Now, I'm sorry, but if you'll excuse us I really do need a few minutes with Lucas."

"Excuse me, everyone." Lucas stepped out of the circle and followed Lacey's black dress as she cut a path through the crowd, checking over her shoulder once to make sure he was following.

"Please tell me that woman is not your date." Lacey's brows puckered as she interrogated him with her eyes.

"I kind of got stuck with her unexpectedly. A favor for an acquaintance."

Lacey flicked open the black folio he hadn't even noticed she'd been holding. She looked down at the run sheet and sighed, and then looked up at him. "Here's a piece of free advice for you, Lucas. Choose carefully. Both your acquaintances and the favors you give them."

Lucas bristled at her condescension. "I'm not some naïve hick guy from Nowheresville. Believe it or not, I am actually a pretty good reader of people. And I've met a few Seonies in my time. I am capable of working out how to handle them."

Lacey looked up. "You're right. I'm sorry. I'm just a little protective, I guess."

Lucas sighed. "You don't have to worry about me doing anything that might compromise the tour. I'm not that kind of guy."

"It's not the tour I'm worried about. Trust me. Donna and I did extensive research before we put all of this in motion.

We probably know more about you than you would ever want us to."

"Well then, you know I lead an exceptionally boring life."

"Surprisingly so." She checked the watch on her wrist, then the piece of paper in front of her. "Now, in about fifteen minutes you and Donna are going to need to say a few words. Welcome people, encourage them to be generous—"

Lucas's attention was pulled away from whatever Lacey said next by a flash of a red cocktail dress through the crowd. His gaze moved straight to the woman's profile. Rachel.

He turned back to see Lacey appraising him with a knowing smile. "Go on. Go talk to her." She nodded in Rachel's direction as she handed him a piece of paper.

Lucas glanced to where Seonie was watching him. "I doubt my handler is going to let me."

Lacey cast a septic look in the woman's direction and clearly saw what he saw. "Fine." She said the words through gritted teeth. "I will go and talk to her, but you owe me."

"I THOUGHT you didn't do schmoozing parties."

Rachel's hand stalled on its path to picking up her glass. She'd know that husky voice anywhere. "Donna made me come and then stole my room key."

A chuckle. "She's a determined woman, your boss."

Her hand found her glass, which she lifted from the bar before she tilted and glanced up her right side.

Crooked grin, eyes the color of an easy summer's day. In a tux. Her breath hitched. *No, Rachel, don't even go there. It's not possible.*

"Lucas Grant." She added a drawl for good measure. "Look at you all scrubbed up in LA."

He tugged at his bow tie. "I could say the same to you." He signaled the bartender. "Orange juice, please."

Orange juice? Maybe Lacey was right about him being a teetotaler. Rachel raised an eyebrow as it landed in front of him.

He shrugged, broad shoulders causing the fabric of his black jacket to ripple. "Not much of a drinker."

"Good." It slipped out before she could stop it.

"Sorry?" His brow furrowed.

"Nothing. So what are you doing—*oomph*." A hard shove from her left saw Rachel flung into Lucas's chest.

His very broad, nice-smelling chest. Like a mix of cloves and—*Stop it, Rachel.* His hands on her waist weren't helping matters at all.

"Dude, show some respect." Lucas glared at the large guy on Rachel's other side, who swayed and muttered something indecipherable under his inebriated breath.

"Come on." Grabbing her wine with one hand and her wrist with the other, he cut a decisive path through the crowd. Her fingers wrapped around his, warmth running up her arm.

When he reached the edge of the crowd, he tugged her into the gap he'd created between himself and one of the many pillars encircling the ballroom. Handing back her wine, he tugged his cuffs so they poked out under his jacket. He caught her gaze and tossed her a grin, and her breath hitched. Lucas Grant scrubbed up more than mighty fine.

"Oh, your juice."

He shrugged. "It wasn't that good."

She tapped her glass. "You know they probably just charged us ten bucks for it."

His jaw dropped. "You're joking."

"High-society prices."

He shook his head. "You realize now I'm going to have to go back and find it. Otherwise I'm not going to be able to sleep tonight."

"Must be nice to live a life where the only thing on your conscience is wasting overpriced juice." Good grief, she was flirting with him. *Stop it.*

His body seemed to stiffen for a second, followed by an easy smile. "Sounds like something far more interesting is on *your* conscience, Miss Somers." He propped an arm against the plaster above her head, creating a shelter for her.

Anyone else and she would have felt trapped, but for some reason, with Lucas it felt safe. She had to extract herself. He was the one person she couldn't afford to feel anything for.

"I wouldn't say that." She leaned back against the cool plaster and gazed up. What was she doing? This was the opposite of extraction. Her head screamed at her to get out, but her heart kept her captured in his eyes. "So what have you been up to today?" She brought her wineglass to her lips, forcing him to shift back to give her space to take a sip.

Again, something she couldn't decipher danced across his eyes. "Um, I guess you could say I'm exploring some career options."

Ahhh, that explained it. "I understand. My lips are sealed."

He grabbed a water off a tray, then leaned against the column next to her. "Thanks. It just kind of recently came up. You know how fickle these things are—probably won't come to anything."

He was so close that if she leaned forward even slightly, she'd practically be in his arms. Again. She grabbed something on a toothpick off a passing tray. Used it to cover for a step back. "Well, for what it's worth, they'd be stupid not to have you. I'm sure Donna would be happy to be a reference if it would help."

He froze with a kind of stricken look, as if she'd just suggested they rob the charity raffle. "Um, thanks. I'll let you know. So how's the tour going?"

She shrugged her shoulders. "Oh, you know. Hotels, planes, bookstores, they all start looking the same after a while. You'll discover that this week."

Lucas closed his eyes for a second as if something she'd said had pained him.

"Are you okay?"

He looked at the room filled with people in gowns and black tie and more bling than Fifth Avenue. "How did I even get here? I'm just a guy from Wisconsin with a sports show. This," he tugged at his bow tie again, "isn't me."

"Don't sell yourself short, Lucas. You're more than just some guy with a sports show."

Lucas looked around. A couple of yards away, a blonde in a dress with a neckline that practically went down to her waist gave him a smile. He gave her a quick nod, then turned his attention back to Rachel. She felt a childish sense of satisfaction at the blonde's look of disbelief.

"Want to help me out with something?" He took out his phone and pulled up the home screen.

"That depends on what it is."

He leaned a little closer as he tapped the screen, his breath brushing her cheek. "The radio station is on me to take some photos of the tour for social media. Want to take one together? We can tag it to Dr. Donna's page if you like."

A photo with Lucas was a bad idea. Especially one of just the two of them. "I'd rather not. I'm a strictly behind-the-scenes person. You should get one with Lacey. Tag it to her PR company." A photo with an up-and-comer like Lucas would surely only help her chances at the promotion she'd mentioned.

Lucas looked up, his phone showing a blurry view of both their feet. "You know when a man's been propositioned twice in the space of a few hours, it's very disconcerting having someone not even want to be in a photo with him. Should I be taking it personally that you don't want your Facebook friends seeing us together?"

Rachel forced a casual shrug. "I'm not on social media, so they wouldn't see it anyway."

His brow crinkled. "What do you mean you're not on social media?"

"I mean obviously I have an administration log-on to manage Donna's pages, but I'm not on it personally." She tried to keep her voice breezy, like it wasn't a big deal.

He looked at her like she'd suddenly started speaking in a different language. "You're not on Twitter? Or Facebook? Or Instagram?"

"No." She didn't get the appeal. The thought of being

virtually connected to people she hadn't spoken to since high school weirded her out.

"But how do people find you?"

"Everyone in my life knows how to find me." A number that took up less than two hands.

"But what do you do with all your spare time while the rest of us are looking at cat memes and random videos?"

"I read books. Watch movies. Bake."

He looked at her like he still wasn't sure if she was serious, but he slipped his phone back into his pocket. "You're a very unusual woman, Rachel Somers." But the way he said it made her feel like he thought she was intriguing, not like a weirdo, so she just smiled and shrugged.

He knocked back his water. "Okay, next matter. You booked me business-class tickets."

And? "I did. And fair warning: all the rest of your flights will be business class too. I told you we have a generous budget."

"Honestly, I'm fine in coach. They're my people. Can't you just book me on the cheap tickets and make a generous donation to the kids?" His breath wafted up across Rachel's cheeks and her toes curled in her too-tight shoes. "That way everyone wins."

Who was this guy who was practically begging to fly with his knees up to his eyeballs? She was pretty sure she was the only assistant in the history of the world ever to be asked to downgrade someone's flight class.

Rachel shook her head. "Hate to break it to you, but it's not quite that easy. Besides, Donna will have my head if she finds out you're flying in the back."

"Fine." Lucas's mouth tipped up. "Guess I'll just have to find someone worthy to swap seats with. That will be fun."

"Go for it." He'd never do it. Not now that he'd had a taste of flying up the front. "Do you want this?" She held out the bacon-wrapped-something canapé she'd grabbed.

"Sure." Lucas grabbed it and popped it in his mouth, barely bothering to chew. "So what else do you do when you're not being the world's best assistant? Are you auditioning for Britain's Hottest Home Baker or something? Is that what you do while I'm blocking Twitter trolls?" He looked only at her, like he had all the time in the world.

Either her radar was totally broken or he was flirting with her. The thought flooded her with both delight and dread. Might as well play along. "Yes, that's exactly it. I spend hours in my kitchen perfecting my Italian meringue."

"Your family in Denver as well?"

Now it was her turn to freeze, mind scrambling for an answer that wasn't either a lie or enough of the truth to ruin the moment. "Colorado Springs."

His gaze drifted above her head and narrowed. "Oh blast, Lacey's giving me the eye. Apparently I'm supposed to say a few words. Help charm the cash out of this crowd. I have to go." He reached into his pocket, then slipped something into her palm.

She looked down at it. His phone. "Wha—"

"Shhhhh." A finger landed on her lips. Lingering. Then his lips brushed her hair, a tantalizing whisper almost taking her out at the knees. "My password is Woofy7. Capital *W*. There's tons of games. Don't tell Donna."

A laugh burst from her lips. "Woofy?"

He made as if to take back the phone. "Fine. Mock my password and no games for you, Miss Somers."

"Okay, I'm sorry, I'm sorry." She held up her hands in surrender.

"Sure you are." He cast a grin over his shoulder that had her wishing she'd said yes to that photo after all.

- *18* -

The hotel bed was so large Lucas could spread out across it and only just reach all four corners. Mmmm. Bliss. Except for one thing.

When he'd first walked in and seen the perfectly made bed with no pillows, he thought it had been a housekeeping error. Then he'd discovered the pillow menu, propped up against the naked headboard. What genius had come up with that great idea? The pages of choices had done his head in. Soft, super soft, firm, orthopedic, down, feather in a hundred combinations. What ever happened to just giving a guest an ordinary rectangle of synthetic fibers to lay his head on?

So, taking the route of passive resistance, he'd chosen the only option not listed: none. He punched the small, pathetic cushion he'd taken off the armchair under his neck, trying to give it some oomph.

This morning his neck muscles hurled abuse at him, bunched up tight and angry. Looked like tonight he was going to have to man up and take on the pages of pillows.

He flopped onto his back and stretched his arms up, locking them above his shoulders and pushing against the headboard. The day stretched out in front of him. There was nowhere he had to be until some media thing with Donna in the afternoon. Maybe a run, a luxurious breakfast in the hotel restaurant, coffee with Brad. The man had arrived at the gala late and stayed for maybe twenty minutes. Their only interaction had been Brad telling him he'd give him a call in the morning to schedule coffee. Lucas rolled over, scanning the bedside table. Where had he put his phone last night when he'd come in?

Not there. Or on the table on the other side. He flipped up, feet over the side of the bed, sending the sheets falling to the floor.

He pulled his suit jacket off the back of the chair and checked the pockets. Empty except for a piece of folded paper. He flipped it open. A phone number. With an *S* and a heart at the bottom. So that's what Sloany, or whatever her name was, had been up to, suckered to his side, as he was trying to make his escape. Crumpling it, he pitched the unwanted advance into the bin.

For all her surgically enhanced assets, she had nothing on Rachel.

Rachel. Phone.

He hadn't remembered to get it off her before he'd left. Hmmm. He was going to have to find her so he could claim it back. A smile quirked. What a shame.

Grabbing a gray T-shirt from his duffel bag, he slipped it over his head. He'd shower after breakfast. He should probably go grab the phone after that, before he met Brad. *Brad.* He froze, T-shirt halfway down his torso. Oh no. Brad had said he would call with the details. He had to get it off Rachel before he called.

Yanking the T-shirt the rest of the way down, he shoved his legs into his jeans, jamming his favorite pair of Tigers on his feet.

Shoving his wallet and key card into his pocket, he grabbed his sunglasses off the desk and strode to the door, flinging it open.

Whoa! He pitched back, almost tripping over his own feet.

"So." Brad stood in the doorway, a huge grin on his face. "Who was the lucky lady? Do I get to meet her?" His eyes scanned the room behind Lucas, as if expecting some damsel would be standing there, clad only in a sheet or something equally compromising.

"What are you talking about?"

"The girl who answered your phone this morning. Said you weren't available. I bet you weren't." He gave a wink that alluded to far more R-rated content than Lucas had any interest in contemplating.

"Sorry, Brad, not that interesting. Just a friend I lent my phone to last night."

Brad's eyes slid over to the closed bathroom door.

Seriously? "You want to come in and do a search?" Lucas opened the door wide.

Brad clapped a hand on his shoulder. "I'm just surprised is all. An eligible bachelor such as yourself. It's not right you having to spend a night by yourself. Especially not in LA. I'm surprised our ladies weren't more hospitable."

If they'd been much more hospitable he would've had to press charges. "Not really my thing, Brad."

"Oh." Brad's eyes narrowed. "You don't play for the other team, do you?"

Had he really just asked that?

"Not that it's a problem if you do," Brad added quickly. "I just hadn't realized."

Lucas's teeth clenched, his fist itched. "No, Brad. Just because I don't have one-night stands doesn't mean I'm gay. It just means my mom raised me better."

Brad chortled, then dropped an expletive. "I didn't realize they still made guys like you. Are you a virgin, too? Waiting for that right special lady?" He waggled his eyebrows.

What was he doing? Was he seriously thinking about going to work for a guy who made him want to take a shower after just a couple of minutes in his presence? *Remember the dream, Grant. And the money to give Joey a sibling.*

"Sorry, bad joke." Brad held up his hands, clearly registering that he might have just crossed a bridge too far. "Let's go get some breakfast and talk about what you've got on Donna."

Thirty minutes later they sat under an umbrella in the courtyard. Even before eight the sun was inviting, the air warm. Crazy.

Lucas tilted his head back and let the rays soak in. Now this, he could get used to. Taking a long slurp of his orange juice, he tried to ignore Brad for a second. Which was difficult, because he seemed to be unable to control himself from commenting on every female within a forty-foot radius.

"So Lucas, what have you got for me?" Brad stabbed a piece of toast into the yolk of a sunny-side-up egg.

Lucas chewed on his piece of bacon for a moment, buying

time. How could he tell Brad that after almost a month he had found nothing that cast doubt on Donna's story? Not only that, but he was pretty sure this was just a wild goose chase. Unless Brad knew more than he was telling him as some kind of test.

"Honestly Brad, don't you think that if there was something big there, someone would have discovered it by now?" He shoveled in a big piece of toast to buy himself some more time, in case Brad's answer was short.

"Look at the moon landing." Brad waved his fork around. "It's been like fifty years and people still believe that happened."

Lucas almost choked on his mouthful of carbs. A conspiracy nut. The guy just got better and better.

"She's just too good, too wholesome. It just doesn't feel right."

Maybe not when your proclivities had you living in the gutter. "Look, I'm doing my best, okay, but I have to tell you, from what I've seen so far, I really don't think there are any skeletons to be found." The only thing that had seemed odd was the twenty-year gap between Donna getting her undergrad psychology degree and starting the blog that got her noticed. But that was no doubt explained by the time she wasted on the loser who eventually abandoned her and their kids.

Brad didn't answer, his eyes off over Lucas's shoulder. "Would you look at that?"

Lucas didn't even turn his head. It was bad enough to have one person at their table unable to control his gaping.

Brad let out a low whistle, jowls trembling. "I'm telling you, dude, you want to check this one out. Now she isn't

exactly a pinup, but there is something about her that is—"
He flapped his hands in an awkward motion that Lucas pre-
sumed was meant to indicate heat.

"No thanks." Lucas pinched some bacon and popped it in
his mouth.

Brad's eyes bounced back. "She's coming our way." His
attempt to suck in his midriff was laughable. Lucas rolled
his eyes. Great, some bimbo recognizing Brad and coming
to paw all over him. He threw down his last piece of toast,
stomach unable to take any more.

"Hi, Lucas." He jolted up in his seat.

He was in so much trouble. His eyes crept up. "Rachel,
hi." His voice croaked. He coughed, trying to clear it.

Floaty navy sundress, lots of lean tanned leg, hair down,
sunglasses perched on her tousled hair. No wonder Brad
looked like a frog trying to swallow flies.

Lucas sprang to his feet, chair almost tipping before balancing itself on the back of his knees.

She smiled, dimples and all. "I'm so glad I spotted you.
Sorry I forgot to give you back your phone last night. You've
had a few calls and messages. Hope you weren't expecting
anything too important."

"No, not at all. Thanks."

She dug around in the cream bag she was holding, fishing
his phone out and placing it in his palm. Was it his imagina-
tion or did her hand linger, just for a second?

"Brad." The bullfrog lurched up, thrusting a sweaty palm
toward Rachel.

She looked at it with distaste, before good manners took
over and she allowed her hand to be manhandled. "Rachel."

She extracted her hand, looking at Lucas with pity in her eyes. "I'll see you at the studio this afternoon."

Lucas's stomach clenched. Donna had insisted he join her at some talk show appearance this afternoon. Why did he say yes? His first TV interview, and Rachel would be there to witness him making a fool of himself. "See you there."

"Great!" She flashed him a bright smile and spun around, her skirt lifting slightly in the breeze.

Lucas looked down to see Brad ogling. He wanted to rip his eyes out and use them to play marbles. "Seriously. Show some respect."

Brad ignored him. "Who. Is. That?"

"That's Rachel."

"And where did you find her, you crafty fox?"

It was like he'd been hit with a brick. He was going to have to tell. No doubt Brad would find out eventually and wonder why he hadn't mentioned it. "She's Donna's assistant."

Brad's gaze snapped back to his, eyes changing from lewd to calculating. "Lucas, my man, I was beginning to doubt you, but you are clearly far more devious than I gave you credit for."

Lucas slumped back into his chair, Brad's words a sobering indictment of his good character.

- *19* -

"*H*i." The whisper went in one ear and straight down her spine, puddling into a warm glow in her stomach. Rachel kept her eyes straight ahead, to where Donna was being fussed at with a makeup retouch. "Hi."

Lucas stood next to her, his arm grazing hers as he lifted a Styrofoam cup of coffee. A slurp. Still she refused to look. She couldn't afford to be undone by his ocean eyes any more than she already was.

She'd spent the rest of her morning digging through her archives from when she'd been an intern to a renowned advice columnist. The discarded letters and emails that never made the newspaper had provided the basis for both her blog and their first two books. She'd been hoping they might spark another idea. Instead she'd spent most of the morning thinking about the same blue eyes she was currently trying to avoid.

"How was your morning, Miss Uber-assistant?"

Rachel tried to smother her smile but failed. "Good. They'll be ready for you soon. Thanks for last night, by the way."

"You're welcome. Though couldn't you have left my ego with even one high score?"

She couldn't help but glance up at the tease in his voice. Mistake. Eyes filled with laughter and, yes, even admiration stared back.

"I would have if any of them were actually a challenge." She would never admit that she had played one level of Flinging Frogs for an hour before she'd managed to beat his score.

"Ouch. Really know how to make a guy feel good about himself, don't you."

"It's a specialty of mine." She couldn't help the smile playing on her lips.

"Can you help me with something?" There was no teasing now.

She turned, her arm grazing against his. His skin was coarse yet soft. Thank goodness. She couldn't abide the plucked and waxed LA men. *Stop thinking, Rachel!* "Um, sure."

He held out his cupped hands, which were piled with a receiver, transmitter, cordless mic, and an earpiece. "What do I do with these?" His bewildered expression was comedic. "One of the guys with headsets gave them to me and just disappeared."

"You um . . ." She took the receiver in her hand and pulled the cord to the earpiece out. "You need to drop this down your back, then you plug it into the receiver and clip it onto your belt."

He took the cord in his hand and reached his arm back, popping one end down his collar. "Like this?"

He did a little dance, trying to shake it down his back.

"Here, turn around."

Lucas turned and Rachel watched the line of the cord snake down under his shirt, getting stuck just above his belt. "Almost there. Can you pull it down the rest of the way?"

He untucked his shirt, his hand reaching up to tug the end of the wire all the way down.

She averted her eyes, but not before catching a glimpse of his tanned, muscular back. The back of someone who knew hard work.

"Rach?" She looked up. "Can you plug it in for me?"

Her hands fumbled with the box, and it took two attempts before she managed the successful click of the plug into the receiver.

"Thanks." He took the box from her, his fingertips dancing along hers. He clipped it onto the back of his belt and did his best to retuck his shirt.

He turned, the earpiece now trailing out of his collar and down his shoulder.

"Okay, now you need to tuck that into your ear."

He groaned. "You mean like a stupid Bluetooth thing?" Plucking it up, he pushed it into his right ear.

She nodded. "Yup. Fine."

"And these?" He turned his attention to the transmitter and cordless mic remaining.

"That one." She pointed to the transmitter. "Clip on the belt too."

Obediently he reached behind and tucked it in.

"And the mic you just clip to your shirt."

With a smile of exasperation, he clipped it onto his collar, then threw his hands up. "Okay?"

Tilting her head, she studied the small black bug-like object. It looked wrong. Clipped to his collar, it would be too high to catch his voice properly.

"Everything okay?" This time, his eyes held hers, searching.

"Um, it needs to . . ." She pinched the mic between her fingers, tugging it down and positioning it to attach on the button seam. His chest rose and fell in time with the warm breath on her cheek. It was broad, safe.

Every fiber in her being yearned to lay her head on it. To have him cradle her in his arms.

She forced herself to focus. She clipped the mic, allowing herself a quick stroke with her palm, like she was smoothing his shirt. She stepped back, lifting her eyes to find him studying her, a smile on his lips. As if he favored what he saw.

"You know, I had to post a solo selfie last night on social media. I looked very sad and pathetic."

"You know what you should do?"

"What?"

"Take a selfie with your arm like it's draped around someone's shoulder and then invite all your fans to Photoshop themselves in. They'd love it."

He let out a surprised laugh. "Or . . . how about if we took a photo and I promised not to publish it anywhere."

"I'm just the assistant, Lucas. I'm no one special."

"Now that clearly is not true." He looked at her and, for the first time in a long time, Rachel felt seen.

"There you are!" A heavyset production assistant appeared, all officious, as if having a headset made him ruler of the universe. His advance broke the spell. "We're ready for you now. Good grief, who on earth miked you up? It's a disgrace!"

HE'D ALMOST forgotten how to breathe. Watching her long, delicate fingers on his chest, her face just a whisper away, brow wrinkled in concentration.

Like the night before, all he'd wanted to do was wrap his arms around her. Although last night it had been out of a desire to wipe away whatever it was that caused pain to etch itself across her face when he asked about her family. Today it had just been the straight-out fact that having her that close scattered his emotions like freshly shelled peas on a wooden floor.

He couldn't explain the effect Rachel had on him. It made no sense. But he couldn't seem to help himself. If that grumpy little tech guy hadn't come and interrupted them, who knew what might have happened. At least today he didn't have to worry about glancing up to find Sloany coming after him like a piranha.

Get a grip, Grant. He shook his head, fingers desperate to scratch his forehead. The infernal makeup they'd plastered his face with was driving him mad. And the lights. Did they really need to light up the set like it was an operating room?

He didn't even know what he was on this show for. According to Lacey, all the scheduled *Feelings and Football* events were already sold out, so it wasn't as though they needed the publicity.

His gaze found its way over to Rachel. She was chatting to a production assistant, laughing at something he had said.

He forced his eyes away. He couldn't let himself get distracted. Not by anyone, but especially not by her. Not when she was his best shot at finding out if Dr. Donna did have a big skeleton in the closet.

He shoved his discomfort away. Silenced his conscience whispering that he was using Rachel to advance his own career.

As far as he could see, there was nothing there. Brad was mistaken. He just needed a little more time, to ask a few more questions, and then he could go back. Tell Brad there was no scandal to be found. No double life being lived. Donna and Rachel would never even know.

"Lucas, darling boy." Donna dropped into the couch beside him, her back ramrod straight. He found himself sucking in his stomach and pulling back his shoulders. "How did you find the rest of the gala?"

His fingers worked their way under his collar, attempting to suction it loose from the sweat ring forming. "Um, fine. They're not really my thing, though."

She pulled her face into a grimace. "You and Rachel both. That girl needs to get out more. I do my best, but . . ." She shrugged her shoulders and gestured in a "what can a woman do?" kind of flap. "Even my powers have their limits."

"You must be happy with all the money we raised for such great causes." Hundreds of thousands of dollars. The zeroes that people had been scrawling down without so much as an intake of breath had caused him to feel lightheaded.

Donna shrugged. "It wasn't bad."

Lucas stretched out his legs, then caught his reflection in a screen. He looked like a frat boy. Pulling them in, he tapped ankle to knee. Better. He tried to remember how he'd seen guys sit on chat shows. Except he didn't watch any.

"Now what's this I hear about Brad Shipman courting you?"

Lucas's mouth went dry. How did she know? Brad had said no one was to know. He licked his lips, mouth parting. "I, um . . ."

Donna's hand fluttered to her impressive bosom. "Oh, I'm sorry, I've put you in an awkward position. Forget I said anything." Her eyes crinkled, a pensive look passing across her face. "Though one piece of advice. Keep your eyes wide open. The man has the golden touch, I'll grant you that, but he would eat his own young if he thought there were ratings in it. I wouldn't trust him as far as I could throw him."

"Do you know him?"

Donna paused. "He was working in marketing at my publisher when I signed my first contract. He was assigned to work on the first book but there was a falling-out, shall we say."

Interesting. Brad definitely hadn't mentioned that little piece of shared history.

"Moving on." Donna plowed ahead before Lucas could ask a follow-up question. "What do you think about taking Rachel on a date?"

"Excuse me?" This was all too surreal.

"C'mon, Lucas. Humor me. You're a nice young man, and I know my Rachel has a bit of a prickly exterior, but I promise underneath it is the best woman you could ever hope to meet. You are single, right?"

"Um, yes, but . . ." How could he get the words out that he didn't really date, when the idea of being able to have more time with Rachel made him short of breath for all the right reasons?

Though he wasn't sure he would manage to last through a whole dinner when simply a few minutes with her made him feel like his heart was about to burst from his chest and run down the road.

"Now, Rachel won't stand for it."

Lucas felt a jolt run through him. Not stand for it? Maybe he wasn't the best-looking guy on the block, but he liked to flatter himself that he was okay company.

Donna caught his reaction. "Nothing to do with you. My ex-husband and Rachel's father unfortunately came from a line of cads. Fortunately, the good Lord was merciful and only allowed two of them to be born. Who knows how many broken hearts would be splattered across the country if their mother had gotten her wish for more."

Lucas rubbed his forehead. His mind was spinning. "I'm sorry. You and Rachel are . . .?"

She laughed. "Sorry. I forget sometimes that people don't know. Related, yes. My ex-husband is her uncle."

Brothers presumably would have shared a last name, but Rachel and Donna didn't. Though they were very close. How hadn't he noticed that before? "So what's with the similar-but-different surnames?"

Donna flicked her hand. "Some research about people perceiving people with three syllables in their last name to be more authoritative. When we got the first book contract the publisher asked whether I'd consider it. Donna Somerville tested much better with focus groups as a self-help author than plain old Donna Somers. Plus, there's a singer called Donna Summers and they wanted to avoid any confusion. Anyway, since Somers was one of the few things Oswald had left me with, I was more than happy to be rid of it. It's just a shame Rob didn't come along before the books took off. Otherwise I'd be Donna Higgins. Though I'm not sure how that would have gone down with the focus group. I did try for Donna Somerville-Higgins, but apparently that was seen as too pretentious."

Lucas's brain was buzzing, overloaded from the information that had been delivered to him in the space of two minutes. He tried to sift through it all. Rachel and Donna were related. Donna had changed her name because of some focus group. Was there something there? Was this the kind of thing that Brad was looking for?

He couldn't see it. It clearly wasn't a secret when she was sitting here, telling it to him all miked up with a bunch of studio staff roaming around.

Donna tapped him on the knee. "So what do you say? I see from your face a date might be pushing it, but will you at least join us for dinner?"

- 20 -

"We're in trouble."

The sharp edge in Lacey's voice swung Rachel around to stare at their flustered publicist. She knew Lacey wasn't exaggerating when she saw that almost half of her immaculate chignon was tumbling down the side of her face. "What is it?"

Lacey gestured to the set, pulsing with action, and grabbed Rachel's elbow. "Not here."

Rachel tossed a glance to where Lucas and Donna sat chatting. Filming hadn't started yet, so she had at least twenty minutes before she'd be missed. "This way."

Retracing her steps through the soundstage, she led Lacey through the tunnel she and Donna had entered half an hour earlier.

Which door was it? All the doors lined up like identical sentries. Taking a stab, she opened the third one on the right. A startled gasp met her and she yanked her head out before even registering what she'd interrupted.

A knock at the next one and then a more cautious crack. A glimpse of Donna's coat thrown over the back of a black leather sofa. *Got it.* "We should be okay in here."

Lacey locked the door behind them. She ran her fingers through her hair, causing the remains of her updo to collapse. With her hair all messed up, tumbling over her shoulders, she lost ten years.

"What's happened?"

"I've double-booked her."

"Just cancel one of them." But even as she said it, Rachel knew that if there was any way she could have, Lacey would have done it.

Lacey shook her head. "It's one of those once-upon-a-wish ones."

Rachel collapsed onto the couch like a sand castle hit by a rogue wave. "No. No, I can't. I won't." It was one of the few remaining pieces of self-respect that she had left. Never would she be the substitute to some terminally ill woman whose dying wish was a phone call with Dr. Donna.

"I'm so sorry." Through the slits of her fingers, she could see Lacey ringing her hands like a dishrag. "I don't know how I missed this in the schedule."

"I'm not doing it. We must be able to reschedule. A personal call later today, fly Donna out to meet her. Whatever it takes!"

Lacey kneaded her bottom lip with her teeth. "She's dying, Rach."

"Which is why I don't do these ones!" She bolted up from the couch, slamming her palm against the cold wall.

"No, I mean she's *dying* dying. This was originally scheduled for next week, but I got a call from the station this morning. She's been slipping in and out of consciousness the last few days; they're not sure if she'll even make it to tomorrow."

"Okay." Rachel forced a breath. "It's okay. Donna will be done in fifteen minutes. Twenty max. She can call her then."

Lacey didn't say anything.

"What? You can't be telling me they think she might die in the next fifteen minutes." And if she was that close to death, wouldn't she want those last moments with her kids? Not some stranger on the end of the phone, no matter who it was?

"Noooooo." Lacey dragged the word out. "But when I spoke to her hospice nurse a few minutes ago she seemed to think they didn't have much time before she lapsed back into unconsciousness, and that she won't wake up again once she does."

Tears tumbled down Rachel's cheeks. Memories of her mother's last few days, flitting between oblivion and the painful shackles of earth, assaulted her.

Lacey held out the phone. "All she asks for when she wakes up is whether Dr. Donna is about to call. I'm so sorry, but please, Rachel, don't do it for me, do it for Suzanne."

The phone burned into her palm, the numbers already lined up along the screen. Just waiting for her to hit the green button. She drew in a shuddering breath. "Tell me about her."

"Her name is Suzanne Moralis. She's forty-four years old. Single mom with three kids."

"Names and ages?"

Lacey looked at her iPad. "Tyler—fourteen, Izzie—twelve, Gabby—nine."

"Partner?"

"Doesn't say."

"What's she got?"

"Breast cancer. First diagnosed when she was thirty-five, went into remission, thought she'd beaten it, then it returned super aggressive just under a year ago."

The numbers on the screen taunted her. Could she do it? Put on Dr. Donna's voice and talk a woman through some of her last moments of life?

Her mom's last wish had been to talk to her and she hadn't gotten it. Rachel had found the string of missed calls from the hospice on her father's phone the next day. Forced the truth out of a nurse who'd tried to protect her from what she'd missed.

Even if it didn't make any sense to her, was she really going to deny a dying woman her last wish? Especially when she had been haunted for years by the knowledge that her own mother had been denied hers?

The room shouted with the force of the door hitting the wall. Her feet raced down the tunnel back to the set. Bursting out between studio audience stands, she stumbled for a second over the spaghetti of electrical cords, the bright lights blinding her.

On the stage, Maggie was in full-on interview mode. Donna looked relaxed, while Lucas had the wild-eyed look of a raccoon caught in an electric fence.

Someone grabbed at her elbow, but she shoved the person off with a shoulder move that would make a defensive coach proud.

She took the steps to the stage before anyone else could stop her. Donna and Lucas's stunned faces loomed closer.

No doubt this would be the gossip of the week. Deranged assistant storms TV show filming.

It didn't even matter. None of it mattered. Except that somewhere out there three kids were about to lose their mom, and before she died she deserved a call from the real Dr. Donna—well, as real as she got. Not some imposter.

Donna stood up, eyes locked on hers. "What is it? What's happened?"

Rachel thrust the phone into her aunt's hands. "I don't do dying people."

THE STUDIO was in an uproar. As Rachel had stormed the stage, Maggie had cut herself off mid-sentence. As soon as the cameras stopped rolling, she'd lost all resemblance to convivial talk show host and started screaming about sacking the entire security team.

Donna had gone into a quick huddle with Rachel and a very stressed-looking Lacey, then strode off down the tunnel with Lacey in tow.

Rachel paced a path across sprawling camera cords, elbows poking out like she was doing the chicken dance, fingers digging into her scalp. From the time she had bolted from the tunnel clutching the phone like she was Jack Bauer in *24* and it was a nuclear bomb, everything kind of meshed into a distortion of sound and motion.

I don't do dying people. At least that's what it had sounded like she'd said.

He looked around. After all the drama she'd caused, she was alone. Whether by accident or design. Grabbing a bottle of water off a table, he ground to a halt a few feet away, seeing what he'd missed from the stage. Gray lines streaked the side of her face, evidence of tears shed.

One foot shifted, then another. Crying women on radio he could handle. At least they were at the other end of the phone. He could be objective and not emotionally entangled. Now that he was here, she was the best way for him to achieve his dream.

The way his heart thudded at each heave of Rachel's shoulders skewered him with the knowledge he was deluding himself. His arms ached to pull her to him, cradle her to his chest and make everything okay.

Shoot. He was in trouble bigger than Texas.

"Is there anything I can do?" His words fell to the concrete floor. Inadequate. Pathetic.

Her head jerked around, red-rimmed eyes wide with . . . what? A tangle of emotions raced across her face in a split second. She looked around, as if she had forgotten where they were. A look of horror rearranged her features. "Please tell me I didn't do what I think I just did," she said, waving a hand around the set.

Lucas allowed his chin to dip. "The good news is at least it wasn't live TV."

She groaned and collapsed into a vacant producer's chair, burying her head in her hands.

He crouched down so his face was level with hers. Her nose poked out between the gap of her shielding hands, just like Joey's when he was counting down for hide-and-seek.

His fingers flew out and pinched its tip. Oh dear Lord, he hadn't just done that. He hadn't just pulled the trick he used on his nephew on a crying woman. Was he crazy?

Instead of using the moment to find out what was wrong, make sure she was okay, he'd poked Rachel in the face. *Excellent work, Grant.*

Her hands fell away from her face and she stared at him, mouth an *O* like a clown at a fair. "Did you just . . . *pinch my nose?*"

He bolted to his feet, hands shoved in his pockets, where they couldn't get him into any more trouble. "Um, yes. Yes I did." Heat seared up the back of his neck. What was it about this woman that turned him into a sixth grader? What would be next? Tugging on her ponytail?

She swiped away the remaining tears on her cheeks as she hopped off the chair, landing only a foot or so away from him. A smile flickered at the edges of her lips, then a laugh bubbled out. "Is that the traditional way to charm women in Wisconsin?"

He couldn't stop himself from grinning. He'd behaved like an absolute moron and she thought it was funny. What were the chances? "More like a Lucas Grant special."

"You are special, I'll give you that." Her tone was teasing, but there was something in her gaze that caused his heart to react like a bull out of the gate.

His breath stalled, every atom in his body suddenly aware of how close she was. This couldn't be happening. He was supposed to be trying to find out Donna's alleged secret, not developing some ridiculous crush on her assistant! "Is everything okay?"

She studied him for a second, as if measuring whether he was just being polite or actually wanted to know. A sigh escaped her, like a deflating balloon. "Yes, no . . ." She paused and frowned, as if trying to order her words. Gosh, she was cute when her brow wrinkled like one of those shar-pei dogs. *Pay attention, Grant!* "Donna is involved with a charity that grants terminally ill people wishes. Sometimes they want to meet her. She was scheduled to meet this one lady next week, but they called to say she's probably not going to make it."

"So that was you—"

"Storming the stage and disrupting your interview to make Donna call her." She finished his sentence with a grimace. "Sorry."

She bit her bottom lip and looked at him with pensive eyes, as though thinking he might be mad. Who had made her so afraid of doing the right thing? "This—" He gestured around them. "None of this really matters. You just made a dying woman's wish come true. Don't you dare apologize for that."

She smiled. "Okay then, I'm not sorry."

"Good."

"Good."

The words hung in the air between them, as if suspended on the arc of electricity that seemed to fill the space. He couldn't tear himself away from studying her unwavering gaze. Who was this girl who scattered his senses like dandelion tufts on the wind?

Reality slammed into him a split second before he did something really stupid. "Well, I um, should be getting back." He jerked his thumb in the general direction of the stage.

She blinked, stepping back. "Yes, of course. I have some stuff I need to get done too."

He turned and walked away, his feet thudding against the hard floor in rhythm with his heart. He had to get it together. A relationship was the last thing he was interested in. And even if he was, Rachel was the last woman in the world he could even contemplate one with right now.

- *21* -

"Hi there. Reservation for Somers?" The waiflike host-ess was so small, she had to stand beside the podium to be seen. Rachel glanced around the restaurant. Red and gold was the dominant theme. Bold lanterns hanging from the ceiling, wall hangings draping the elegant paneled walls.

As long as she'd been working with Donna, she'd never known her to have a penchant for Thai food. But her aunt had announced she was in the mood to live daringly and so here they were. Or, rather, here she was.

Shaking her watch free from under her gauzy olive-green sleeve, Rachel checked the time. Five past seven. Her aunt had texted saying she was running late, but ordering Rachel to be on time so their reservation wasn't given away. Something about the restaurant being the latest big thing. Judging by the empty tables scattered around the room, someone had forgotten to tell the general public that.

The hostess bowed, laminated menus clasped in her hand. Rachel hoped it wasn't one of those newfangled fusion restaurants that would serve her panang up as deconstructed sushi. All she wanted was a simple, tasty curry.

The hostess wafted her way around tables. Rachel had to weave her less delicate limbs between chairs and a stroller. Reaching the side of the room, the hostess gestured to a small curved leather booth, a single tea light flickering in the center of the table. Vertical slats wrapped around the booth, sheltering it from the rest of the restaurant.

What a waste. This spot deserved to go to some smitten couple. Not to dinner for a more-than-middle-aged woman and someone who hadn't been on a date since Obama was in the Oval Office.

Rachel turned, mouth opening to suggest to the hostess that a perfectly average table would be fine, but she'd disappeared.

Oh well. Good thing she loved her aunt, because she wasn't the smallest woman in the world, so it was going to be an intimate dining experience.

Shimmying between the table and the bench, she shrugged out of her coat, tucking it in between one of the slats and the edge of the seat, squishing her bag down on top.

Ahhh. The soft leather enveloped her, cushioning her aching shoulders. If the food was as good as the seat, she was going to leave one happy customer.

Rachel picked up a menu, scanning the wine list. If there was any day that deserved a glass, this was it. Thank goodness the second half of the filming had gone well. Donna, of course was a pro. But Lucas . . .

Eyes the color of a Caribbean ocean flashed into her mind.

Examining her as she'd retracted her apology. Lips so close that if she'd leaned forward—

Her phone trilled, saving her from herself. She flicked it open. If Donna was more than five minutes away, appetizers would be ordered. She was starving.

Sure enough, it was a text. *Sry. Smthgs cm up. Cnt make it. Bt dnt wry, hve sub ;)*

What? She had Subway? As per usual, Donna's inability to grasp text language required a clarifying phone call, defeating the whole point. Why would she have Subway when they had booked a perfectly nice restaurant?

Rachel pressed Donna's number and lifted her phone to her ear. It rang through to voicemail. What on earth was she up to? They needed to debrief. Especially after today. They hadn't had a chance to after the debacle that was filming *Hello LA!* since Lacey had lined up more media for the rest of the afternoon. For some reason, people couldn't get enough of the whole *Feelings and Football* thing.

A judder of unease coursed through her. She had to find out what had tumbled out of her hysterical mouth when she stormed the stage. What if further damage control was needed to smooth over anything Lucas had overheard?

After he'd gone back to the stage, she thought she'd managed to cover their tracks. Until she went to the restroom and discovered the snail trails of mascara streaking her cheeks. He was a smart guy. How could he not suspect that there was more to the story than a stranger on death's door?

She examined the text again. It wasn't like her aunt to be so circumspect. What could have come up? They had nothing going on tonight. Lacey had something on for another client and Donna had said Lucas was catching up with a friend.

Unless . . . maybe Rob had paid a surprise visit. A smile slipped up Rachel's face. Her aunt's second husband was the real deal. Between his stud ranch and Donna's publicity circuit, they didn't get to spend nearly enough time together. Oh well, good for them if he had managed to sneak away from the corral for a couple of days.

But in the absence of a good man, she was going to have herself some good Thai.

"Hi." Rachel's whole body froze. She didn't even need to look up to know who was standing beside her. The shirt she'd gotten up close and personal with a few hours before was branded in her mind.

Her aunt's text hadn't said Subway, it was *substitute*. She was going to kill her.

"Hey." Her voice sounded normal, at least.

"So, um, where's Donna?" He looked around, scanning the restaurant.

"Not coming." Rachel flattened both palms on the table, spreading her fingers and trying to ground herself. "It would appear that my meddling aunt has set us up."

A smile slid across his face. "Ahhhhh." He didn't look in the least bit surprised. "She's really not a woman who gives up easily, is she?"

"What do you mean?" Rachel picked up her bag and coat and moved them to the floor next to her.

Lucas hesitated, then slid into the booth. Their knees touched. It was the best of two unthinkable options. The only way their knees couldn't touch would be if they sat side by side. Or if they contorted their bodies at some ridiculous angles so that one set of limbs faced into the booth and one set faced out.

Lucas cleared his throat. "So, what's good here?"

Rachel could tell a diversion when she saw one. The question was whether she was going to pursue it. Might as well know what it was. "What did she say?"

Lucas took a drink of water.

"C'mon, Lucas. If we're going to be doing these events together for a couple of weeks, you might as well tell me now. Did she ask you if you have any single brothers? Friends you could set me up with?"

The man cleared his throat as he set down his glass. "Actually, she asked me to take you out on a date."

She did not! That was brazen, even for Donna. No wonder the woman hadn't shown up. She knew she would be facing death by chopsticks. "I'm sorry. Despite being a relationship expert, my aunt sometimes flings herself over personal boundaries."

"Don't worry about it. There are way worse things in life than Dr. Donna thinking you're good enough for her niece." He cast her a quick smile, then lifted his menu and studied the options.

He shifted slightly, and now her right knee rested against his lower thigh. A hot flush crawled up her spine. Lucas's lashes were so long they cast shadows on his cheeks as he studied the menu. His elbow rested on the table, thumb and pointer finger splayed across his cheeks as he pondered.

She tried to drag her eyes back to her own menu, but they

refused. Ruffled hair, firm forearms, a quirk of a smile. If she weren't so mad at her aunt, she'd kiss her.

What on earth was Donna doing? Did she want to ruin everything? One screw-up on her part and Lucas could unravel everything. Being a matchmaker was one thing. But with a guy who could bring their world crashing down? Certifiable.

Not to mention the one guy who made her wish for everything that wasn't possible.

Her menu misted in front of her. She scrunched her eyes for a second, forcing the tears away.

She had no right to tears. She'd chosen this. Earned it. Her father, for all his faults, deserved a better daughter. Instead he'd gotten one who'd left him to die in a gutter on a stormy night.

"Rachel? You ready to order?" Lucas's voice cut through her regrets.

Her gaze skittered up to see the waitress tapping her pencil against her order book. "Um, yeah. Can I have the panang with chicken and a glass of Oyster Bay Sauvignon, please?"

Pencil scratched across paper as Lucas added his order, then the waitress disappeared.

Rachel searched her mind for something, anything, to take her focus off Lucas's close proximity. "So how did it go today?" Why would she even ask that? What could he say? *Well, it was all going really well until this mentally unstable woman stormed the stage and ruined the interview?*

A slow smile eased across his face. "You're the pro. Shouldn't I be asking you that?"

Okay. Well, if he wasn't going to mention the elephant in

the restaurant, she'd play along. "You did great." She couldn't exactly admit that for the last half of the interview her mind had been lingering on how good it had felt to be so close to him. But what she had seen had been surprisingly smooth. "You never would've known it was your first TV show."

"You think?" Uncertain eyes, searching for reassurance. Surprising. She wouldn't have picked Lucas Grant to have any insecurities. It was nice. Made him more human.

"I know." The way his eyes widened with gratitude, as though she'd given him an unexpected gift, warmed her right through.

He ran a hand through his sandy hair. "I was freaking out. I'm a radio guy. Used to being trapped in a small closet with Ethan. The lights, the cameras, it just all seemed so . . ." his hands stretched out, ". . . big. Like the whole world could be peering in at me. On radio it's just voice. If you get that right, nothing else matters. On TV—some wardrobe assistant tried to make me change my shirt based on the image they wanted me to project. My shirt! Apparently the one I was wearing was 'too country.'" His fingers bunny-eared the words, his expression somewhere between wonder and disillusionment.

A giggle burst up from inside of her. A girlish one. She couldn't even remember when that had happened last. The poor guy. Should she be the one to break it to him that the shirt was just a cube off the iceberg?

"If I tell you something, do you promise not to tell?" She leaned in, breathing in his woody, spicy scent. What was it about this guy that made her feel like she could tell him anything and it would be safe?

"Scout's honor." He placed a hand over his heart, his shirt pulling to emphasize his broad chest.

She tore her eyes away. Lordy. She needed to keep herself away from Lucas Grant. No good could come from this. "About five years ago, when the publisher realized Donna was becoming a big deal, they brought in an image consultant. For about three years she dictated everything from Donna's hair to her weight."

"Her weight!" Lucas looked genuinely offended for Donna.

"Well, apparently she couldn't be too skinny because Middle America wouldn't relate, and that is her core demographic. But too heavy and they would be put off. Would ask themselves why they should trust someone's advice with relationships if she couldn't manage her own weight."

Lucas leaned back against the booth and took a long pull of the Coke that had appeared in front of him. "Man, it is one messed-up world we live in."

"Tell me about it." And he didn't even know the half of it.

He leaned forward, slipped the wooden chopsticks out of their paper packet, and snapped them apart. "So, um, today . . ." He didn't look at her, focusing on spinning the flimsy sticks around his fingers.

Rachel's lungs contracted. What was she going to say? There was nothing more she could tell him that would make sense of the total meltdown he'd witnessed. She didn't even know what he'd heard, if anything. Wasn't even sure what she'd said in that hysterical moment when she'd stormed the stage and pretty much thrown the phone at Donna.

He stood the two sticks in front of him, like sentries at attention, and looked up. "Look, I know it's none of my business and I'll understand if you tell me to butt out; I just want to check that everything is okay."

It was the way his eyes probed her, as if uncovering secrets she didn't even know she had, that undid her. She couldn't add more lies on top of the ones that were already between them.

Placing her palms flat on the wooden table, she forced herself to look at him. "The woman who was dying, she had young children." Her voice stalled at the last sentence. *Stop it, Rachel, don't cry. Not again.* Unable to withstand his concerned gaze, she took a slug of the wine that had appeared in front of her.

"How many?" Something about the way his voice wavered forced her to look up.

She nodded, sucked in a breath. "Three. Two girls and a boy. I just . . . when there's kids involved, losing their mom . . ." Like hers. Stolen away in the middle of the night. No final good-byes. Thanks to her father being passed out unconscious on the sofa when the hospice rang to say she wasn't going to make it to morning. "My mom died of cancer when I was twelve. She asked for me and I wasn't there."

She didn't even register what she'd said until her words resounded in her ears. When they did, it was like the world screeched on its axis. She was hot, she was cold. Waves surfed across her wineglass as her hand shook. What had she done? She had never told anyone that. Not even Lacey or Anna.

Her hand was empty. She watched as Lucas set her wineglass to the side, safe from harm's way.

"I'm sorry, I didn't mean to land that on you." She grasped

for a way to take back the words. Why him? Of all people, why did it have to be him?

The tips of his fingers tilted up her chin, forcing her to look into his eyes. They crinkled at the corners, like messy sheets on an unmade bed. "Hey." His words were soft. "It's okay, I get it." He took his hand away, returning his attention to the chopsticks. After a couple of seconds of spinning them on the table, he looked back up. "Mine died when I was nineteen."

The sadness in his gaze sucked her breath out of her chest. How was it possible? How could he keep getting better, when it just made everything so much worse?

LUCAS'S HANDS clenched around his chopsticks as he plunged them into his Massaman beef. This was a spectacularly bad idea. He'd known it from the second he'd seen Rachel and been mesmerized. The booth, the flickering shadows thrown by the candle, her brow furrowed, rosebud lips pursed at something on her phone. She was wearing some sort of blouse with filmy sleeves that highlighted her lean arms. For a second he'd let himself dream that this was a real date. That this beautiful woman was waiting for him. Lips pursed because he was late, wishing he would hurry up and arrive.

Which, clearly, was about as far from the truth as it was possible to get. When he'd finally made her aware of his presence, Rachel couldn't have looked more unimpressed if he'd been a process server slapping court papers on the table. Which was fine. Because he wasn't interested in anything with anyone anyway. Though the words rang hollow, even in his own head.

He was supposed to be trying to see if he could dig up any information that might suggest Brad's hunch was right. He had to at least report back with a clean conscience that he hadn't been able to find anything. Rather than admit that he didn't even try because her assistant had mesmerized him with her quick wit and take-no-prisoners approach that hid a sadness that ran as deep as the Pacific.

He wasn't even going to begin to analyze what had compelled him to tell her about his mom, because he knew he wouldn't like the answer. Fortunately, the arrival of dinner had diverted them onto much safer matters. Well, for one of them anyway . . . He struggled to keep his smile under control.

"Stop smiling, it's not funny!" Rachel's splutter merged with the tears streaming from her eyes, as she tried to stem the river running from her nose. Either she could not handle her curry or she'd been served up something hotter than the surface of the sun.

With her spare hand she forked rice into her mouth, sucking in air between bites. She leaned over the table, whether because it hurt to sit upright or to minimize the distance between the rice and her mouth, he wasn't sure.

"Here." He pushed his Coke toward her.

She waved it away. "Bubbles worse, need milk."

Her eyes landed on his plate. And before he knew what had happened, she'd reached over and swiped the yogurt-dip thing that had come as a side to his appetizer.

And it was gone. Down the hatch. Thrown between her lips like it was the elixir of life.

Finally she sagged back against the booth, trying to mop up her sweat-beaded forehead with the tattered remains of her napkin.

"Here." He offered over his.

"Thanks." She used it to blow her nose with an almighty honk. "I'm just going to go to the ladies' room." She bolted from the table faster than a green filly.

Lucas studied her dish from across the table. It looked innocent enough. Chicken, some vegetables, and some kind of sauce. Nothing to suggest it contained the kick of a small cannon.

He reached over with his fork, spearing a small piece of broccoli. Popping it in his mouth, he received something mighty reminiscent of the time one of Scott's calves had hoofed him in the mouth.

His lips tingled, eyes watered, and he knocked back the last of his Coke in a gulp. And she was right: bubbles made it worse.

If he'd had a whole mouthful of this stuff, he wouldn't have been weeping, he would have been on the floor begging the good Lord for mercy.

His breath came out in puffs, tongue hanging out. Air, he needed air. Something, anything. Ice—there was ice in his glass. He crunched down on a cube, tongue wrapping around the broken shards. Ahhhh. Relief numbed his blazing taste buds. *More, need more.* He poured the rest of the ice into his mouth.

What had they done? Pureed chilies and just poured them straight on? He was sorry for smiling now. He was lucky she hadn't clocked him. He deserved it.

He waved down a waitress. "Excuse me?" His words came out in a croak. "What is this?" He waved toward the dish of torture.

The waitress glanced over and a smile started up her face. "That is Pezang Curry. Our spiciest meal. Most people, they think they like hot food, but that dish—" She pointed toward it and shook her head. "*I* won't even eat that. But it's great if you have a cold—it will blow it right out!"

She wasn't wrong there. Someone needed to call NATO and tell them the next weapon for their arsenal could be found in downtown LA. "Do you happen to have any milk? Two glasses."

The woman nodded with a smile that notched up into gleeful.

Rachel returned and slid back into her seat. Her eyes and nose were still dripping, but her face had lost some of its fire-like flush. Lucas sucked air through his curled tongue, still trying desperately to cool it down.

Rachel looked at her plate, then at him. "Really? After watching me almost spontaneously combust you still just had to try it?"

Two glasses of milk appeared in front of them, and he grabbed his and gulped it down in three chugs.

"You probably don't—okay, you did."

Lucas looked at Rachel over the rim of his empty glass. "What?"

"Adding a quarter gallon of milk to the mix may pay dividends you're not expecting, but too late now." Rachel took a delicate sip of her milk and right as she did, Lucas's stomach let out an almighty grumble. "We should probably get you some Pepto-Bismol on the way back to the hotel if you don't have some. Just in case."

"It'll be fine. I only had a piece of broccoli."

Rachel tipped her glass at him. "To each his own indigestion. Just don't come knocking on my door at two a.m. begging for some of mine."

The thought of knocking on Rachel's door at two a.m. for *any* reason sent his mind to places it shouldn't be going. "So, what do I need to know about tomorrow?"

Rachel shrugged. "Nothing really. The setup is pretty much identical to the first one. Sellout crowd again. Lacey wasn't sure with it being an afternoon event, but tickets sold out in a couple of days. Oh, I got her to plant a couple of sports questions. Just so, you know, there's at least one mention of football among all the feelings. No need to thank me. I'll just add it to the tab of all the things you owe me for."

"I have a tab?"

"Yes. The present for Donna. That's a lot of debt right there just for that. The questions I'm getting Lacey to plant for you. My flying you in style. Plus tonight, you turned down my aunt's kind offer of a date with my spinster self, watched me leak snot all over my dinner, and somehow got me talking about my dead mother. Which, for the record, I never do. So that's a pretty long tab already and there's still two weeks to go."

"Okay, Miss Awesome Assistant, I know you have a pen and paper in that bag, so why don't you get them out and we can settle this tab right here and now." She gave him a look under her eyelashes.

"Go on." He nodded toward her bag. "I know you have them in there. Get them out and write down your list."

Lifting up her purse, Rachel rummaged through and extracted a notebook and pen. She scrawled down her list and pushed it across the table. "There you go."

Picking up the pen, Lucas looked at the items listed neatly in a vertical line down the left-hand side of the page in precise handwriting.

"Okay. So, I sent you the best ribs in Texas. I'm going to say that cancels out the planted questions. I loaned you my phone last night so that you could hide in the bathroom and ruthlessly decimate my high scores. So I'm pretty sure that cancels out the gift. I also told you about my long-departed mother who I never talk about, so they cancel each other out. And yes, you did snot all over your dinner, but I procured your milk, so I think we're even there. And you did fly me in style, but last night I raised over fifty grand so that underprivileged kids can have access to sports. I feel like they balance out quite well." He put lines through her list as he spoke. "And that one . . ." He circled the last item and pushed the pad back over to her. "That was Donna, not me. But even if it was mine, it wouldn't count. Which means we're even."

Rachel looked down to where she'd written *Mortifying attempted setup*. "Why wouldn't it count?"

He smiled at her confused expression. What he should do was say something safe like *it doesn't count when you don't know about it*. But there was something about the booth and the way the candlelight was flickering across her confused face that made playing it safe distinctly unappealing. "Because I didn't turn her down."

- 22 -

"The guy is a rock star." Lacey murmured the words to Rachel as they stood backstage in San Francisco and watched the live feed of Donna and Lucas onstage. Lucas held two thousand women in the palm of his hand. Again. "And that face. Wasted on radio. He's so made for TV I could just cry. And he's actually a stand-up guy. It's not often in this business those things combine."

Onstage, Lucas leaned back on the couch, ankle tapped to knee and a relaxed smile on his face as he turned some woman's question about dating into a sports analogy.

"I still can't believe he actually swapped his seat." Rachel had almost choked on her champagne when a heavily pregnant woman lowered herself into seat 1B next to Lacey. A few passengers later, Lucas had strolled past with a wink and a grin on his way back to coach.

"That baby is totally going to be named Lucas if it's a boy." Lacey whipped out her phone and tapped open her Twitter app. "She didn't know who he was, but I made sure to fix that. All going well, it will be all over social media before the day is out."

Rachel snagged a cookie off the catering table in the green room. She side-eyed their publicist. "When are you going to put feelers out? Or have you already done it?"

"What do you mean?" Lacey turned to her all wide-eyed and innocent.

"Come on, Lace. I know you better than you think. You have the future *New York Times* bestseller look glowing in your eyes."

Lacey pivoted on her heels. "Lucas couldn't write a book by himself. Not even with a ghostwriter. He doesn't have enough to say. But . . ." She let her words linger.

"But what?"

Lacey raised her eyebrows at Rachel. "He could do one with Donna."

Rachel said nothing. Just stared at her as she ate her cookie.

Lacey leaned back against the edge of the couch. "Just think about it. You still don't have an idea for your last book, do you?"

"I've been working with a few. Donna and I have brainstormed some." She'd also watched a lot of reality TV. Which had sparked the idea for their fourth book, but apparently that was a one-time-only deal.

"And how many of them have gotten past five thousand words?"

Rachel didn't say anything.

"Exactly. I bet if Max took it to Randolph, he could renegotiate a better deal and an extension on your deadline. There is no way Randolph would let something this big get away. Especially if he knew it was going to be the last book."

"What would this book even be about?" Rachel asked the question grudgingly. Her pride wanted her to insist that she would get the book done. Just like she always had. But she'd never been this close to a deadline and not had the high-level concept well advanced.

Lacey shrugged. "We could use a whole lot of material from the next two weeks. Then you, Donna, Lucas, and his writer could hole up in a room for a couple of weeks and hey, presto. A number one bestseller is born. Straight to the top of the charts. Guaranteed."

"Lucas has shown absolutely no interest in doing a book. He's only on this tour under protest."

"Lucas would make a basket load of money. Who's going to say no to that? Plus you and Donna get to go out on a high with the last book."

Rachel grabbed a bottle of water. Twisted the top off with a crack. "I really don't want to involve Lucas in all this any more than he already is."

"If it helps your conscience, we can tell him that you're Donna's ghostwriter. It's really not a big deal."

"It's not the books I'm worried about. It's the other stuff." She could be wrong, but somehow she instinctively knew that while Lucas might not give peanuts about Donna having a ghostwriter, he would give a whole lot more if he found out it hadn't been Donna calling in to his show.

I didn't turn her down. Lucas's words from the night before had her tossing and turning half the night. Trying to work out what they meant. The moment interrupted by a phone call he'd had to take.

"Anyway, let's talk about it with Donna when we get to Sacramento tonight. I'm sure she will have a view."

Given this whole tour was Donna's brainchild, she knew the woman would leap at it. "Fine." At least that bought Rachel a few hours to process it herself and decide what tack she wanted to take.

Donna and Lucas writing a book together. It would definitely solve one very large problem. But would it create even more?

Lacey glanced up at the screen where Lucas and Donna were wrapping up their session. "There's one other thing that I wanted to show you."

"What's that?"

Lacey was tapping on her phone. "Just give me a couple of seconds to find it again. Here it is." She held her phone out to Rachel. "I know how much you hate being in the limelight, so I thought you'd probably want to know about this."

Rachel glanced down at the phone and felt her knees give way. It was a photo of her and Lucas together at the gala. On the Facebook page of one of the country's largest gossip sites.

CALIFORNIA WOMEN were not his thing. He'd suspected that at the gala and now knew it for a fact. Security guards. There had been six of them stopping screaming women from stampeding the stage at the end. It was more nuts than a Snickers bar.

Lucas blew out a breath as he reached the door to the

green room. He'd made it to the end of the first quarter. Chicago and San Francisco down, six more stage shows to go.

"I don't understand why you're freaking out. It's just a photo. Your name isn't even on it." Lacey's words hit Lucas as he opened the door.

Lucas stepped into the room. Lacey and Rachel were huddled together on the couch. Rachel was holding a phone, her body almost folded in half over it. Lacey's hand kind of hovered over Rachel's shoulder. As if she was trying to work out whether to make physical contact or not.

"Is everything okay?" Lucas closed the door behind him. Donna had gone to sign some books for her adoring fans, so she might be a while.

Rachel's head jerked up. "Fine." But she dropped the phone and it skittered across the floor toward Lucas. He leaned down and picked it up to find him and Rachel staring at him.

It was a photo of the two of them snapped at the gala on some Facebook page. Paparazzi style, from someone's phone, judging by the angle. Him leaning toward her, Rachel laughing. He scanned the short blurb about Lucas Grant and some "mystery woman" being spotted getting cozy at the gala. He'd had far worse and far more inaccurate.

He studied the photo. It was a nice image. They looked very *together*. And he had absolutely no idea how he felt about it. Just like he wasn't sure whether he'd been wretched or relieved when Brad had phoned at the most inconvenient moment ever last night.

"It's a great photo. I should share it on the station's Facebook page. Put up how much money we raised." Maybe if women thought he was seeing someone, that would help quell some of the insanity currently unraveling at these things.

"No!" Rachel's exclamation was so vehement he almost dropped the phone.

Lacey held her hand out to him as she stood. "I agree with Rachel. Part of your charm is that you're an eligible bachelor. If you get asked about the photo, it would be best if you say she's just a friend."

"How about 'no comment'?" He took one last look at the photo as he handed Lacey back her phone. Memorized the Facebook page so he could look it up later.

Rachel stood. "Look, I'm sure you get photographed with random women all the time, so this probably isn't a big deal to you, but it is to me."

Lucas's hackles rose at the insinuation that he was some man-about-town with a different woman every week. "Firstly, completely untrue. Secondly, I'm pretty sure you know that, because you wouldn't have invited me on this if I were. Giving a platform to a playboy wouldn't exactly be a good fit with Donna's brand."

Rachel at least had the grace to look slightly ashamed, her cheeks pinkening. "Sorry, I didn't mean it like that. I just mean that you have a public profile. I don't. And I'd really prefer to keep it that way. So I'd really appreciate it if you didn't share it."

Lucas wasn't sure whether his ego should be dented or not, but one look at Rachel's folded arms and hunched shoulders told him she was deadly serious. This wasn't some weird female game where she wanted him to share the photo and was just playing hard-to-get.

"Fine. We can be 'just friends.'" He put bunny ears around the last two words, and that at least got a hint of a smile out of her. Their gazes tangled, and if it weren't for the fact that Lacey was watching them with undisguised interest, he'd have closed the gap between them and tried to uncover what it was about this photo that bothered her so much.

A knock on the door interrupted his thoughts. Breaking his gaze away from Rachel, he turned to open it. On the other side, a heavyset man stood holding a large bunch of flowers. His weathered face spoke of years in the sun and his bushy gray mustache belonged in a good, old-fashioned western.

"Hey, son. Do you mind if I come in there? I want to surprise Donna when she's done with the signing."

"Um . . ." The guy didn't look dangerous, but you never knew these days. For all he knew, the guy could be a stalker or some other brand of weirdo. "Can I ask what your business is with her?"

A brush of warmth lit up his side as Rachel squeezed between him and the door frame. "Rob!" She grinned at the man and Lucas felt irrationally jealous. "I thought that was your voice. Come in!"

She looked up at him and her smile took on a hint of teasing. "You can let him in, Mr. Rent-A-Guard. Rob's Donna's husband."

For a second Lucas got distracted by her full, smiling lips that were so close to his that a lean on his part and a tilt of the toes on hers and they would meet.

"Lucas?" Rachel tilted her head at him.

"Right, sorry." He stepped back and opened the door wider as the man—Rob—gave him a knowing look.

"Much obliged that someone is watching out for my wife."
He clapped Lucas's shoulder with a meaty hand as he entered
the room. "Lacey. Lovely to see you again."

Lacey looked up from her phone and flashed him a quick
smile. "You too. Donna shouldn't be too far away and I hate
to be rude, but I just need to make a couple of calls before she
gets back." She had her phone to her ear and was opening
the door on the opposite side of the room before she'd even
finished the sentence.

"Do you want a water? Coffee? Something to eat?" Rachel had stationed herself by the catering table and already
had a mug in her hand.

"Coffee would be great." Rob settled himself onto the red
couch and placed the bouquet beside him.

Rachel picked up the coffeepot and tipped it over a mug,
but just a dribble came out of the spout. "Let me just go refill
this. It'll just take a couple of minutes."

"Don't w—" Rachel was gone before Rob could stop her,
and Lucas was left alone with him.

The man leaned back in his seat. "So, you must be Lucas.
My wife is quite the fan. Apparently you have an excellent
credit score."

What?

Rob chuckled. "Yes, I'm sure my face probably looked
very similar when I discovered how thoroughly my background had been interrogated before we'd even been on our
first date."

"How did you meet?" Lucas settled himself into one of
the chairs as he made a mental note to call Ethan later and see
if he knew anything about a background check.

"My sister is a huge fan. A couple of books ago, Donna was in town for a signing. Laurel was desperate to go but broke her ankle a couple of days before. Somehow I got shanghaied into going to the signing for her."

"Was it love at first sight?" Apart from the mention at the TV studio, Lucas didn't think he'd ever heard Donna talk about her husband.

"It was for me. I was expecting some kind of skinny Botoxed East Coast type and when I got to the front of the line, I found Donna with a grease stripe right up the front of her jacket. Their car had gotten a flat on the way to the signing and the driver was some millennial who'd never learned how to change a tire so Donna did it."

That sounded exactly like something Donna would do. "And then?"

Rob took a stroll to the food and helped himself to a donut. "She signed the book. Gave Laurel her best wishes. So I went back and bought another book and joined the line again. Got it signed to my other sister. Then the third time I got it signed to my cousin, and she cracked a smile and asked if I'd run out of sisters."

Lucas's phone buzzed in his pocket and he pulled it out. *Brad.* He sent the call straight to voicemail. "Sorry, go on."

Somehow in the space of him checking his phone Rob had demolished the donut, sugar coating the tips of his mustache. "Donna didn't smile as much back then. She was very professional. That smile felt like a medal, so I summoned up the courage to ask her if she had dinner plans. She did. Then I asked if I could take a rain check for the next time she was back in Texas."

Lucas had to give the man credit for persistence. He probably would have cut his losses at the second sister if he wasn't getting any hint of interest in return.

"Want to guess what that got me?" Rob picked up another donut and a bottle of water, then wandered back to the couch.

"I'm going to guess it wasn't a yes."

"She asked for a copy of my driver's license and took a photo of it. Then gave it back to me and said someone would be in touch. Which I thought was code for me having just triggered some kind of security flag and that 'someone' would be the police." He twisted open his water and took a gulp. "Four months later, I got a call from Rachel saying Donna was going to be in a town about fifty miles away and asking if the dinner invite still stood."

The door opened and Rachel stepped in, pot of coffee held out in front of her. "Ah, Rachel, perfect timing. I was just telling Lucas how Donna and I met. Do you want to tell him what Donna came armed with to our first date?"

Rachel shook her head as she poured a cup of steaming coffee. "You do it. You tell the story much better."

"Was it you?" That wouldn't surprise him. Donna taking Rachel to dinner to vet Rob was exactly the kind of thing he could imagine.

Rachel placed the coffeepot back on the table. "Not me. Though I wish I had been there."

"Close. It was one of those big folders. Filled with information about me. She knew things about me that I had forgotten. Here I was all love at first sight, while she had a PI verifying my land taxes were all paid up before I was allowed a first date." Rob leaned back his head and roared with laughter.

"You didn't think it was a bit extreme?" By which he meant extremely terrifying.

Rob shrugged. "Sure. But people often do things that seem extreme to protect themselves or the people they love. You just have to be willing to persevere to find out what sits underneath."

Well, it had sounded like her first husband was a piece of work, but hiring a PI? "So now she recommends doing background checks on all potential dates?"

Rachel arched an eyebrow at him. "Not at all. Just some due diligence. You'd be surprised at how a little bit of digging can often save a whole lot of heartache. Donna wrote a whole book on it. You might want to think about reading it."

Now that she mentioned it, he vaguely recalled an early book along those lines. But how was he supposed to do any digging at all when the woman didn't have so much as a Facebook page?

Lucas stood and walked over to Rachel as she tipped creamer into the coffee. "I hear I have an excellent credit score. What's that worth on the Dr. Donna scale?" He murmured the words and watched as his breath lifted a strand of her hair.

If he'd hoped that that was going to throw her off kilter, he was sorely mistaken. Instead she just gave him the smug smile of someone who was already a step ahead. "I wouldn't go that far. Now, Rob had an excellent credit score. Yours is just okay. Though with the size of your mortgage, you might want to think about some income protection insurance."

For the second time in five minutes, Lucas was lost for words.

There was a snort from the couch. For a second he'd forgotten about Rob. "Looks like there's a folder with your name on it, too."

He looked at Rachel. "Is there?"

She flashed him a grin, and he knew what Rob meant about it feeling like a medal. "I couldn't possibly comment."

- 23 -

"*H*ey." Rachel stuck her head in the door of room 401.

"Hey!" Anna slapped her magazine closed and lifted her feet off her husband's bed. She was alone. "Welcome back. Where did you just come from?"

"Sacramento." Rachel stifled a yawn. "How's Cam doing?"

Anna ran a hand down his pale bare arm as she stood. "No real change. Some of the brain swelling has gone down, but," she shrugged, "apart from that, still just hoping and praying. Want to chat for a while?" She gestured to the other easy chair in the room. "Or are you going to see your dad?"

Rachel slipped through the door and closed it behind her. "Actually, I came to check on you." She held out the Panera bag in her hand. "I brought you this in case you hadn't had dinner."

"Thanks." Anna took the bag and peeked inside as she settled back into her chair. "I had something earlier, but this will be perfect for later." Closing the bag, she placed it on the table next to Cam's bed. "Soooooooooo . . ." She drew the word out and looked at Rachel with a raised eyebrow.

"So?"

"You're on tour with Lucas Grant. You didn't mention that in your texts."

Her two pitiful, stilted, and awkward texts. "I'm not on tour with him, Donna is."

Anna rolled her eyes. "Irrelevant detail."

Rachel crossed the small room and settled into the chair Anna had offered. "I didn't realize he was a thing outside of Wisconsin."

"Well if he wasn't, he sure is now. One of my friends shared a clip of him at one of the Q-and-A things, and wow." Anna fanned herself. "Plus I may have also found a few other videos on YouTube."

Rachel swung her legs over the arm of the chair and just looked at her.

"What?" Anna gave her wide eyes. "Lacey mentioned he'd been added to the book tour, and I happen to have a lot of time to internet-stalk quasi-celebrities at the moment. So is he as great in person as he seems on screen?"

Rachel tilted her head and stared at the ceiling for a second. Lucas's stunned face when she'd told him he needed income protection insurance was still making her smile two days later. He'd spent all of the previous day trying to find out what else she knew about him.

It had been way too much fun to confess that the income protection thing was entirely a guess based on the statistics of American men under forty being chronically underinsured.

"Oh no. Is he a jerk?" She looked back to see Anna's face had fallen.

"Nope." Rachel sighed. The woman's husband was probably dying. The least she could do was distract her for a few minutes. "He's even better in person. Unfortunately."

"Tell me!" Anna's face looked just like it had when she was twenty years old and demanding all the details from a date. Always Lacey's, though, not Rachel's. She leaned back and studied Rachel. "Are you two . . ."

"No! It's probably nothing. Definitely nothing." Or it would be, if she could stop replaying in her head the shared looks that seemed to have enough electricity to start a wildfire.

And that was before the photo now crawling across the Web that made them look like a couple. And not just some couple posing for a photo at a charity gig, but a captured-unawares-completely-into-each-other couple. Seeing herself look so happy was terrifying.

Thank goodness Lacey had managed to help cover her complete overreaction.

"C'mon, Rach. Puhlease."

Rachel focused on the highest light. Squinted until it danced and spun. She didn't even know how to do girl talk anymore. But what did it matter if she told Anna? She'd already proven she could keep secrets.

"It's all stupid. Nothing could ever happen. He lives in Wisconsin and I, well, clearly don't." She wriggled her shoulders against the chair. Wisconsin. All she knew about the state was that it produced a lot of cheese.

"Mah, details. So how did he get to be on the tour?"

Rachel bit her bottom lip. She couldn't lie to Anna, but she couldn't exactly tell the truth, either. "Through Donna. She goes on his show to promote her books. He has a sports show but gets heaps of women callers asking for relationship advice. Lacey and Donna were smart enough to work out how to spin it into something big." She couldn't tell Anna how deep the deception had become. Couldn't risk their teetering friendship on the chance Anna's religion thing was more than desperate platitudes.

Anna propped her head up on one hand. "And?"

And whenever she was around him, all she wanted to do was throw herself into his arms and experience what it felt like to feel safe. "And . . ." Rachel shrugged, tapping her palms against the spongy seat. "I don't know. He's nice, and he's funny and he seems like a decent guy, and Lord knows there aren't any of those beating a path to my door."

"Does he like you too?"

"No!" She paused at the memory of the way his eyes captured hers, then lingered, when they'd had dinner. Until she'd taken one bite and turned into a gasping, wheezing, snot-producing machine. "Maybe. Possibly. I don't know. We had dinner. Donna was supposed to be there and she set us up, but he didn't make an excuse to leave." She was kidding herself. The guy was probably just hungry. Or too scared to leave and get on Donna's bad list.

"Have you kissed?" Anna punctuated her question by pursing her lips and making sucky sounds like she was thirteen, not thirty.

"Of course not!"

"All power to you then, because if some guy looking like

Lucas crossed my path, I'd lay one on him, and I'm a married woman."

Rachel's cheeks flushed just at the thought. She put both hands against them, trying to cool them down.

"Aha!" Anna's voice held a note of triumph. "So you *have* thought about it." It was a statement.

Thought about it. Dreamed about it. Visualized it. And it didn't help, as her luck would have it, that the PR train was heading to Madison next week and he would be on his home turf. "Yes." Rachel groaned. "It's so ridiculous. There's no way in a million years it could ever happen. But then he looks at me with these all-seeing blue-gray eyes and I almost keel over."

"Why wouldn't it happen? You're a catch!"

Rachel choked back a bitter laugh. "His star is on the rise. You said it yourself. Lacey thinks it's only a matter of time before he's a really big deal. I have nothing next to that. Not to mention I was so rude to him the first couple of times we met."

"Sounds like a good start. Give him a bit of a run for his money. Bit of a chase. Guys like that." Anna flopped back in her chair. "Lord knows I had to make Cam think he had one on his hands, even though if he'd proposed on the second date I would've hightailed it off to Vegas in a heartbeat."

An image of Cam and Anna being married by Elvis popped into Rachel's head, causing a spurt of laughter to burst out.

"You laugh, but Cam is crazy about Elvis, and I would've married that man dressed as Priscilla if it would make him happy."

"Has he been to Graceland?"

Anna grinned at her. "He makes a pilgrimage every year."

"He does not!"

"Everyone has their faults. Look at you, lining up as a Packers or Badgers supporter."

"What? Who?"

Anna shook her head. "Oh Rachel. If you're going to go fall in love with a sports guy from Wisconsin, you're going to have to learn up on the football teams. Green Bay Packers and UW Badgers."

"I don't do football."

Anna shook her head. "Oh but you will, my friend, you will."

She guessed it couldn't hurt to Google them when she got home. Hold on. What was she doing? She didn't care about stupid football teams; she needed to write a book. That was it. That was the whole reason for this whole crazy thing.

Anna was still staring at her with an irritating smile on her lips. "You were thinking about it. I saw you. You're a goner."

Secrets and relationships can't coexist in the long term. Eventually you will have to choose one over the other.

Her own advice, which had been so easy to type onto the screen when she had no skin in the game, was coming back to haunt her.

- 24 -

"*L*ucas, my main man. How's it going?"

Lucas winced at the sound of Brad's voice. He knew he shouldn't have answered the call without checking the screen. "Fine. Thanks." Swinging open his door, he jumped out of his truck.

"Look, no pressure, but I need to know how you're doing with Donna." At least Brad was kind enough not to torment them both with small talk.

Lucas shifted on his feet. "You know how things like this are, Brad. Two steps forward, one step back." Closing the door with a thump, he leaned against the side of the vehicle and scuffed a couple of pebbles with the toe of his boot.

"So you're making progress on finding out, then? That nice little piece of assistant given you some good leads?" Brad's interest was piqued.

Lucas's neck prickled at the way Brad's voice had lingered over the first three letters of "assistant." "Well . . . not exactly."

"I get what you're saying, Lucas, but I have to be honest with you and let you know that I don't have months to wait around for you to get the job done. I want you on the team, I really do, but I have other options. So if you're not going to be able to deliver for me, just tell me."

Lucas shot out a breath, kicked another stone, and watched as it skittered and bounced across the parking lot. "Brad, of course I want to deliver, if there's something there. But nothing I've seen and heard indicates Donna is lying."

Brad let out an ominous chuckle. "Lucas, I love that you small-town folk are so trusting, but I'm telling you as someone who hasn't gotten where he is without a good radar for secrets, there's something."

"Why don't you tell me more about that, since you worked at Randolph when Donna signed her first book deal?" Lucas threw it out there. Brad's LinkedIn profile hadn't contained any mention of a job at Randolph, but he couldn't think of any reason Donna would have had to lie to him about that.

There was a pause at the other end. "I'm impressed. You *have* been doing your research. Yes. You're right. I was on the marketing team. She came to our attention after a blog post she wrote went viral. It was all very odd. Soon after we approached her, I heard that the deal wasn't going to happen. That she wasn't suitable. Then suddenly it was back on, but only the VP of marketing was privy to the details."

"Why didn't you just say so in the beginning?" He didn't appreciate being played like he was some kind of puppet on a string. Not to mention that every time he was around Rachel, he found himself losing his grasp on all the reasons why he wanted what Brad was offering.

"I guess I didn't want you to think I might have some kind of personal vendetta or something from back then. To be honest, I didn't think that much of it at the time. Publishing is full of quirks, and I left soon after."

His explanation conveniently omitted the "falling-out" Donna had mentioned. "She's approached me about possibly cowriting a book based on the tour." Lucas winced as the words fell out of his mouth. He hadn't been intending to mention that. Donna had only mentioned it in an offhand way. Joked that she was having trouble coming up with an idea for the final book in her contract and they should join forces.

Silence for a couple of seconds. "Are you still on board with me on this, Lucas? A couple of weeks on tour is one thing, but a book? That's forever. Do you really want to be permanently connected to her if she is hiding some kind of double life?"

A memory blindsided Lucas. Coming home from school. Finding his father carrying suitcases out of the house, his mother pleading with him that they could work it out. His dad peeling out of the driveway without a backward glance. Leaving them behind for a life he'd built without them.

A bitter stew rose in his throat. Brad might be crass, but he was right. If Donna wasn't who she said she was, then people deserved to know. "Of course not."

Rachel's face appeared again. The laughter in her eyes as she teased him, the whisper of her hand as she helped him with the mic. The way she bit her lip when she was concentrating. The total vulnerability in her eyes when she'd told him about her mom.

He shook it away. Surely that made him the best person to do this, to try and find out. Because he cared about the truth, not just about bagging a big career move.

"Good man. So what next?"

"They're in Madison this week, so I should have plenty of time to do some digging."

"But you're still thinking the hot assistant is your best bet?"

"Yeah." Lucas could barely force the word out.

"Great, great. Keep in touch. Ciao."

Lucas shoved his phone back in his pocket and slammed the back door with a crunch. He was doing the right thing, he was. But if so, why did he feel like he needed to take a shower *before* his workout?

His pocket buzzed again. Could the guy not leave him alone? Yanking it out, he put it to his ear. "Yes, Brad." His words landed harshly. Probably not the best way to talk to the guy who held his dream in the palm of his hand.

"Who's Brad?" Scott's voice rolled across the line.

"Oh, just some guy at work."

"Is now a bad time? I can call back later." The stress vibrating off his brother's voice contradicted his words.

"No, of course not. What's up?" Lucas slumped back against the door of his truck. At this rate, his gym hour would be up without him having progressed beyond the parking lot.

"We're at the hospital."

Lucas was reopening the truck door before he'd even fully registered what Scott had said. "What?!"

"It's nothing serious. Joey fell out of a tree and broke his arm. Nice and clean, though."

Well, it had to happen sooner or later. His nephew's utter lack of fear, combined with a deeply held belief that gravity didn't apply to him, made that a certainty.

Throwing his gym bag back in the passenger side, he slipped his key into the ignition.

"The thing is . . . I, um, I forgot to pay our health insurance last month."

Lucas stilled, key partly turned. He had never heard his brother sound so defeated. "Forgot, Scott, or couldn't?"

A shuddering sigh was his only response.

Starting the truck, Lucas backed out of the lot. "Okay. I'll need to stop at the bank on my way. How much do you need?"

"They're saying they need a grand up front." His brother answered the question but didn't. Lucas would bet his truck the insurance could take a number in a long line of bills that were knocking on his brother's door. "And Luc, um, Grace doesn't know."

"Got it." Lucas flipped his indicator to turn onto East Washington Avenue. It would be killing his brother to be keeping the reality of their situation from Grace. He was the most honest guy he knew.

He had to find a way to get some money in. His family depended on it. He'd sell his house, but in the current market he doubted he'd even get enough to pay off the mortgage, let alone enough to help Scott. His savings were all he could offer, which might cover an insurance bill and some back taxes, but they certainly weren't up to saving Scott's ranch.

Either the Brad option or the Donna option had to pay some

dividends. He was going to need to decide soon which way to jump, and that meant he needed to stay objective. Which could only happen if he kept his distance from the woman who had the ability to unravel the knots he'd tied around his heart with a glance.

- 25 -

"Want to know how many billboards of you I counted on the way in from the airport?" Rachel leaned against the wall beside Studio 1 and gave Lucas a smirk.

"Not at all." Rachel and Donna had been in the station for all of ninety seconds and Lucas was already losing the battle to remain aloof and objective.

"Madison is proud of their homeboy. There are worse things in life." She looked through the glass to where Bree and Jack hosted the lunchtime show. "Is this the studio you usually broadcast from?"

"Why do you ask?"

She shrugged. "You referred to it at some point as a closet. Even Donna's closet isn't this big."

"Well, you're right. My place is a little smaller." He held his thumb and pointer finger about an inch apart. "Ethan and I, we don't need much space when it's just the two of us."

She quirked an eyebrow at him. "The two of you prefer

something a bit more intimate, huh? To give each other back rubs during the show maybe?" Her eyes sparkled.

"That's enough sass out of you, Miss Somers."

"I'm just saying." She waggled her eyebrows. "Here you are, Madison's most eligible bachelor and all these poor women ringing up, trying to win your heart, probably don't imagine you're all cozied up with Ethan the whole time."

"I'm not cozied up with Ethan." He growled the words.

Rachel clamped her lips together, but from the twitching of her mouth to the shaking of the shoulders, she was having a hard time keeping back the laughter. At least Donna was too busy on the phone to hear the aspersions her assistant was casting.

"Come on." He marched ten yards up the hall and threw open the door to Studio 2.

"See?" He pointed at the tiny production booth. "Ethan sits in there and I," he gestured at the seat right in front of them, "sit here. Though when we debrief he sits there." He quirked his own mischievous smile back at her as he gestured at the only other spot in the small room. "So I guess we could have a game of footsies if we wanted."

Rachel spun around, taking in the cramped space. Her perfume smelled like flowers and summer. "I like what you've done with the place." She gestured to the red-and-white Badgers pennant hung on the wall, directly underneath Ethan's old moth-eaten moose head.

Lucas took a step back, then a half step, until he stopped by the curved edge of his desk. What a genius! He wasn't asking for trouble inviting Rachel into a small, intimate space, where the most they could ever be from each other was all of about two feet. No, not at all.

His carefully laid plans involving being cool and professional and never being alone with her all dashed in the first few seconds by his big mouth.

"So when you and Donna are doing the show, this is where you are?" She ran her fingers along the console, leaning over on tiptoes to look at the side where Ethan sometimes sat. Pulling back, she perched on a clear space on his desk, toes swishing along the ground as she swung her legs.

Lucas fisted his hands in his pockets. He couldn't sit down, not in his own seat. It would put him directly eye height with her chest, and his end of the desk was stacked with papers. The fridge broke the silence with its whirring hum. A drink! "Would you like something to drink?" Hopefully Ethan had it stocked with more than just cheap beer.

"Sure."

Reprieve. Lucas skirted around his end of the desk, ducked under the moose's nose, and pulled open the tiny bar fridge shoved between two filing cabinets. Pay dirt. Grabbing two sodas, he passed one to Rachel over the console and leaned back in Ethan's chair as he cracked his own open. Perfect. The instrument panel between them meant she only came into view at shoulder height.

The Mountain Dew bubbled down his throat, icy cold.

"Why don't you drink?" Rachel didn't even look at him as she asked the question, piercing the pennant with her gaze as she took a sip from her can.

Lucas coughed and spluttered, the fizz hitting his nose. "To prove I'm nothing like my dad." The words fumbled out of his mouth. The truth. But he'd never admitted it that bluntly to anyone.

Rachel ran a finger around the rim of her can, a Mona Lisa smile on her face.

"What?"

She looked across at him, brown eyes shadowed. "I was just thinking how ironic it is."

"What?"

"Well, that you don't drink to prove you're nothing like your dad, while I do, to prove I'm nothing like mine."

The haunted look on her face robbed him of his breath. "I'm sorry."

"Yeah, well, life happens." She took a slug this time, then swallowed. "Have you seen yours since he left?"

He opened his mouth to answer, but nothing came out. How did she know? He didn't talk about his dad to anyone. Except . . . that time with Donna. Was nothing sacred?

He looked across at her.

Eyes stricken, cheeks flushed. Realizing that maybe she wasn't supposed to know. "Oh my gosh, I'm so sorry." She stuttered a little, falling over her words. "Donna, Donna just mentioned it in passing and . . ." She trailed off, studying the top of the can clenched between her hands.

"It's okay." And weirdly enough, it was. Sure, it had been a personal conversation, but it was hardly like he was alone in having a deadbeat dad. In Donna's world it was probably a case of draw a ticket and get in line. "Sorry, I was just surprised. It's not exactly a state secret. It's, um . . ." Now it was his turn to study the silver circular can lid. "It's complicated." Not that it was. He'd been perfectly happy not even knowing if his father was dead or alive, then Scott had to go and try to build some kind of bridge to nowhere.

She looked at him, all big eyes and woebegone face. Lord help him, she was going to be his undoing. He chucked his soda can in the bin and stood, striding back around to her side of the room.

"Hey." Now she studied the tips of her shoes. Or maybe his, which could really use a clean. "Rach." His hand reached out, tugged a wayward lock of hair behind her ear. It was soft and silky and—he shoved his hand back in his pocket before it could get him into any more trouble. "So my dad was a loser. We managed without him." He tried to put a smile in his voice. "Some crazy people even seem to think I still turned out okay."

She looked up at him, the mist of a smile in her cheeks. "They do say there's a fool born every minute."

"Ow, straight to the heart." Lucas clutched his chest. "Here I am being all vulnerable and bam, she just socks it to me."

She pushed herself off the desk and landed within inches of him. Tilting her head, she looked up at him with mischief in her eyes. "Okay, you're right. I'll say something nice."

Lucas crossed his arms. "Go for it."

She crooked a finger. "Come closer."

He leaned down. Her shampoo smelled like apples and his heart was beating so hard, he wouldn't be surprised if he woke up with a bruise on his chest.

She leaned in, her hand reaching up to his shirt and tugging him even closer. "I'm really sorry your football team wears pink." She whispered the words. Then she turned and tried to dodge past him, but his arm flew out and caught her around the waist and reeled her in like a fish at the end of the line.

"You didn't just do that. You did not just insult the mighty Badgers."

Rachel was laughing, and he suddenly realized that she was flush up against him, her face tilted up and her lips so close to his he could feel her breath on his face.

"Are you going to take it back?" Lucas had his left palm planted firmly on the small of her back, but his right hand traveled up her side. Rachel swallowed but shook her head. But her gaze wasn't on his eyes. It was firmly on his lips. The chemistry arched between them.

He was going to kiss her. Lucas knew it with the same certainty that he'd known the Astros were going to win the World Series. It had been a long time since he had kissed anyone. And something instinctive told him it had been a long time for Rachel, too.

He let out his breath slowly. He couldn't kiss her when he was still on the fence about what he was going to do. And if Donna was hiding something, he certainly didn't want the way that he got to it to be by taking advantage of Rachel.

"What are you and Donna doing for lunch tomorrow?"

"Nothing that I know of. Why?"

"Want to come and meet my family?"

- 26 -

The bunch of calla lilies on Rachel's lap were clenched in a death grip she couldn't seem to release. They were only halfway to Lucas's brother's house and already the flowers slumped across her legs, limp and mangled.

"Lordy, girl. What have you done?" Donna surveyed the damage from the driver's seat. "There's a pair of nail scissors in my purse. See if you can find them and give those poor stems a trim."

Rachel reached down and picked up Donna's enormous brown leather purse. Fishing around inside, she pulled out a pair of nail scissors. She peeled back the layers of wrapping and trimmed the first broken stem.

"So what's got you wound up tighter than a piglet's tail?" Donna checked the rearview mirror, then overtook the car in front of them, her lead foot pressing Rachel into her backrest. Her aunt drove like she had frustrated ambitions to be an Indy 500 racer, and she had acquired speeding tickets in all fifty states to prove it.

Rachel swiped her damp palms on the car seat. No way was she going to encourage Donna by admitting the angst that had been feeding her ulcer all night. "I was thinking about the book."

It wasn't a complete lie. At the moment, all roads to Lucas also seemed to end up at the book. It was doing her head in.

Actually, it was doing her heart in. Her head insisted on reminding her that only disaster could come from letting him get close.

Donna could not have looked less concerned. "Did I tell you I mentioned Lacey's idea about doing it as a joint project to Lucas?"

"You did not." She should probably put up some sort of protest, but she couldn't summon up the energy.

"It was very offhand. Just to see if I could get a read on any interest."

"And?"

Donna gained ground on the next car ahead. "He said that he didn't know the first thing about writing a book and I told him that was what collaborative writers were for. He didn't jump at it but didn't dismiss it, either."

"Huh." That was all Rachel could think to say. If there was a collaborative writer at Lucas's end it could be doable. Once they agreed on an outline, he'd never need to know that Donna didn't write her half of the book.

Donna looked across at her. "You don't sound as against it as I expected."

Rachel tried to focus on snipping the next broken stem. "Did you hear all the screaming women last night? The sales in Madison alone would probably put it straight to number one on the *New York Times* list." They'd ended up putting on two events in Madison after the first one had sold out in forty-seven minutes.

"Yup. I'll talk to him about it some more this afternoon if we get the chance. Or before the show tonight. I put out some feelers to Max, and he thinks Randolph would jump at the chance to acquire a book by the two of us. It's the perfect solution."

"Yes, well, let's not count any chickens." Outside the streets were changing into farmland. Scott and Grace. Lucas's brother and sister-in-law. Joey's parents. She smoothed her palm across her green-patterned wrap dress. Hopefully he wouldn't think this one looked like haberdashery.

"How's your father doing?"

Rachel's gaze lurched across the seat. They'd long since stopped talking about him. Ever since it became clear his limbo was a more than temporary state. "No change." She returned her focus to cutting the final few stems, then rearranged the stumps.

Donna's fingers tapped on the steering wheel. Her tell that she was looking for the first opportunity to overtake the driver in front of them committing the sin of driving the speed limit. "So, you planning to stop using him as an excuse to live anytime soon?"

What? "I'm not!" Her words came out in an indignant splutter. "You of all people should know why my life is what it is."

"And soon it will all be over, and so will all of your excuses for hiding. What then? Are you going to make up some more reasons to run or are you finally going to deal with why you've held yourself hostage for years and move on?" Her aunt said the words slowly, but they hit with the force of a sledgehammer.

"This isn't—"

"Turn right in a quarter of a mile," Siri interrupted them, and Donna slowed. A white fence with a red mailbox. Those were the instructions Lucas had given them.

Donna put on the blinker and made the turn. "Sweetie, I love you like the daughter I've never had. And I worry about you. Because when this is all over, I go home to my sweet Rob and a wonderful life, but who are you when Dr. Donna gracefully retires from the public eye? There is a big life waiting out there for you, Rachel, and I'm not going to let you watch it go by because your father was too drunk and too stupid to stick to the pavement."

Rachel gaped at her aunt. Who did she think she was?

"You have no idea what it's like!" The words exploded from Rachel's mouth. "You're not the one who has to live every day knowing what you did. To be living in a decrepit condo with no close friends because you can't afford to take the chance that someone will betray you. To—" She stopped at the self-satisfied smile on her aunt's face. "What are you so happy about?"

"That you're angry. Because you have every right to be. You've had a lot taken away from you. And it's a heck of a lot better than the passive acceptance that you've majored in. Oh look, we're here."

And with that, her aunt swung into a driveway, came to a sudden stop in front of a ranch-style house, and jumped out of the car, leaving Rachel mid-meltdown, with nowhere to melt.

ONCE SHE'D calmed herself down from Donna's unwelcome lecture, lunch had been surprisingly fun. Joey had bounced among all the adults like a pinball, which had been a welcome distraction, and Scott and Grace were the epitome of gracious and hospitable. Though she hadn't missed the inquisitive looks that both of them had bounced between herself and Lucas at different times.

As for Lucas . . . Rachel had thought Lucas couldn't look any more attractive than he had sitting in the sun, laughing with his family around the picnic table, but there was something about the wrinkle in his brow, as he now scrubbed the silverware like the President himself was coming for dinner, that made it a mighty tight competition.

If there was anything sexier than a man as cute as Lucas doing dishes, then she sure couldn't come up with it. "Well, well, a man who knows how to wield a dish brush. Aren't you just full of surprises, Lucas Grant."

He startled, barbecue utensils crashing back into the sink.

"Need any help?" She moved around the island, placing the empty salad bowl and meat dish on the counter.

"Almost done, but thanks." He placed a pair of tongs on the drying rack.

Plates caked with coleslaw and sauce glistened up at Rachel from the open dishwasher. Plates crying out for a rinse. Should she?

"You guys didn't have to do that, but thanks." Grace bustled into the kitchen, flip-flops slapping across the wooden floor. "I was just going to get us some more iced tea." She rounded the island, coming to rest in front of the fridge. Grabbing the handle, she turned to face them. "Do you—"

Her gaze landed on the plates, then bounced up to Rachel, and they shared a conspiring look of two people acknowledging that Grace would be unloading her dishwasher as soon as Lucas left.

"All right, you two, what is it?" Lucas stood, arms crossed, looking back and forth between the two of them.

"What?" Their response in unison made it sound suspicious even to her own ears.

"You look like you're trying to work out how to tell me my dog died or something."

"I have no idea what you're talking about. I'm just getting some more tea." Grace grabbed the jug out of the fridge and bolted. *Traitor.*

"Rachel." He raised an eyebrow, his tone one that a parent might use on a wayward child.

She held her palms up in surrender. "I have no idea what you're talking about. I'm just here to help." Avoiding his gaze, she reached past him for a couple of glasses and stacked them in the top rack. "See?"

"Miss Somers." His whispered voice crept down her neck and danced down her spine. "Don't make me bring out my secret weapon."

She fought to stop herself from turning to look at him. "Mr. Grant, I'm just a humble lunch guest trying to help clean up. There's no need for weapons here." Another glass in the rack. Hopefully he wouldn't notice it shaking just a little.

"Well, you can't say I didn't warn you." Against her will, her gaze skidded up. To hooded eyes and lilting lips. He slid the top rack away and kicked the door up with his foot. *Oh dear.* She stepped back, again, until she was trapped against the counter in the corner.

He leaned in, placing one hand on the countertop beside her, the other hanging loosely at his side. She had nowhere to go. He leaned in close, the scent of something spicy but subtle wafting up.

"So . . ." His voice lingered in her ear, filled with promise. *Eject! Eject!* her mind screamed, but her body leaned toward him, lips parting in anticipation. "One last chance. We can do this the easy way or take the longer route."

She stared up at him, mute.

"Okay, you can't say I didn't warn you."

He leaned in, and her eyelids fluttered. "The plates!" The words shattered the moment. For a second she didn't even realize it was her voice that had uttered them.

Lucas started, eyes flying open. "The what?"

"The plates need to be rinsed, otherwise the barbecue sauce will set like glue." What was she doing? The hottest guy she'd ever laid eyes on was about to kiss her and she shot him down with dish scum?

"The barbecue sauce will set like glue." He repeated her words, running a hand through his hair, causing parts to stick up on end. His expression was half bewilderment, half . . . relief?

He stepped back and pulled open the dishwasher door. "Well, we wouldn't want that, would we?"

She just watched, feet glued to the floor, as he started pulling out plates and piling them in the sink, whistling as if he had not a care in the world.

"I can help." She pushed herself off the counter and moved to stand beside the dishwasher so she could take the plates as he finished rinsing them.

He looked over at her and smiled the kind of smile that almost had her sagging back against the counter. "I have a question."

"Okay." There was something about the way his eyes glinted as he said it that made her nervous.

"Are you going to keep sabotaging our first kiss? I mean, don't get me wrong. I'm a patient man. I'd just like to know what kind of time frame we're talking here. Days? Weeks? Months?" He shrugged his shoulders as if it were all the same to him and handed her a plate. Which she almost dropped.

He'd done it. He'd put all their near-kisses on the table. Who did that? He did that. Rachel felt something well up in her chest as she looked at him, dishwater up to his elbows, looking at her like he had all the time in the world.

"I . . ." She looked at the shaking plate in her hand, then bent over and slipped it into its slot before she really did drop it. "Lucas, I haven't kissed someone in a really long time. And I haven't kissed someone who mattered in . . ." She closed the dishwasher door that separated them. "Well, it feels like forever."

"So you're saying I matter." Lucas quirked a smile at her as he placed some clean cutlery in the second sink.

"Yes." It was only three letters, but it felt like everything.

"So is it a Dr. Donna rule? Does she have some rule like no kissing before the third date or something? I knew I should've read one of her books."

Yes, she did. *Don't go kissing anyone until you've established some baseline compatibility. Great physical chemistry too often helps mask incompatibility.*

It was an excellent piece of advice. One clearly written when she wasn't in danger of kissing anyone, let alone a man who made her toes curl with longing.

But it wasn't that. She was all too aware of the things that stood between them that a physical connection was only going to make worse, not solve. "It's not that. I guess I'm just afraid that once we get past that first kiss, then it's just the beginning of the end."

Lucas leaned his hip against the sink. "But what if it's not? What if it's just the beginning of the beginning?" He studied her. Genuinely interested in wanting to know the answer. Not trying to get the chitchat out of the way so he could try again. "It's not like I don't come with baggage. My father was an adulterer and a drunkard and he abandoned us. But I had the same dad as Scott, and look at him." He pointed out the window to where his brother wrestled with Joey in the grass. "I have to believe that I have a chance at that. And right now I want that chance with you."

The way he looked at her made her lose all sense of anything except him. "But what if you change your mind?"

Lucas reached out and tugged her to him. His wet hands plastered her blouse to her waist, but she leaned in. "What if *you* change your mind? You could hurt me too. Either of us could change our minds. Or both of us. But what if we don't? What if we fall in love and have six kids and in fifty years I tell my grandchildren about how my legendary sports-commentating career started with a grumpy personal assistant and a bunch of women wanting my advice on their love lives?"

"I'm not having six kids."

"I'm negotiable down to four." He tilted his head down. "But then your all-knowing folder probably told you that already."

"I can neither confirm nor deny." He was going to be sorely disappointed one day when he found out there was no such folder. Let alone one that detailed his preferred number of progeny. Unless Donna had been up to something she didn't know about.

"Well, at the rate we're going we're not going to have any at all, are we? Remember what Joey said the day you flung yourself into my lap?" He murmured the words against her lips, and Rachel had never wanted anything as much as she wanted him to kiss her.

Then he grinned at her and pulled back a little.

"What!" She almost exploded with pure longing.

"I've been here a few times before. You can't blame a guy for being a bit gun shy when he was left hanging a mere five minutes ago."

Rachel looked at the glint of challenge in his eyes. "Fine." She dropped back to her heels and stepped back to open the dishwasher. "Shall we continue, then?"

A rumble of laughter echoed up from his chest. "You are something else, Rachel Somers."

She tossed him a wink. "Just wash the plates, Lucas Grant. You're not a big radio star in this kitchen."

At that, before she even realized what was happening, he kicked shut the dishwasher door, picked her up, kissed her, put her down, and opened the dishwasher door again.

"There," he said calmly. Rinsing off a plate as if nothing had happened. "It wasn't the best first kiss in the world, but I'm sure we can make up for that next time. By the way, I'm going to do the book. With Donna. So we'll be seeing a lot more of each other."

THE SOLID oak door closed with a thunk. Lucas rested his head against it for a second, the cool wood soothing his warm face.

He'd kissed her. And he wasn't sure if it had been the right call. A groan escaped. Maybe he should have waited. For a better moment. To take her on an actual date like most sane people.

"So." Lucas turned his head. His brother stood behind him, face pasted with the big-brother smirk that he had perfected over thirty-four years.

"What." He was not in the mood, not now. Not ever.

"You going to prop up our front door all day, or come fill us in on the mysterious love life of Lucas Grant that you appear to have forgotten to mention?"

Lucas slid his face off the door and turned. "I have no idea what you're talking about." He made a show of looking at his watch. "Thanks for lunch, but I need to go prep for the show."

Scott laughed in his face. "You have Donna on your show tonight. You don't need to prep."

Oh.

"Uncle Lucas!" Jocy ran in from the family room, shirt undone, pants streaked with dirt, and skidded to a stop in his socks at Lucas's feet.

Saved. A triple scoop for that boy the next time they went out.

"Yes, bud?"

"Are you and Rachel going to get married?"

Lucas's jaw unhinged. "What?"

Grace appeared behind her son, her eyes twinkling.

Joey looked at him like he was the five-year-old. "Because you were kissing, and Mommy says that only people who love each other kiss."

"I never . . . We didn't . . ." The words spluttered out of his mouth like a misfiring engine. They weren't kissing. It was just a single kiss. One that lasted all of a second. Maybe.

Scott was no help at all, laughing so hard the only sound coming out of his mouth was the occasional gasp for air.

His wife also wasn't going to be saving him, propped up against the doorway to the family room, shoulders shaking, tears now running down her cheeks. She wiped a trail from her cheek, then padded over to stand by her son. Bobbing down to his level, she tousled her son's hair. "Joey, I think Uncle Lucas just might be a little disappointed that we know. I think maybe he might have been wanting to make it a surprise."

His nephew pondered this for a second. "Like when you said that I couldn't have a puppy, but then Daddy brought Nelson home?"

Grace nodded. "Just like that."

"Oh. Okay." Joey nodded as if it made perfect sense. "So then I probably shouldn't call her Aunty Rachel yet?"

There was a thud as Scott buckled against the wall, clutching his tummy, entire body convulsing as he sucked in air. Lucas hoped he was getting a kick out of this because the next time he needed help, he could go whistle in the wind for it.

Grace nodded seriously. "I think that's a very good idea. Why don't you go see what Nelson is up to?"

The words were barely out of her mouth before Joey was off skidding down the hallway and calling for his dog.

Lucas took one look at them and knew there was no chance he was going to escape the house without giving them something. "I'm just going to grab a Coke."

The two of them followed him into the kitchen like they thought he might be planning to bolt out the back door. Pulling open the fridge, he palmed a can of Coke and then pressed it to his face for a second.

Synchronized scraping chairs told him the inquisition awaited at the dining table. Pulling out a seat next to Scott, he propped his elbows on his knees and took his time cracking open the can. This was new territory. It had been years since he'd even insinuated he might have met someone, let alone let them meet her.

Not that today was that. No, as far as they were supposed to know, Rachel was just Donna's assistant, nothing more and nothing less. How could he have been so stupid as to forget about the big bay window in the kitchen that overlooked the yard? What a great show that must have been! No wonder

Scott was grinning like he'd won best calf at show. Lucas resisted the urge to slap himself upside the head. What a mess!

"Just to clarify," he said, running a finger up the side of the can, leaving a snail trail in its wake, "there was no kissing."

"Really." Scott quirked an eyebrow.

"No, we um . . ." Lucas took a slug of his Coke. "It was just a moment. So fast I don't think it even qualifies as a kiss."

Scott took a draw of his Sprite. "Is there something I'm not seeing here, little bro? She's a great gal. Even before the cutesy little romance scene, it was obvious to everyone that you two have a connection. So where's the problem? Lord knows we've been waiting for you to find someone you like enough to sneak a smooch in our kitchen."

"And feel free to bring her around as often as you like if it means the dishes get done as a bonus." Grace was positively giddy. Possibly at the prospect of a future life where she wasn't outnumbered three to one.

How was he going to explain this without looking like a total cad? "It's . . ." His top teeth found his bottom lip. "More complicated than that."

"Actually, it's not; it's pretty simple. You like her, she likes you—everything else can be worked out."

"I live in Wisconsin; she lives in Colorado."

"Gah, details." Scott flicked a thousand miles away with the wave of his hand.

What could he say? Since he'd decided in that split second to do the book with Donna, Brad was out of the picture. And surely a book with her would bring in enough money to help out Scott and Grace. The woman did spend her life on the bestseller charts. That had to mean she sold a lot of books.

"Is this about Dad?"

Lucas just looked at Scott. He chose now to bring up their old man?

Silence smothered the room.

"I'm just going to check on Joey." Grace stood up and pushed her chair out. "This kind of quiet usually means trouble." She scuttled out of the room like a sand crab chasing a wave.

Their father. The King of Liars. He hadn't served any use in twenty-odd years, but he might just provide Lucas with the escape hatch he needed. How ironic, the one person he refused to talk about now being the preferred subject.

"Luc, you look like Dad but you are nothing like him. You will never be anything like him."

"You don't know that. Dad wasn't anything like him either, until he was." The words landed hard, a harsh reminder of the fact that their family had lived a pretty good life before their father blew their world apart. Sure, he drank a bit too much, but it was the nineties. Almost everyone's dad came home and had a few too many beers.

Only half an hour ago he'd stood in this very kitchen and told Rachel he was nothing like his dad. He looked at his Coke. A scotch or a whiskey would be good right now. Conversations about their father always triggered the desire for a hard drink. As if some burning liquor could wipe away that taste of abandonment that still lingered in his throat almost twenty years on. Bitterness overtook the taste of the sugary soda in his mouth.

"Yeah well, little bro, you never have to worry about that, do you. Unable to let yourself love one woman, I'd say that makes you a hundred percent safe from ever keeping two."

Scott's soft words whistled through the air like a knife. He leaned forward, clasping his hands in front of his knees. "The ironic thing, Luc, is that in your attempt to be nothing like him, you could end up exactly like him."

"Well I guess you'd know. The two of you being so buddy-buddy and all."

"Don't be stupid, Luc. I've seen him all of twice and I'm not going to apologize for that. And do you know what he is? An old man, lonely, estranged from both of his families, filled with regrets that choke him every day. That will be you too in thirty years if you let what he did stop you from letting yourself fall in love."

A lonely old man filled with regrets. The words bounced around Lucas's brain like an out-of-control pinball. Rachel's eyes filled his mind, her laugh, the breathless look on her face when he had her cornered. What would it be like to come home to that every night?

Speaking of which. "You told Grace yet?" He nodded toward the doorway she'd exited through.

His brother's face seemed to collapse. "I can't. Not right now. She's already struggling to accept that another round just isn't financially viable. If I told her how bad things were . . ." His explanation trailed off as he studied his tented fingers.

Lucas took a sip of his soda. Scott had no idea the unpaid vet bills, power, land taxes, and insurance Lucas had finally gotten him to own up to had cleaned him out of almost all his savings.

He'd talk to Donna tonight. See how fast they could get him a contract and a check.

- 27 -

This was it. The last night on Lucas's show. Standing at the studio window, looking up and over Madison's jagged skyline, Rachel drew in a ragged breath, trying to get her scattered emotions under control.

Donna hadn't said a word the entire way back to the hotel. Just smiled smugly to herself. Rachel put her fingers to her lips. Who would've guessed a few short weeks ago she would fall in love with Lucas Grant?

In love. The words screeched through Rachel's brain like a needle across a record. No. She wasn't. Couldn't be. She didn't love Lucas. It was ridiculous. She barely knew him. But if he did do the book, then they would see a lot more of each other.

It seemed too crazy to wish for. That all the things that had kept her up at night might have been solved in one afternoon.

The worst part of deceiving Lucas was over. No more calling in to his show pretending to be someone else. No more trying to remember what he'd told her as Donna and what he'd told her as Rachel.

She was done with that game. No more pretending to be Donna. She turned around to face inside Studio 1. "I'm only going to be your assistant from now on. No more subbing in for publicity stuff."

"Okay." Donna barely even glanced up from her phone, not looking in the least bit worried.

The clock above Donna's head ticked over to seven thirty, making Lucas officially late for pre-brief. Where was he?

Back to Denver. Then Kansas City. Then Tulsa. Three stops. This time next week, Lucas's place in the tour would be finished. He'd be back here while Max ironed out a deal with Randolph. Which shouldn't take very long, but still. What if something went wrong? What if he backed out of doing the book? What if he'd second-guessed everything in the last few hours?

The door opened and he walked in. His grin filled his face when he saw her and she felt her lungs infuse with hope.

"Hey." Lucas was so close, the word wafted down the side of her face like a feather. She felt the strength of his presence right behind her.

"I'm just going to find the bathroom. I might be a while," Donna announced loudly as she opened the studio door. The woman had all the subtlety of a machine gun.

"Hey." Rachel couldn't stop her smile. "How was the rest of your afternoon?"

"About what you'd expect when your older brother catches you making out in his kitchen."

Rachel raised her eyebrows. "We made out? Why do I feel like I missed that part."

Lucas leaned in. "We could make up for that. Your aunt did say she might be a while and we do have, like," he glanced over his shoulder, "a good twenty minutes before the show starts."

"I'm not making out in front of your producer."

"Ethan!" Lucas lifted his voice and looked toward the sound booth. "I'll pay you a hundred bucks to go find something else to do for twenty minutes."

Rachel raised her voice too. "Ignore him, Ethan." She leaned against the window ledge. "We've got plenty of time. Especially if you do the book."

Lucas propped himself next to her, his arm brushing hers. "About that. What's the process for getting that done? How long will it take?"

"It depends. We have a great literary agent." Rachel almost choked as she realized she'd said "we," but Lucas didn't appear to notice. "I'm sure he'd be happy to talk to Randolph about renegotiating the deal to bring you on board given how successful the *Feelings and Football* events have been. Unless you want to get your own agent and they can work together on the renegotiation."

"Nope. I'm happy with whoever Donna has. Then what?"

"Well, it depends. The original deadline is only a couple of months away, so Max will need to negotiate getting that extended. Agree on who your collaborative writer will be. Negotiate you an advance."

"How does that work? The advance." Lucas shifted slightly as he turned toward her, his hand brushing across hers as he did.

Rachel tried to focus on his questions. "You get half up

front when you sign the contract and half when they accept the book for publication."

"And how long will it take? To negotiate the contract?"

Rachel shrugged. "Honestly, I don't know. It depends on so many things. Randolph will want to sort it quickly, since there's already a deadline in play in Donna's contract."

"What if they don't go for it? Randolph, I mean?"

Rachel laughed. "They would let Donna cowrite a book with Kermit the Frog if that was what she wanted. You don't have anything to worry about there."

"Okay. Sounds good." There was something unsettled in his expression, but maybe that was to be expected. A couple of months ago he hadn't been involved in any of this, and now suddenly he was about to cowrite a book.

"Oh, I have something else. I found you a present for her." She crossed the room and opened her tote, pulling out a square box a little larger than a tennis ball. Turning, she held it up, the gold wrapping catching the studio lights. "Ta-da!"

A slow smile inched across his face. "You are wonderful."

"I know."

"Am I allowed to ask what it is?"

"Donna likes to collect a Christmas decoration from every city she visits. She doesn't have one for Madison."

His eyes boggled. "You spent two hundred bucks on a Christmas decoration."

"Have you ever tried to find one in June? Scratch that. Have you tried to find a classy one ever?"

His right cheek rose. "Point taken."

"And no, of course I didn't. Where do you think I shop? Tiffany's? It was fifty, plus five for the wrapping stuff."

He closed the gap between them and lifted the box from her hand. "And she'll like it?"

"She'll love it," she promised.

He lowered his hand, ocean eyes staring into hers. "Thanks. Really, I know it must have taken time to find this for me."

It had actually been pretty straightforward once she'd thought of the Christmas decoration idea, but no need to tell him that.

"You're welcome." She tried to unhook her eyes from his. To come up with a neutral topic of conversation.

"Sooooooo." He drew out the word, his eyes locked on hers. The atmosphere was suddenly charged, her emotions flying in all directions. "Denver's next."

"It is." She could barely get the words out.

He launched an easy smile at her like a missile, the corners of his eyes folding like rumpled sheets. His breath floated across her face, minty and fresh. "I was thinking . . ." He left it hanging, the sound of a question unspoken.

"Yes?" Her voice wasn't even hers. Breathless, eager.

"I've never been to Denver before. Do you want to head out tomorrow night after the show? You could show me all the cool hangouts." His words were casual, but his eyes and the way he now worried his bottom lip between his teeth said his intention was not.

Don't run away because you're scared. Her aunt's words appeared, as if written across the canvas of her mind. Maybe she was right. Maybe it was time to take a chance. She was so tired of being alone. And this guy standing in front of her, for once he made it seem like the impossible might not be.

She wanted to say yes, but fear caused the simple three-letter word to jam in her throat. "Can I think about it?"

COULD SHE think about it? Could she *think* about it? Lucas struggled to keep his attention on whatever soothing advice Donna was caressing her latest caller with. It was hardly a difficult question. Either she wanted to go to dinner with him or she didn't. Why did women always have to make everything so complicated? What was there to think about? Call him arrogant, but he'd thought a date was a sure thing.

Hopefully he had managed not to convey his shock in his attempt at a casual shrug and "of course." Good thing Donna had chosen that moment to walk in, saving them from having to try to pretend the situation wasn't as awkward as it was.

He put his fingers to his temples, gave them a circular rub. How could he have misread Rachel so badly? It wasn't like he was some guy who thought every woman he met was into him. In fact he'd been accused of being too oblivious in the past. He'd thought a blind man could've seen there was a spark between them, but clearly the blind man was him.

Except that made no sense with everything that had happened between them the last few days. The conversation in the kitchen. Had she already changed her mind?

"Lucas, honey, you okay?" Donna's voice cut through his pity party. She tugged her lilac-colored wrap around her shoulders and peered at him with knowing eyes.

"Fine. Why?" An ad for a cleaning service was playing. Had he just missed a whole call?

"Well, this is your show and all, but you wouldn't know

it. You haven't uttered a word to the last three callers and you haven't even tried to get in a sports update in the last half hour."

He groaned. "I'm sorry, Doc, I must've gotten distracted."

She shot him a knowing look. "You're not the only one." She tilted her head sideways and he glanced over to the sofa. Rachel sat, legs crossed underneath her, nibbling her bottom lip and staring into space.

"Back on in five." Ethan's voice echoed into their headphones.

Lucas's eyes found the clock. Ten to twelve. A couple more calls and they were done. No more Dr. Donna on *Sports with Lucas.* He should be relieved, but it felt a bit weird coming to an end. He'd started enjoying the advice-to-the-lovelorn thing much more than he'd expected. Maybe the book would be a fun thing to do. Not just a good moneymaker.

A sharp elbow in his side jolted him back out of his musings.

"So Lucas, what do you reckon? Should Annie take back her boyfriend who cheated on her?" Donna pinned him with a "get it together" look and shook her head with a vengeance, in case he'd missed the first time what his answer should be.

Ten minutes later he'd rescued the Annie call from disaster, managed to stick it out through two others, and presented Donna with her Christmas decoration on air. The glass globe, decorated with some kind of sparkly silhouette, had gotten the rapt reaction Rachel had promised.

Lucas flipped off the various switches at the console. Donna had disappeared off to the ladies' room and Ethan had mumbled something indecipherable under his breath and fled after her. Leaving him and Rachel alone. At least they'd saved him from being officially denied in front of an audience.

To buy more time, he tapped the keyboard and pretended to be engrossed in important radio-show business, when he was only reading what songs Ethan had lined up for the next twenty minutes until the graveyard host arrived.

"Lucas?"

He turned and looked up. Rachel was just behind him. He stood. He was at least going to be standing like a man for the pronouncement. "It's fine. Don't worry about it." His pride jumped in, preempting her words.

"What?"

He shrugged. "I just thought it could be fun to go out together. Sorry, I didn't mean to place you in an awkward position." His words were terse, clipped.

Rachel's eyes narrowed, snapped. "Lucas Grant, want to stop being such a jerk and let a girl give you her answer?"

Had she just called him a jerk? "Go ahead." He turned back to the console, flicked another few switches.

A tug on his elbow swung him around.

"Yes."

"What?"

She started to laugh. "How on earth did you get to be who you are when you don't have a clue? Yes, you idiot, I'd like to go out with you tomorrow night."

"Really?"

She nodded, her smile lighting up her face. "Really."

He needed to make sure they were clear before his heart raced away into the distance and he never got it back. "Just to make sure we're on the same page, I, Lucas Grant, am asking you, Rachel Somers, on a date. A proper one, where I pick you up and take you somewhere nice for a late dinner and pay the tab and, in return, you bat your eyelashes at me and simper and tell me how wonderful I am. Is that what you're saying yes to?"

She pulled out a smile he'd never seen before. Sultry, full of promise. The kind of smile that could make a guy lose his mind and run off to Vegas. "Well, that depends. Will there be a kiss good night?"

His mouth lost all its moisture at her words. Who was he kidding? This woman already had his heart. Along with every other atom in his body. He looped an arm around her waist and pulled her toward him, eyes on her full, rosy lips. "That's a possibility, Miss Somers. If you play your cards right."

She reached up, ran her fingers from his shoulder to where his hand rested on her waist, and let them linger there. "I'll meet you in the hotel lobby at ten." And with that, she spun out of his grasp and walked toward the door, leaving him standing by himself with the world's stupidest grin on his face.

- 28 -

A jaunty tune made its way through Rachel's pressed lips as she finished wanding her eyelashes. Blinking once, twice. She had to give it to Maybelline: her lashes were indeed both fuller and longer.

Lipstick. Two tubes stared at her from the bathroom counter in Donna's suite. The red she'd bought in a fit of daring was more her color, but definitely a bit more "come and get me." Hmmm, maybe the pink. A little less obvious. Lord knew she didn't need any help when it came to being obvious about how she felt about Lucas.

He'd been perfect, again, tonight. Denver had loved him just as much as every other city. He could write sports commentary in the book with Donna and it would fly off the shelves. And there *would* be a book. Lucas had spoken to Max first thing in the morning. Signed the contract for representation in the afternoon, and Max had promised he would be getting straight on the phone to Randolph to renegotiate the deal. He seemed to think they could have something ready for signing within a couple of weeks.

Rachel didn't know herself without the looming deadline hanging over her head.

Contouring her lips with liner, she dabbed a cotton bud into the tube of dusky rose. Painting it on, she pressed, blotted, and pressed. Her eyes sparkled back at her in the mirror. She hadn't even touched her cheeks and they were already flushed like she'd been on a long run.

Maybe it was time to let herself believe that something good could happen in her life.

The carpet swished as she padded back into the bedroom. The perfume she had spritzed on a few minutes earlier had settled into a lingering scent of summer and promises.

The clock blinked nine forty-seven. Thirteen minutes to go.

Shedding her bathrobe, she dropped her dress over her head, the fabric whooshing as it billowed over her hips. She'd found it earlier in the day. Yet another sign of good luck. She was ordinarily jinxed when it came to finding a new outfit when she really needed one. A deep blue like midnight but shot through with some kind of silver thread, the V-neck gave her cleavage that didn't naturally exist, the waist flaring out into a fifties skirt.

Was it too much? The mirror reflected someone looking like a starlet from a bygone era. One not out of place crooning "Happy Birthday, Mr. President" into a microphone.

Her gaze fell to her second outfit option laid out on the bed. A muted green wrap shirt and a black skirt. Much more her, much more . . . ordinary.

Come dressed for a good time. It wasn't his words as they'd parted after the show so much as the promise in Lucas's voice that popped into her head.

She swept the ordinary outfit onto the floor, sitting in its place to slip on her silver shoes. She was done with ordinary. At least for tonight.

No thinking about deadlines, or deception, or deadbeat fathers. Tonight was just about possibilities. No backing out, no getting afraid and running away. Time to listen to her own bestselling advice. To take a chance and believe that it might be her turn, for once.

Walking across to the dresser, the silver heart-shaped locket blinked up at her. As she lifted it, it spun, as if knowing it had been taken out of retirement for something special. Unlatching the clasp, she settled it on her chest. The one thing she had left from her mother that made her smile when she saw it, instead of wanting to cry.

Her phone rang, the screen flashing a Colorado area code.

"Hello, Rachel speaking."

"Rachel, Dr. Lockhart from Sunhaven here."

She sank to the bed, heart free-falling like a crevice had just split through the room. Unbelievable. He'd always known how to time things for maximum destruction. If he'd gone and died, she was going to kill him.

"Is he dead?"

"Oh, I'm so sorry. No, your father's fine." She didn't have time to diagnose why her heart sank at the news. "No, it's Cam Grayson. His wife, Anna, asked me to call you."

"Is he okay?"

A pause. "No, I'm afraid not. He's suffered a significant

and irreversible brain bleed. We've advised Mrs. Grayson it's time to take him off life support."

Rachel's body folded over until her head touched her knees. There truly was no justice in the world. "Please let her know I'm on my way. I'm in Denver, but I'll be there as soon as I can."

"I'll let her know."

"Thank you, Doctor." Rachel threw the phone on her bed, kicking her shoes off just as there was a hammer on the door.

Flinging it open, she found Lacey standing there. "Anna needs us. Cam's not going to make it." The publicist looked as harassed as Rachel had ever seen her.

"I know. The hospital just called me. Just let me get my coat."

Rachel jammed her phone against her ear as she threw her wallet into her purse. Lucas, she had to tell Lucas. His phone went straight to voicemail. "It's me. Um, Rachel. I'm really sorry, but I'm not going to make it tonight. Something's come up. I have to go and be with a friend."

She was such an idiot. What on earth had inspired her to think things might work out for once?

LUCAS GAZED at his Rolex as the minute hand moved from its position on the three. Rachel was only fifteen minutes late, but it felt like a lifetime.

How could he have let his phone go dead? Tonight of all nights. How could he not have registered the red bar, oh, at any time today, and given it some juice? Even ten minutes' worth. Just enough for a quick "Hey Rach, just waiting in the lobby." Or, heaven help him, receive a "Running a bit late, be down soon" from her. Instead here he was, sweating it out like a soon-to-be convicted felon.

He tugged at his cuffs. Stared at the delicate posy of spring blooms wilting on the chair beside him. He'd never been a flowers guy. Always swore he would never waste his money on something that would die in a couple of days. But for Rachel, somehow he'd found himself in a florist shop, clucking over buds like they were his grandchildren. Fretting over combinations until the salesgirl took pity and suggested he go for a stroll while she put something together.

He'd handed over the thirty bucks without even blinking. It would be worth ten times that if they made her smile the smile that he now saw every time he closed his eyes at night.

Relax, Grant. She's coming. Women always run late. Especially for dates. Better get used to it.

He bounced his useless phone in his hand. He'd sent two calls from Brad to voicemail earlier. He could wait another day to hear Lucas was going to go with the book deal. He'd spent two weeks with Donna and she was exactly what she seemed, but Brad was clearly determined that wasn't an acceptable answer.

All he had worked toward for the last decade was syndication. And yet, compared to the thought of the chance at something with Rachel . . . everything faded in comparison to that.

His black shoes tapped the carpet, his eyes focusing on a small checked pattern.

Scott and Grace would be so happy. Already were. When he'd mentioned to Scott that he was taking Rachel out, his brother had whooped so loud, the whole state was probably roused.

Long distance. He let his mind meander over the logistics. Denver and Madison weren't that far apart. It was hardly a West Coast/East Coast divide.

"Lucas, honey?"

He jolted at Donna's voice. She had changed into a purple pantsuit but still had the hairdo from earlier that reminded him of fairground candy floss. "Oh hey, Doc. Is Rachel on her way down?"

Her eyes crinkled. "Did you two have plans?"

"Um, yeah." He gestured at the flowers. "Dinner . . . we were meant to be having a late dinner."

Material rustled as she sat on the bench beside him. "I didn't realize." She peered at him closely.

"Has something happened?" *Please let her be okay.*

A sigh. "I don't know, but I suspect so." The look on her face snuffed out hope. It was the look he imagined a vet might have before they put down a small sick animal. Compassion, pity.

Something snapped in her eyes, as if she'd made a decision about a debate he hadn't even known was happening. "Lucas, I love my niece, and for the last ten years I've done my best to not interfere."

A smile slipped onto his lips.

A flash of one on hers, too. "Done my best, but there may have been a little interference here and there. If I tell you something, do you promise not to tell another soul, no matter what does or doesn't happen with you or Rachel?"

The hair on the back of his neck prickled. He was on the

brink of something important. Something that might change everything. "I promise."

"As you know, my ex-husband and Rachel's father are brothers." She took a breath. Wrapped her arms around herself, clutching her elbows. "It would be fair to say that when the chips were down, neither of them stepped up. My husband left me bankrupt with three young boys to raise alone, and Rachel's father, well, her mother was the glue that held that family together. Kept him semi-decent. Once it became clear her mom wasn't going to beat the cancer, her father pretty much disappeared."

Donna peered out the window at the dark sky. "Oh, he was still present in body. He paid the bills at least. But he drank. The Somers boys could always hold their liquor, but he hit the bottle like it was the elixir of life."

"He didn't . . .?" Lucas's insides roiled just at the thought. If he had laid a hand on Rachel, he would hunt him down and . . .

"No. Not that she's ever told me anyway. Pretty much every night he would drink until he passed out. Sometimes on the journey there he would say horrible things that no daughter should ever hear from a father's mouth. But as far as I know, he never touched her."

Thank God. The thought of Rachel bearing the brunt of someone's fists, or worse, on top of everything else she'd had to endure—he didn't know if he could bottle that up.

"After she went to college, things got worse. He lost his job. Linda's life insurance money disappeared down the toilet of his addiction. Every night was a different bar, another strip club. Every night he would ring Rachel at some ridiculous time of the morning and order her to make the hour drive to pick him up and take him home. And almost every night she did. For two years. Extracted him from whatever flea-bitten sleazy joint he'd crawled into and took him home. Then turned around and drove an hour back home."

A tear trickled down Donna's cheek, leaving a dark trail in its path. "Then one night she finally put her foot down. Said no. It was a friend's birthday, and she told him to call a cab and make his own way home. She told me that was the first time since her mother died that she had felt free. Deciding that her father didn't get to control her life anymore. The stubborn old codger didn't call a cab. He decided to walk."

Lucas had a gut-wrenching feeling that he knew where this was going.

"Witnesses say he was weaving down roads like they were sidewalks. Yelling abuse at Rachel."

A deep breath. "He was in a hit-and-run. Rachel was the one who found him. She'd called to check that he'd gotten home and when he didn't answer, she'd driven there. When he wasn't there, she combed the streets looking for him. She found him in a gutter, left for dead."

Lucas didn't realize he was crying until a tear slid down his neck. His Rachel. His beautiful Rachel. How could anyone do that to another person?

He realized Donna was still talking. ". . . uncontrollable brain swelling, permanent damage."

"Hold on. He's still alive?"

Donna blew air out her nose. "'Alive' is stretching it. In possibly the cruelest thing ever, his body still functions, to a point. But for all other purposes he's as alive as your average turnip."

So many things finally clicked into place. "She blames herself."

"'Blames' would be kind. She is obsessed with living in her own kind of purgatory on earth as penance. That's why she never lets anyone close. Runs away from any possibility of happiness. She's convinced herself that she deserves nothing good from life. I thought that maybe that had changed with you, but if she's not here . . ." Donna's voice trailed off.

The desire to find her was so strong, he struggled to keep himself seated. "Where is she?"

Donna cast him a knowing look. "Probably at his care facility. It's where she always goes when something good happens. Something like you."

"What do I do?" Was Donna really hinting he go gate-crashing into Rachel's father's care facility?

"I'm afraid that if you don't talk to her tonight, by tomorrow she will have convinced herself of what she always convinces herself of. That she has to spend her life paying penance for what happened to her father. That she doesn't deserve anything good."

He was already on his feet. "What's it called?"

"Sunhaven." The words carried on the wind behind him, chasing him into a cab.

RACHEL'S FOREHEAD left a smear on the cab's rear window. She'd spent most of the journey from Denver with it pressed against the glass, watching the scenery blur by. At least her cab driver was happy. He'd hummed pretty much the entire seventy miles. She'd be humming too if she were him. Probably the easiest three hundred bucks he had ever made.

The cab crunched into the driveway. The driver peered through the glass, and she did have to admit the place did look pretty eerie in the middle of the night. "Is this right?"

"Unfortunately." She handed a twenty over as a tip. Her credit card had taken the battering in Denver. Couldn't blame the guy for insisting on proof they were good for the fare before he drove over an hour to the destination.

Lacey was already getting out the other side of the car. She'd barely uttered a word during the ride. If Rachel didn't know better, she'd think she was praying. But Lacey had even less use for religion than Rachel did.

The gravel shifted beneath her flip-flops. Of all the shoes she could have chosen, what on earth had possessed her to grab flip-flops? She clutched her coat tighter, making her way to the front doors. She didn't need to look hard to find the security buzzer; it was lit up like Christmas. She pressed her thumb against it, waiting for a disembodied voice to ask who was mad enough to be visiting this late. Instead the doors simply clicked and whooshed open. Creepy.

The reception area was empty, the only real light coming from the glow of the computer screen on the desk. Turning left, she padded toward the passageway to Cam's room.

"Hey, honey."

Rachel jolted. "Loretta, you scared me."

The nurse with a smile like melted butter on grits wrapped a cuddly arm around her waist. Rachel leaned into her softness and closed her eyes for a second. Man, she was tired.

"This is Lacey. Another friend of Anna's." Lacey just nodded.

"Anna's in his room. She'll be glad to see you." Loretta used her swipe card to open the door into Cam's wing. "How're you doing, sweetness?"

Rachel rubbed her gritty eyes. "Fine. I guess."

They stopped outside room 401, its door ajar. "You go on in there. That girl needs her friends tonight. You and me, we'll talk later, Little Miss Not Fine."

Rachel opened her mouth to protest, but Loretta had already disappeared as quietly as she'd arrived. How did such a large lady manage to move like a ghost?

She pushed the door open with her fingertips, allowing it to slide on its hinges until the space was large enough for her, then Lacey, to slip through.

In the dim light Anna lay curled up on the bed next to Cam, her head on his chest, arm across his torso. The remains of a shredded tissue rested by her fingertips, the rest of it scattered across the pale blue sheets like confetti. Above them, the ever-present monitors beeped and flashed.

Heart rate, oxygen levels; Rachel scanned for the one showing brain activity. *Dear God, let there be a mistake.* There wasn't. The lines that had shown enough activity to allow the smallest sliver of hope last time now showed almost nothing. Blips similar to those of her father, but Cam's were from the ventilator forcing air into his lungs to make his chest rise and fall. It was a cruel hint at life.

Cam was even thinner than when she had last seen him. Cheekbones set like peaks against the landscape of his wasted face. Eye sockets sunken like craters.

Rachel took a step back toward the door. An intruder in a sacred space. The last night between a wife and her husband.

"Let's go." She whispered the words to Lacey, who stood like a statue by the door. They could haul some chairs from the activity room, and she and Lacey could stand guard outside.

Her hand hit the handle just as Anna stirred from her slumber. Her body stiffened, as if sensing someone else present, then relaxed as her gaze landed on them. "Hi," she whispered. As if Cam were just asleep and a loud noise might wake him up.

"We can go," Rachel said, gesturing toward the door. "Come back later."

Anna shook her head. The movement wrinkled the sheets drawn across Cam's chest. "Don't be silly. Come in, sit." She tilted her forehead to the chairs on the other side of Cam.

Rachel slid across the room, her footsteps alternating with the beeps of the monitors. Curling her body into the easy chair next to Cam, she looked at Anna's fingers wrapped around his now skeletal forearm, rings glinting even in the dim light.

"C'mon, Lace." Lacey finally walked the few steps.

The three of them were finally back together. By Anna's dying husband. Could life get any more unfair?

"I just, um, need to find a bathroom. I won't be long." Lacey had barely finished her sentence before she was slipping back out the door, but not before Rachel managed to catch her stricken expression.

"Should I go after her?" Rachel looked toward the door.

"No. Just give her a few minutes." Anna propped up her

head in her hand and peered at Rachel across Cam's chest. "You look nice. Hope you didn't leave anything special for me."

Rachel looked down at the blue of her skirt fanned across her knees. She'd almost forgotten what she was wearing. All three calls to Lucas had gone straight to voicemail. She shrugged. "Nothing important."

"Thanks for coming." Anna's voice was tinny, apologetic. "I have people who offered to come in but, it's just that . . . you know, you get it."

"What happened?"

"Nothing . . . everything. We were here. Thank goodness Dad had taken Libby off to get a snack, and suddenly some of the alarms started going mental. Of course everyone came pouring in. We had to go. After, well, I don't know how long—it felt like hours—they came and told us that Cam had suffered a bleed, some kind of clot must have come loose, and that there was nothing they could do." Anna's thumb rubbed her husband's hand, as if apologizing for talking about him like he wasn't there. "They ran some tests, which all came back saying the same thing. Complete and irreversible brain death."

It wasn't fair. "I'm so sorry." Rachel somehow managed to force the completely inadequate words out.

Anna blinked rapidly. "We'd talked about organ donation. We agreed it was what we both wanted if something like this ever happened. But we were young; it was a theoretical conversation. I never thought—" Anna's voice broke. Then a breath shuddered through her lips. "They're not equipped to do it here, so they'll transfer him in the morning. So I have tonight." Even in the dim room she could see tears pouring down Anna's face. "I mean, it's stupid—I know he's gone. That I'm lying here with a dead man, but I wasn't ready. I've had weeks, but I hadn't said good-bye. And how do you explain to a three-year-old that even though her father doesn't look any different to her than he did yesterday, today he's gone?"

Rachel tugged her coat closer. "I don't know."

Anna swiped a hand across her cheek. "In the morning Mom and Dad will bring Libby, and Cam's parents will come too, and one of us is going to have to find a way to explain to her that it's time to say good-bye. He's her whole world. She's never stopped believing one day he would wake up." She buried her face in her husband's shoulder and her back heaved.

Rachel stayed lodged in her chair, keeping watch as Anna battled her grief. After a few minutes, the sobbing subsided and Anna wiped her face on the top of the sheet. "Sorry about that."

For what? "Don't ever apologize for loving your husband."

A tremulous smile. "Okay." She stared up at the ceiling. "I don't know how to do this. I don't know how to be a parent without him. I don't know how to do life without him." She pushed herself up and looked straight at Rachel. "I don't know if you've ever forgiven us for what happened to your dad, but please, will you stay?"

LUCAS PRESSED the buzzer outside the dark hospital. *Please let someone answer, please let someone answer.*

"Hello?" A woman's voice came through the crackling intercom.

"I'm here to see Rachel Somers."

"Young man, do you know what time it is? Visiting hours start at nine."

"Please, can you just let me in so I can explain?"

Silence for a couple of seconds, then a buzz, and the electronic doors slid open. He walked through them and then through a second set. "I hope it's a really good explanation." A middle-aged nurse standing guard looked pointedly toward a security guard, who had his hand resting on his holster.

"I just need to see Rachel. Please. It's important."

"More important than a woman whose husband will be taken off life support in a few hours?" The nurse's ebony curls sat tight against her head, bristling as if already offended.

"Um, no."

"Well, then you can't see Rachel."

Lucas shook his head. The nurse wasn't making any sense. "I'm sorry. I don't understand. Isn't she with her father?"

"No. Her father is here, but that's not why she's here tonight. She's with a friend whose husband didn't make it."

Lucas's shoulders sagged. She hadn't come here to hide from him. To talk herself out of giving them a chance. "I'm sorry. I misunderstood. We were supposed to go on a date and when she didn't show up . . ." He gestured with a nonsensical hand wave. "I'm crazy about her. And I'd heard that she has a tendency to shut people out when they get too close. Because of what happened with her father."

The nurse's face softened. "Well then why didn't you say

so, son. Lord knows we've all been prayin' for years for a decent man for our Rachel. Look, I didn't let you do this, but there's a lounge you can wait in. If you happen to still be here in the morning waiting to talk to her, then so be it. Garrett, show him the visitors' lounge."

She cast the poor security guard a glare as if blaming him for keeping them apart.

His feet swallowed up the carpet, paintings zooming past in a blur. He'd spent the ride thinking of eloquent words, but now his mind was empty.

"You can wait in here." The security guard opened a door to a dimly lit room. "There's tea and coffee and some snacks in the kitchenette."

"Okay, thank you." Lucas stepped through the door into a room filled with chairs and couches. He didn't know if he should stay or go. Rachel wasn't here because she was bailing on him. She was here for a friend. If he charged his phone he would probably find messages telling him exactly what had happened.

But if he didn't stay, when would he see her again? They were due to fly to Kansas City at lunchtime, and then Tulsa was the last stop for his part on the tour. Surely Rachel wouldn't be coming, with a friend to support and a funeral to attend.

Finding the light switch, he flicked one of the buttons and a couple of ceiling lights flickered on.

The door opened behind him and he turned to see Lacey walking in. "Lacey?"

"Lucas? What are you doing here?" Lacey stepped into the room and closed the door behind her. He had never seen her look so disheveled. Her shirt half untucked and makeup smeared.

"Rachel and I were supposed to be going on a date, but she never showed up and my phone is dead and Donna said . . ." He realized he was rambling and stopped.

"Ahhh." Lacey rubbed both her temples. "Well, that explains the dress, then."

"Are you okay?"

"I—" Lacey sagged against the wall.

"Do you want to sit down?" She looked like it was possible she might slide down the wall and onto the floor.

Lacey shook her head. "I just can't believe I'm here. Again."

"Again?"

Lacey looked around the room. "The wallpaper was different last time, though."

He really wasn't following.

"Do you know Rachel's father is here?"

"Yes."

She looked at him, clearly expecting him to elaborate.

"Donna told me a bit about what happened to him. She thought that maybe Rachel had stood me up because she blames herself for what happened to her father and sabotages things that give her a chance at happiness."

"It wasn't Rachel's fault. It was *my* fault. Everything about that night was my fault. If it weren't for me, we'd all be living different lives right now. We'd probably all still be friends."

This was making no sense. "How could it possibly be your fault?"

He didn't think it was possible that Lacey could fold even more into the wall. "The night of the accident was my birthday. The three of us were out when her dad called. I chucked a massive fit when I could see she was thinking about leaving to go and collect him from whatever sleazy joint he was in this time. Anna took my side, so she didn't go, and he got hit and . . ." She swiped a hand across her eyes. "Well, here we are."

Lucas was trying to put the pieces together. "So it's Anna's husband who's here?"

Lacey nodded. "I walked into Cam's room and it was like everything that happened with Rachel's father all over again. I felt like I couldn't even breathe. What are the chances that the two of them would end up in the same place? And in a few hours Anna is going to have to turn off his life support. I don't know what to say. I don't know what to do."

Lucas lowered himself down onto a couch. "Well, as someone who has lost a few people close to me, can I offer up some advice?"

Lacey didn't say anything but gave the smallest hint of a shrug. He took it as permission to continue.

"You have to go back into that room. Because this isn't about you. It's about Anna. And she is about to go through one of the worst things that can happen to any human. You don't get to opt out because it's uncomfortable or you don't feel equipped."

"Ouch. Why don't you say what you really think?" But a faint smile hovered on Lacey's lips.

"Sorry."

"Don't be. This is exactly why your book is going to be a hit."

"Can I be honest? I don't really care about the book. I mean the money will be good, but I'm mostly doing it because it means spending more time with Rachel."

"I know." Lacey pushed herself off the wall. "Okay, I'm going back. Do you want me to let her know you're here?"

"No. I'll wait. For as long as she needs."

- 29 -

"Mommy!"

Rachel cranked open one eye just in time to see a Libby-shaped blur disappear behind the foot of her father's bed.

Rolling her head from shoulder to shoulder, she attempted to dislodge one of her feet from under her behind. *Ouch.* It cramped like, well, a foot that had been holding her body weight for hours. "Hey, Libby-Belle."

"Shhhh." Libby's carrot curls sprung up on the other side of the bed. "Mommy's sleeping."

Sure enough, Anna lay curled up on her side, head tucked into Cam's shoulder, arm flung across his chest, little purrs emitting from her half-open mouth.

"Who's this?" Libby pointed to where Lacey slept curled up in her chair. She'd gone on the longest bathroom break in the history of the world, but she had come back.

"That's Lacey. She's a friend of your mom's too."

Cam's parents stood framed in the doorway, gazes stuck

on their son, faces that had been buoyed by hope now collapsed and shriveled like a pair of old balloons.

Out, out! Rachel stamped her foot on the floor, trying to bring feeling back into her leg. She stood, knee buckling for a second before it agreed to hold her up.

Next to her, Lacey had opened her eyes and taken in enough of the situation to stand too, her clothes rumpled and hair askew.

Outside the sky was gray and stormy, threatening rain. Appropriate. At least they wouldn't have to say good-bye with the sun shining and birds singing.

"I want to get up with Daddy too." Libby looked up, bottom lip starting to drop.

There was no space next to Anna, but on Rachel's side there was a small patch of real estate. Right under the "no sitting on the patient's bed" placard.

"Come around this side, honey."

Libby's head disappeared, replaced by the pitter-patter of little feet. She reappeared around the end, a smile on her face.

Rachel ducked down, tip of her nose almost touching Libby's. "Okay, I'm going to pick you up so you can sit next to your daddy, but you have to be very careful not to knock any of his tubes, okay?"

While Lacey had been gone, Anna had talked about the comfort of knowing that at least Cam's death would be able to save other people's lives. The last thing they needed was for something to go wrong with his ventilation and for Anna to lose that as well.

Solemn eyes studied hers. "Okay."

"Okay." She placed her arms under the armpits of Libby's pink polka-dotted dress and picked her up.

"Ooof." The kid was a lot heavier than she looked.

Checking that they were clear of tubes and wires, she settled the little girl on the bed. It creaked underneath the added weight.

Libby balanced on her side, but she couldn't quite manage to reach her father's face.

"Let me help, honey." Wrapping her arms around Libby's torso, Rachel lifted her up above the wires and tubes and held her face close so she could brush a kiss across Cam's cheek. "Hey, Daddy. It's Libby." She whispered the words, but they lingered in the room as if carried by angels. "Mommy and I miss you. And Grandma and Pops, too. So please wake up soon."

A muffled sob came from behind. Rachel turned her head to see Cam's mother shove her fist in her mouth, tears streaming down her face.

Placing Libby back at her father's side, she wiped her palms on her crumpled skirt.

On the other side of Cam's chest, Anna's eyes fluttered for a second, then opened.

"Hi, Mommy."

"Hey, baby." Anna directed a dozy smile at her daughter, then froze as reality registered.

"'Achel picked me up so I could say hi to Daddy too."

Anna's unreadable gaze met Rachel's. Uh-oh. Had it not been a good idea? Then she smiled. "What a good idea. I know Daddy will be very happy that you're beside him." She reached up and tugged one of Libby's curls. "Just like we used to do, huh?"

Libby stroked her father's hair, then his cheek. "Do you think he'll wake up soon? I asked Jesus last night please before my birthday." Her lower lip wobbled.

"Oh baby." Propping herself up on her elbows, Anna spun her feet to the floor and stood up slowly.

And this would be the moment Rachel exited stage left. Picking up her purse from where it had fallen on the floor during the night, she dropped a kiss on Libby's head, then swapped places with Anna.

Anna grabbed her hand, and Rachel squeezed back. "I'll be at the hospital. I promise." She glanced at the clock. Just after eight. UNOS would have sprung into action overnight. Now, coming into hospitals all over the country this morning were people about to get a new lease on life, knowing that their second chance had cost another family everything.

"Thanks." Anna's voice was calm, steady. "For everything."

Passing Cam's parents in the doorway, Rachel tried to find some appropriate words of condolence to utter, but they lodged in her throat like cement slippers.

Behind her, Lacey gave Anna a hug and whispered something in her ear before following Rachel.

Lacey slid the glass door closed behind her and pressed her forehead against the wall.

"Are you okay?"

"No." Lacey sucked in a ragged breath. "I have never seen anyone love someone the way Anna loves Cam. And the way he loved her back. I don't know how she's going to make it through this."

Lacey pulled out her phone and stared at the screen lit up with notifications and missed calls. "I just can't even." For the first time ever, she put it back in her purse without checking a single one.

Last night felt like another lifetime. Rachel pulled her phone out and checked the screen. No missed calls. One new message from Donna. She didn't even bother to read it. If it was important, she'd call.

Should she call Lucas again? Explain her garbled voice messages? No. If nothing else, he would be able to decipher that she was sorry and hadn't stood him up. Ball was in his court now.

Wasn't there something else she had to do? She sifted through her brain, trying to assemble the neurons buzzing around containing her next task. Money. It had to do with money.

Hopefully Cam had been a smarter guy than her father and had enough insurance that Anna and Libby would be taken care of after the medical establishment had taken their cut.

"Is everything okay?"

"Look where we are, Lace. Nothing is ever okay here." Rachel snapped the words and immediately felt horrible. The last time she and Lacey had stood in this exact hallway she'd said even worse things.

"You're right. I'm sorry." Lacey dragged her hand through her hair. "I have something to tell you."

What else could there be in this day that hadn't really even begun and was already horrible?

"Lucas is here."

Rachel didn't say anything.

"Rach? Did you hear what I said?"

Rachel shook her head. Was this a dream? Did she need to

wake up? "What do you mean Lucas is here? What are you talking about?"

Lacey gestured down the hall. "He's in the lounge. He's been here all night."

Rachel stared at Lacey. "Lucas Grant. Is here. In the visitors' lounge."

"Yes. I saw him last night when I went to the bathroom."

"Why didn't you tell me then?" Lucas had been down the hall all night and she hadn't known?

Lacey gave her the glimmer of a smile. "Because he told me not to. He said he'd wait for you."

"LUCAS?" FOR some reason she'd thought Lacey had to be wrong, but Lucas was right there. Asleep in a wingback chair in the lounge. Legs stretched out, little snores rumbling from his open mouth. There were already a few residents dotted around the room, including her father.

Her hands gripped a chair back, grasping for something concrete to hold on to. Her two worlds had just collided. How? How did he know?

"Lucas, wake up." She reached down and touched his shoulder. "It's morning." She didn't even know what time it was. She looked around for a clock. Just after eight.

"Hey." He blinked. His words were soft, his eyes softer.

"What are you doing here?"

"I . . ." He looked around them like he had something he'd rather not say in front of others. The absurdity of it all almost made her laugh. They were surrounded by people but not one of them was cognizant of anything, let alone them.

"Can we talk?" His hands tumbled over themselves.

"I um . . ."

Lacey's voice sounded from behind Lucas. "Go for a walk in the garden." She appeared beside him, all no-nonsense. "Shoo, out."

"But, it's . . ."

"I'll let you know if Anna needs us. But you two need to talk. So scat."

A smile quirked up Lucas's cheek. She could lose herself in that dimple forever.

Without even knowing how, they were suddenly outside, Lacey closing the door with a thump of finality behind them, and Rachel's flight instinct kicked in.

She wrapped her coat around her and stalked across the grass. Distance, she needed distance. If he was here, then he knew something about her father. And if he knew anything, he knew that she'd failed him as a daughter.

"I didn't know. I never thought for a second that he might be in danger. I know that might be hard to believe." The words tumbled out of her.

Lucas walked across the grass. His legs ate up the distance between them. "Rachel." Her name fell from his lips so quietly, it almost got stolen away by the wind before it reached her ears.

Reaching out, he ran his fingers down the side of her face, tilting her chin so she was forced to look at him. "I know that you twist your hair when you're nervous or stressed. I know you don't suffer fools. I know when you laugh hard, you snort like a baby rhino and it's the cutest thing I've ever heard." His eyes darkened and smoldered. "I know you look smokin' hot in a red dress." One hand was around her waist, drawing her in. "I know you are protective and sassy and funny and smart. I know you drive me crazy and when you're in the room I can't think about anything else. I know I would rather have a two-minute conversation with you than an entire date with anyone else. I know that *that*," he pointed at her father through the French doors, "was not your fault. No matter what you think."

Her mind scrambled. What did he know? Who told him?

"Rachel . . ." He searched her eyes, then paused. "What's your middle name?"

"Elizabeth." She barely managed to get the word out.

"Perfect." His fingers tucked her hair behind her ears, caressed her cheeks, captured her chin. "Rachel *Elizabeth* Somers. I know we haven't known each other that long and I know I still have a lot to learn about you, but I'm crazy about you. And you can run as hard and as fast as you like, but I will run harder and faster."

"Lucas . . ." She managed to get a word out.

"Shhh." A finger settled on her lip. "I'm not finished." His fingers gathered her hair. With a will of their own, her hands encircled his neck, lifting her heels from the ground.

The tips of their noses grazed. He stared at her with such intensity she almost believed nothing else mattered.

"Rachel." His voice was husky. "Don't fight me, because this is one battle I intend to win."

His mouth quirked, then everything collided as his lips brushed hers. His hands traveled down her sides, resting on her hips for a moment, then wrapping around her. It wasn't anything like the split-second affair in the kitchen. She couldn't even remember the last time she'd kissed anyone properly, but she knew it had never been like this. The kiss deepened until her knees gave out and she almost forgot her own name.

Her shameless fingers ran through his hair, the way they'd wanted to do from the first day they'd met. Her body melded against his. Finally, she knew that what she'd spent a decade writing about was worth holding out for.

The kiss broke off and Lucas looked at her with the kind of shaken smile she'd waited her whole life to see. "Is this it?" He murmured the words as his nose touched hers.

"What do you mean?"

"Is your dad your last secret? Nothing else I need to know?"

His words struck her like a hand grenade. She lurched backward. Palms on his chest.

His eyes were still glazed. He was still in the moment, didn't even know she was already running. From him. About to ruin the best thing she'd ever had a chance at. She had to tell him. She couldn't stand here and tell him there was nothing more. It would haunt her. And then it would destroy them.

Her head was already shaking. Even as her heart screamed at her to find a way, to *try* and find a way. Everything she'd ever wanted was standing here in front of her and she was about to give it up for what? The truth? Surely she deserved a trade-off. Surely her conscience would let her get away with it.

But her heart thumped in her chest, telling her that she had to tell him. And she had to do it now.

"Rach?" Confusion clouded ocean eyes. "What's wrong?"

She forced herself to step back. "I can't do this, Lucas. I—" She couldn't even get the rest of the words out.

She didn't even know what they were going to be. Her feelings she couldn't, wouldn't, deny. She had too many lies in her life as it was, without piling more on top.

His shoulders tensed, as though ready to take on whatever it was pulling her away. "So, what? You're telling me you work day in and day out with Donna and yet when a guy who just wants a chance and puts everything on the line, is right in front of you, it's all too hard?"

Hysterical laughter. Right in front of her. Shame he couldn't appreciate the irony. "It's all a lie, Lucas. The whole stupid mess is one big, fat moneymaking lie. What do you think pays for all of this?" She waved her arms around to encompass the manicured gardens, the immaculate buildings. "An assistant's salary?" The truth tumbled from her lips. Oh, it felt so good to finally say it out loud.

"I don't understand."

"*I'm* the one who created Donna."

Lucas was as gray as the clouds rolling above them. "I still don't understand."

She couldn't look at him.

"What do you mean you 'created Donna'?"

"I write the books. Donna was, *is*, the front person." The words came out mumbled.

"What?"

She forced herself to look at him. Into his face that stormed with emotions like squalls across a sea. "I write the books, Donna is the front person. Well, mostly. We collaborate a lot."

"So, you're her ghostwriter." He didn't look angry so much as just a little confused. "For how long?"

"Since the beginning." The breeze picked up and the skirt

of her dress whipped around her legs. The dress that was supposed to mark a new beginning. Not this. Not here.

Lucas squinted at her. "I'm sorry. I'm really not following. Donna wasn't famous in the beginning. Why would she need a ghostwriter? What got her the publishing deal if it wasn't her writing?"

Rachel blew out a breath. No turning back now. "When I was in college I interned at a newspaper one summer. Part of my job was filtering the mail for the advice columnist. She didn't care about what happened to the letters she didn't answer, so I started a blog. I called it *Ask Donna*." It had been meant as a tribute. After her mom died and everyone else had gone back to their lives, Donna was the only relation who even checked up on her.

"Why?"

"I guess because I know what it feels like to be invisible. And I hated that there were people who might be opening their paper every day hoping for an answer that never came. I guess it was my way of trying to help them be heard." It had given her purpose. Even though she knew the people would probably never read it. Might not even recognize themselves if they did since she changed some of the details.

"Rach—" Lucas reached out his hand and stepped toward her, but she pulled back. If he touched her, she might leave it there. At only half the truth.

"About a year in, I wrote a post that some celebrity tweeted and it went viral. Suddenly I had all these social media followers and requests for Donna to appear on shows, and it all just spiraled."

Lucas ran a hand through his hair. "I still don't understand why the need for the whole ghostwriter front-person charade. People use fake names on the internet all the time." He didn't sound angry, just puzzled.

"When the acquisitions team at Randolph found out how old I was, they said I had no credibility. That I was too young. Donna knew about the blog. She had a psychology degree gathering dust so she helped me out sometimes with answers I was struggling with. She had three kids and was in huge debt. I . . . My dad had just had his accident and insurance didn't even come close to covering his care. So we put together a proposal for me to write the books and Donna to be the face and when the head of marketing met Donna, she loved her. All we were hoping for was a bit of breathing room. We had no idea how big it would get."

"Okay." Lucas said the words slowly. "But lots of people like her have ghostwriters, right? I mean, isn't the plan that I'm going to have one, or at least someone to help me?"

"Yes."

"What am I missing, Rachel? I feel like I'm missing something."

She scrubbed her hands through her hair. This was it. If she continued from here he would never look at her the same way again.

"Rach?"

"We also shared some of the media stuff."

"Shared some of the what? What do you mean?" Lucas probably didn't even realize it, but he shifted back as he said the words, already putting distance between them.

Why had she added that? She couldn't say it. Couldn't say the words that would make him hate her with every ounce of his being. Because she knew that even if the ghostwriting didn't matter to him, *this* would.

"I had voice training. To sound like her. Sometimes if the schedule was tight or there were two things we wanted to do at the same time, I would do radio slots for her or phone interviews." She watched the pieces click into place across his face like a perfectly aligned Rubik's Cube.

Lucas didn't say anything for a few seconds. "That night . . . the night that Donna was on my show and she talked that woman off the window ledge. Was that her or was it you?"

Rachel sucked in a breath. That was the night that changed everything. When she had woken up the next morning, Dr. Donna was a household name. Randolph had gone from saying they weren't going to offer them another book contract to throwing a six-figure advance at them.

"It was me."

When he spoke his voice was choked, eyes haunted.

"Did . . ." His breath shuddered. "Did you know about my father because Donna told you?"

The shame was so heavy she could barely stay on her feet. Her head turned left, then right. "I'm so sorry. We never meant to hurt anyone."

"How many? How many times were you on my show?" The last sentence came out in a roar of fury.

Tears pooled in her eyes. "Probably most of them."

"I trusted you. How could you?"

She had no answer. What was she supposed to say? That he was supposed to just be a conduit to kick-starting a stalled book? A book that he was now going to be cowriting.

She forced herself to look into his wrung-out, haunted face. "I'm so sorry."

He looked at her, a flicker of the old Lucas in his eyes. "Was any of it real, Rach?" He waved his hands around. "Or was this," he swallowed, "was I just being played for a fool the whole time?"

"It was all real. Every single second."

He blinked, then his eyes hardened and his soul put up shutters. "Huh. Well, forgive me if every second of a well-orchestrated web of lies doesn't mean a whole lot."

"We . . ." Her breath came out in gasps, words having to fight their way around the boulder crushing her chest. "We never meant to hurt anyone."

"This book. That Donna said she was struggling with ideas for. Was this the plan the whole time? The reason for bringing me on the tour? For all of it? To get me as a coauthor? Save you from being in breach of contract when you had no book to deliver?"

"No. No. We never planned for it to happen like that. That was all Donna and Lacey. The tour. I had nothing to do with it. And they definitely didn't plan on that. They hoped that maybe it would give me some ideas. And what was the harm? Your ratings are up. Once the book is out, you'll practically be able to pick your path."

"Once the book is out?" He spat her words out like they tasted bad. "You can't seriously think I'm going to do this book now? I'm not even going to do the last two stops of the tour."

Not do the book. For some reason that hadn't even occurred to her, even though it should have. "But Max is renegotiating the contract right now." She couldn't hide the panic in her voice.

Lucas shrugged. "I haven't signed anything."

June. They were in June. If Lucas didn't sign, she had less than eight weeks to deliver a book or they'd have to give the advance back. Hundreds of thousands of dollars. Rachel felt her knees start to give way just thinking about it.

"You don't mean that. Think of all the good you could do with a book. I get that you may never want to have anything to do with me again, but whether you like it or not, I saved that woman that night. I've written thousands of words that have helped people."

"So the ends justify the means." Lucas shook his head. "You're just like him. I don't believe it. How could I have been so stupid?"

His words didn't make any sense. "Just like who?"

"My father." He barked a harsh laugh. "You should meet him sometime—the two of you could swap tales of your best tricks."

The conversation had stopped making sense. What did his father have to do with anything? She opened her mouth, not knowing what would come out. "I—"

"I'm not even sure which one of you is more impressive. I mean you, you've managed to fool the whole country, but he had two wives and two sets of kids to fool." He shook his head, eyes spitting condemnation. "I hate to say it, but I think my old man might have met his match in you two."

Her head spun like a roulette wheel as she tried to process what he was saying. "Please, just let me explain."

"You've explained more than enough." He turned away, crossing his arms across his chest.

Something stirred in her chest, anger bubbling up and out. "Tell me another way, Lucas. You got any better ideas for how I could have made a million bucks? Because it's either this, or my father eventually ends up in an institution where he will be left to fester in his own bed sores because the staff aren't paid enough to give a fig!"

He turned to her, eyes dead. "Just leave, Rachel. Go away."

"Lucas, please." But he turned away again. Her anger disappeared, replaced by desperation. It couldn't end like this, after everything, not this.

He turned back to her, eyes blazing. "Just leave me *alone!*" He roared the last word with a raw fury she hadn't seen since she was eighteen and her father discovered she had poured out all his liquor.

Resisting the urge to run, Rachel turned and made her way back to the door, her flip-flops slapping against the dew-drenched grass.

She had to go to the hospital. She had to go to the hospital and stand in a sterile waiting room while her friend's husband's organs were harvested.

And when she woke up tomorrow, she might have a broken heart. But at least she still had one.

- 30 -

"All right. What happened?" Scott's voice cut through the haze.

Lucas lifted his head, opened one eye a slit, grunted, and dropped his head back down. "Who let you in?"

"I did." The jangle of his spare key being tossed permeated his brain. "Seriously, little bro. You stink, and as for these . . ." Scott gave his sweatpants a tug. "Thank goodness I didn't bring Grace with me. No one needs to get a bird's-eye view of their brother-in-law's family jewels."

Oh. He'd forgotten about the slight hole in his pants. "Ventilation."

"I'll give you ventilation." He cracked open one eye to see Scott throwing back his curtains and flinging open both windows.

"Show some respect for the man cave."

Scott picked his way across a variety of take-out containers spread across the living room floor, picking up a couple of pizza boxes as he went. "Have you eaten anything in the last couple of days that wasn't from Pizza Hut, Mr. Chow's, or . . ." He eyed a wrapper on the floor, still showing the remnants of what had been a pretty average beef burrito. "Mexican Express?"

Lucas groaned. "I can neither confirm nor deny."

"And I can neither confirm nor deny that if you do not get up off that couch in the next ten seconds, I'm going to make you."

"Give it your best shot." Lucas leaned back and closed his eyes again. He had two inches and twenty pounds on Scott. His brother had no chance. And he still had a good two days of vacation time left to wallow away.

"Argh!" *What the . . . ?* He blinked. He was on his feet, ice-cold water pooling on the floor, dripping off his arms, running down his back. His pants were barely holding together under the onslaught and wow, that hole was a lot larger than he remembered. He clasped his hands in front to protect what little modesty he had left.

Scott stood at the end of the couch, bucket in hand, self-satisfied smirk on his face. "I'll brew the coffee while you hit the shower."

"I'm going to get you back."

"Yeah, count me scared, big guy. Go." He pointed to the doorway.

Lucas looked at the floor, now polka-dotted with splashes of icy water. What had his brother done, brought a melted iceberg with him? Brat. "Fine. But revenge will be sweet."

Half an hour later, the brothers sat at the rickety dining table in his kitchen, two mugs of steaming black coffee clasped in their hands.

Lucas ran a hand across the three days of growth. A shower he had managed, but a shave required more effort than he possessed.

"Don't even think about it." His brother took a sip of his brew.

"What?"

"You'd look horrible with a beard."

"I'm pretty sure I'd look like Brad Pitt in *Seven Years in Tibet*, but even more manly."

"Let me know how that works out for you." Scott lifted his *World's Bestest Uncle* mug back to his lips and slurped.

Lucas tipped back and eyed the congealed food on the dishes littering almost every surface. Including a half-eaten bowl of cereal, which he couldn't even remember starting. Gross.

"So." Scott placed his mug down.

"So." Lucas walked to the counter and dumped the bowl into the sink, turning on the tap and letting the stream wash away gluggy rice crispies and semi-fermented milk.

"What happened?"

"I've been offered a job by Brad Shipman." He almost did a double take at his own words. That had not been what he was planning to say.

Scott's brow wrinkled. "Should I know who that is?"

Lucas shrugged. "No, but he's a bit of a big deal in radio land."

"What's the job?" Scott tipped back so he was balancing on two chair legs.

"A show in LA."

The front two legs of Scott's chair landed back on the floor with a thud. "Wow." His brother kept his face in neutral. "So what are you thinking?"

"It's complicated. I mean it's a great opportunity, but it would mean leaving you guys and . . ." He trailed off, something stopping him before he told his brother about what else it would require.

Scott's gaze probed his face and he opened his mouth to say something, then closed it.

"What? So what do you think?"

Scott leaned forward. "Well, of course we would miss you a lot, but you have to decide what is the right thing for you."

"That doesn't help."

His brother pushed his chair back. "Good, I didn't want to. This is one thing you have to decide for yourself."

"Thanks."

His brother gestured around them. "So now how about you tell me what's really going on. I'm assuming something went wrong with Rachel."

He was sure the taste in his mouth was mighty similar to the curdled milk he'd just poured away. "She was a fraud."

"Rachel?"

He nodded. Unable to even say her name.

"What happened?"

He stacked the bowl on the counter and emptied two glasses of water down the drain. A bitter laugh left his lips. "I told her I was crazy about her. That I wanted a chance at something with her. And in return—" Ripping open the dishwasher door, he tipped the two glasses into the rack. "In return, she told me she and Donna are just a couple of cons."

"You've lost me."

Lucas turned, leaned against the cupboard, and ran his hand through his still damp hair. "Well, big bro, turns out that Dr. Donna isn't Dr. Donna, she's just a front. Rachel is the one who writes the books."

Scott's face creased for a few seconds while he processed this. "So Rachel writes the books, but everyone thinks Donna does because she's the one who does all the talk shows and stuff."

"Well, that and they're in *her* name."

"Gotcha." Scott leaned back in his chair, hands folded behind his neck, looking completely unperturbed.

"'Gotcha'? I tell you that America's number one relationship coach is a complete and total double-life-living fraud and all you've got to say is 'gotcha'?"

"Nope. Unless I missed something, you just told me that Dr. Donna has a ghostwriter. And I may be just a small-time farmer from Wisconsin, but I'm pretty sure none of those *Duck Dynasty* people wrote their own books. The second thing I have to say is, why does this result in you going into hibernation, eating junk food and pouting like a three-year-old?"

How could his brother, of all people, not get it? "Because I made an idiot of myself. I told this woman I loved her and it turns out she's been taking me for a ride. Rachel even called in to my show pretending to be Donna. Playing everyone for fools. Just like . . ." His words trailed off.

"Just like Dad." Scott said the words with understanding, but not with agreement.

"Your words, not mine." Lucas busied himself stacking the dishwasher.

"Did you give her a chance to explain herself? Why she did it?"

"Her father was drunk, got hit by a car, brain damaged. She did it to pay for his care."

"Oh. So she's nothing like Dad, then."

"What?"

"Seriously, Luc. The two are nothing alike. Our father cheated on Mom, had a second family, emptied the bank accounts, and then took off, leaving Mom to raise us on the poverty line."

"But—"

"Not finished." Scott held up a roughened hand. "Meanwhile, Rachel lives a lie in order to pay for the care for a guy who doesn't sound like he was exactly the world's best dad to start with. Yeah, sounds like the two of them are real alike."

"You don't get it."

"What? I wasn't there too when Dad walked out? I didn't quit school before graduation so Mom didn't have to get a *third* job to put food on the table?" Scott pushed back his chair. "Seriously, Luc, I love you, but sometimes you need to get over yourself. Give me a call when you're ready to behave like a grown-up."

He slammed the door on the way out. Like he hadn't been the one to barge in uninvited in the first place.

Lucas went to pick up the laundry he'd brought downstairs. The holey gray sweatpants collapsed like a pile of cobwebs in his hands. Nope, nothing could save these babies. Time to go. He opened the kitchen cupboard and stuffed them in the trash.

Needed to get over himself? Whatever. Just because Scott was a big softy who cried watching *Terminator 2*.

He did have to get out of his funk, though. He'd been played. No point sitting around feeling sorry for himself like the Packers had lost the Super Bowl.

Grabbing his phone off the countertop, he plugged it into the charger. He hadn't even realized it had gone flat at some point in his self-imposed sulkathon.

The screen tumbled and then lit up with a list of missed calls. Lacey, Lacey, Donna, Brad, Brad, Rachel, Scott, Brad, Ethan, Rachel, Brad, Brad. His stomach clenched. What was he going to do?

He hadn't spoken to any of them. The only communication he'd had was a text message to Donna to say he was out of all of it. The tour. The book. He didn't even know if the shows had gone on without him or if they'd conjured up a reason to cancel them.

He might not ever want to see Rachel again, but did he hate her enough to destroy her? And Donna?

He tried to pace, but his socks stuck to the linoleum, issuing up a slurping sound as they unpeeled with every hobbled step he took. The money. The dream. Living in LA. Actually, that didn't really appeal at all. He'd have to see if he could negotiate to stay in Madison, at least until they knew if the show was going to get wings or flop.

But then there was Brad. *Urgh.* Did he really want to be beholden to someone who made his skin crawl? And that was presumably him at his most charming.

But syndication. The opportunity to reach hundreds of thousands more people. To be something a little different. He had enjoyed himself on tour. Even if he hadn't exactly enthusiastically signed up for it.

Scott and Grace could pay off the loans they'd taken out over the ranch. Afford better, more cutting-edge, fertility treatment. Joey might finally get his little brother or sister.

His phone flickered to life on the countertop, vibrating across the surface until it skated close to the edge. He didn't even have to look at the screen to know who it was. It was a sign.

The book deal was off the table. He didn't owe Rachel or Donna anything. But he owed it to Scott and Grace to do everything he could for them.

"Hello." He had to contort himself to get the phone to his ear.

"Lucas! I was getting worried my favorite host had gone off reservation on me! What's going on? I heard the last two *Feelings and Football* events were cancelled." Brad's attempt was jovial, but there was definitely an edge running underneath.

"I just had something come up and needed to come back home. Nothing for you to worry about."

"Excellent, excellent."

Man, this was awkward; he was half kneeling, neck contorted. Lucas squinted at his battery bar—2 percent—nope, no chance he could take it off charge. He stabbed the speaker phone key and put it back on the counter.

Deep breath, Lucas. You're the one in the right. America deserves to know the truth. "So, I've—"

"So how's that cute little assistant? I saw that photo of the two of you online. I'm assuming all the secrets have come out now in your pillow talk. Or has there not been much talking?" Brad's accompanying chuckle was pure poison.

Lucas stood. Socks glued to the sticky floor. He did not just say that. He. Did. Not. Just. Say. *That*. "Excuse me?"

"What was her name? Raquel? Rochelle?"

"Rachel." Lucas corrected Brad before he even thought about it.

"Rachel! That's it! Man, those were some killer legs. I bet between the sheets—"

Lucas's finger darted out and stabbed the loudspeaker off, bringing the room to blessed silence. He wanted to rip his ears off. Unwind the last minute and unhear every syllable out of Brad's mouth. He felt violated just being in the same room as the guy's voice.

What was he thinking? How could he have possibly thought that anything would be worth having to work for this scumbag? And to hand over Rachel and Donna to be publicly crucified by him?

He picked up his phone, threw it out his front door, then sank to the floor, folding his knees into his chest. *God, forgive me*. He had been so stupid. So blinded by chasing his dream and the money, he'd almost been prepared to sell out at any cost to get it.

It took him a few seconds to realize he'd just made his first request to the Almighty since his mother died and he'd stopped asking God for anything.

- *31* -

Rachel had been to one funeral in her entire life. A depressing, dreary occasion that maybe fifty people attended and lasted less than an hour. She'd survived thanks to sedatives, while her father hadn't even tried to hide the hip flask he'd taken regular slugs from.

Cam's funeral couldn't have been more opposite. Hundreds of people. So many they'd had to set up an overflow hall. Everyone in bright colors, on order of Libby and Anna. The tributes alone went for almost two hours. And Anna somehow in the middle of it all, holding firm under more weight than Rachel thought it was possible for one person to bear.

The whole thing had left her feeling disoriented. She'd steeled herself for heartbreak, but it was the undercurrent of hope that had left her floundering. The pastor talking about eternal life like he actually believed it.

Rachel pushed her feet against Anna's porch boards, using the leverage to rock the swing back and forth. Lifting her feet, she savored the breeze whooshing past her calves. She grasped her teacup and watched as the remnants of the tea inside swished around.

Next to her, Lacey rocked in a chair. Hair pulled back in a tight bun, eyes with black shadows underneath. "Have you heard from Lucas?"

"No. I doubt I ever will." It had been four days. Lucas hadn't returned any of her calls, which had gone straight to voicemail. Both of the final shows had had to be cancelled. Max was trying to hold the book deal option open just in case Lucas needed a few days to cool off, but she'd told him there was no point. She'd driven him away.

You're just like him. The accusation rolled through her head as if on repeat. Taunting her. There hadn't been time to process the revelation during their scorched-earth-style battle, but now the words, and the storm of repulsion and contempt in his eyes as he said them, haunted her.

But it would fade. She'd never been married to Lucas. Had a child with him. Unlike Anna, who now had to navigate the rest of her life without her husband. She'd had to buy another freezer to hold all the meals that had shown up. She and Libby would be eating lasagna for months. Yesterday, more worker ants from the church had shown up. Cleaned the house from top to bottom. Taken care of the yard and garden. Some teenage boy had told Anna he was going to mow her lawn every other week for the next year.

It was almost enough to restore Rachel's faith in humanity. It certainly didn't look anything like the angry protesting, picketing Christians who popped up in the news with monotonous regularity.

"Do you think it's true, Lace?"

"What's that?" Lacey's hands twitched. Like she didn't know what to do with her fingers without her phone in them.

Rachel shrugged. "God. Heaven. All of it."

Lacey considered the question for a long second. "No." She said the word softly. "But I'm really glad that Anna does."

"Here you are." Anna stepped out onto the porch. "Scoot over." She yawned as she sat down. "Sorry. I'm exhausted."

Rachel shifted farther to the left and Anna settled in beside her. After a couple of seconds, she pushed her feet against the porch boards, keeping the swing rocking in perfect rhythm.

"Gloss?" Anna offered her a small tube.

"Thanks." Rachel swiped some across her lips, then passed it back. "It was a beautiful service."

Anna closed her eyes and leaned back. "Pastor Dave did a great job. I know it must have been hard for him."

Hard for him? What about her? The woman who'd just had to bury her husband? Been left with a little girl to raise alone? "How do you do it?"

"God." That was it. No explanations, no preaching. Just one word.

"Really?" Rachel couldn't stop the skepticism that leached into her voice.

"I get that may sound a little hokey to you, but the truth is that if it weren't for Him, I wouldn't be rocking in a porch swing with you, I'd be sedated. Or possibly in a psych ward somewhere."

"You really believe that?" *Really? Now is a good time to grill someone about her spiritual beliefs? She's just been made a widow at barely thirty. Let her find her comfort wherever works.*

Beside her Lacey just watched, silent.

"I *know* it, Rach. Don't get me wrong. Most of the time I can't breathe, because it feels like I can't shove the air past the shards of my heart. And I have a little girl who doesn't have her daddy anymore." A lone tear meandered down her cheek. "And I will probably never understand why God let him fall. Or not make him land any other way. But I know that when nothing makes sense and life is as hard as it's ever been, God is even more present in the middle of all the brokenness. Because Jesus changes everything."

"I wish I could believe that." For the first time in years it was true.

Anna's hand closed over hers. "Faith is a lot like love. It's a big, scary leap that requires you to hold nothing back, throw yourself off the precipice and believe you'll be caught."

"I tend to run away from precipices."

Anna yawned and settled her head on Rachel's shoulder, her curls tickling the small space where her scarf didn't quite cover her neck. "Is that what happened with Lucas?"

Rachel mulled her answer. "Something like that."

"Can you fix it?"

"I don't think so. I . . . I kept something from him, something big, and I don't think he'll ever forgive me for it."

"But you told him the truth?"

"About that, yes."

"Did you tell him you love him?"

"No."

"Well then . . ." It came out like a little sigh. "You should tell him the whole truth. You might be surprised."

"How can I, when he isn't even returning—"

A purr from Anna, followed by a snort. She'd fallen asleep.

"My calls."

- 32 -

"*H*ey." A week later, Anna opened her front door and stepped aside. "Come on in." Her damp hair trailed water patches across her shoulders and her T-shirt and sweatpants had clearly seen better days.

"I bring supplies." Rachel held up her grocery bag containing Anna's favorite apple pie and ice cream.

Anna peeked inside and smiled. "I love you."

Rachel stepped over the vestibule and found herself in a hallway lined with photos on both walls. She must have walked through it the day of the funeral, but it was all a blur.

She paused and looked at a picture that must have been taken just after Libby was born. In it, Cam stared down at a beaming Anna, the only sign of Libby the tip of a tiny nose peeking above the swaddle of blankets.

"What's it like? To have someone love you that much?" The words just slipped out. "I'm sorry."

Anna laid a hand on her arm, fingers curling around her

elbow. "It's fine. I'd rather talk about him than have people not mention him, like they're afraid I'll fall apart if they acknowledge his existence."

Lifting the photo off the wall, Anna's fingers danced lightly over the surface. "No matter what, I had eight years with a guy who made me happier than I knew was possible. Which is more than a lot of people ever have in a lifetime."

The parade of memories marching down the hall overwhelmed Rachel. What would it be like to have even a tenth of them?

What did she have? Nothing. She'd betrayed the one guy she'd ever loved. And when she didn't deliver a book in less than two months, she would have to return her half of their substantial advance. Eventually her father would have to be moved to another care facility. The magnitude of her failure threatened to overwhelm her.

"'Achel!" Little arms wrapped around her knees and she shook off her melancholy to swing a pink-pajama-clad Libby into her arms.

"Hey, angel. Whatcha doing?"

"We're having sleepover day because we ran out of clothes."

Anna tousled her daughter's hair. "Thanks for that, honey."

"That sounds like an excellent idea. I wish I'd known—I would've brought my pajamas."

Libby regarded her jeans and sweater. "I know! You can use some of Mommy's."

Rachel looked at Anna, who laughed and shrugged. "Works for me, if you don't mind slumming it in an old pair."

"Sounds perfect."

Two hours later, three loads of washing were in various

stages of the laundry process and Libby peered over a dessert bowl that was almost bigger than her head.

Her elbow poked straight to heaven as she dug into her pie and spooned it into her rosebud mouth. Licking the melted ice cream off the back of her spoon, she smacked her lips, then burped.

"Libby Evangeline!"

Rachel pressed her lips together so she didn't ruin Anna's parenting moment by laughing.

Libby's bottom lip wobbled and her eyes filled. "Daddy would say, 'Libby, Libby, you're so silly.'"

Anna put her spoon down and held out her arms. "Come here, baby."

Her daughter scrambled off her chair and flung herself into her mother's lap. Arms folding, Anna pulled her close and pressed a kiss into her copper curls.

"I miss him. Why didn't he wake up?" The broken little girl's voice was Rachel's undoing.

Smooshed pie crust and melted ice cream swam in front of her face. Who was she to be privy to such an intimate moment?

"I'll be back in a sec." Anna stood, Libby curled tightly in her arms like an early rosebud, tears glistening at the tips of her long lashes.

"Okay." Rachel whispered the word, not wanting to interrupt the sacred moment.

Anna disappeared through the doorway, a few seconds later her footsteps echoing up the wooden stairs.

Gathering up the dishes from the table, Rachel scraped the remains into the trash then rinsed them, stacking the plates beside the sink. Pausing, she leaned against the stainless-steel sink and stared into the inky night.

During the afternoon, a pain had worked its way through her like a phantom and wrapped around her heart like a vice. Here she was, on what was supposed to be some sort of new-widow mercy mission, and instead she was . . . *jealous.*

The word jarred in her brain. It was ridiculous. Jealous of someone whose husband had just died, leaving her with a small, bereft child to raise alone. What was wrong with her?

She stared at her reflection. "Get a grip, Rachel." She had no right to feel sorry for herself, let alone envious of Anna and Libby. She had chosen this life. She *deserved* this life. She'd known better than to let herself fall for Lucas, yet she had. What did she expect? Happily-ever-after?

Wrenching the door of the dishwasher open, dishes and cutlery clattered against each other as she jammed them between the already resident dirty dishes.

"Want a coffee?" Anna wandered past, hair now up in a high ponytail, and pulled two mugs out of a candy-cane-pink cupboard. She hadn't been joking when she'd said the kitchen repaint was a disaster. It looked like someone had put a live grenade in a hot-pink paint can and closed the door on their way out.

"I'm fine, thanks." Rachel shoved the top rack back but it refused to go in, catching. "Come on." She tried again with more force, but it just bounced back again.

Anna paused and surveyed the scene in front of her. "Whatever you are, 'fine' is not it. So would you like some kind of beverage in your hand while you tell me about it?"

Rachel blew a breath out between her teeth. She couldn't exactly lie to Anna, not when the big guy upstairs practically sat on her shoulder. "Can you do cocoa?"

Anna beamed a beatific smile. "Can I do cocoa? You're not allowed to leave the hospital with a baby if you can't do cocoa."

"That would be great." Rachel bent down, shoved her sleeve up to her elbow, and plumbed the depths of the dishwasher, fingers grasping for the obstruction.

Anna moved around the kitchen, opening and closing drawers and containers. Teaspoons clinking in mugs, water pouring.

Where was it? Getting down on her hands and knees. Rachel peered into the bowels of the machine. Ah, there it was. A spatula had fallen halfway down the back. Twisting sideways, her fingers inched forward until she could tug it free.

"So whatever happened with Lucas?"

Rachel's head jerked up, connecting with the front edge of the top rack. "Ow!" Extracting herself, she landed on the floor on her rear end, legs under the open door.

Anna leaned down, poured powder into the dispenser, and closed it in one fluid motion.

She looked down at Rachel and grinned. "Would you like to talk about it on the kitchen floor? I have spent a fair amount of time down there myself. Though I have to say, I do offer some comfier options."

"Glad you think it's so funny." Rachel grabbed the side of the counter and hauled herself up.

Anna laughed. "If you could have seen yourself with your butt hanging out of my dishwasher you would have thought it was funny too. Come on." She handed Rachel a green mug and padded across the floor toward the den.

Rachel froze, stomach wrenching. This wasn't the plan. Sure, she'd known there might be a deep and meaningful discussion, but it was supposed to be Anna wringing tissues and crying. Her, the supporting act. Doing whatever it was that you did when a friend becomes a widow.

All of her self-preservation instincts were screaming at her to escape. Padding through the doorway and down the hall, she peered into the den.

Anna sat on a well-worn brown leather couch, legs curled underneath her, mug clasped between two hands.

"You know, it's late, and you've had a long day." Rachel took a sip of the hot, sweet cocoa. "I should just finish this up and go."

"No. You should sit down, and we're going to talk about what's going on." Anna gave her a look saturated in determination and gestured to the spot beside her. "Sit."

Rachel's feet propelled her into the room, cocoa sloshing. What was she doing? She didn't talk. Not about things that mattered. She wouldn't even know how. Perching on the edge of the cushion, she focused on the bookcase in front of her. Authors she'd never even heard of lined the shelves. No surprise, since most of the books seemed to have "God" in the titles.

"So." Anna's voice was soft. "What happened?"

Rachel shrugged, kept looking straight ahead. "It just didn't work out."

"Why not?"

Because nothing in her life ever did. She opened her

mouth to tell Anna he wasn't interested. "Because I lied to him. He hasn't spoken to me since." Cocoa spilled from the mug and coated her hand. She pulled a tissue from the box on the table next to her and swiped at it. What had she done? Now she was going to have to come up with more lies to explain the truth.

"Did you tell him why? Did you tell him you're sorry?"

"I tried, but he wouldn't accept my apology. I broke his trust. For Lucas, if you do that it's over."

"I'm sorry."

"Me too."

Anna settled back. "I want you to be happy. But I think that's more complicated than whether or not Lucas and you ever work things out."

She was right. "I don't know how to forgive myself for that night. Or him."

She wasn't sure which she found the most unforgivable: the joints that had started as "high class" and degraded to the scummiest, slimiest pits of depravity toward the end, or the fact that it had been her mother's life insurance that had paid for it all.

If there was a God, He was probably the one who deserved credit for the fact that she'd managed never to experience anything worse than a lecher pawing her behind as she waded through the worst of humanity trying to find her father. Occasionally Anna or Lacey with her.

"What about Lacey and me?" Anna took a cautious sip as she softly asked the question.

Rachel was struck by an overwhelming sense of loss as she stared at her friend. Ten years. She'd missed out on almost a decade of Anna's friendship because she'd unfairly blamed her for what happened that night. And Lacey.

She hadn't been around for her meeting Cam. Getting engaged. Married. Her pregnancy. Libby being born. Any of it. And that was just Anna. Lacey was a closed book to her too. She didn't know much more about her than a prospective client would reading her online bio.

"Rach?" Anna reached out and touched her knee.

"I'm sorry. It wasn't your fault. I know I blamed you, but he was my responsibility. My father was left on the side of the road to die because I wasn't there for him. Now he exists in some kind of limbo land. What's forgivable about that?"

"You didn't make your father go to a bar. Or drink. Or walk home instead of catching a cab. You weren't responsible for him. Entirely the opposite. *He* was responsible for *you*. And he let you down every day."

Rachel was back at that night. The emptiness of his filthy, run-down house. The pouring rain as she drove through the streets searching. The first glimpse of what looked like a trash bag in the gutter. The crashing realization it was a person. The screeching of her brakes, stopping the car in the middle of the street. The look on his face when she reached him, picked up his head, and cradled it in his arms. His mouth opening as she leaned in close to hear his words.

"The last thing he ever said to me was, 'You never could do anything right.'" Since Anna was religious now, she left out the expletive he'd included between the last two words. She shook her head. "And the funny thing is, even if he'd known that would be the last thing he ever said, I'm pretty sure the only thing that would have changed is he probably would have thrown in a few more curses for good measure."

"Ouch." Anna breathed the word out.

Ouch. That pretty much summed it up. One four-letter word that encompassed the last decade of her life spent trying to assuage the bottomless pit of guilt that consumed everything she touched.

Her fingers rubbed circles into her temples. "It's been almost ten years. I keep thinking that one day it will magically get better, but it doesn't, and I don't know what to do."

"Why don't you start from the beginning? Tell me everything about Donna and Lucas and your dad. Because it sounds all intertwined, but I don't know how."

Once she told Anna the truth she couldn't take it back. Might lose their fledgling relationship. But she was so tired of pretending, and everything she'd done it for was gone anyway. What did she have to lose at this point?

So she told her. Just let everything spill out and land where it may. If they were going to be real friends again, she wanted there not to be any secrets. She didn't leave anything out, including the fact that Lucas had refused to return her calls since she'd left.

"So now I have six weeks to turn in a book that I haven't even started. And if I don't, then we're in breach of contract and have to give the advance back. And if I have to do that, then I eventually won't be able to afford Sunhaven. I could never forgive myself if I have to put him into one of the awful places that Medicaid will pay for."

"Rach." Anna leaned forward, grabbing her hands. "You were his daughter. He should have been the one looking out for you, protecting you. It wasn't your job to babysit him, be his chauffeur, or scrape him off a bar. What happened that night was not your fault. The fact that you've managed to keep him in Sunhaven for as long as you have is amazing. He's in a vegetative state. So whether he's there or somewhere else, it matters a whole lot more to you than it does to him. And until you figure out how to forgive yourself, everything else will be like dust."

A tear slipped down Rachel's face. Slid down her cheek. Anna's voice only echoed what Donna had been telling her for years, but for some reason, this time, it connected.

"I don't know how."

"Ask God. He'll always help."

She looked at Anna. Took in the sincerity in her face. Six months ago she would have tossed her words off like a sweater in August. Now they sat, until she found herself mentally shrugging her shoulders. Why not? It wasn't as if anything else had worked.

Rachel burrowed her head in her hands. "I don't know what to do."

"Here's the thing. No matter how hard it is, no matter how much it hurts, no matter how many ugly layers of lies, you have to deal with it. The truth will always set you free."

Maybe it would, but it could also get her sued.

- 33 -

The truth will always set you free. The words vibrated in Rachel's head as she unlocked the door to her condo the next morning, kicked off her flats, and switched on the light.

She shrugged off her coat, tossed it over the back of a chair, and pulled out her phone. Max had called while she'd been talking to Anna and she'd ignored it, along with his voicemail.

Tapping on the screen, she put the message on speaker. "Hey, Rach, it's Max." He cleared his throat. "So I've reviewed the ideas you sent me."

She'd only just sent them yesterday afternoon. A mishmash of false starts and premises that couldn't even carry a chapter, let alone a book. She'd known they were awful, hadn't even bothered to hope she was wrong.

"So, um, I see what you mean about them being a bit rough. I mean, they're fine. No, good, they're good. I'm sure we can find something to work with from them. They're just missing that something your writing usually has. I have to admit that I am hoping that once Lucas has a chance to cool off, he'll be willing to reconsider the book deal. Anyway, I've talked to Kelly and . . ." His voice sort of skipped, jumped, then crashed into a gaping moment of silence. "Um, I'm sorry, it's not great, kiddo. She said she had to clear it with some higher powers and when she called back, all they would give was an extra month. And that was really begrudging. She said they were adamant about holding to the release date."

Her phone hit the counter. A month! That was even worse than a flat-out no. All it did was delay doomsday by thirty days.

He was still talking. "Maybe just take a week or so. Get away. Take some time to get a fresh perspective. If this is going to be the last one, then I just think you owe it to yourself to exit with something you'll be proud of."

Something she'd be proud of. She couldn't care less about that. If she didn't deliver, they would ask for the advance back.

Pulling her MacBook out of her satchel, she flicked the lid up and opened a new document. Stared at the white screen, flashing cursor taunting her.

Tilting her head back, she surveyed her ceiling. *Maybe? Don't be so stupid, Rachel. Got a better idea?* Silence.

She clasped and unclasped her hands. Looked at the floor. Was she supposed to kneel? This was ridiculous. "Okay." She directed her words to a spider web that traversed the corner above the front door. "I don't know if You exist, and it's really nothing to me whether You do or not. But I hope You do for Anna's sake. And I know You don't owe me anything, and I'm not going to make any stupid promises like if You help me out here I'm all in. But I'm here, and I really need to write a book, and You're pretty much my last chance. So . . . okay, then."

Anything? The cursor still taunted her. The page was still blank. She was still stuck. No buzzy vibes she'd heard some televangelist harping on about. Nothing was any different than thirty seconds before.

Anna's words repeated in her head like a catchy pop song lyric. *The truth will always set you free.* What would it be like, just for once, to tell the truth? The whole truth. Words appeared on the screen, her fingers racing ahead of her brain.

> I was six the first time my father told me I'd been a mistake. I didn't even understand what he meant. Having no knowledge of the birds and the bees, it had never entered my mind that some children were wanted and others arrived in their parents' lives an unwelcome intruder, besting all obstacles in the path to their existence.

She leaned back and absorbed the memory. Her sin that night had been forgetting to collect the mail. Her father had crouched down to her level and pinched her chin between his thumb and forefinger. She'd steeled herself, ordered herself not to cry when his hand carved a red path of rage across her legs. But the stinging slap hadn't come. Instead he'd looked deep into her eyes, his face so close that when he spoke, spit rained down across her face as he told her very softly that she was a mistake and should never have been born. That there hadn't been a single day in her whole useless life that he was glad she had.

Her fingers found the keys again and words started spilling onto the screen.

My mother didn't believe in abortion. Nothing quite like knowing your place in the world is the result of pure dumb luck. Landing in the womb of someone who didn't really want you, but wouldn't get rid of you.

She paused again, the words burning her eyes. Was she being unfair to her mother? It was not that it wasn't true, but she knew her mother had loved her and done the best she could. Despite the resentful, brooding presence that filled the house.

Placing her fingers back on the keyboard, she sucked in a deep breath and started to type.

Six days later, Rachel's eyes stung as though she'd run a marathon through a sandstorm. Her neck and shoulders were locked, muscles screaming, as she'd been crouched over her laptop for days on end. She ran a hand through her hair. *Ick.* Stringy, greasy strands swam past her fingers. Her screen blinked *4:32 a.m.* She clicked over it to check the day. Sunday.

When had she last had a shower? She lifted an arm up and took a whiff. *Argh.* Her stomach rumbled, reminding her that a shower wasn't the only thing that had been missing lately.

The words had tumbled out, falling on top of each other. Her fingers stumbled over themselves trying to keep up. Spell check was going to have a meltdown trying to make sense of it all.

The cursor in the middle of the blank page blinked at her. Waiting for her to finish it. Her part, anyway.

Her hands hovered over the keyboard. Mind trying to come up with the right words. The only words that hadn't landed on the page like someone had already written them and she was just filling in the lines.

She hit seven keys. *For L.G.* Looked at the words. Deleted them. Any semiliterate tabloid reporter would be able to work out what they meant. She had done enough without unleashing the never-satisfied paparazzi on him. Her fingers drummed on the surface of her desk for a few seconds. What was something that would have meaning for only the two of them?

She cast her mind back through their conversations, trying to ignore her heart constricting as she played back some of the best moments of her life. *Gone.* Finally she got it and typed out the words, fingers heavy on the keys. A token gesture, all for nothing. He was so repulsed by what she and Donna had done, even if by some miracle it was published, he'd never read it.

God . . . A prayer hovered, but she cut it short, refused to allow herself to think it, let alone ask the Almighty for any more assistance. She hadn't even stopped writing long enough to unravel the implications of His appearing to have answered her pathetic, half-hearted request for help the week before.

It seemed too improbable, *impossible*, to believe. But deep inside she knew it was more than a fluke coincidence that she hadn't been able to write anything for eight months and minutes after asking for help, words had been pouring out of her.

She pushed back her chair and strode to the kitchen. The fridge was a tomb of rancid milk and shriveled produce. The cupboards were persuaded to part with the dregs of a packet of crackers, a half jar of peanut butter, and four semi-stale Oreos.

Dipping the crackers into the jar, she chewed and swallowed, the taste barely registering. It was all about calories, an attempt to prevent her cotton jammies, once well fitting, from slithering to the floor and puddling around her ankles.

Tucking the boxes under her arm, she grabbed a glass of water and wandered back to her desk.

Her phone blinked. Donna. Three words. *All done. Sent.*

She clicked open her emails and waited for five days' worth to unravel down her screen. Finally, Donna's popped up at the top and she clicked on it.

You know I'm not a writer. So you have to promise to fix it.

Opening the document attached, Rachel started scanning the first page. Her aunt telling her part of their deception, in all its ugliness, for the whole world to know.

After a couple of pages, she didn't know whether to laugh or cry. Whether she knew it or not, Donna was a great writer. Oh the irony.

Putting the two documents side by side, she set to work copying and pasting Donna's chapters into the manuscript. A shower would have to wait. The truth had already waited long enough.

- 34 -

Lucas flung open his front door and slammed it shut again. "Lucas, open the door." Scott's voice was determined, no-nonsense.

"I will to you, but never to him!" Lucas yelled the words, hoping their force knocked his father straight off his porch and back into whatever hole he'd crawled out of.

"Lucas, if you don't open the door right now, you're not taking Joey out this weekend."

Lucas wrenched the door open so hard it barreled into the wall. A cracking sound let him know he'd be digging the handle out of plaster. He seared his unflinching brother with a glare. "Didn't know you had it in you to be so low."

"And I thought you were smart enough not to let him ruin the rest of your life." Scott jerked his thumb back toward their father, who stood behind him, weathered face unreadable.

Scott couldn't have come up with something with more tinder in it if he'd tried.

"You're deluded." Lucas dropped a curse for effect, but neither man even blinked.

"You want to have this conversation yelling at each other on the porch, little bro? Because I'm more than happy to."

Lucas stepped back and Scott, then his father, crossed the threshold. He had lost his mind. What we he doing letting *him* into his house?

Scott paused under the arched doorway to the den. "You don't look so good. Have you been on a bender or something?"

He wished. "No. I haven't had a single drink. As much as I would desperately like to."

Lucas crossed his arms and stood in the doorway. Nothing could be between him and the exit. "What is *he* doing here?" He didn't even look at his father—who now sat in his favorite armchair—as he barked the words.

Scott settled into the sofa, making himself comfortable. "He's here because you need to forgive him, and clearly you have some things to get off your chest in order to do that."

"I have nothing to say to him."

"Son——" The word was tentative at best.

A sliver of something pierced his conscience. *No. Don't let him get to you. Remember what he did. He could be dead for all you care.*

For the first time in years, the familiar words held a hollow ring. His eyes trailed sideways to where his father's boots scuffed the carpet.

"We need to talk." This time his father's tone was stronger. His chair creaked as he stood.

Lucas turned his head at the sound, palmed his hair, and clasped his hands behind his back.

"Leaving you boys and your mom was the worst thing I ever did. And I wish every second of every day that I could take it back. I would give anything, do anything, to change what I did. But I can't."

The fury that had simmered inside Lucas for almost twenty years exploded. His feet took him across the room until he stood less than a yard away from his father. "Do you know what you did to us? Mom cried every day for a year. Begged God to bring your lying, cheating carcass back. We had to live in a trailer. She worked two jobs to make ends meet. She died because of you. She got sick and—" His voice broke and he spun around, picked up the lightweight coffee table in front of Scott, and threw it against the opposite wall.

The table gouged the wall, then hit the floor, bouncing once before settling on its top.

He shook his head at his father, who still stood, face sagging under the weight of accusation. "We were a family and you left. And now you're back? For what?"

"I want to ask for your forgiveness."

Lucas laughed. A harsh, scornful bark that echoed around the room. "You have got to be joking. Are you in AA or something? Working your twelve steps? My name on your list of people to make amends to?"

"Lucas." He'd almost forgotten Scott was even in the room. "Hear him out."

His father sat down, kneading his hands in front of him. "You don't have to ever see me again. I know I don't deserve to know you. And I—" His voice stalled and he brushed a hand across his cheek. "And you're right: it's my fault your mom is gone. But please, Lucas, I want you to have a good life, the best one, and as long as you hate me, you're never going to be free."

Lucas slumped down on the sofa next to his brother. "You know who you sound like? Dr. Donna." He fisted his hands. "Turns out she's a liar too."

"People make mistakes. Sometimes big, ugly ones that can never be undone. But please don't throw away the woman that you love because you hate me."

Lucas turned on his brother. "You told him about Rachel? How dare you!"

"Because you love her, and you've walked away because you can't move past him."

"She lied to me. She deceived me. She used me. And not just me—everyone! And you're sitting here wondering why I don't want to have anything to do with her?"

Scott pushed himself up off the couch. "Yeah. Because if it weren't for him, you might have some perspective. Like the fact that her mother died. Sound familiar? And her father turned out to be a loser. Déjà vu at all? And his farewell gift was to load her up with medical bills that she had to contort her life into a lie to pay for. Any other guy might have had a bit of compassion, but not you. No, poor Rachel has committed the unforgivable Lucas crime of not being perfect."

How could he ever think his brother knew him? "That's not it at all."

"Really? Because the only other option I can see is that you're just as big a hypocrite as you say she is. You who went on tour with Dr. Donna and handed out advice to everyone else all about forgiveness and second chances. Sounds like a perfect match to me. She writes her lies, you transmit yours. Or are you just jealous that she makes more money off hers?"

"Out." Lucas launched up from the sofa and marched to the front door. "Both of you. Get out."

- 35 -

"Are you sure you want to do this?" Max turned, checking one last time.

"I'm sure." The words echoed in the elevator, bouncing off the walls.

"It's going to get ugly."

"Yup." It wasn't that Rachel didn't want to say more; she was just busy clamping her teeth together to stop them from juddering.

Donna reached over and squeezed her hand.

The doors pinged, sliding open to reveal the plush reception area of the president's office. Floor-to-ceiling windows took up one side, reveling in the view of New York's skyline. In the center of the room sat a coiffed middle-aged receptionist at a pristine desk. From the look of her perfect nails, she didn't do a lot of typing.

Rachel stepped out of the elevator, feet plunging into luxurious carpet. She lingered behind Blake, their lawyer, enjoying her last few minutes of anonymity before everything hit the fan.

"Max, Donna—welcome, welcome." Randolph himself strode out from the boardroom before the mannequin even had a chance to open her mouth. Shaking Max's hand, he dropped a kiss on Donna's cheek. His eyes skated across Blake and never even made it to Rachel. "Please, come through." He gestured toward the boardroom. "You know you didn't have to come in and hand deliver it, right? We do accept manuscripts by email." He chuckled at his lousy joke.

Walking the plank. This was it. Her last chance to back out. The boardroom swallowed them all in. A huge table with seating for sixteen, dwarfed again by the same windows. The only other time they'd been here had been to sign Donna's last deal.

Only two other seats at the table were taken. Kelly sat in one, suit pressed, hair pulled back in a French knot. Her face was pinched, despite Donna promising the meeting had nothing to do with her. Poor girl.

The seat on Kelly's right was taken up by an older gentleman in an expensive suit. The firm's lawyer, given that he was the only other person requested.

"Can I get you anything? Tea, coffee?" Randolph gestured to the receptionist, who now stood poised at the door.

All four of them demurred, settling themselves in the seats he indicated to his left. Max, Donna, Rachel, and Blake at the end.

Dismissing the woman with a nod, Randolph took the chair at the head of the table, game face on, drumming right hand the only indication he wasn't the one in control of this meeting. "Well then, Max, Donna, what can we do for you? I've checked with all of my departments and everyone has assured me that we've been treating you well." His tone made it clear that anyone who had made a liar out of him would be packing their boxes as soon as they were back in the elevator.

Max cleared his throat and straightened his jacket. "Theo, your team is wonderful, always have been."

The president's face unfolded a little. "Good to hear."

"The reason we've called this meeting is, well—there are two reasons. The first is that Donna won't be signing another contract."

Randolph paled. "We can match whatever another house is offering her. Both in terms of the advance and favorable terms."

"She's not going to be writing any more books. She's going to be retiring."

"Is this true?" Randolph looked at Donna.

"Very. My husband has a horse ranch. I'm looking forward to spending a lot more time with him and a lot less time on planes."

"Well, let's not be too hasty. You said there were two things?"

"Yes. As we know, your father could be slightly unconventional."

Randolph tipped back in his seat, triangulating his fingers in front of him, tilting his head forward as if to say "go on."

"The thing is that when Donna was signed with you . . . oh blast it, just read this." He handed three copies of their original confidentiality agreement to Randolph, who took one and passed the other two on.

"What is this?" Randolph dropped the stapled pieces of paper in front of him.

"It's the confidentiality agreement that Donna and Rachel first signed, to endure over the first, and any subsequent, deals they had with the company."

"Who on earth is Rachel?" Randolph spat her name out as if it tasted bad.

Max nodded down the table. "Rachel is next to Donna. She's her assistant, but, as you'll see, she's a lot more than that. And up front, I'd just like to state that your company was all for this from the beginning."

Across the table Kelly's lips moved as she read the paper, while the company's lawyer was already scanning the final page.

"Jonathan." Randolph turned to his right. "What is this all about?"

The lawyer threw the papers down on the table, whipped his glasses off, and massaged the bridge of his nose. "It would appear that Dr. Donna is not so much an individual as a team."

Understanding was dawning on Kelly's face. No doubt beginning to click as to why Donna insisted book edits be carried out "through" Rachel.

"Excuse me?"

"I'm assuming Max can fill you in on the background, but the confidentiality agreement sets out that while Donna is the front person, so to speak, this Rachel . . . " he glanced at the top page, "Somers is the author."

"The author?" Randolph frowned.

Max intervened. "To put it bluntly, Donna is the face, but Rachel writes the books."

A vein running through Randolph's forehead started to

pulse, a fat finger stabbed inches away from Max's face. "You're sitting here telling me that my bestselling author is this, this . . ." He was on his feet, arms waving, jacket buttons straining to hang on for the ride. "Girl! This had better be your idea of some sick joke, because if it's not, I'm going to sue every last hair off your head."

A cough from his lawyer. Randolph swung around on him. "Don't you dare tell me I can't. I pay you a thousand bucks an hour to tell me that I can!"

His eyes settled on his poor hapless editor. "Did you know about this?"

"No, sir. They were acquired by Jacqui. She—"

"I don't believe you. You're fired! Get out!"

"Theodore, she—"

"Out! Out! Out!" Randolph roared, and Kelly ran for the door. She'd have a miserable few hours until they were able to get to her with the news that not only had they put some money aside for her, but Max had already gotten results on the feelers he'd put out to some publishing contacts.

"Tell me." He thumped back into his seat.

"Well—" Max started, only to be cut off.

"Not you, you." Randolph pointed at Rachel, eyes like razors. "What have you got to say for yourself?"

What did he want from her? An apology for existing? "Yes, I'm her ghostwriter. It's not like all your other big non-fiction authors don't have them."

"Why?"

Rachel's fingers curled around the arms of her chair, held tight. "I started a blog when I was in college. Called it 'Ask Donna.' A post went viral and I got contacted by a couple of publishers interested in whether I wanted to write a book."

Max jumped in. "Long story short, she found me. When the team that was here found out how young she was, there was a view that she wouldn't have any credibility. So Rachel and Donna came up with a proposal: Rachel could still write the books and Donna could do the rest. Your head of marketing agreed."

"Who?" Randolph demanded.

"Not important. Long gone."

"And what do *you* have to say for yourself?" Donna was at the end of the sausage finger this time.

"My ex-husband left me borderline bankrupt and with three boys to raise. I needed the money. And I'm hardly going to apologize for that when it's not like you haven't made millions out of this as well." Donna's voice was as cool as a chocolate Frappuccino.

"How could I not know this? I'm the president of the company!" The vein throbbed; he looked like he was about to have a stroke.

"Well, whoever drafted this was clearly an idiot, because instead of allocating knowledge to the deal to certain positions, they attached it to people. Your father and a couple of others, who I can only assume are gone too?" Jonathan looked to Max for confirmation, who nodded. "Clearly whoever drafted this assumed your father would retire and pass the knowledge on, not keel over dead while still president."

"But surely they"—a finger stabbed in their direction—"had a duty to tell me after my father died, as the new president."

Jonathan sighed. "I need the time to work through this in detail, but it's complicated."

Randolph tilted, spun, and cast his evil eye across the three of them. "So why now? What do you want? More money?"

"Actually, it's the opposite. We're just here to deliver their last book. I know we'd negotiated an extension, but it turns out we didn't need it. Rachel?" Max nodded at her.

Her hands shook as she reached into her bag and pulled out two copies of the completed manuscript, passing them to Max, who handed one to Randolph and pushed the second over the table to his lawyer. "Gentlemen, the final book to complete their current deal. We'll email you a copy, of course."

Randolph looked at the title and did such a dramatic double take, it would have been funny if Rachel wasn't readying herself to dive under the table for cover.

"You want to tell the truth? *Are you insane?*" He yelled the question at such volume, Donna clamped her hands over her ears. "Why? So we all can get sued to kingdom come? No, no, absolutely not. Over my dead body."

"Think about it. There's no need to rush to decisions. Take a few days. Read the book. Have your people read the book. You might be surprised." Max moved as if to push his chair back.

"Think about it? I don't need to think about it! And you!" He pointed at Donna. "Or you." A wave at Rachel. "Whichever of you it is. You owe me a book. A proper Dr. Donna book. Or else give me my advance back."

"I don't think so, Theo. The contract stipulates three books. You're holding the third, and it meets every contractual requirement. While they only get the second half of the advance if you publish it, the first half is theirs. You're welcome to check the contract. I've highlighted the pertinent section for you." Max extracted another piece of paper from his leather folio and slid it across the table, the yellow stripes across a paragraph a third of the way down prominent. This time Max did push his chair back, straightening his lapels as he stood.

Randolph's body coiled as though he was about to lunge at Max over the table, but he managed to keep himself in his chair. "I'm going to get you for this." He included Donna and Rachel in his glare. "All of you. This isn't over."

- 36 -

*L*ucas dropped onto Scott's front porch, the wood creaking underneath him. The front of the house faced the long, dusty driveway he'd just come up, straggling pieces of grass and the occasional wildflower breaking up the brown.

In the distance you could just make out the blur of traffic zooming by on the road leading from Madison to Fitchburg.

He entwined his fingers and propped his thumbs together. The air shimmered before him with early summer heat.

He hadn't seen his brother, or spoken to him, since he'd ejected him and their father from his house last week.

Instead he'd just replayed their conversation over and over. Half of him wishing he'd never let them in, the other half wishing he'd let them stay.

After sleepless nights, lackluster shows, and days of haunted thoughts, he'd finally just gotten into his truck and driven. Knowing he would end up here, with no clue what he was going to say.

Scott made it all sound so easy. Just forgive him. Go find Rachel and tell her everything was okay.

Did he think he didn't want to escape the anger and resentment that twisted around inside him day in and night out? To think of Rachel and remember her smile and her laugh and not her deception. To look at their father and remember someone beyond the guy who built himself a second life and then left them for it.

The porch sagged, followed by his brother settling down beside him. "You planning to sit here all day?"

"Don't know. Maybe."

"Okay." His brother propped his elbows on his knees and crossed his arms. "Want a drink?"

"Sure."

Scott stood, returning a few seconds later with a couple of icy sodas. Cracking his open, he took a couple of gulps, then placed it on the step his feet rested on.

Lucas rolled his behind his hands, then placed it on the back of his neck. Yesterday he'd gone on a long run, resulting in a very sunburnt neck. *Ahhhh.* Condensation trickled down his back, leaving a trail of momentary icy reprieve behind. Moving the can from his neck, he held it against his cheek for a second, then just held it between his hands.

The silence stretched out. Scott serenely drinking his Dr. Pepper, Lucas trying to come up with words.

"How?"

"How what?"

"How did you forgive him?"

Scott paused, contemplating the distance. "It was just after we had Joey. I realized the only person I was hurting with hating him was me. Well, and Grace and Joey as well. I couldn't enjoy Joey because I was consumed with being angry at Dad for being able to hold his son in his arms and just walk away. And he was gone. It wasn't like I knew where he was and I could just call him up and ask him."

"And?"

Scott shrugged. "I just realized I had to let it go. I didn't know how. And part of me didn't even want to. I felt so entitled to hold onto it all. So I just asked God to help me want to."

He'd known there had to be a sermon somewhere in there. But for some reason he didn't feel annoyed, just more resigned. "But how did you do it?"

Scott bounced his empty can from hand to hand. "Every time I thought about him, or started feeling angry or resentful or whatever, I just asked God to help me let it go. To remember that the only thing I could control was who I was with my family, not who he was with us."

Lucas tried to imagine thinking of his father without a well of putrid emotion overflowing. Even trying to imagine it was beyond him. "And if God and I aren't on speaking terms?"

Scott balanced his can on his pointer finger. "Apart from sorting that out? Remind yourself, you're the one losing out here. If you don't forgive him, what he did wins. Dad has his own demons to live with, and I'm pretty sure they haunt him every second of every day. But whether you like it or not, you have a choice whether you let them conquer you too."

"Are you going to keep seeing him?"

"Probably. He's a lonely old man, Luc. One who has paid

a high price for his mistakes. He's estranged from all our half siblings, messed that up as well. I want to give him a chance."

Not that he deserved one. "And what if he disappears again?"

"Better that than living wondering what might have been if I'd let him in." Scott paused, surveying the grass. "You know, Lucas. Forgiving him doesn't make what he did okay; it just means refusing to carry it any longer."

"Do you really think I'm a hypocrite?"

Scott gave him a measured look. "It doesn't matter what I think. What do *you* think?"

"Every time I think of her, all I can think of is how she lied to me. To everyone. Even if I find a way to forgive him, that doesn't fix me and Rachel. I told her stuff, personal stuff, thinking she was Donna. It's like she was the priest in the confessional, all one-way traffic. I don't even know what was real Rachel, what was Rachel pretending to be Donna, and what was all just spin and PR. How do you think of what might have been, when what you knew was all based on deception?"

"Can I tell you what I think?"

"When have you not?"

"All I know is the woman I met that day, she was sweet and funny and genuine, and I'd bet the ranch it wasn't an act. And she really liked my brother. And he had a pretty big thing for her too. Sometimes things really are that uncomplicated; everything else is just baggage."

Lucas crunched his can in his hand. "And sometimes people aren't who you think they are and you're better off leaving them behind."

His words swirled around them. He sighed, shifting his feet on the step. Maybe his brother would get it if he knew what it cost him as well. "I was going to give you the money, you know."

"What money?" His brother didn't sound nearly as interested as he'd expected.

"The signing fee from Brad." He gestured to the land around them. "So you could pay off the rest of your debts, fund more treatment, whatever you needed."

Scott stilled, his jaw working. Finally he got it. Maybe he wouldn't be so free and easy with the forgiveness now.

"Lucas, you know I love you, but you don't know me at all if you thought for a second I would take money that's come from a cretin like Brad Shipman."

What? "But—"

"I can use Google. Tell you what, little bro—why don't you worry about dealing with your own issues, and let me worry about my family. We don't need you to rescue us. I'm the husband and the father here; it's my job, not yours." His brother's tight tone was the one he used only when he was really annoyed.

"Scott, I—"

His brother stood up and dusted off his jeans. "Don't be late for lunch on Sunday. Joey misses you."

Rachel rested her forehead against the cool wood of her front door. A miracle. That was the only way she could describe it. The royalty checks from Randolph were notorious for being late or wrong. It usually took Max weeks to reconcile them.

For the first time ever, one had showed up on time. It hadn't been huge, as *He Wasn't the One that Got Away* was still earning out its advance, but it was enough to buy another couple of months' breathing space at Sunhaven.

Slipping her key in the lock, she turned the handle and stepped into her small hallway. She slid her coat off her shoulders, and it let out a *swish* as it formed a puddle at her feet. She kicked off her shoes, left them where they'd landed, and padded toward the living area. There was an ice-cold Diet Coke in the fridge with her name on it. After today, she might even splurge on take-out for di—

"Ahhhhh!" The piercing scream escaped her mouth before she'd even processed what was in her living room.

Her heart pounded in her chest like a runaway carriage in a western, while her three intruders sat as serene as nuns in a convent.

She knew she shouldn't have given Donna a key.

"That had better not have come out of my fridge." She pointed at the can of soda sitting next to her publicist, a watery ring visible around its base.

"Whoops." Lacey raised an eyebrow and offered it back up. "You can have the rest."

"Thanks, that's very generous of you." She snatched it out of her hand and took a gulp. Since there was nothing stronger in the house, she was going to at least get a caffeine hit before they officially delivered the news.

"So how much?" She directed the question at Max.

"How much what?"

"How much is Randolph suing us for?"

Max pulled his glasses off and made a show of polishing them with his handkerchief. She mentally added another zero to her guess with every circular motion.

She looked at her aunt. Maybe a hint? Nope, Donna's face was inscrutable.

"He's not." Max deigned to speak, but his words made no sense.

"He's not what?"

"Suing us. Any of us. You, Donna, me. None of us. Not that he ever had a legal leg to stand on, but I did wonder a little if that might not stop him."

"What?" Her body melted, caught, by sheer luck, by her sofa. "He's not. Really?"

"Really."

Her eyes skated across the ceiling, trying to absorb the news. The man was as rich as Croesus. Could afford to hire an army of the best lawyers in the country. "The contract was really that good?" She shouldn't be surprised. Max wasn't one of the best agents in the business for no reason.

"I don't know."

"But it must have been, if he's not suing us."

"He's publishing it."

Donna's words couldn't have had a greater effect if Rachel had stuck a fork in a live electrical socket. Her body jerked, limbs flying, like a flailing marionette doll whose puppeteer was having a fit. "He's not!"

She looked at Max. This was Donna's idea of some kind of strange joke. It had to be. Why would he out his own best-selling author as a fraud?

He tipped his chin. "He is. Or at least so he's saying."

"But why?" Of course she'd always known it was a possibility. That's kind of the chance you took when you handed a book in to your publisher, but she'd never thought for a second he *would*.

Max shrugged his shoulders. "Well, he seems to think his coterie of Harvard lawyers will just slay anyone who tries to sue the company and that even with a bunch of lawsuits, their legal bills will pale in comparison to what marketing are telling him the book will make."

"Tell her the best part." She couldn't tell from Lacey's tone if she was serious or joking.

"It's not in the next Fall lineup."

"Have they moved it back to Spring?"

"Nope. November. Week before Thanksgiving."

She did the mental arithmetic. Almost fifteen months away. She'd have to start hunting for a job. There was no way they could continue the Dr. Donna act in the interim. They'd get crucified.

".. . putting a big rush on it, going to be as locked down as Clinton's memoirs. They want our input on the release strategy."

"Hold on. What?"

"Well, with it being a couple of months away, it's all hands to the pump."

Her stomach rolled like she'd just found herself on Space Mountain. Not next November. *This* one.

Her eyes locked with Donna's, who was studying her with an intent look. "What?"

"The release."

"What about it?" Randolph could do what he liked.

Donna raised an eyebrow at her. "You know where we should go first."

Oh no. No. No. No. No. *No*. Her head shook; her mouth wouldn't even open. She was going to be sick.

"It's the right thing to do, Rach."

"He *hates* me!" Bad enough just knowing it; there was no way she would be able to see it in his eyes. Donna hadn't been there that day. Hadn't seen the look of disgust and betrayal on his face.

Her aunt just looked at her, big, knowing quasi-therapist eyes boring deeper than her fears and speaking to her soul.

The one that knew she had to do it. Even when it meant subjecting herself to the revulsion of the one man she'd ever loved.

- 38 -

TWO MONTHS LATER

Stuck. The door stuck, sucking onto the frame like two lovesick teenagers parting for the summer. Why could nothing just work around here? A hard tug broke the seal, and the door flew backward and clipped Lucas's foot. He stormed through, letting it slam shut behind him, bringing in a whoosh of cold air. Tugging his jacket tighter, he fingered the envelope in the inner pocket. It had been residing there for the last three weeks, just waiting for the right moment to tell Ethan.

Why hadn't he already done it? Every day that he delayed was another show that he would have to endure. It wasn't fair. Not on Ethan. Not on his listeners. His brother was right. He was a hypocrite. People didn't deserve a host who didn't care about his callers anymore. Not the ones who actually wanted to talk about sports, and certainly not the ones who—for reasons unknown—still insisted on calling and asking for relationship advice.

More fool him. Every night his job mocked him. Daring him to tell the truth. That loving someone was about as smart as pulling your heart out of your chest and putting it through a shredder and expecting it to feel good. That only idiots took chances, gave up their dreams in the hope that their love might be returned.

He took the stairs. Pounding upward, feet beating the Formica into submission. One floor, two . . . By the time he reached the eighth he was barely out of breath. If there was one thing he could thank she-whose-name-shall-not-be-mentioned for, it was ceaseless energy that only seemed to grow the more he tried to beat it into oblivion.

Even refusing to allow himself to think her name, his heart still tanked just at the thought of *her*.

He pulled open the door to his floor. Empty. Good. No having to make small talk about a job he no longer cared about. Get into the studio, get it done, and get out—that was all he wanted. He slid his hand into his jacket and withdrew the envelope. It stared back, crinkled and grubby from weeks of being carried around but never delivered.

Tonight. After the show, he'd tell Ethan. Hand in his notice. Offer to help find his replacement. Or replacements. He wouldn't leave them in the lurch. He'd been listening to a new host over on Drive95. She was good, and he'd heard rumors she was open to a new opportunity. He had to do it. He didn't like who he had become. Cynical, jaded Lucas. Even Joey had noticed. Asked him when "old Uncle Lucas" was coming back. He needed to go find him.

How was it only a few months ago that he thought he might be able to get both the woman and the dream? Huh. What a joke. And it was all on him.

He folded the envelope and shoved it in his back pocket.

He reached for the door to Studio 3. Wrenched his shoulder when, instead of turning and swinging, the handle stayed firm. *What the . . .?* The door was never locked. He didn't even have a key. He peered into the darkness, tried the handle again. His foot connected with the door.

"It's closed. Maintenance." Ethan's voice spun him around.

"Maintenance? What kind?" In the five years he'd been here, he'd never known John the janitor to maintain a single thing. He was of the "I'll fix it when it's busted" school of property management.

Ethan shrugged, black leather collar sliding up his neck. "Don't ask me—I'm just the producer. We're in Studio One tonight."

"How am I supposed to do my prep in a studio that's already been used?" Lucas strode down the hall, his funk deepening with every step.

He stopped outside the fishbowl. The empty fishbowl. Equipment glowing in the moonlight filtered through the blinds.

"Jack and Lucy are doing a live show from the Governor's Gala."

"Fine." Lucas grumbled, testing the handle before throwing the door open, sliding his palm down the wall to turn on the lights.

"So, Dr. Donna's new book comes out this week." Ethan swung the words like a baseball bat.

It took everything in him to keep walking, switching on equipment and snagging a bag of chips out of the samples box.

"I've heard it's been shrouded in secrecy. Not even the sales staff know what it's about."

"Good for them." Lucas stuffed a handful of chips into his mouth. Pulling up a stool, he called up CNN and started scanning the sports headlines.

Strange. He'd thought Rachel had said the next book wasn't due out until next year. He tried to push the unwanted thought out of his mind, but it stubbornly remained, taunting him.

She must have written something crazy fast after he'd left them in the lurch. Yet another book of lies. Just in time to fleece the masses for Christmas.

Tell me another way, Lucas. You got any better ideas for how I can make a million bucks? Because it's either this, or my father eventually ends up in an institution where he will be left to fester in his own bed sores because the staff aren't paid enough to give a fig. Rachel's voice decimated his bitter thought, her brimming brown eyes ghosting in front of him.

"Hi."

He ran his hands through his hair. He had to get a grip. Her voice was so vivid, it sounded like it was in the room.

The air in the studio shifted, causing him to look up.

His seat moved underneath him, hands flying out to grip the sides, to stop him from face-planting into the ground.

"Rachel?" The word came out a croak.

"Hey, Lucas." She tried to smile, but the sides of her mouth quivered, causing her cheeks to tremble. Her eyes bounced from his, around the studio, and back to his.

"What are you doing here?" His words sounded harsh and she flinched, jumping back as though he'd struck her.

"I mean . . ." he flailed. No more words coming.

She took a step toward him. "We have a new book."

"So I heard." She was thinner. Her cheekbones more prominent, navy top unable to disguise that underneath it her collarbones stuck out like bridges. He forced his eyes to the floor. She'd broken his heart, and still all he wanted to do was cradle her in his arms and tell her everything was going to be okay.

"It's been wrapped pretty tight. Tonight is the first time we're going to talk about it."

Talk about it? Use his show as an accomplice to their con? Over his dead body. "You have got to be joking."

She twisted her hands like she was wringing wet clothes. "Lucas, I know—"

"No, you don't know, Rachel, you have no idea. Because if you did, you wouldn't be standing in my studio. You'd be as far away from here as you could possibly get." He strode to the doorway and flung his arm through it. "Get out. Over my dead body are you using my show to propagate your lies."

Her eyes widened, then misted. "It's not . . . We're not . . ."

"What Rachel's trying to say, Lucas," Donna said, standing right outside the door, "is that we're here to tell the truth."

YOU WOULD have needed a power saw to cut the tension in the studio. Lucas wouldn't even look at her. They sat less than a couple of feet apart, but they might as well be strangers in a seedy bar on a Tuesday night, each trying to ignore the other's existence.

Her bitten-to-the-cuticle fingers drummed on the console as he scanned the cheat sheet Donna and she had prepared. A copy of the book sat propped in front of him, the title screaming out in gold font. *And the Truth Shall Set You Free.* Huh—so far all the truth had done was give her an ulcer. And almost given Theodore Randolph IV a stroke. Not to mention made lawyers a lot of money as they tried to hash out Randolph's likelihood of getting sued versus a guaranteed payday. A trickle of sweat ran down Rachel's back. The studio was stifling, but that wasn't why. It was the grilling Lucas had served up over the last half hour. It was as though she'd been wheeled into surgery, had her entire body sliced open, and then been left on the operating table for the world to stare at her. Vulnerable. Completely exposed.

From Donna's ex-husband to Rachel's parents. From the blog that started it all, through to how they carried out the deception, including how she'd pretended to be Donna in various publicity interviews. Lucas was determined to leave no stone unturned, no lie left standing, before he turned them over to the hands of their listeners.

Which wouldn't have been so bad if he'd looked at her, even just once—anything to indicate that he gave one iota about her. Not that she was doing this for him. Her attempt at comfort fell flat. For him, no; because of him, yes.

She was an idiot. What did she think was going to happen? That they would show up in the studio with the book and he would take her in his arms and tell her all was forgiven? She couldn't look at him. It hurt too much to see the complete disinterest in his gaze. So she allowed her eyes to linger on the cover. On both her and Donna's names. The first and only time that was ever going to happen.

"Two minutes." Ethan's voice rolled over the console. She plucked up her headphones and clamped them over her ears. Donna caught her eye and mouthed, "It's going to be okay" across the desk. Fine for her to say. She had a husband who adored her waiting back at the hotel, not to mention no expensive care facility bills chewing through her savings at a terrifying rate.

They'd practiced this. Been drilled by Max and Lacey, who, once they'd realized they were determined to start off their publicity tour with the most hostile interviewer imaginable, had set about trying to spin the story as much in their favor as possible.

She didn't care. All she wanted was to be free of this tangled web of lies that suffocated her everywhere she turned. That had cost her the one guy she'd ever loved and smothered her life for years.

"Fifteen seconds."

Lucas still wouldn't look at her, switching on his microphone as the opening music swelled. The music finished, and for a second, nothing. Was Lucas just going to leave them all hanging? Was he still so revolted by what they had done that he was going to choose a show of dead air rather than have her and Donna on it?

"Good evening and welcome to *Sports with Lucas*." Her shoulders sagged as his voice rolled across the airwaves. "I'm Lucas Grant, and you are not going to believe what we have in store for you tonight. In fact, what we have coming up is so mind-blowing that we won't be taking any calls for the first hour because we need to create some space for my guests to tell their story."

An hour. An hour before all of Wisconsin got on the phone and hurled every piece of abuse they deserved down the line.

"So without any further delay, let me introduce the two people here in the studio with me. The first, many of you know and love, Donna Somerville." He left the "Dr." off at Donna's request. An undeserved honorary degree bestowed after their first bestseller. It had gone on books only because Randolph had insisted.

"Good evening, Lucas." Donna's voice was calm, modulated.

"And second, her assistant, Rachel Somers. Who is also a named author for this book." She winced at his sarcastic use of "named author."

"Hi." Her voice boomed back at her, except it wasn't. Croaky and high pitched. She swallowed. Or tried to.

If only she were sitting next to Donna. Donna would squeeze her hand, remind her she wasn't alone. Instead she had a stone Adonis next to her who radiated about as much warmth as Aspen in December.

"So, Donna, Rachel, tomorrow your book *And the Truth Shall Set You Free* releases. There has been a veil of secrecy around this book. So much so that there have been no advance review copies and no PR. In fact, I believe that this may even be the first time the title has been made public, is that right?"

"That's right, Lucas," Donna answered.

"And why is that?"

"Well, Lucas, it's because the truth is that I am a fraud, and since you were one of our many unwitting accomplices, we wanted to start making amends on your show." Her aunt said the words as if they were as ordinary as ordering a slice of apple pie for dessert.

Next to Donna, Ethan's eyes boggled, jaw slack. Good thing he wasn't expected to be doing any talking. When Max had asked him if they could use Lucas's show to release their new book he'd jumped at the opportunity, no questions asked.

"Well, now that you've got everyone's attention, why don't you start at the beginning?"

Donna gave Rachel a nod. This was it, her moment. She leaned forward and centered herself on her aunt's face. *You can do this, Rachel; you have to do this.* "The truth starts with me."

LUCAS HAD to give Rachel some credit. She hadn't held anything back as she'd talked for over an hour.

The only thing she left out was everything that had happened between them. Though they'd openly admitted that he'd been pulled into the web in the hope that he'd help them come up with a book idea.

"Why now? When no one knew. Why tell the truth now? Was it just out of desperation to deliver another book so you didn't have to pay your advance back?" Lucas directed the question to Rachel.

"I fell in love." She looked straight at Lucas and he snapped the pencil he was holding in half.

"I met a wonderful guy and I fell in love. I didn't want to and I tried not to, but I could help it as much as I could turn the sky green. And then, in my fear, I hurt him deeply. I didn't want to involve him in my deception, but I couldn't see any way out when my father's care depended on the advance from this book. One of my biggest regrets will always be that he got caught up in all of this. That I hurt him deeply."

She gambled a glance in his direction, but he couldn't look at her. Was it real or was it all just spin for the PR machine to try to buy a big dose of public sympathy?

Being first with the story is everything. That was one of the few things he still remembered from his PR class on crisis management. If you get in front of the story, you have a much better chance of being able to turn it your way. That could be all this was about. And he was aiding and abetting them in doing so. Again.

"And with that, it's time to take some calls." His voice was emotionless.

Over two hours later, so many calls had descended on their switchboard it caused some sort of network failure. Switching online, Ethan had stopped holding callers there over an hour ago. And every single caller had stayed holding for up to two hours, waiting for their turn to have their say. Now they had time for only a few more.

"Heidi, you're on." He caught his breath. So far, calls had been overwhelmingly supportive. Like Wisconsin had all been boozing at the bar of forgiveness. He didn't get it. Sure, there had been a few angry callers, but nothing like the whirlwind of hysteria he'd expected to be unleashed. Most just had questions.

"Hi." Heidi cleared her throat. "My question is for Donna."

"Go ahead."

"You've sold millions of books; you must have made a lot of money. How can you live with making so much money off people who believed in you when it was all a sham?"

"I can't." Donna said the two words as a statement of fact. "I . . ." She paused for a second, took a breath. "In the beginning, I justified it because I used the money to raise my boys. My ex-husband left us with nothing, and it felt like God had provided a way for me to be able to put food on the table and shoes on their feet. But it always bothered me. And so, when the checks started getting bigger, I started a charity."

"What kind?" Heidi sounded skeptical. He couldn't blame her.

"It's called Hands of Hope. It's in New Orleans."

No way. Even he'd heard of Hands of Hope. The charity established by a mysterious benefactor a few years after Katrina that had done amazing stuff in poor communities.

A sound next to Lucas caused him to turn. Rachel was staring at her aunt, eyes bugging. Clearly this was news to her as well. *"You're* Hands of Hope?"

Her aunt looked across at her. "Not just me; Rob, too."

"Why didn't you tell me?"

Donna shrugged. "The only people who knew were our lawyers and the director. Oh, and our close friends at the IRS. That's how we wanted it."

He had to get a grip on his show. "Thanks, Heidi; let's take another call." He glanced at his call list. "Hello, Olivia."

"Hi. My question is for Rachel."

"Go ahead."

"Is there still a chance?"

"A chance?" Rachel spoke.

"With the guy you fell in love with. Do you think that maybe now that the truth is out, you could find a way to work it out?"

It felt like even the walls held their breath, waiting for her answer.

Rachel breathed out into the mic, a whoosh filling the airwaves. "I don't know. I don't think so. He doesn't want anything to do with me."

"But maybe if you explained."

Rachel kept her gaze straight ahead. "He knows."

"Lucas? You're a guy, what do you think?" Olivia's voice held a ray of hope.

What did he think? He couldn't. "I think that sometimes, sometimes when something is broken, you have to ask if it's worth trying to fix it. Especially when it's trust. Once that's broken it's almost impossible to restore."

"But if he loved her too, surely it's worth a try?"

"Maybe he doesn't know if he loved her; maybe he's not sure if he ever knew her at all." It was his voice saying the words, but his heart screamed at him to take them back. To stomp on his hurt just for a second and let hope speak.

Across the console Donna wore a funeral face, while Ethan glared at him from the producer's booth. Beside him Rachel sat ramrod straight, face unreadable except for a slight tremble in her lips.

His cell phone buzzed on the desk next to him. In all the madness, he'd forgotten to turn it off. *Scott* flashed on the screen. He sent him to voicemail, knowing what his brother was going to be calling to say.

They had moved on to the last caller without him. His mind couldn't even focus on what they were saying, words tumbling past him like comets in the night.

What was he doing? He knew her. Knew the curve of her smile and the way she wrung her hands when she was nervous. The way her laugh tumbled over him like fresh rain and the way she poked her tongue out when she was concentrating. How she fitted perfectly in his arms and made him feel like the world was full of possibilities.

" . . . joining us, folks." Donna had taken over closing the show in view of his stupor. "Thank you for allowing Rachel and me to tell our story. Until tomorrow, this is *Sports with Lucas*."

Ethan cued to the midnight news. Had he just told the woman he loved there were no second chances? On radio?

He pulled his headphones off. Took a couple of breaths. He just needed a minute to find his bearings. To work out what he really wanted to say. Picking up the copy of the book they'd given him, he flipped it over, stared at her face.

He opened the front cover. *For Woofy. The guy who introduced me to the kind of love I wrote books about waiting for. I'm sorry.*

The words burned into his brain, then his heart. What had he done?

"Rach—" The words died on his lips; they'd gone. The empty room stared back at him, mocking.

"They left." Ethan glared at him from the doorway like he'd just shotgun-married his daughter.

"They what?"

Ethan took a step into the room. "What did you expect, Lucas? That she would come here, put herself on the line for you, have you shoot her down, and hang around so that you could pulverize her heart into even smaller pieces?"

His breath caught. "Where is she?"

"No idea, and wouldn't tell you if I did. Who do you think you are? Sure, she made some mistakes. But at least she had a good reason. What about you? Sitting here spewing out relationship advice seemingly under protest but secretly loving it? The woman who is the best thing who ever happened to you shows up and puts everything on the line and you shred her like confetti. Who needs the paparazzi when the great Lucas Grant is all set up as judge and jury? You're a good guy, Luc, but what happened tonight, I had no idea you had it in you to be so cruel. Not to mention blind."

"What do you mean 'blind'?"

Ethan huffed out a breath. "Seriously? You love her. You are crazy stupid in love with that woman. And if your pride stops you from seeing that, then you shouldn't bother coming back tomorrow."

A burst of panic sent him flying off his seat. He had to find her, had to fix it. Had to tell her he was wrong, so wrong. If required, he would run every street in Madison until he did.

"YOU SURE you don't want to come in the Uber?" Donna shook out her umbrella, peering at Rachel with crinkled eyes.

Rachel shook her head. "It's fine. The hotel isn't far and

I've got Bruno." She gestured to the brute of a man that Max had hired to watch over them. For a few days, he said, just while public reaction played out.

The personal protection officer—apparently that was what they were called these days—crossed his arms, muscles rippling through his jacket. No thug in his right mind would take him on.

She needed to walk. Needed the air. To process the way Lucas couldn't even look at her. "I'll see you in the morning."

Donna pulled her close and kissed her on both cheeks. "It'll be okay, Rach. Whatever happens next, it will be okay. Maybe he just needs some more time. To process everything."

Rachel just shook her head. She wasn't holding out any more hope for Lucas. She'd known that tonight would be it. Whichever way the chips fell, she would at least know. She could now move on.

Bruno held open the door for both of them, light rain misting under the streetlights. Donna made a run for her car, which was idling at the curb.

Rachel pulled her coat close, shoving her hands under her armpits.

"Umbrella?" Bruno already had one up, holding it over her.

"No thanks." The water landing on her face felt good. A much needed shower after four hours of being bathed with Lucas's loathing. He hadn't even bothered to say good-bye, staring down at his fingernails like he couldn't even bring himself to acknowledge her presence.

How could she have been so stupid? To allow even a small part of her to think that maybe, just maybe, this would fix it.

That they would sit in his studio and, as they unfolded the truth, he would catch her eye and, with a tug of his lips, let her know that all was forgiven.

Her wilder fantasies had involved him sweeping her up in his arms and making some kind of crazy public declaration on air. Like Hugh Grant and Drew Barrymore in *Music and Lyrics*.

A short, sharp laugh left her lips. Not even her worst-case scenarios had painted him so cold that the Arctic seemed like a summer vacation.

God, I don't know how to do this. She directed her prayer to the pavement, where puddles parted beneath her shoes.

She loved Lucas. After everything, she still loved him. She'd known that the moment she walked into the studio and saw him. But she was going to have to get over him. *If you can love the wrong person, imagine how it will feel when you finally love the right person.* She'd written that once. Now she was just going to have to take some of the medicine she'd doled out to thousands of other women.

"Rachel!"

His voice echoed behind her. Proof she was still holding on to delusions. The hotel loomed a block away. A warm bath would be first. Followed by a good cry. She would allow herself just one. Then it was time to move on, navigate whatever lay ahead. Maybe go hide somewhere in Africa for a while.

"Rachel!"

"Get behind me, ma'am." Bruno ushered her with his tree trunk of an arm, unclipped his holster, and pulled out his gun.

She peered out, mist obscuring her vision.

"Sir, please don't come any closer." Bruno barked the words out as Lucas emerged from the fog.

Rachel didn't know if Lucas didn't hear him or if he just didn't realize what was going on, but he kept moving toward her and the next thing she knew, Bruno was right in front of her with his gun raised.

"Whoa." Lucas slammed to a stop and threw both hands in the air.

"He's okay, Bruno. He's safe!" She put her hand on his arm. "Put your gun down." Lucas getting accidentally shot. That really would be a fitting ending to this whole saga.

Lucas's hair was slicked to his head, he didn't even have a jacket, and his shirt was soaked through.

"What on earth are you doing?" She stepped around the guard, who moved a few feet away. But he kept his gun in his hands and watched Lucas like a hawk. A fact that wasn't missed by either of them.

"There's something I need to say." His voice was rough, like he'd eaten gravel for breakfast.

"Really? And what could that possibly be?" She took a step back, as if maybe an extra foot might somehow shield her from whatever arrows he had left in his arsenal. "You were pretty clear where we stood a few minutes ago. Crystal, in fact."

"I'm sorry. You took me by surprise and I let my pride and ego talk, instead of my heart." He ran a hand through his hair, causing it to stick up on end.

The fact that he looked adorable made her even angrier. "How many times do you want me to say I'm sorry, Lucas? I'm sorry I hurt you. I'm sorry I'm not who you thought I was. I'm sorry you clearly can't even stand being in the same room as me. Do you want me to grovel from here to eternity? Because I can't . . . I won't . . . do it." Her coat squelched against her, rain beginning to work its way through the lining. "I've spent too long as a living, breathing apology to my father. And look where it's got me. I'm done."

"Rach, I—" They were in between streetlights and she struggled to make out the expression on his face.

"Spit it out. Because I'd quite like to get a few hours' sleep before I have to talk about the worst moments of my life to a bunch of reporters tomorrow."

At least she still wasn't on social media. The Twitter trolls could go for their lives and she would never know 99 percent of it.

He stepped toward her again and this time she didn't back down. Standing her ground.

"So, here's the thing." He stopped about two feet away, hands fisted in his pockets. His eyes caught hers for a second, then jittered to the ground. "I haven't been completely honest with you either."

"Oh?" She hadn't been expecting that.

"I, um . . ." He shuffled, feet splashing in spreading puddles.

Rain slicked down her neck. Why hadn't she accepted Bruno's offer of an umbrella?

"Do you remember when we were in LA and I was having breakfast with that guy?"

She cast her mind back, scraping together a scattered memory. "Fat guy with sweaty hands?"

A quirk of a smile. "His name was Brad Shipman."

It was a name she'd heard before but she couldn't place it. Rachel turned and gestured to the hulk. "You know what,

Bruno, I think I will have that umbrella, please." She was already soaked through, clothes slurping with every movement, but at the pace Lucas was telling his story, she'd be dry again by the time it was over.

A second later, there was a whoosh as the umbrella popped open and the handle landed in her palm. "Thanks." Bruno gave a nod and melted away.

"So Brad, he um, well, you see, the thing is . . ."

She had to lean forward to try and grasp what Lucas was stuttering. This was ridiculous. She looked up. The umbrella was huge; there was plenty of space for them to both be under it without it getting cozy.

She took a couple of steps and thrust the umbrella into his startled hands. "Don't read anything into it. I just can't hear whatever the heck it is you're attempting to spit out. So go: the thing with Brad is?"

He took a jagged breath and looked down at her. "Brad Shipman is a big producer in LA. Kind of like the Simon Cowell of radio. So he came to me just after Donna—you— whoever—started coming on the show and offered me my own show with him, with a chance at syndication if it went well."

Foreboding curled in her stomach as the name connected with the past. "Donna got a Brad Shipman fired at our publisher. She said he was a lecherous creep. Please tell me it's not the same guy."

He tugged at the neck of his T-shirt with his free hand. "I didn't know any of that when he approached me."

There was more. She could tell by the way Lucas diverted his gaze. "How is this connected to me?"

"His offer of the show came with a catch."

She tilted her head, studied his face. "What kind of a catch?"

"He was convinced Donna had a big secret. Something that would destroy her. To get the show I had to find out what it was, or else convince him he was wrong." Lucas finally looked at her again, his gaze wretched.

It was like someone had just scratched a fingernail down the blackboard of the universe. She stared at him, every synapse in her body firing a million messages. A sensation that she would hazard a guess was close to being Tasered. "All those odd questions about her. You were . . ."

He sighed, nodding. "Trying to find out if there was a secret. I never guessed, not for a second, that it was you. You have to understand, it looked like Scott was going to lose the ranch. The money that Brad offered . . ." He blew a breath out. "It was enough to fix everything."

Memories stormed her mind. The ribs delivery in Houston. The party in LA. The Thai dinner. That whole time he'd just been . . . using her. Playing her to get information. The way he'd looked at her had made her feel like she mattered. It had all been make-believe. The truth ripped her breath away. Tore her soul down the seam and surfaced every bit of pain and hurt she'd been carrying her whole life.

Rachel forced the hurt down. She couldn't give him the satisfaction of making any more of a fool of herself. Bad enough she'd already done it on the dedication page. For him to have forever.

"Well, I guess congratulations are in order." She spoke to his chin. If she looked him in the eye, it would all be over.

"You got me, Lucas. I thought I was good at playing the double game, but you, you win. Congratulations on your new job. When do you start?"

She stepped back. He'd played her, and yet some insane part of her still wanted him to find a way to say something, anything, to give her a reason to hope they could find a way through. She just needed to get away from here, from him.

His fingers landed on her forearm and curled around it.

"Get your hands off me."

"Rachel, please." There was something in his voice that caused her to look up and find herself engulfed in his eyes.

She wrenched her arm out of his hand and looked away. "There's nothing left to say. I, of all people, get prostituting your conscience to pay the bills. Is that why you're so mad at me? Because we've just beat you to it? What was the plan? To wait for the next book and then do the big exposé right before it released from your new fancy LA studio?"

"I didn't tell him."

"What?" Her head jerked up, searching his face for any sign of deception. Not that she'd even know what it looked like on him. "But what about the money? Saving the ranch?"

"Don't get me wrong. After that day I was so angry. And hurt. You deceived me. I told you things, personal things, thinking you were Donna."

Rachel's cheeks flushed with shame. "So why didn't you?"

"I was about to. I was on the phone to him and he said something that made me see, properly, what a repulsive human being he is. Not that he ever hid it, but I kept glossing it over. Chose to ignore a bunch of things that I never should have because I was so focused on the end goal. And then I got there and discovered having the big show wasn't worth what it was going to cost me."

"I'm sorry."

"I'm not." He cast her a sad smile. "Not about that, anyway."

"What about, then?" The question floated from her lips before she had time to censor it.

He tugged her toward him, using her lapels as anchors, the umbrella pole bumping against her shoulder. "I've spent months trying to forget about you. About us."

"And how's that working for you?" Her words were so soft, she barely heard them above the now pelting rain on the canvas above them. Her gaze traveled his face, bouncing around it, except for his lips. Looking at those always got her in trouble.

A wry smile. "Well, I'm fitter than I've ever been."

He wasn't wrong about that. It was hard not to notice when his shirt clung to him like sugar to a donut.

"Rach." His touch feathered the side of her face. His eyes searched hers. She didn't want to think about what they said back. They no doubt gave away her last remaining secret. "I am crazy about you. And turns out, without you, I'm just plain crazy. And I know we both have enough baggage to keep FedEx in business for years, but my life just doesn't make sense without you."

Thunder cracked above them. She didn't care. She drank him in. From his crooked nose, to his strong chin, to his perfect long lashes dripping raindrops. "You realize I'm probably going to get sued, right?"

"Don't care."

"And I live in Colorado and you live in Wisconsin."

"I'm sure we can make arrangements, since I believe you're soon to be unemployed."

"And that if my father lives for more than another five years, he is way more expensive than if I had credit card debt or a penchant for Macy's sales?"

He tugged at her hair. "We'll have lots of kids and send them to work the fields to pay for Granddad's care."

"And—" She was cut off by a finger over her lips. Which went on to trace their outline, before his hand captured the small of her back and pulled her close.

"Rach?"

"Mmm-hmm." She couldn't tear herself away. From his eyes, which looked right into her heart, or from his arms, which lifted her heels off the ground.

"I've wanted to kiss you since the first time we met." His voice was husky, shaded with longing.

"But I was awful!"

"You were feisty." His nose grazed hers.

She snuggled in close, rain pouring into her collar and down her back. "I've wanted to kiss you since the first call-in we did together."

"But every time we've gotten close, it's been sabotaged, usually by you."

She opened her mouth. Had he forgotten about their scorching kiss at Sunhaven?

He read her eyes and shook his head. "Doesn't count. And neither does the kitchen. That wasn't a proper kiss."

Okay, if that was how he wanted it to be. She would have first-kiss do-overs with this guy as many times as he wanted.

"Now, where were we?" His hand feathered the side of her face, disintegrating her ability to think straight. "Ah yes, you and your sabotaging."

Her hands ran up his arms. "I was trying not to fall for you."

A smile quirked. "And how did that work for you."

"Not at all." She loped her arms around his neck, running her fingers through the hair at the nape.

"So Rachel Somers, in about three seconds I am going to attempt to kiss you. But before I do, are there any dishes I need to rinse, or sports teams you need to insult, or secrets that need to be revealed?"

She shook her head, emotion clogging her throat.

"You promise?"

He was so close, his breath tickled her lips. Unable to resist any longer, she tugged him down the final inch and answered without words.

His lips were strong and firm, and he broke the kiss off way too soon. Tangling her hair in his hands, he gazed at her for a second before pulling her closer for another. This one longer, adding new shades of promise and longing.

She held on tight to his neck, sure her legs wouldn't hold her up if she let go.

He groaned, pulling himself away. "You are going to get me into trouble, Miss Somers."

She pulled him back. "You're already in trouble."

He smiled the kind of smile that would have them heading to Vegas if he used it too often. Then his face settled and he stared at her with something she couldn't quite interpret. "I love you." He breathed the words out as if it was a prayer.

"I love you too." The words rushed from her lips, as if they'd been sitting there, just waiting for permission to be uttered.

A grin split his face. "You sure? Because if you don't take it back, you're going to be stuck with me forever."

"Forever sounds just about right." She tugged him down and silenced him with a kiss that left no room for misunderstanding.

Acknowledgments

Every book feels like a miracle and *One Thing I Know* is no exception!

I have the privilege of writing books with imperfect people and messy faith, and none of that is possible without God. In every single book there are many moments where I'm convinced that *this* is going to be the book I can't finish. Or that it will be a huge disappointment. But the ultimate Creator always carries me through.

I am beyond grateful for the insight and perseverance of my incomparable editor, Beth Adams. Lucas and Rachel's story is not only so much better and stronger because of you but the conversations that we have in edits where things aren't translating from New Zealand English to American English is always one of my favorite parts of the process. One day you have to come to New Zealand where we will eat hot pudding and you will discover what you're missing out on!

To my agent, Chip MacGregor: This time last year the future of my writing career was unclear but you never stopped believing in my stories and that they would find their place (again) in the traditional publishing world. Thank you.

My husband, Josh, is the only reason these books even exist. Keeping all the balls in the air is only possible because of his unfailing support and boundless enthusiasm for books that he has absolutely no interest in ever reading. ☺ I love you.

To the small people, Buddy, Buzz, and Boogles. It has been a year of change for our family and I know the whole "Mummy juggling a 'real' job and deadlines on two books at the same time" thing has meant that you guys have missed out while I've been bunkered down with my imaginary people. You three are the best thing I've ever (co-)created and I hope that one day me chasing my dream encourages you to chase yours.

I am always indebted to my "SisterChucks" Jaime Jo Wright, Laurie Tomlinson, Halee Matthews, Anne Love, and Sarah Varland for the daily Facebook messages, the cheering on and the picking up, the friendship that covers all aspects of our lives, and for telling me what I'm writing is great even when it's not even close. Thank you for being such an unwavering part of every adventure.

My crazy, fun family and family-in-love is spread all over the world. What we lack in physical presence we sure make up for with random WhatsApp conversations! Thank you for your never-ceasing love and support even though I'm sometimes so busy with the imaginary people I forget to tell the real people minor things such as that I have another book coming out and you find out from my newsletter (sorry!)

Finally, to my readers. I am convinced that I have the best readers in the world. Thank you for your enthusiasm for my books, your encouraging emails and Facebook messages on the days when the imaginary people are defeating me, and for helping to spread the word. I know I speak for every author when I say we appreciate everything that you do to support us and our stories.

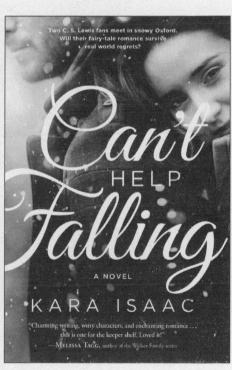